They a
        fig...
without losing control of their
own. . . .

ELIOT WOLFE, M.D. The privileged son of a family of doctors, the chief administrator of Harmony Hill fears he may be the first member of the Wolfe family to fail—in the eyes of his family, his wife, and the hospital.

TONI ROMANO, M.D. Named one of New York's ten best doctors, she runs the Women's Health Center after hours, saving teenage mothers and their babies. But Toni's clinic is threatened by her husband's financial policies, and this is taking its toll on their marriage.

HAMILTON PIERCE The "people's reporter," he's out for himself first and the story always. But his latest obsession is the hot pursuit of Toni Romano—and the inside information he can get from her.

BETTY STRONG CANNON Eliot's no-nonsense secretary, she's privy to the most confidential information—which she uses in her own private battle against the horrors of the inner-city.

DEEDRA STRONG, M.D. Her lifelong dream of becoming a doctor, encouraged by her devoted older sister, has now come true. But her patients are crack addicts and malnourished, abused children. Can she really make a difference?

KING CRAWFORD A handsome young paramedic who's fallen in love with Dr. Deedra Strong, one question still haunts him: the identity of his real parents. And the truth is closer than he thinks. . . .

Also by Marcia Rose
Published by Ballantine Books:

ADMISSIONS
CHOICES
CONNECTIONS
SECOND CHANCES
SUMMERTIMES
ALL FOR THE LOVE OF DADDY
SONGS MY FATHER TAUGHT ME
A HOUSE OF HER OWN

HOSPITAL

Marcia Rose

BALLANTINE BOOKS • NEW YORK

Copyright © 1992 by Marcia Kamien and Rose Novak

All rights reserved under International and Pan-American Copyright Conventions. Published in the United States of America by Ballantine Books, a division of Random House, Inc., New York, and simultaneously in Canada by Random House of Canada Limited, Toronto.

Library of Congress Catalog Card Number: 91-58981

ISBN 0-345-36829-0

Manufactured in the United States of America

First Hardcover Edition: June 1992
First Mass Market Edition: November 1993

This book is for all the children:
Sarah, Julia,
Laura, Richard, Neil, Susie, Melanie,
Leila, Mara, Mitch,
and—the newest and the latest—
Gareth Novak-Miller
born January 30, 1992

1

June

Eliot Wolfe rounded the corner at 100th Street and instantly caught sight of the crowd gathered in front of the hospital's ornate front entrance. It was a large crowd, and—he could hear as he got closer—a noisy one, even though it was barely six o'clock in the morning. As president of the hospital, he always felt obligated to be at his desk by six-thirty A.M., when his surgeons started work, but what were all these other people doing out in the street at this hour? He had already guessed the answer: they were getting ready to give him hell, that's what!

He began to walk faster, and then he spotted Channel 14's van, with its signature black rooster against a big red sun. Damn! Better slow his pace; he couldn't let any television reporter catch him out of breath. Especially not that royal pain in the ass Hamilton Pierce, who was standing on the front steps of Harmony Hill, holding forth into a mike. A camerawoman moved around to get a flattering angle on his handsome, deeply tanned face, with its chiseled cheekbones, tightly curled blond hair, and odd, slanting eyes of startling light gray.

Eliot had come to hate those eyes; they told you nothing. They only reflected back the light. Yet, he was sure they missed very little. It was always a challenge, being questioned by Pierce. The man was quick-witted and always, it seemed, armed with inside information. Eliot would give a week's pay to know who his sources were.

He was almost at the hospital when Pierce spotted him and, with a wolfish grin spreading across his face, trotted over to meet him. You could practically see him licking his chops! What a nuisance, being put on the defensive by a TV commentator—

not a Ted Koppel, not a Walter Cronkite, not even a Gabe Pressman—but a glamour boy, a former basketball star, who had appointed himself the champion of the poor, minorities, the disabled, women, crime victims, you name it.

Eliot *could* sneak in the emergency entrance and avoid this confrontation— Hell, he thought with a laugh, this *was* an emergency—but he had promised himself he would never run and hide. The last president had been famous for that, and the hospital had enough problems without getting more bad press. He pushed his shoulders back, lengthened his stride, put a presidential smile on his face. And cursed. Now he could read the placards being hoisted. One in particular immediately caught his eye: SAVE OUR BABIES. And another one: MURDERERS.

The story had been a front-page item in yesterday's *New York Times*, as well as the *News, Newsday*, and, most irritatingly, the *New York Post*, where the entire first page was filled with big black letters declaiming NYC KILLS BLACK BABIES. Figures had just been released showing that infant mortality in Harlem was greater than in Bangladesh. Hospitals were named, and Harmony Hill was one.

"Dr. Wolfe!" Here it came: the mike under his nose, the famous Ham Pierce smile.

"Could you spare a moment, Doctor? For the eight million viewers who watch 'Voice of the City' every night? We'd all like to learn why, in your hospital, black babies die at a higher rate than in the Third World."

As usual, he didn't bother to wait for an answer but just kept pressing. Damn the man!

"Or perhaps you can tell us why last night, a black woman in labor was forced to sit and wait in a hallway for three hours! Why do things like this always happen to African-Americans, Dr. Wolfe?"

Pierce stood with his long legs planted apart and his head back, the very picture of aggrieved self-importance. He had movie-star good looks and the faint trace of a Southern accent. Long before Eliot took over as president, Pierce had decided to "look into" the rotten state of health care at Harmony Hill Hospital. So Eliot had inherited his attentions along with the disintegration of the hospital. That meant finding himself constantly on the defensive. He'd discovered that you could say,

"That was a decision of the previous administration," only so many times before it got to sound very lame.

Damn it, the truth was, he *had* found Harmony Hill in a shambles. So much so, it was almost comic: cost overruns, rampant waste, shortages of everything, discontented employees, overcrowding . . . all the usual, plus the pressures brought about by the AIDS epidemic, the crack epidemic, the homeless epidemic, hell, the poverty epidemic! He needed more time; what he *didn't* need was a hotshot television personality hounding him.

"A woman in *labor*, Dr. Wolfe, a woman in pain, a woman about to give birth to a child—ignored and neglected by your staff! And what do you say to *that*, Dr. Wolfe? My audience is waiting. Well, Dr. Wolfe? May we hear from you?"

Eliot forced his face to remain pleasant and calm. He was aware that the camera had now turned to him and was running.

"It seems strange, Mr. Pierce, that *you* keep getting reports about this hospital before *I* do."

He would bet that, sitting on his desk at this very moment, was Betty Cannon's memo about this incident. His secretary was a model of efficiency. But how the hell did Pierce keep getting the advance word on every goddamn thing, big or little, that happened at Harmony Hill? He must have some network of informants!

"It seems obvious, Dr. Wolfe, that reports on abuses suffered by black patients are rarely brought to your attention!"

He did not say "Bullshit," which he badly wanted to do. He even managed to look calm—at least he *thought* he looked calm, he *hoped* he looked calm. Goddamn it, he'd *better* look calm.

"Harmony Hill has no, I repeat *no*, racist policies. You know as well as I do that every hospital in New York City is in crisis. We are fighting as hard as we can, but there are not enough doctors, not enough funds, not enough beds—"

"Speaking of beds, Dr. Wolfe, how about Harmony Hill's plans to eliminate all their maternity beds?"

Now he was *really* mad. "That is absolutely not true! And if I were you, Pierce, I would not report every rumor, not until I had the facts. If any woman has had to wait for a labor room, that is unfortunate, and it will be corrected."

Who knew what the real story was? It could be any damn thing, from an addict-mother too stoned to ask for help to a recent immigrant whose command of English wasn't good enough to explain her predicament. Why the media always had to focus on one small negative item, he didn't know. What had happened to the appeal of the success story, anyway? People were treated every day in Harmony Hill, sometimes they were cured, and most times they left better off than when they came. For a moment he considered sounding off, and then he thought better of it. Somehow, some way, Hamilton Pierce would turn it against him.

"Now, if you'll excuse me," he said brusquely, "I have a hospital to run." He knew he sounded blunt, and he didn't care. Damn it, enough was enough!

But apparently enough was *not* enough, not for Hamilton Pierce. As Eliot started up the flight of steps into the front lobby, the reporter was right with him, matching stride for stride . . . and the camera was rolling right along behind them.

"I heard—"

Now he turned, laughing. "Mr. Pierce, didn't your mother teach you not to believe everything you hear?"

There was a murmur of laughter from the crowd, and Pierce sliced the air with his hand—the order to cut the camera. Eliot looked at him, smiling. Pierce smiled back. Eliot was sure it was phony. The reporter never showed an emotion that wasn't deliberate. He wondered if the man *had* any real feelings. Maybe if you performed for an audience long enough, you forgot what the real thing felt like.

Ostentatiously, Pierce handed the mike to one of his many assistants. In a much different tone, he said, "I believe we have an appointment, Dr. Wolfe."

"And now we're both late."

Pierce shrugged and smiled. "It's my job, Doctor. Each of us has a job to do in this life."

"Indeed," Eliot murmured. Without waiting for further comment, he turned, took the shallow flight of stairs two at a time, and pushed through the heavy front doors. Pierce could damn well run after him, if he wanted to talk. Eliot hated to be late. He had a full calendar today, with the usual round of people to see and problems to solve—not to mention spending his lunch hour with his mother, a real-estate agent, and the Perfect Apartment.

As he had done at least once a day, every day since he got

here, Eliot asked himself *why*? Why had he taken this job? Why was he back in this hospital, after he'd stayed away so long?

There had been a Dr. Wolfe at Harmony Hill ever since it had been built at the turn of the century—too much history for him to handle, too many expectations, the result of overblown myth and legend.

The sainted Dr. Eli Wolfe, his grandfather, had been one of the founders, a great healer who was far ahead of his time. He believed in a balanced diet and exercise and felt that proper nutrition could prevent most illness. He also went every week to the teeming slums of the Lower East Side, where he performed free abortions for poor women—yes, even Eastern European women. This at a time when Russian and Polish Jews were considered to be barely a cut above Negroes by the German Jews who had already settled comfortably into their own New York society. The sainted Dr. Eli had been jailed six times for his charity; it was a story Eliot had heard many times as a child.

Then there was Dr. Philip Wolfe, his father, who was such a brilliant diagnostician, he had potentates from Saudi Arabia of all places; presidents of major corporations, movie stars, mothers with their children—anyone who had a mysterious ailment. They would sit outside his office, waiting for hours to see him. Although his father was eighty-three now, he still got letters from physicians all over the world, asking his advice. Eliot had grown up so in awe of these two men, his forebears.

When he was eleven or twelve, his father would proudly take him around, showing him everything in the hospital, explaining what each department did, introducing him as "the next Dr. Wolfe." For a long time, Eliot treasured those rambles around the hospital, those few minutes when he could feel close to his father. Of course he would carry on the family tradition. As the only child of his parents, it did not occur to him that he might do something else—not until much later.

He shook the memories away like a dog shaking off water. He had more important things to think about . . . and number one was getting Hamilton Pierce off his case. Just how he was going to accomplish this feat, he had no idea.

He strode into his suite of offices. He really didn't need all this space, but your authority was reckoned by how long it took people to walk to your desk. And, secretly, he was beginning to like it.

Betty Strong Cannon was already ensconced at her large, neat desk, murmuring into the phone. Her voice was so low, he could hear nothing from a few feet away, but, on the telephone, she came in loud and clear. Where did she learn that trick? he marveled.

As Eliot walked by, Betty covered the phone with one hand and said: "Dr. Wolfe, you told me to remind you you're having lunch with your daughter today."

Eliot swore, then laughed. "Too many women in my life, Betty. I also promised to spend my lunch hour with my mother—and I had to sign it in blood."

Betty rolled her eyes expressively. She knew Mrs. Doctor Philip; everyone in the hospital knew Mrs. Dr. Philip Wolfe and knew that whatever she wanted, that's what got done. "I'll call your daughter," she said, laughing.

He turned to look back down the hall. "Oops. Here comes Ham Pierce, the rabble-rouser."

"The rabble around here needs a little rousing, that's what *I* think. And not everyone thinks he's a troublemaker. He's very popular where *I* live," she added, somewhat defensively.

She spent most of her spare time leading drug-busting patrols on her block of West 122nd Street. Every night she was out, armed with only a radio and her convictions, chasing the pushers, threatening the cars from Jersey and Long Island that came cruising around for a fix. A woman in her middle years, for God's sake!

"I'm sorry, Betty. That was a feeble attempt at a joke. Feeble, because he caught me outside and I'm already in a weakened condition."

He got a little laugh from her, which relieved him. He didn't want Betty to get the wrong idea. He was a staunch believer in civil rights; and many were the times, in Southern-mentality Washington in the 1960s, that he had defied the unspoken rules, giving the same attention to black patients as to whites, the same care. He had paid a high price for that. It had kept him from being promoted at John Quincy Adams Hospital.

He had never thought to find himself, at the age of fifty-four, dealing once again with the same old bigotry—embroiled in it! But since he had come to Harmony Hill, there was always some kind of demonstration out in front, and it always boiled down to racism. It was annoying, but people had a right to march and picket and protest and demonstrate. The real headache was the patient-load of crack addicts and alcoholics and malnourished, abused children: all the diseases of despair.

As soon as Pierce arrived, they went into his office. "I know you want to get right down to it," he said. "And so do I. Just give me a moment to check my schedule."

He crossed his daughter's name off the desk calendar. He hated to break a date with her. But he had no choice this time. He took in a deep breath, swiveled his chair around, and prepared to do polite battle.

Dr. Wolfe was sitting in what Ham always thought of as the Confidentiality Position: hands folded in front of him, leaning forward but with an acre of desk between them. Sure, Ham thought, secretly amused, now the Man will take a deep breath and then tell me something very important. He had to hand it to Wolfe; the guy was good. He was trying to play it very cool, very confident; but there was agitation underneath. Ham could feel it, could *smell* it. He had always been able to size people up in a few seconds. You had to get up very early in the morning to put something over on Mrs. Pierce's little boy!

He looked across the desk at his adversary. How could a privileged, rich, white man who had never known a moment's anxiety over hunger or shelter or sickness—how could *he* be making the life and death decisions for a whole neighborhood of black and Hispanic people who had known nothing else since the day they were born?

"The Rodriguez baby, Dr. Wolfe," Ham said suddenly, taking the other man by surprise. It pleased him that he had the power to do this. He enjoyed the look of helpless dismay that crossed, quick as a flash, over Wolfe's face and was instantly wiped away. "Why is a white baby who is legally dead being kept alive—I say 'alive' in quotation marks—when so many black babies are dying in the hospital. Where are the tubes and technology for *them*?"

Wolfe colored and, for an instant, Ham was afraid he had gone that little bit too far. But to hell with it; it was a real question, a legitimate question. The doctor leaned back in his big black leather chair, running a hand through his thick white hair. He was a well setup man, for sure. If you asked most people to picture a doctor, they'd describe him: tall, solid-looking, maybe even some muscle under the padding, strong features, strong jaw, deepset eyes under definite dark brows. Hell, if you asked most people to describe the ideal president of the United States, they'd describe someone like Eliot Wolfe!

But Ham Pierce wasn't fooled by appearances. If this guy was full of shit, like Dopey Don Delafield, the late unlamented president of Harmony Hill, Ham would expose him, and it wouldn't take five years either!

Wolfe cleared his throat. "This has nothing to do with color! God knows we have enough real problems serving everybody who comes here, problems we're working like hell to solve. If you keep this up, next thing we know, there'll be pitched battles between Hispanics and blacks in the waiting rooms. I wish I could figure out just what in hell you're *up* to."

Too bad he couldn't tell this bland Ivy League–type the truth. But keeping him guessing and off-balance made it more interesting. "I think I'm getting to the truth, Dr. Wolfe. Facts are facts. Black babies die here; white babies get life-support systems."

"Black babies do, too." Wolfe's voice was tight. It would be even more interesting to see him lose his cool, but Ham didn't think he was dumb enough to do *that*. "As for the Rodriguez baby . . . the parents asked that everything possible be done."

"Surely the head of the hospital gets to say no. Especially when it's a hopeless case."

"Who is to say it's hopeless? There is still some brain activity. As long as there is brain activity, the state of New York says the person is alive. The problem has just been exacerbated by the 'miracles of modern science'—and that's in quotes, Pierce— which have clouded the issue by making it possible to prolong quote 'life' unquote . . ."

Ham tried very hard not to show how this condescension turned him off.

"My very point, Dr. Wolfe. What would happen if the Rodriguez baby were taken off life support?"

"I don't know. And, may I add, neither do you, Pierce. I know you think he would die, but you can't be sure. Remember Karen Ann Quindlan? And furthermore, I'd like to remind you that, since Baby Jane Doe, interference by outsiders is prohibited."

Ham kept his face straight and his mouth shut, but his hackles were on the rise. His daddy always did that to him, backed him into a corner and lectured him into a stupor. Reverend Albert Pierce, graduate of Duke University, a cultured man, a well-read man, a man of enormous pride and anger and no patience whatsoever. A man with a guilty secret. His mentor and his tormentor.

He always told the little boy, ''You've got it in you to be the best. And you *will* be. God has given you the gift of high intelligence; but the *will*, the desire to succeed: that's up to you, son.''

His daddy felt it was his duty to force-feed that will into this weak and recalcitrant vessel. The young Hamilton was expected to achieve, no exceptions. Every childish endeavor was scrutinized and judged. Every report card was inspected as carefully as if it were a legal document . . . no, as if it were Scripture. If he didn't get all *A*'s, all 100s, the massive brow would wrinkle and the heavy eyebrows would draw down and the mouth would tighten; and, then, discipline would be meted out.

He had spent many hours of his childhood standing without moving, facing a corner of the dining room, until his legs ached. More hours than that memorizing pages of the Bible, mostly about sinners and their punishments. God, Ham learned very early, was a Father very much like his own.

So of course he was always very good, always perfectly behaved, always first in his class. Until eighth grade, when suddenly thoughts of girls, of naked breasts, of fleshy thighs, filled his prepubescent mind. His grades fell. His chores were neglected. And then came the dreadful day when his daddy found his centerfolds, which he had hidden under the neatly folded, snowy-white underwear.

''Are these yours?'' his father, in a voice of doom, asked him, downstairs in the front room. By this time, Ham was at a defiant age, and he had decided not to let the old man terrorize him. So he lifted his chin and said, smartly, ''Yes. These are mine. Why do you want to know?''

Daddy lifted his right arm, hand tightly fisted, his eyes blazing. He was sure that muscular right arm would come crashing down on him. But then his father took himself visibly under control, trembling a little from the effort. ''No, boy, I'm not going to hit you. You're too big for that.'' But, oh God, it was much worse. His father shut the door and began to lecture him. Ham would rather have gotten a beating.

The process was sadistically slow. First they knelt and prayed together for the salvation of his eternal soul. Then his father ranted. Then he preached in a soft, gentle voice. Then, thunderously, he quoted the Bible. A lot about Aaron and the golden calf and worshipping false gods. Then he went on to the purity and sweetness of good women . . . of mothers, of sisters, of *his* mother, *his* sisters!

And, at last, after what felt like eternity, he finally got to the point: that filth Hamilton had hidden in his dresser drawer, that filth Hamilton had in his mind that must be cleansed and purified.

"Temptation is always with us, son. The world is full of temptation. Our job, as men made in the image of the Almighty, is to resist that temptation, yes, resist all the blandishments that beckon to weak flesh. Especially those of us in whose veins there runs a hotter blood. Do you understand, boy?"

He would never forget his father's piercing eyes, drilling into him, reading his mind, on and on and on. In the end, he was ready to promise anything, anything at all. But what he really learned was that he had to be more careful, he had to learn to hide everything. And that day, he also realized, for the first time, that his father's long-kept secret wasn't locked away. It drove him, it controlled his whole life. His grandmother, his father's mother, had been a black woman. His father, alone of the four children she had, was able to pass for white. And so he did. But he suffered for it; his life was one long expiation for his guilt. He had to be better, stronger, more virtuous than any man—and that went double for his son.

Any time Ham heard that certainty in a man's voice, of knowing the Truth . . . any time he heard that patronizing tone, his back went up.

"You wanted to talk to me alone, Pierce. I'm glad because I have a question for you." The good doctor paused, his handsome brow furrowing in thought. Now what bullshit was he going to hand out, Ham wondered. "Why are you hounding this hospital? I mean, you must have a reason, because surely you know that if you keep on digging into every little flaw—no, don't laugh. I know there are big ones, too, but I'm talking about the constant picking at things like the garbage not being picked up on time, or beds in the halls, or this one woman you mentioned before, the one who sat for hours in labor—and, by the way, there's a good explanation for that . . .'' He tapped a typewritten memo sitting on his desk. ''. . . But we'll get into that later—Surely you know you could help bring about the demise of this hospital.''

''Excuse me, Dr. Wolfe, but isn't that bullshit?''

Wolfe did not stiffen, as Ham had thought he would.

''No, off the record, it is not bullshit. Do you know how many hospitals, major hospitals, have been forced to close down? Twelve in the past five years. It's the old bottom line, Mr. Pierce. The paying customers stopped coming and the state was late with Medicaid and Medicare payments and pretty soon . . . bankruptcy.''

''You mean the white patients stopped coming and, of course, who the hell cares about a bunch of sick black people? Let 'em die! There's too many of them anyway!''

Wolfe rose from his chair and loomed over Ham. There was a look on his face that sent a shiver down Ham's spine.

''Where do you come off, talking to me that way? What makes you think you're the only white man who has compassion for minorities? I was in Mississippi to register black voters when you were still wetting your pants!''

Ham stood up. ''My father marched right behind Martin Luther King to Montgomery. He was the only white minister in our county who stood with our black brothers and demanded equal rights!''

''What is this, a contest?''

They glared at each other, both obviously trying to stay in control.

''For Christ's sake, Pierce, you *know* we aren't racist here. I don't intend to bury you under a bunch of statistics. The point is, we treat whoever comes here, period.''

Meet an offensive with your own offensive. ''What about that woman in labor!''

Wolfe slid a paper across the desk. ''As you will see,'' he said, ''the woman in question is a South American immigrant—maybe illegal, I don't know. In any case, she never told anybody she was in labor. Even when she knew the birth was quite imminent, she said nothing, whether from a lack of English or a fear of the authorities, I don't know. And when she finally did speak up, someone misunderstood her.''

Hamilton was instantly alert. "Someone? Who?" Into the even longer pause, he said, "I get it. It was a doctor, and you doctors always protect each other.''

Wolfe colored just a little. "As a matter of fact, yes, it was one of the interns, a first-year man.''

"And exactly what was it he misunderstood?''

"*He* is a woman—a black woman in fact.''

"Oh great. And what's that supposed to do to me!''

"The patient had a heavy accent, apparently, and was agitated and spoke very rapidly and . . .'' He spread his hands. "Not at all a plot against anyone. Goddamn it.''

"I see what goes on . . . not just here in your hospital. Everywhere. No cab will take anyone uptown. Prices are twice as high up there as they are in your elegant neighborhood! White men assume every woman in Harlem is for sale!''

"What has that got to do with Harmony Hill?''

"Harmony Hill is part of the system. Hell, Dr. Wolfe, you yourself have been part of the system since the day you were born; no wonder you're blind to it.''

"You know, Pierce, frankly I find you insulting.''

"The truth is insulting?''

"You don't give a damn for the truth, Pierce. As for minorities, you don't give much of a damn for them, either, in my opinion. You're on a power trip, Pierce, why don't you admit it. It's not justice you're after . . . it's *ratings*!''

"You can go to hell!'' Ham pushed himself out of his chair. What a waste of time, trying to talk to this Jewish American Prince. "Maybe you should be more careful what you say to me, Dr. Wolfe. Remember, I have millions of people on my side.'' He slammed the door behind him.

Eliot stared for a moment at the door. Oh hell. What did Pierce want, anyway? He tried to calm himself by turning his attention to the array of objects artfully and discreetly on display and realized that his mother had put his whole life before him, like fetishes to protect him from evil.

There, as a paperweight, was the medal he had won in track and field in high school. His baby shoe, bronzed. His diploma from medical school, engraved on a brass plaque. And an assortment of photographs. Lillian and Philip, with Grandpa Eli and Grandma Bettina, in front of the hospital, posing by their brand-new Packard, circa 1934. His three kids, as youngsters in bathing suits, on some beach or other. And then, the separate photos in a modern curved-Lucite triple frame: David, looking very like the young Eliot. In the middle, a snapshot of Carolyn, suntanned, laughing, taken on a ski trip. And then Eric, the image of his mother, with the same fair curly hair, the same deep dimples.

He moved his eyes quickly to the ornate silver frame that held his wedding picture. He and Toni, his second wife, holding hands, he in his tux and she in her white lace dress, her dark, pretty face alight with her happiness. She was an extraordinary woman, intelligent, ethical, witty, honest, and loving. And she was *his*, that was the miracle. They had been really happy then, and he was flooded with a sudden certainty that they could be happy again.

He reached out to his phone and called their number in Georgetown. Toni might be home; she still had a lot of packing and stuff to do. When there was a click after two rings, he smiled in anticipation. But it wasn't her, after all; it was her canned voice, saying, "Hello, there. Neither Eliot nor Toni are here right now, but you know what to do. Well . . . *do* it." And her little giggle.

"Damn it, Toni," he said into the phone. "Where are you? I'm all alone, and I *need* you."

2

June, the same day

The living room of the Perfect Apartment was very large, with huge windows overlooking both West 94th Street and Central Park West. It was on the twelfth floor of an old prewar building, one of the truly elegant old apartment houses; the view out the windows was spectacular: Central Park was an endless expanse of green lushness that melted into a hazy skyline.

Eliot threw open one of the windows and leaned out, breathing in deeply the still summer air. Up this high, it was fairly cool and smelled good. He would probably like living here, but really, it was ridiculously large for just the two of them.

He turned away from the window, to meet his own startled reflection in the wall of mirrors opposite. His eyes immediately slid away; he rarely looked at himself. Instead, he eyed the gleaming expanse of glass and thought, *Is it too glitzy for Toni?* He liked it okay; but would *she*? God, he wished he knew. God, he wished she was here with him. *Instead* of him would be even better!

He stifled a yawn, so his mother wouldn't notice. She'd be sure to tell him he hadn't had enough sleep last night. He hadn't, but the last thing he wanted was to let her know that there was anything wrong. And besides, he wasn't even *sure* anything was wrong. Not really. He just had . . . an uneasy feeling about his marriage. But he could never tell Lillian even that much.

Christ, he was a big boy now. Fifty-four . . . and that made Lillian, oh my God, could it be? Seventy-nine? Eighty? Hard to believe, looking at her: small, trim, no stoop, no dowager's hump, no sign of age, really, except for her close-cropped hair, a blaze of white waves. As far back as he could recall, his mother

14

had always been beautifully turned out. Today, she was resplendent and businesslike in a navy blue Chanel suit—he knew that for sure, because she had told him—and Barbara Bush pearls; although she'd kick him in the slats if she ever heard that description. "Excuse me, Eliot darling, but Mrs. Bush's pearls are fake," she would say disdainfully. And, of course, hers were not. His mother would have nothing to do with costume jewelry; and those two words were always laden with the same scorn she saved for "silverplate," "murder," or "capital gains tax."

Stop picking on your mother, he chided himself. Remember, it's Lillian who's been doing all the work: picking out apartments, checking them, and winnowing out the losers. She seemed not to mind. She certainly never complained. He should be grateful. But what was he thinking? He knew she was enjoying every single moment of being in charge.

Right now, she was discussing the fine points of parquet floors versus wall-to-wall carpeting with the real-estate agent, a hyperthyroid blonde with a first name like a last name . . . Carter, Marshall. Something like that. What did Toni prefer? Wood, he thought. If Toni were here, it would be so much easier. He really shouldn't be spending his time this way. He knew damned well there would be a dozen new problems on his desk by the time he got back.

There were *always* new problems for the president of Harmony Hill Hospital. He said it to himself again: president of Harmony Hill. The place he had run away from, where he had vowed he would *never* work. Well, he had been hoisted on his own petard. Not only was he back in New York, working at Harmony Hill, but he had been forced to grovel for his job, to evoke the magic of the Wolfe name to sell himself. If his parents ever found out . . . Christ, if his parents ever found out he'd been passed over for promotion at John Quincy Adams, it would kill them!

He glanced at his watch, impatient with his own thoughts. He had never told Toni the truth. He had let her believe that Harmony Hill came running after him. He had joked a lot about how they probably thought anyone at all was better than old Don Delafield.

He squirmed inwardly. It was so dishonest, and he was ashamed of himself for running down poor old Don . . . for a *lie*! Irritable, he paced the room, catching sight of himself in those damned inescapable mirrors. He was frowning deeply, he saw, and he immediately smoothed out his expression. He also straightened his shoulders; now that he was in charge of a major metropolitan hospital, as his mother had told him, he had to stand straighter. She had even gone with him to buy this magnificent and overpriced midnight-blue suit at Barney's. Barney's . . . God, the last time he lived in New York, Barney's was just Barney's Boystown, a kind of schlocky discount place way downtown. And now, it was the epitome of expensive elegance.

He studied himself for a moment. It *was* a proper power suit. For five hundred bucks, it had better be! He even gave himself a little smile in the glass. His old friend Sam had teased him, saying, "I'm not quite sure what your other qualifications are, but you certainly look the part." He was not exactly handsome—not with the hawk nose he had inherited from Philip—but women still gave him the eye from time to time. Did that mean he had a presidential look? And why was he thinking about women, anyway? Toni had better get herself up here!

He consulted his watch again. How long could two women discuss the pros and cons of one apartment? He yawned, and this time he didn't bother to hide it.

"Eliot," his mother said, in an amused tone, "stop complaining. Now, the mirrors will be taken down, and I'm sure Bailey can arrange any changes Antonia might want."

Bailey. Bailey Myers. *That* was the agent's name.

"Certainly." Bailey beamed with delight at the thought of taking down twenty-five feet of beveled glass. Eliot wouldn't be surprised if she grabbed a screwdriver and did it herself. Seven percent of a million-dollar sale was not to be sneezed at, especially in this market. Bailey Myers had a lean and hungry look— a *very* lean and hungry look. "Whatever Dr. Wolfe wants."

Lillian made a little noise in her throat and set Bailey straight. "*Two* doctors. My daughter-in-law is a *very* well known obstetrician in Washington, which is why she's not here with us."

"I do hope I'll meet Mrs. . . . er, um, the other Dr. Wolfe . . . er, your wife, Dr. Wolfe."

"She uses her own name," Eliot said. "She's Dr. Romano."

"Oh. Romano, did you say?"

"That's right." If by any chance she was wondering how a man from one of New York's old Jewish families came by a wife with an Italian name, he would tell her "by marrying twice,

that's how. By finally marrying for love." His first wife had
been of the proper age, religion, socioeconomic level, and intelligence. He had ended up hating her.

Poor Arlene. It wasn't her fault. She was a sick woman. But
it had been horrible, living with her. He shook his head impatiently. If there was one thing he tried to keep out of his thoughts,
it was his ex-wife and the lost years.

On the other hand, it wasn't much better, these days, thinking
about his second marriage. He missed Toni. He loved her. But
he was getting mad. He wanted her here with him. Was that so
terrible? Her devotion to her patients was admirable, of course
it was; but right now, when their own lives were in such an
uproar, he found it excessive and maybe even a bit obsessive.

There were other doctors in Washington; there were even a
few, so he had heard, capable of delivering a baby. Which he
had said to her again last weekend. She hadn't even smiled.
"Give me a break, will you?" she had snapped. "These are not
normal pregnancies, and you know that. I am committed to be
with these women when they deliver. You're not a woman, but
even so, you should understand. You *are* a doctor."

Yes, he was; but he was not the super-dedicated doctor she
was, not by a long shot. He had never enjoyed practicing medicine, not from the first. For a long time, he had thought there
must be something wrong with him; he didn't find each patient
a challenge and a joy. He just didn't really *care*! What *he* wanted
to do was reorganize his department at the hospital; he wanted
to redesign the nursing station so that it worked right!

His new job: that was more like it! Harmony Hill was like a
volcano about to blow, and he found he *enjoyed* the danger. He
relished dealing with 1099, the local chapter of the hospital
workers union; he loved dueling with the politicians; he enjoyed
all the conflicts; he liked delegating authority; he took delight
in every single difficult decision he had to make.

At last, he was where he belonged, doing something he was
really good at. For the first time since he was twelve years old,
he woke up every morning with a strange feeling he had finally
identified as joy. And then he had to laugh at himself. Big talk
from a man who had been doing this for a whole six weeks! He
could imagine his feelings this time next year. When you were
in the hot seat, on top of a smoldering volcano, you were bound
to get your butt burned sooner or later.

"And the kitchen . . ." burbled the agent, gesturing him through a pair of swinging doors. "Isn't it gorgeous? All Italian tile, and the refrigerator's a Zero King, the stove, a Garland, of course. . . . They did it over just a year ago; it cost over $50,000."

The refrigerator looked like any refrigerator to Eliot, only a hell of a lot bigger. And the stove, whose name had just been spoken in reverent tones, was just a big, black, ugly stove. "There's just two of us. We're not planning to open a restaurant," he said, and was immediately sorry when the agent's face fell and his mother shot him one of her looks.

"Pay no attention to this man," Lillian soothed. "He doesn't know the first thing about kitchens."

Now he had to laugh. "Worse than that! Neither does my wife! She never cooks! I don't think she knows how!"

He remembered quite well the first meal she cooked for him. He had waited a long, long time for that meal. Years.

When he had first met Toni, she had been a nurse, the best nurse on his service, although the newest. She had just graduated, and she was so eager, so full of energy, she fairly crackled. Patients loved her because she seemed to be there before they even knew they needed her. And downstairs, in the big hospital cafeteria, he had become very aware of her voice, which was husky and theatrical and carried her very definite opinions to the far corners of the room—even above the clatter and clamor of a mob of several hundred medical students, doctors, nurses, salesmen, visitors, and patients. She was for socialized medicine, against capital punishment, and thought President Johnson should be shot as a kindness to the country. She also knew the very best places for pizza, take-out Chinese, and deli sandwiches.

At the time, he had been bored, restless, and sexually starved at home. Arlene, whose life was hemmed in by dozens of rigid rules and regulations, was smothered by her depression and was beginning to smother him. So he began to "just happen" to eat his lunch in the hospital, at the hour when Nurse Romano took hers; and, since she worked on his service, it had been perfectly natural for him to suggest they sit together.

That year, they became friends. He would never forget the day he remarked on this and she had said to him, "Oh yes, we're on a first-name basis. You call me Toni, I call you

Doctor.'' He loved her humor; he enjoyed her directness; he admired the way she took care of her patients.

"Toni, you're wasted in nursing," he said to her one lunchtime. "You should be a doctor." And he meant it. He only wished the interns he got were half as competent as she was.

He had expected her to protest, but she surprised him—not for the first time, and certainly not for the last. "I know that," she said. "It's my dream."

"Then do it! I'll give you a recommendation. I know people—"

Toni laughed. "Recommendations and people, *I* got. My problem is money. Or, rather, *no* money."

He didn't know where the words came from. "I'll give you whatever you need." And then the swift succession of emotions that swept across her face made him realize how that must sound.

"What in hell are you trying to pull on me?"

"Nothing. Really. Look, Toni, I'm serious. I'm . . ." Hell, he might as well take a page from her book and say it straight out. "I've got plenty of money. And . . . I'd like to do it."

She had been leaning forward, elbows on the table, intent. Now she sat back and regarded him, her eyes narrowed. "Yeah, sure. And . . . what do *I* have to do? Oh Jesus, you're blushing! Does that mean I've put my foot in my mouth, as usual?"

"No . . . No." He felt so stupid and inept. And, damn it, he *was* blushing; he could feel the heat across his cheekbones. "Look. We're friends; I *thought* we were friends. I . . . I've needed a friend this year, and, well, I've come to care about you. Look, Toni, are you going to take me off the hook, or not?"

She laughed and patted his hand, clenched into a fist on the table. "Take it easy, Doc. We *are* friends. And I'll take a loan from you. A *loan*. Once I'm a doctor, I can easily pay it back, right?"

"Not if you have your way and we have socialized medicine!"

"That's not a joking matter, Doctor. Listen, in England . . ." And they were off and running, carrying on one of their favorite arguments.

She left at the end of that year, and he didn't see her again until 1971, when she came back to the hospital as an intern.

He knew that she had done well in medical school. She had sent him postcards, twenty-three of them, which he had saved, secured by a rubber band. He also knew because, unbeknownst to her, he had made regular phone calls to the dean there, an old classmate of his at Columbia Med.

But he was completely unprepared for the surge of pure delight that swept over him when he saw her at the entrance to the cafeteria, just standing there, waiting for him, in her white coat, with the stethoscope slung ever so casually around her neck, and the biggest, broadest, brightest smile lighting her face. He had forgotten how pretty she was . . . or had he ever known? He had forgotten her eyes were green; he had forgotten the thick black lashes. He had forgotten the proud Roman nose and the high cheekbones. And her mouth, with its full lower lip. His heart was hammering behind his rib cage; he felt like an overheated teenager, and more than anything he wanted to take this woman in his arms and taste her mouth.

What he *did* was to take control of his crazed emotions, thrust out his hand, and say in his best colleague-and-friend voice, "Well. Doctor Romano. Welcome back to John Quincy Adams Hospital."

She took his hand and then, standing on tiptoe, kissed him. Lightly, briefly. But it burned. Eliot's heart beat faster than ever; his whole body was shaking, and he was afraid she would notice.

"I missed you," she said.

"I missed you, too," Eliot said. "I didn't realize quite how much." Damn it, he was going to make a fool of himself. And then he *did* make a fool of himself. "Have dinner with me tonight," he blurted. "At Duke Zeibert's. I'll give you a steak."

Toni grinned. "Why don't you come to Toni Romano's? I'll give you spaghetti and meatballs."

They stood there by the cafeteria, heedless of all the people brushing by, bumping into them. He remembered later thinking, *Is this real? Is she really saying this?* And then, with a rush of excitement, remembering that Arlene had gone to New York to visit her parents and had taken the children with her. He was alone. He was free.

He arrived at her door ten minutes early, a huge bunch of roses in one hand, a bottle of Chianti nestled in its straw basket in the other. He stood there feeling like an idiot. He had no hands to knock on the door. But the door opened, and she was there, gazing up at him with those amazing green eyes. She was wearing a gauzy green thing . . . robe . . . something that seemed to float around her.

"I heard you coming up the stairs. So. Come in! You don't have to wait until exactly seven o'clock. Come on, come see the world's tiniest apartment."

The bed seemed to dominate the room; it was all he could see, for a moment or two. Then she took the flowers from him, and the bottle of wine. She was laughing, looking into his eyes. "I should put them in water before they die."

Eliot looked around. His thoughts were flying all over the place. He couldn't seem to concentrate, to do anything normal. It was a small all-purpose room, the bed pushed into one corner, draped with a blue bedspread to look like a studio couch, and piled with pillows. In another corner was the kitchenette, with a curtain you could pull across, and in front of it, a gateleg table—fully opened and set for dinner—and two straight chairs. And there was the bed, her bed. There was a desk, he saw, and photographs, framed, on the wall. And the bed. He was so scattered; he felt as if he were about to fly apart.

She turned back to him, the roses stuffed into a vase, and as she looked at him, the expression on her face changed completely. She made a soft little noise in her throat. "Oh," she said. "Oh Jesus." And then, instantly, magically, she was in his arms.

She was soft and fragrant with the scent of lilies or roses or something wonderful. Her mouth was satin and tasted of something delicious. His head was reeling with the smell and the feel and the taste of her. He pulled her closer into him, needing to have her body, her whole body, next to him. He had been lost in a desert . . . for so long! and now he was in a lush oasis. He drank of her mouth, he put his hands into her cloudy hair, he pushed his hips into her. Someone was groaning with pleasure; suddenly he realized it was himself. He needed her, he wanted her, everything else in the world had disappeared.

When she started to pull away from him, he fought her for a blind moment and then, alarmed, stepped back. "I'm sorry, I'm sorry."

She was laughing, tenderly. She laid her hand along his cheek. "I'm not. I've been waiting a long time for this."

Eliot could not believe what he was hearing. She had never given the slightest hint; and he said so.

Again, she laughed and tugged at his arm. "Men are idiots," she said. "I've had a crush on you from the very beginning. But, today . . . well, today you had a different look. Today . . . never mind. Come to bed."

Their clothes flew away; later, he could not remember undressing. He really wanted to make love to her slowly, sweetly. He wanted to take her clothes off and kiss each part as it was revealed. He wanted to stand her off and look at her body, touch her and caress her. And then, he wanted to lie down next to her and kiss her, and with his hands, get to know the contours of her loveliness . . . and then, and then, slowly, lovingly, enter her.

Instead, they crashed together, mouths open, tongues searching, arms pulling tighter and tighter until they lost their balance and fell across the bed. All his thoughts of prolonged, lingering lovemaking vanished like a fog burned off by intense heat. He plunged into her, in a frenzy of lust, and she cried out, her hands cupped tightly around his buttocks, pulling him into her, deeper and deeper. He closed his eyes, he bent his mouth to hers once more, and exploded, red flashes of light behind his eyelids.

He collapsed over her, breathing heavily, kissing her neck and her shoulder in gratitude. He was depleted, emptied of tension, completely happy. He had never known this kind of joy, this warmth, this comfort. He had forgotten a woman could make him feel this way. He could feel the tears forming in his eyes, and he moved to hold her in his arms, thinking that he would never have this, never again. Moments later, he was fast asleep.

He awakened quite suddenly to her touch. She was sitting on the edge of the bed, wearing nothing but his shirt, rubbing his chest, grinning at him.

"The pasta's glue, the sauce is burned, and the meatballs are rubber."

Eliot grinned up at her. There was a stirring in his loins. "And I'm so hungry," he said, grabbing her and pulling her down. "For you . . ."

"Eliot!"

He jumped. "What? Oh." He had been very lost in his memories, and it was a jolt to find himself, not in the rumpled sheets of Toni's bed on Q Street, but in an empty, echoing apartment in New York City.

"Well? What do you think?"

He had a hard time remembering what it was she wanted him to think about. Oh yes, the kitchen. "Very nice. Very nice." He and Toni had made love that whole night; they never had gotten around to eating; they didn't need food back then. Somewhere in the wee hours of the morning, she confessed to him that she didn't know how to cook; she'd invited him for dinner because, well, she couldn't exactly invite him to fuck, could she?

Damn it, what had happened to those days? What had happened to *them*? The woman who had always been so eager, so hot for him that they even screwed standing up in the linen closet at the hospital . . . *often!* When had she changed, become disinterested, preoccupied, and driven?

Maybe in a new place, in New York, they could make a new start. Why not? He already felt like a different man, a happier man, a younger and more energetic man.

Quite suddenly making up his mind, he turned to the two women and announced, "Okay. This is it. I'll take it."

His mother gave him a look. "Of *course* you'll take it," she said. "Didn't I say so?"

And so he left, laughing.

3

End of June

The rain beat in solid sheets against the windshield, running in thick streams over the glass. Eliot squinted, trying to see. He'd be grateful to see *anything* out there, in the unfamiliar dark streets, pointing him in the right direction. He had taken a wrong turn, trying to find the Marine Air Terminal, and now he was lost in the wasteland of rainswept residential Queens.

Toni had insisted on taking the shuttle from Washington, saying, "I won't step foot on or in anything with the name Trump on it, you know that. If I do, my hair falls out."

They had both laughed. Now, though, lost in the storm, Eliot wished she were coming in at LaGuardia. He knew the way there, and he didn't want to be late, not tonight. He wanted to be waiting for her when she walked in, so he could go right up to her and grab her and give her the smooch of a lifetime. He laughed aloud. Oh, she'd be surprised, all right. The Wolfe men did not usually show emotion in public. But tonight was different. Tonight was the first night of the rest of their lives.

He turned left, for the fourteenth time, and at last: an arrow pointing the poor weary traveler in the right direction. In a few minutes, he could see the lights, sort of. A quick glimpse as the wipers pushed the water away. But he had faith; he just kept going, and in less time than he had figured, he was there. No creeping and crawling down the ramp, like at LaGuardia; no going round and round, looking for where they had hidden the entrance to the parking lot this time.

This was nice! This was like the old days. You drove up, you found a parking space right in front of the terminal, you cursed the rain, opened your umbrella, ran for the front doors, cursed again, ran back, put a quarter into the meter, and *then*, finally, you got inside the terminal.

And stepped right into the past. This was an airport like the airports in all the old '30s movies: contained, quiet, *pretty*. An Art Deco air terminal. He half expected to see flyers in leather helmets and white scarves come ambling out. A mural depicting flight through the ages—well, through the decades, anyway—curved around the walls. He stood there for a minute or two, letting the umbrella drip dry, enjoying the old-fashioned feel of the place.

And then they told him that Toni's plane was delayed and he looked around, annoyed, itchy, wanting her to *be* here, god-damn it. *Now* what was he supposed to do? He hadn't brought anything to read, and this place was a desert. No coffee shop, no newspaper stand, no little café, no nothing; just a clump of disgruntled, damp people standing near the gate, complaining to each other.

Eliot asked a pleasant young woman behind a high counter just how long this flight from D.C. would be delayed. "I'm sorry, sir, we really can't say. There are a number of storms between here and Washington. Everything's backed up. Could be an hour."

He did not say "Shit," but he was certainly thinking it. He marched around the small terminal a couple of times, became bored with that; studied the mural a bit, became bored with *that*; tried people watching, making instant diagnoses, an old medical-school game. That woman should do something about her edema; he was sure the teenage girl with the skinny legs was anorexic; he wondered if the older man realized one hip was higher than the other. And then he became bored with that, too.

He checked his watch for the umpteenth time. Almost ten o'clock; the plane was already half an hour late. And then it struck him; ten o'clock here was seven o'clock in California. His son Eric might be home. He performed at nightclubs and didn't start until ten or eleven o'clock. He hadn't talked to Eric for quite a while.

He found a phone that would take his credit card and punched out Eric's number. It rang four times, and then made the little click that meant you would be hearing a recorded monologue. Every time he called Eric, there was a new message. They were all amusing. But now he wanted to talk to the real Eric, and he was not amused. He left a brief message: he'd call another time . . . "Or you *could* try *me*, Eric." After he hung up, he thought, *That was stupid, taking that tone.* He thought of calling back, but instead he dialed Carolyn's home phone. Again, the faint click, the musical background, the canned voice inviting him to leave a message after the beep. Damn it. This time, he just hung up.

He looked at his watch again. Oh boy, he'd used up all of four minutes playing telephone tag with his kids. Not David, of course. It would be fruitless trying to figure out if he could call David in Africa. Time zones were not his strong point. And in any case, David was more than likely not in the clinic, but on his eternal rounds of remote villages that knew no other doctor but him.

And here he was again, walking aimlessly around the terminal, looking out at the endless downpour, wishing Toni were here. He couldn't wait to take her home. *Home.* It had a nice sound to it. She thought they'd be going to his parents' apartment; but surprise, surprise. That apartment he'd seen was too big, too glitzy, and too expensive. So, of course, he had bought it. He laughed, remembering the little smile of triumph on his mother's face.

Lillian—he had never called her mom—was a character, no doubt about it. Even after all these years, she still missed nothing about him—as he had discovered all over again these past six weeks, staying with his parents in the oversized apartment on Riverside Drive where he had grown up. You'd think, with him ensconced at the end of the hall, far from the master bedroom suite, he could evade her scrutiny. But no. She knew exactly when he skipped breakfast and how often he went to the bathroom. And she scolded him when he groused about his wife's absence. "You're a doctor," she told him. "You understand." Yes to the first, but no, he did not understand why Toni had to stay behind in Washington so long.

But that was over, now. Toni had closed out her practice, quit her job, and was coming home. To him. And he was taking her to the new apartment, empty save for a brand-new big bed, a big bottle of champagne, and a big something else she was sure to be thrilled with.

He paced back and forth near the gate, willing that damned

plane to come in. Damn it, he wanted his wife, and he wanted her *now*!

Sitting in seat 2A, with a magazine open on her lap, Toni Romano stopped making believe she was reading, pushed her new glasses up onto the top of her head, sat back, and closed her eyes. She was not reading; if anything, she was praying. The plane had been going around and around and around since the beginning of time, she had seen a lot of lightning out there, and she didn't like any of it.

She didn't like flying, to begin with. There was something impossible about this huge thing lifting itself into the air and staying *up* there. She knew it was because of the Bernoulli Effect but, even though the guy was Italian, what did he know? Leaving the earth and lumbering along through the air was *dangerous*. No matter how many statistics she read that you were more likely to get killed in your car, in your neighborhood, she *knew*, in her bones, that God had never intended people to sit 20,000 feet in the air, circling Baltimore, Maryland.

And anyway, she didn't want to be on this plane, leaving her practice and her patients and her friends—her whole life. She didn't want to be going to New York. If she told the truth, the whole truth, and nothing but the truth, she'd have to admit that being alone in the house, without Eliot around, had been a relief, really, after all those months of misery.

It was his misery, really, but it had become hers, too. What a hideous time! He had expected to be named chief of his service at John Quincy Adams; in a way, he had every reason to expect it. But there was another doctor who was willing to work harder than Eliot Wolfe, who was willing to put in more hours, see more patients, woo more members of the board . . . kiss more ass, that's what it amounted to. So the other doctor got it. She knew Eliot would be terribly disappointed, but she was totally unprepared for his response.

She got the word while she was working, and she ran for a telephone, just as soon as she was free, to give him a call, ask him if he wanted to meet her for a quick drink before she headed out for night clinic. He wasn't in his office; he wasn't home, either. So she left him a tender message and went back to work. She did leave earlier than usual; she wanted to hold him in her arms and give him comfort.

She found him sitting in the dark, in their bedroom, wide awake, staring at nothing. She knelt by him and took his hand. "Eliot, Eliot, I'm so sorry. They're stupid, obviously."

He didn't answer her for the longest time; he didn't move a muscle; she was beginning to get nervous. And then he said, in a dead voice, "I can't stay at John Q."

"Eliot, don't be ridiculous. Chief of service isn't the be-all and end-all."

"It was, for me."

He sounded like a child, not a grown man. Her husband, her strong, capable, supportive husband, was allowing himself to be defeated by a fucking *promotion*? It was something of a setback, and it was terrible for him, but the end of the world?

"Eliot, come on. You can't mean that. I know you wanted it very badly, but since when have you been a quitter? 'You can't stay there!' That's not you talking!"

"That's me talking."

He meant it. Oh God. She'd never, ever, seen him like this! What was happening to him? She felt a chill climbing through her bones, and she made her voice stay even. She couldn't let him see how frightened she was.

"You want to leave the hospital where you've spent your entire medical career?"

"I'm a failure. I left New York, I left my opportunity to be the Wolfe heir to the throne at Harmony Hill, because I was so sure I could do it on my own. I was going to prove—to my father, to Lillian, to all of them—that I could do just as well on the outside. I was wrong, Toni, don't you see? I failed, and now I'm too old to start all over again."

"You're not too old; that's nonsense. You're still young and vigorous. You have a good reputation, you're respected—"

"Who'll have me? Christ, how can I tell them?"

"Tell who?" Toni said, but she knew who. Dr. Philip Wolfe and Mrs. Dr. Philip Wolfe, that's who. She didn't wait for an answer, but put her arms around him and said, "Lie down with me. Let me hold you."

She held him in her arms all night. She hardly slept, he was clinging so hard to her. And in the weeks that followed, she felt him hanging on to her, emotionally if not physically, twenty-four hours a day. He was that close to a nervous breakdown, and she didn't know what to do about it. He put on a pretty good imitation of his normal self, in the hospital. To everyone else, he seemed about the same: calm, laid back, purposeful. But she knew he was gibbering inside, unable to concentrate on anything for more than a few minutes at a time. His colitis kicked up on him—no surprise there—and their sex life became non-existent.

He wouldn't talk about it; he wouldn't talk about anything. He was her mentor, her idol, her model! He was supposed to be *better* than she was, and bigger and stronger and smarter. And here he was, becoming more and more infantile, letting life happen to him, instead of getting on with it. She found herself falling out of love with him and then feeling so horribly guilty about feeling that way!

He wouldn't go for therapy in D.C., of course not. All the psychiatrists knew him; he had a certain image to maintain. But his friend Sam Bronstein was a good shrink, and Sam was his best friend, more a brother, really, and, best of all, he was in New York. Eliot had said yes, it was a good idea, but the days went by and he didn't call and he didn't call. Finally, he admitted to her, "I can't. I just can't." So *she* did it.

Eliot and Sam talked for over three hours on the telephone. She never found out what was said, on either side. It didn't matter because when they were finished, it was pretty much the old Eliot who came striding into their bedroom. She was lying on the bed pretending to watch television when he threw himself down on her, biting her neck, kissing her all over, eager and passionate.

She couldn't remember whether it was during that telephone call or another one when Sam let Eliot know that a search had started for a new president at Harmony Hill Hospital, and that he should make himself available. "My name came up!" Eliot said with the biggest smile she'd seen on his face for a long time. "Sam thinks I have a very good chance. Don Delafield . . ." Here, he paused and made a little face, shaking his head. ". . . is not doing such a great job, Sam says."

At the time, she thought it was a godsend that he was able to concentrate on something. There was his résumé to be worked on, papers to be got together, calls to be made, and trips to New York and meetings and interviews and dinners and cocktail parties.

She encouraged it; she did everything she could to help it

along. But he wasn't supposed to actually *get* the job! She just never thought that far ahead. It was all this game, called Going After the President's Job. Jesus, he even said it himself: ''My chances are probably somewhat less than fifty-fifty. But, hey, it's worth a shot.''

Well, here she was up in the sky circling over Baltimore, heading for New York City. Yes, folks, he got the job. He was so happy, she had to be happy for him. But she was being forced to leave her life behind, in Washington, a life she loved.

Then again, she might learn to love it in New York. She even had a new job. Eliot had told her about a program at the hospital—a failing storefront clinic for poor women. ''They could really use you,'' he said to her. And he was right. From everything she was reading and hearing about New York these days, they weren't standing in line to work in the dangerous neighborhoods, with the lowest of the low. So she had gone up for an interview, and they had offered her the position on the spot. Lousy pay, miserable surroundings, difficult job. Who else would want it?

Now the loudspeaker in the plane cleared its throat, and there was the captain, drawling that the storms had passed over and he expected to get into the Marine Air Terminal in New York City in about thirty minutes.

The minute he said it, she began to feel excited at the prospect of seeing Eliot. She loved him; he was so dear to her, and even though it had been nice, being alone in the house without having to worry about him, it would be even nicer to be with him again, making a new life together. Making love, yeah, that would be good, too. It was *all* going to be good; it *had* to be.

The plane came in an hour and five minutes late. Eliot, who had been fighting sleep, came instantly awake. Soon, his honey would walk out of that door . . . and then, suddenly, there she was! One of the first ones off. God, she was sexy! Little, dark, vivid, with a thick sweep of dark hair and a mouth you could die for! Men always looked twice at her; he loved walking into a restaurant or a party with her on his arm. He knew he was envied.

He found himself pushing past the other waiting people, eager to get to her. He grabbed her, pulling her in as tight as he could. ''Eliot!'' she protested, but she was laughing, and when he backed away to look at her she reached up on tiptoe and pulled his head down to kiss him. The touch of her mouth made him dizzy.

It had stopped raining when they got outside with her suitcases. They were both talking as fast as they could, talking over each other. He walked so their bodies could touch; and when they had tossed her cases into the trunk, he turned and grabbed her again, thrusting his tongue deep into her mouth. He hated moving away from her to get in behind the wheel.

He drove with one hand, the other holding hers. "God, it's good to have you home," he said; and she said, "It's good to be here."

"You'll never guess where we're going. No, no, you're wrong—"

She laughed. "How do you know what I was going to say?"

"Give up, Toni! You'll never guess, not in a million years! We're *not*, repeat *not*, going to my parents' place."

"Oh Eliot, you clever boy! You got us a suite at the Plaza, just like I always wanted!"

"You won't stay in a Trump building, remember?"

"Jesus, he bought that, too? Is there no safe place for me in New York City?"

They were both laughing so hard that when he said, "No, sweetheart, we're going to our new apartment," she leaned forward to peer at him, quizzical.

"What did you say? Did you say 'our new apartment'?"

"Yes!" He squeezed her hand. "Aren't you proud of me? It's gorgeous; it has the Good Lillian Seal of Approval. Central Park West, Toni, with an unbelievable view over the park and—"

"How can we possibly go there, without furniture, Eliot?"

He thought there was something strained in her voice. But why? She should be overjoyed! "It has all the furniture you and I will need tonight." When she didn't respond right away, he added, "A bed." And he brought her hand to his lips.

"You really bought an apartment, Eliot?"

"Yes, that's what I'm trying to tell you." He recounted his lunch hour with Lillian and Bailey, complete with sexual revery. "So I said I'll take it. And I took it."

"Isn't it mine, too?"

"Toni, what's the matter? I thought you would be so pleased!"

She sat quietly for a moment, and then said, "Of course I'm

pleased that it's done, and I'm sure it's a beautiful apartment. Your mother has wonderful taste. But, Eliot . . . don't you think I should have had a chance to see it before it was a done deal?''

"I . . . I . . . I don't understand. You told me you were dreading that whole business. You told me you didn't want to have to schlepp around and shop—!''

"I just think it would have been nice to have had some input.'' Her voice was tight, and she removed her hand from his.

"Toni! We've only been together fifteen minutes! Come on!''

"You're right, of course, you're right. I'm a little nuts from that airplane ride: five thousand miles in circles. Sorry, sweetie.'' She leaned over and kissed his jaw. "Better?''

Yes, it was better. It was much better.

He took the turn to the Triboro Bridge, and there it was: the skyline of New York, all lit up, looking like fairyland against the stormy sky where clouds swiftly broke apart, came together, fled into the distance. "Look at that!'' he said.

"Hey, man, I've seen that skyline before! I come from New York too, you know.''

"Brooklyn!''

"Yo! Don't make funna Brooklyn, or you'll have trouble wit' de mob!'' She put on her best Brooklyn voice, and Eliot laughed, glad to feel the mood in the car lighten.

"Toni, you're going to love the apartment, I promise you! Eight rooms, a library with the most gorgeous brass-trimmed bookcases . . . a view of Central Park . . . oh God, it's just so grand, I can't think of what to describe first. . . . Three huge bedrooms . . . God, there's room enough for an army. As a matter of fact, did I tell you that David's coming home from Africa? Well, I figured he could stay with us, till he decides what he wants to do. I think he needs some TLC, and some R and R; he sounds a bit depressed.''

"Eliot, in case you're thinking that we're the ones to cure a twenty-eight-year-old man of his depression, let me tell you, I haven't got it in me, not with everything else on my plate; and personally, sweetie pie, I don't think it's such a great idea for you, either. Maybe David should stay with Philip and Lillian. There's nothing she likes better than to have someone to take care of—''

He interrupted her, hating the tension he could hear in

his own voice, but unable to get rid of it. "Uh, Toni, the thing is, see . . . I already told David he could stay with *us*."

"Without consulting me?"

"What's to consult?" He had to fight to keep his voice under control.

"Why did you leave me out of the whole decision?"

"What would you have said if I'd asked you?"

"Of course I would have agreed, but—"

"Then what's all this about?"

"I *wasn't* asked, that's what this is all about!"

Now he was getting pissed. "I'm not going to ask your permission to have my own son, exhausted from two years of grueling work in Ethiopia, come to stay in *my* home!"

"Excuse me. It's not my home, too?"

"You know damn well that's not what I meant. I don't know why you're being so difficult about this. I thought you loved David!"

"Oh, for Christ's sake, Eliot!"

"We've been married for twelve years! You *know* how I feel about my children!"

"Eliot, David is a grown man! He's not your little boy anymore!"

"I don't care how old he is. I'm not going to change the way I treat my child, just because it might inconvenience you."

There was a long, long silence. He drove crosstown, his hands tight on the wheel, wondering how in hell they'd screwed up this homecoming so badly. Agh, maybe it was his fault. Maybe the car wasn't the place to start discussing household arrangements, especially not their first night together in their new home.

He reached out for her hand again and said, "I'm sorry, Toni, that was stupid of me. Will you accept an abject apology?"

She squeezed his hand. "Depends," she said. "*How* abject?"

"How abject do you want?" he said, pulling into the building's garage, smiling to himself.

"Will you grovel and cower and fawn?"

"Absolutely!" He paused. "Well, maybe not cower." He parked and turned to her. "Toni, are we okay?"

She laughed a little and laid a hand along his cheek. "We're okay. Don't worry. We're better than okay. And what I suggest is, you take me upstairs to our place so you can start your fawning and groveling just as soon as you possibly can. Know what I'm saying?"

He reached for her. "Let's go!"

4

July

The nasal voice over the loudspeaker singsonged "Dr. *Wong*, Dr. Wong . . . Dr. *Wong*, Dr. Wong . . ." Toni Romano glanced up the moment the sound began and then relaxed. She had thought they might be calling Deedra Strong, her chief resident. They were almost finished with rounds and she didn't want to lose Dee just now. She wanted her here particularly, when they went in to see the Rodriguez baby.

But now, on to the next mother in maternity. As they walked into Room 411, she checked the patients' charts for their names. Simms and Meade. What a contrast! Karen Simms, twenty-nine years old, overachiever, bank vice-president, rock climber, Yuppie from the top of her frosted head to the tips of her beautifully pedicured toenails. Imogene Meade, seventeen years old, unmarried, uneducated, unloved. Imogene was six feet tall and nearly as wide, with skin so dark it was almost purple. Her mother's last boyfriend, she had told Toni, had said she was "so damn ugly, you could haunt houses!"

Karen Simms, closest to the door, was sitting up in bed, reading the *Wall Street Journal*, her burgundy leather attaché case open on the bed next to her. Toni smiled to herself. Karen had given birth at 4:28 A.M., and here she was, not two hours later, wide awake and working.

The minute she heard Toni's voice, she put the paper down and announced, "Well, I blew it."

"Excuse me?" What in hell was she talking about? Maybe the stock market went up or down or whatever it took to ruin a deal?

35

"I really messed up. You're not supposed to take medication when you do natural."

Oh. "You had some Demerol," Toni said patiently. "You gave birth five minutes later. You were awake for the birth. You saw your daughter as soon as she was born. You held her. You talked to her."

Stubbornly: "I had drugs. It's like giving up. I thought I was better than that. But look, the first time it got difficult, I turned into a quitter. I messed up."

Dee looked over at Toni, the irritation clear in her eyes. If Deedra Strong had a major fault, it was that she did not suffer fools gladly, and it was clear that she considered Karen's upper-middle-class perfectionism foolish. Dee was going to have to learn that every anxiety was important and real to the person who had it, and a good doctor did· not judge and dismiss. Quickly, before Dee could open her mouth, Toni sat on the bed and began to talk.

"Karen, please listen to me. Your childbirth instructor told you it wasn't a competition, didn't she?" A nod. "That's right. Your instructor urged all of you not to be rigid, but to work with whatever happened. Am I right?" Another nod. "The bottom line, Karen, let's keep our eye on the bottom line." She squeezed Karen's hand and smiled into her anxious eyes. "Alyssa Jane Simms-Shannon—your daughter, your beautiful, healthy daughter."

Briskly, Toni stood up. Enough of this, she thought, a trifle wearily. She could see she hadn't convinced Ms. Simms, not one bit. Maybe she ought to take her up to neonatal intensive care with them this morning and let her see for herself what real mess-ups were—as in crack, as in AIDS, as in alcohol abuse.

"And now—" Toni turned and walked to the other bed. "Ms. Imogene Meade, who was delivered of a six-pound, three-ounce son, let's see now, was it really two days ago?"

The girl in the bed grinned. "That's right, Romano Abdullah Meade. He's thirty-two hours old, and we're leavin' at noon."

Toni regarded Imogene. Imogene was built like a football player; she had a large, flat face devoid of makeup, and she had hacked her thick hair short. If it weren't for her massive breasts, it would be difficult to tell her sex.

She had come to the hospital, to the ER, already in labor. She hadn't had even one prenatal examination, and in spite of her considerable bulk, she was anemic and poorly nourished. The baby was born wizened and grayish, although now he was plumping out.

The father was nowhere to be found. "Harlan, he got himself on crack," Imogene had explained. "Nobody knows where he got to." And when Toni asked her, gently, didn't she mind, Imogene shook her head, saying, "He wasn't no boyfriend, not really. I never had no boyfriend. He let me sleep on the floor in his place after my mother's new boyfriend threw me outa the house. He was right, Dr. Toni, I'm ugly, all right." It was said so matter-of-factly, it hurt Toni's heart. "But that don't mean he got the right to make me leave my own mother."

"You're right," Toni had told her. "You're absolutely right." She wanted to ask why her mother hadn't protected her, but she knew better. Neglect was a way of life in these disintegrated families. It was no different, really, than in D.C., just more visible, more pervasive, more devastating. Still, each sad tale, like Imogene's, tore at her. Imogene was sharp. She somehow caught Toni's thought and patted Toni's hand. "Yo, it's cool. She wasn't so nice to me anyhow."

"Do you have a place to go, Imogene?" Toni searched the dark, unreadable face. She hated thinking of this incompetent child taking her baby out into a hostile and dangerous world. Imogene was not stupid, but she had no education past the eighth grade, no skills, and no self-esteem whatsoever. It was the same old question: why had she had this baby when abortion was available? And, unfortunately, it was the same old answer: to have someone who would love her.

"I'm goin' to my grandmother's," Imogene said, proudly. "She said we're welcome. I can get a job at McDonald's and my grandmother will mind the baby."

Toni had met that grandmother, a tough little bird, probably not even fifty years old, but worn and out of patience. She hadn't been talking welcome, not when Toni walked into the room. She'd been laying down the law. No this, no that, no the other thing . . . "or out you go, girl, you *and* your baby!" Imogene, like so many of the teenagers Toni had seen here, was full of fantasies.

"I'll be comin' to your clinic, Dr. Toni," Imogene was going on, "just like you said, get birth control and learn about taking care of a baby and family planning and everything.'' She was nearly out of breath from the effort.

''That's good, Imogene. You have the paper I gave you?''

''With all the times and where it is and everything? Yep, I got it in my wallet!'' And as Toni and the residents filed out, she called out, ''See you real soon, Dr. Toni!''

Toni marched them down to the end of the hall, where they could not easily be overheard. ''Comments?'' she said.

Gilbert Reid was fresh out of medical school. Usually, interns were terrified of giving a wrong answer, but not young Dr. Reid.

''I must say, I was impressed with that Negro girl,'' he said. There was a murmur of agreement from the rest of them, and Reid preened himself a bit. ''Seems to me she's ready to be a responsible mother.''

Toni kept her face blank. ''And the rest of you? All impressed with Imogene?''

Dee burst out before anyone else could answer. ''You're all so goddamn naive! Honest to God, don't you see who you're dealing with? Obviously, you don't know thing one about living in the ghetto! 'Responsible!' In your *dreams*, Dr. Reid. Let me tell you what's really gonna happen. She'll move in with her grandmother and next thing you know, she'll be out in the street, hanging out, getting stoned. And then you know what will happen? She'll get pregnant again! I know these girls! They never learn!''

''You don't know that!'' Reid snapped. ''She could be the exception!''

''Whoa!'' Toni said. ''Let's not get embroiled in an argument over this. Dee is right, and so is Gilbert. However,'' she added, looking Gilbert in the eye and speaking very clearly, ''it is important to remember that our teenaged mothers, of whom we have far too many, deny and fantasize. Imogene really means to come to the clinic and to take good care of her baby and to finish school and make a better life for herself. But her chances of being able to do it are . . . oh God, *miniscule*. If we had good follow-up . . . but there's not enough money, there's not enough staff. . . .''

She paused and smiled slightly. ''Don't worry, I'm not going to mention the Women's Health Center—not more than six to seven more times.'' They all groaned.

"And now," she went on briskly, "let's talk about Ms. Simms for a minute."

"What she needs is a shrink, not an obstetrician!" That was Alan Pasternak, small and dark and wry and dry, her second-year resident. Toni found him very interesting. His mind took odd little twists and turns, and she never knew quite what to expect from him at any moment. She had once come up to the nursery and found him, in a rocking chair, holding one of the boarder babies, singing softly to it. The infant was nearly three months old and languishing for lack of love, a very dark-skinned baby the Social Service people were having trouble placing with a family. Even black families, apparently, did not want a baby who was "too dark."

"Alan's right," Dee said. "I don't know how you kept a straight face, Dr. Romano. Of all the crap—!" She stopped as Toni raised an eyebrow.

"Once again, I will remind you, *all* of you: every problem is real and important to the person who owns it. Can we all try to remember that?"

Dee pressed her lips together, and the rest of them didn't look at one another. Toni hated calling Dee down. She was going to be a marvelous doctor, but she had to conquer her impatience. She was extremely directed, and she expected the whole world to be the same. She was the kind of self-possessed young woman who seemed to strut through life: brilliant, young, tall, and athletic. She certainly moved swiftly and deftly around the hospital. Few young women were as disciplined. Toni had to admit that Dee reminded her of herself.

"Okay then, people, let's continue to the neonatal ICU."

The neonatal nursery was in the far side of the building, away from the maternity unit, with only a series of offices nearby. It was a quiet section of the building, so that when they rounded a corner and came across a cluster of nurses, it was something of a surprise.

"Dr. Romano, do you have a minute?" someone hailed. It was Janet Rafferty, the head of nursing, looking like a storm cloud.

"Sure." She turned to send the residents on ahead, but Janet stopped her with a chop of her hand. "No, no, let them hear. Let them learn what really goes on in a quote 'major metropolitan hospital' unquote."

"I hate to ask, but . . . what now?"

"I just got the agenda for the board meeting next week, and I can't believe it! They just won't give up, those idiots! It's on there again! Again! They've been told every time they bring it up and—"

"Whoa, wait a minute," Toni said. "What? What can't you believe!"

Janet Rafferty took in a deep breath and closed her eyes briefly. "Sorry," she said, "but I'm so angry. It's the maternity beds. Some of the men on the administration committee feel that we don't really need a maternity floor in this hospital."

Almost in unison, the residents began to protest.

"Yeah, that's how I feel, too. It's nuts. No maternity floor! What in hell is this hospital for, if not to take care of people who need it—as it has carved in stone over the goddamn front entrance!"

"Dr. Wolfe would never allow that to happen," Toni said, adding with a grin, "I know him."

"He may have no choice. I'm telling you, Dr. Romano, you and the other doctors are going to have to join forces and stop this stupidity!"

"I'll do what *I* can, you can be sure of that, Ms. Rafferty."

"It's very subtle, you know. Every month, it's on the agenda. Not to get *rid* of maternity, oh no. But the beds should be cut down. The staff should be cut. The medications are costing too much. But you and I know, we all know, what it's really all about. Am I right, ladies?" She turned to her group of nurses. They all nodded and agreed.

"What it's all about, Dr. Romano, which you've probably discovered already, is uninsured, poor, nonpaying patients. Those guys want to get rid of them." She stopped, her face pink with exertion. "Our ambulances have already been turned back too many times because there's no room for a mother giving birth. What kind of a country is this if there's no room for a mother to give birth?" She took in a breath, to say more, when around the corner came Conrad Havemayer, chief of pediatric surgery and a major power at Harmony Hill.

"Okay, women, back to your battle stations!" Janet sang out. The sudden change in her voice startled Toni a little, as did the subtle softening of her features. Where, a moment ago, a firebrand had been holding forth, there now stood a femme fatale who tossed her mane of red hair so that it rippled over her shoulders.

Oh my God! Toni thought. Nurses still have to do it, still have to play handmaiden to great white god doctors! Because surely this transformation was for the benefit of Dr. Havemayer who strode by, bestowing upon the little group a godlike inclination of his leonine head. Well, kiss my little pink tush, Toni thought. She hated doctors with an attitude, and this one had it in spades. She was just glad that, unlike the nurses, she didn't have to simper and coo at him.

"Good morning, Dr. Havemayer." Yes, it was definitely a coo.

"Nurse Rafferty." Brusque and businesslike. And then, in a crackle of starch, he marched past them into one of the offices.

Janet turned to Toni, grinning. "Nurse Rafferty," she said, imitating his deep baritone and the touch of accent, to perfection. Both laughing, they said good-bye, and Toni hurried her group along. She knew they were eager to take a look at this highly publicized infant. She held up her hand and said, "Okay, we've come here to see Steven Rodriguez, twelve days old . . ."

She paused as a murmur went through the group. "Let's hold it down, ladies and gentlemen. There'll be plenty of time for discussion afterward."

The little group pushed through the door that read NEONATAL INTENSIVE CARE UNIT and, led by Toni, made their way to the double sink just past the entrance. There, they all washed their hands and put on scrubs. Anyone who entered this place had to do the same, even the parents.

Even though the tiny patients here were all desperately sick, there was nothing gloomy about the ICU. All was bustle and brightness—yellow walls, cheerful curtains imprinted with brightly colored balloons on the windows, a crepe-paper clown hung from the ceiling—punctuated by the tweets and bleeps of the monitors at work. It looked more like a nursery school than a place for the sickest babies in the hospital. Even the scrubs— instead of the usual white or green—were yellow, blue, and pink.

Toni sought out Marie Campbell, the head nurse. "How's Steven doing?" she asked. She kept her voice very low; his mother and father were bent over his basinette, cooing at him, reaching down to touch him every few seconds.

Marie, a good-looking black woman from St. Bart's, glanced quickly over at him and gave a slight shake of her head. "The same. You know. But they won't see it. They keep telling me how he's opening his eyes, and he's grabbing their fingers." She stopped and sighed. "I haven't got the heart to tell them they're imagining it. Let them have a little hope for a little while longer."

Again, she sighed. "It's tough. She had so many misses and finally, this one made it, and they can't accept the reality." She paused and added, "You know, I love this job—as demanding as it is—because we get most of them to live. But this time. . . ? This time, my heart is breaking. If they ever let us turn off the respirator—"

"I know," Toni said. "I know."

"All they see is that he's there, and he's breathing."

Toni sighed and ran her fingers through her already tousled hair. "Damn it. And that reporter . . . Ham Pierce . . . he isn't helping. Every night on TV, there it is: an update on Steven Rodriguez, the Miracle Baby." She made a pained face.

Marie rolled her eyes. "That Ham Pierce!" she said, turning away so that the Rodriguez couple could not possibly overhear her. "They gave him permission. He talked them into it. We couldn't do anything about it. Well, we *did* keep him out of the room, but he just shot his pictures right through the window." An entire wall of the unit along the hall was glass. "Nothing stops that man!" Marie said. "But you know? He's really not pushy, he's, I don't know, forceful. And his show is certainly popular! Everybody wants to come take pictures of us, now."

Toni put a hand on Marie's arm. "Well, let them come look. They'll only see excellence. You run this place beautifully." They smiled at each other. "And now comes the hard part, talking the Rodriguezes into leaving for a while so I can discuss Steven with my residents."

"Suggest that they go get something to eat. They've been here since six o'clock."

Toni braced herself, thinking how it didn't get any easier. Somehow she didn't seem to get tougher with the years. Where was the objectivity, the professional distance, she had been promised when she was an intern.

Taking a deep breath, she walked over to Steven Rodriguez's basinette: a box of clear lucite, bravely festooned with hand-lettered signs, proclaiming his name in large letters, with many hearts drawn around it and the slogan, THE LONG-AWAITED STEVEN DAVID. The teddy bear propped up at the foot of the crib, a bright blue ribbon tied in a bow around its neck, was larger than the infant it seemed to be guarding. In fact, Steven was so tiny, he could be held entirely in one hand.

He had been born prematurely, his umbilical cord wrapped around his neck, and not breathing. Thanks to quick intervention, he had not died . . . that is, he had managed to give a weak cry or two and start breathing, more or less. But the only thing that kept him breathing was the respirator, and the skinny white tubes that snaked all over his wizened little body, feeding oxygen into his lungs, feeding nourishment and medications into his bloodstream, monitoring his every function. Because, having kept him alive in the first place, they had found more and more defects. Immature lungs. Bowel obstruction. It was heartbreaking.

Joe and Alice Rodriguez were an attractive couple, very attractive, Toni thought. He was short and dark and dimpled. She was slim and elegant with a serene oval face, her black hair parted in the middle and pulled back. She was a pediatric nurse from St. Vincent's. It made Toni feel terrible when Alice turned to her with dark, haunted eyes. Alice, Alice, where did all *your* objectivity go?

Toni liked Alice and Joe. They were the epitome of the American Dream come true: children of the working class, brought up in the barrio. And they had pulled themselves up, right into the middle class. They both worked. They had a nice apartment, a nice car, a nice savings account, a nice life. This tragedy wasn't supposed to happen to people like them. Inwardly, Toni sighed. But it had.

She and the young couple said their good mornings, and when she suggested they might be hungry, they glanced beyond her. They knew that little Steven was going to be her subject on this morning's rounds, and they were happy to go, she thought, because they didn't really want to hear the truth.

They wanted to go on believing the unbelievable, and they had said as much to her when she first suggested that Steven "might never really recover": a little play with words. Steven was brain dead. Oh, the EEG wasn't *completely* flat; there was some activity in the brain stem, the most primitive part of the brain. But he would never be capable of thought or feeling or emotion. And, if he were taken off the respirator, he would most likely cease breathing. He would be dead.

Toni's patient load consisted almost entirely of difficult cases, the same as it had been at John Q. She had a small reputation of success with high-risk births, so Alice Rodriguez had been referred to her.

Alice had already been pregnant seven times and had miscarried every time in the first trimester. When she had been twenty-six weeks pregnant, she'd been filled with joyful hope— "I can hardly believe it. But God has answered my prayers." That was just a few weeks ago. Well, it looked like God had other plans for Alice and Joe Rodriguez. Alice had wept the last time Toni very gently tried to tell her the bitter truth, that it was hopeless.

"And even if by some miracle he's able to breathe without help, Alice," Toni had explained, "his lungs have been ruined. He'll suffer for the rest of his life." The poor little fellow. He'd already been under the surgeon's knife twice, once for the bowel obstruction and then for a colostomy. Havemayer was a fantastic surgeon, but good God, what was the point! She didn't want to distress Alice even more by telling her what was in store for them, if this damaged child managed to stay alive. But a moment later, she wished she had been more direct.

"He's breathing," Alice had sobbed, over and over. "I can see him breathing. He's alive. I don't care what's wrong with him! He's my baby; he's the only one who lived! Don't ask me again, Dr. Romano, don't ever tell me again we ought to take him off the respirator. God had a reason to put Steven here on earth; He must have had a reason!"

Toni had reached out to put a hand on the shaking shoulders. So many parents said the same thing: that God had a reason for giving them a handicapped baby. What kind of God would do a thing like that to innocent people! But, if it gave them comfort, who was she to say they shouldn't believe what they believed? So she said nothing more to Alice and Joe.

She had gone to Havemayer; she told him exactly what she thought. And when he just kept shaking his noble head, she had found herself yelling, "Don't you realize what this is doing to those poor people! This is torture, and the longer you drag it out, the worse it's going to be for them!"

Conrad Havemayer had gone pale with passion, gritting out between clenched teeth, "As long as I am chief of pediatric surgery, Dr. Romano, every child I can keep alive, I will keep alive."

She had stood up, feeling the blood drain from her face. "No matter what?" she had demanded tightly; and he had replied tightly, "No matter what."

Somehow, Ham Pierce got wind of the story, and before you could say "Channel 14," he was there with his crew. One thing quickly led to another, and now they had a lawyer who regularly spoke to Ham Pierce and any other reporter who came his way, always ending with the same statement: "As far as Mr. and Mrs. Rodriguez are concerned, they see Steven breathing, he's alive." It had gotten to the point where Toni was hearing that nasal New York lawyer voice in her dreams.

As for Eliot, it seemed all *he* could think of was the hospital's image. Privately, he agreed with her. But for the record, he was totally noncommital. "For the present, Harmony Hill will support the parents of this baby."

And when, in private, she had protested, "Eliot, this baby is brain dead!" he had said, "Then he will eventually die. I cannot push this thing, Toni. I don't want the hospital embroiled in a long, messy court battle."

She had thought she knew him so well! But now he was ready to compromise his deepest beliefs for expediency! She stared at him, willing him to admit his true feelings to her. But his face remained impassive.

"But with every day he's kept artificially alive, Eliot, his parents have more and more false hope! It's cruel!"

"What's cruel, Toni, is to arbitrarily decide that *we* always know best, because we're physicians."

"Eliot, that's sophistry!"

"You've never had a baby, Toni. You don't know how the parents feel."

She stood stock-still, staring at him in disbelief. He had told her so many times it was okay that she didn't want children. It was a goddamn lie, she suddenly realized. He was still disappointed about it, after all these years. And now he was hitting her over the head with it.

Should she calmly and reasonably tell him that was a hurtful thing to say? Should she tell him to go fuck himself? Should she explain that, as an obstetrician, she damn well knew how parents felt about their babies? Should she remind him that he had been passed over, at John Q, and add that *she* had been offered a promotion, and that *she* had given up *her* promotion to follow him here? Should she tell him that he was wrong, she *had* had a baby?

Of course, she ended up saying nothing at all, slamming out of the library, still steaming, mad at herself as well as him. She should have told him about the baby long ago. Why hadn't she? It was so dumb, so damned dishonest. They'd been married for twelve years, and for twelve years she had kept her secret. Every year in February, when it came close to Valentine's Day, the baby's birthday, she thought that this time she would tell him. And each year, she just couldn't. She would wait patiently until her sadness went away again. Which it always did.

She had been only nineteen when she met Arch Williams. She was a student nurse, and he was an intern at Flower and Fifth Avenue Hospital. God, she was young, young and cock-sure. She felt indestructible. Her father had said no college for her, and she *had* gone to college; her father had said no nursing, it was a dirty business, and she had become a nurse. And her father hated black people, "nigs," he called them. He would certainly have said *no* to Arch Williams, who was big and tall and very definitely black. Which made him all the more attractive to her, probably. As if Arch needed anything to make him more attractive to her!

He was a doll, a doll with dimples and a sweet way of talking. Everyone loved him: the patients, the other interns, the nurses. He was totally good-natured, not a mean bone in his body. She came from Bensonhurst in Brooklyn, a tough Italian working-class neighborhood if ever there was one, and she hadn't thought men like him existed. Oh, God, if her father had ever found out she wasn't a virgin anymore! And with a colored lover! He would have had apoplexy, and then he would have killed Arch, and then he would have taken her straight to the nuns.

She and Arch in bed together. He would kiss every inch of her body, top to bottom, and then ask her if she'd like him to make his way back up. By that time, she was usually so frantic to feel him inside her, she'd grab his head and haul him up, at the same time wiggling her body down to meet his stiff cock. It was never enough, never. He was an intern with no time and no privacy. She was living in the nurses' residence. They had to find free time at the same time, and then they had to sneak around, so they would never be seen together. It was *never* enough. Was that why she thought she was so madly in love?

Dumbbell that she was, she had lost track of her period and thought she was putting on weight. And then she realized. She'd never forget the feeling: as if the entire top half of her body had collapsed into her stomach. She had trouble breathing for a moment and then her pulse began to race. What was she going to do? She was pregnant, she was going to have a baby, but she couldn't be. She could never marry Arch! Her mind was gibbering. *What* was she going to do?

"An abortion. Of course, an abortion," Arch said, when she told him. "Hey, don't look like that, sugar." He hugged her tight. "I'll go with you. I know a safe place, a doctor. It'll be fine. It'll be okay."

To her amazement, she couldn't. Oh, she knew she should; she knew she ought to. What chance did a half-black child have in this world? But when she thought of doing it, she froze. She *had* to get an abortion. She was three weeks away from graduation, three weeks away from beginning her real life. But she found herself shaking her head, heard herself saying, No, no, no.

She never had been able to figure out why. But she certainly had learned over the years that simply keeping a baby alive was not nearly the end of the story. And that brought her right back to the Rodriguez baby.

"Steven Rodriguez," she said to her group, all looking down at the wrinkled little body, "was born with a gestational age of twenty-six weeks and weighing six hundred twenty grams. The umbilical cord was wrapped around his neck, and he was probably oxygen starved at birth. He was delivered by a paramedic in an EMS ambulance, and there was no monitoring of the fetal heartbeat. However, the paramedic"—she consulted her notes—"reported that the infant was not breathing at birth. CPR was applied as they rushed the baby into the E.R., where he was successfully resuscitated."

Toni paused, choosing her words with care. "Successfully. I want you all to think about that word. Not so long ago, a six-hundred-gram baby would have died, no question. This infant has been saved by our modern technology." She reached down into the bassinet and held one tiny foot in her fingertips. "But for what kind of life? If he survives, he will be a vegetable." She paused long enough to let her last words sink in and then signaled that it was time they left. En masse, they left the nursery and walked down the hall to the same quiet spot where they had bumped into the nurses.

"Should this child have been saved?" she said, without preamble.

"Absolutely not!" said young Dr. Reid. "A doctor's job is to save lives, yes, but not artificially. Anyone who believes in God must believe that some things are out of our hands and beyond our understanding."

"Oh, you're on speaking terms with the big guy in the sky?" He'd done it again: set Pasternak, one of the other interns, off.

Gilbert's lips thinned out. He did not approve of anyone speaking lightly of his lord. "His will be done; you've heard of that, surely."

Ruth Singer, another first-year "man," quickly said, "But Gilbert, look, they've found a way to regenerate severed nerves, and we thought that was impossible. If we keep baby Rodriguez alive long enough, maybe we'll be able to help him. Surely God gave us our intelligence in order to use it?"

"It seems a terrible waste," Dee put in, "to use so much of our resources on what is essentially a hopeless case—"

"Exactly what I was saying!" Gilbert said.

"On the other hand," Dee continued easily, not even raising her voice, "it is our job as doctors to treat our patients humanely, and that means we have to know where they're coming from. In this case, we know that Mr. and Mrs. Rodriguez have had multiple pregnancies, none of which have gone to term. Now they finally have a baby, alive and breathing. All their hopes and dreams are fixed on this infant. I doubt very much they can even hear reality." She shrugged her shoulders.

"This is of course one of the major issues in medicine today," Toni said. "You are going to be confronted with these conflicts all the time. It's well worth discussing, over and over again. Ultimately, each physician has to decide for him or herself—"

"How do *you* feel, Dr. Romano?" Ruth asked. "About this case? This baby?"

"I feel this baby should be taken off the machines and allowed to die, or live, naturally."

"Then why is he still on?"

"The parents' wishes are paramount, as Dee so eloquently explained. And I'm not the pediatrician. I'm Alice Rodriguez's doctor. Dr. Havemayer is Steven's."

"And Dr. Havemayer," Deedra said, "will tell you if you ask—and even if you don't—'Every child has a right to life, period.' "

"I don't—"

"There are two sides to—"

"But on the other hand—"

Toni held up a hand. "Enough, enough. I must get back to my patients, and you, to yours. We will have many, many discussions on this issue. Now, let's talk center hours." She smiled at their stifled groans. The storefront Women's Health Center on 123rd Street was nobody's idea of a wonderful place to work. Its patient load consisted largely of society's leftovers, the poorest of the poor, the most ignorant of the ignorant. "I know, I know . . . it's a pain in the neck, and it's voluntary, and who has time? Well, I have time, for one. And, Doctors, the need is so great. There are too many teenage mothers, and if we, you and I together, don't *try* to have some impact . . ."

It was just as she had expected. Pasternak, Singer, and Strong were willing to do it; Reid, grumbling, finally said he'd fill in if needed. And when the others turned to give him basilisk stares, he glowered and said, "Well, I'm a married man and my wife works and I have two little kids and—" Then he broke off and said, "I *said* I'd do it!"

A few minutes later, she was striding down the hall alone, on the way to the elevators, mentally reviewing her day. It was ten o'clock; she had patients waiting in the clinic downstairs; then a quick lunch; and then the Women's Health Center until God only knew when. Just thinking about it made her weary. It was hard work, dealing with people who were so beaten down and hopeless.

Many of the women who came into the Women's Health Center were alcoholics and/or addicts, and that made them night people. She'd be working until at least nine o'clock, and Eliot wasn't going to like it, not one bit. He had some big affair on tonight, some kind of dinner dance or something.

Last night, he had complained, not for the first time. "Damn it, Toni, you haven't been to a single one of these hospital functions, do you realize that?"

"With gratitude," she answered, trying for a light note. "You know I hate getting dressed up. That's why God gave you a mother."

"It's not funny, Toni. The president's *wife* is expected to be at his side, at least every once in a while."

"Come on, Eliot, I'm just getting started here." What she did not say—and she was very proud of herself for keeping her mouth shut!—was, "It wasn't *my* idea to come here." She also did not tell him what she really thought: that working in the clinic, maybe helping a patient or two, was more important than grinning mindlessly at a lot of rich people whom she didn't know and wouldn't like if she did.

She had behaved very well—for her. Toni Romano was not a diplomat. But poor Eliot; he really deserved a normal wife. She moved close to him, putting her arms around his waist and tipping her head back to be kissed, murmuring, "To be continued, later, in bed . . ."

The elevator finally arrived, and for a change it was nearly empty. Only two young nurses bent over an International Male catalog. "Have we had a bomb threat?"

She expected at least a giggle, but they both stared at her with mild alarm.

"It was just a feeble empty-elevator joke. Never mind."

She got off at the ground floor. What kind of a wife *was* she, working night after night, never available to her husband when he needed her, madly in love with her work. She had *once* been madly in love with Eliot, and she had thought that feeling would never, never go away.

She needed a cup of coffee, she decided suddenly. Instead of going to the clinic, she turned the other way and headed for the cafeteria. It was noisy, as usual, with the clatter of silverware and the buzz of conversations and that horrible Muzak that was never quite loud enough for you to make out what song was playing. And, of course, the clumps of med students, residents, and nurses, all talking and laughing as loudly as they could. It was annoying, but she still remembered that need to horse around, to let off steam.

Carrying the hot container of coffee gingerly in one hand

while she balanced her briefcase under the other arm, she searched for a table where, God willing, she could be alone. There was Dr. Voorhees, sitting bolt upright, eating his lunch with great precision, eyes down. Funny, there wasn't a relaxed muscle in the man's entire body, and he the sports medicine *maven*. Physician, heal thyself, she thought. And, oh, God, of all the damn people, here was Ham Pierce. Maybe if she turned and went in the other direction . . . but no such luck.

"Dr. Romano!" Why didn't he yell a little bit louder, so they could hear it in New Jersey? "Dr. Romano, just one moment of your time." He was swift, and he was deft. He had done an end run around the cluster of drug salesmen by the Coke machine, jumped over a chair, wriggled through three tables crowded together, and here he was, standing right in front of her.

"Dr. Romano, I've been trying to get in touch with you." He waited for her nod. She knew; she had been given all the messages. "What I have to ask you, I think you'll like," he said, with that charming smile that made her feel like Little Red Riding Hood with the wolf. "I hear such good things about your center."

Again, a pause. He was waiting for his applause. "You hear good things about the center because I don't spend my time talking to reporters," she said. "I spend my time taking care of my patients." She was smiling at him, waiting to see what he'd do.

He never batted an eye. "Good for you, Dr. Romano. But, you know, I've been thinking . . . if I featured the center in one of my regular health segments, don't you think it would bring more patients in? Everyone uptown watches my show, you know."

Toni stood there, looking at him, feeling the coffee growing colder by the minute, wondering if she should take a chance on telling him straight out what she thought; and then, almost instantly, decided yes.

"Frankly, Mr. Pierce, I don't trust you. I'm sorry, but I don't. I watch your show, too. I know what you do in your medical segment, and it's generally sensationalism. If I ever let you in, you'd find *something* to pick on." She shook her head. "No, thanks. The clinic could use publicity, but not *that* kind."

Pierce grinned, but his eyes were angry. "Dr. Romano, I don't fabricate. The camera doesn't lie, you know."

"Maybe not, but the camera doesn't walk itself around, either. It follows your orders and sees what you want it to see. And shall we discuss editing and what *that* does to the truth?"

She waited for him to continue the battle, but to her surprise, he stepped back, holding both hands in the air, palms up, in surrender. "Okay, okay. I don't want to argue with you. I'm sure you're very busy. But I'm not giving up, Dr. Romano. That clinic is too important to my people."

Watching him walk away, Toni shook her head over his gall. Give me a break, she thought. *His people!* He talked as if he were a pharaoh. In fact, he looked just like her idea of a pharaoh: tall, broad-shouldered, with that well-tanned skin TV people always seemed to have, and almond eyes. She shook herself. Come on, Toni, enough of *that*! And then she continued her search for a table. Yes, there was an empty one, in a far corner near the kitchen. She pulled out the molded plastic chair, glancing down at the seat to make sure someone hadn't left crumbs or a puddle of milk or, as had happened to her once already, a fork. Nothing. Good. She sat down, thinking she should really get to her paperwork. But her mind was drifting, refusing to settle down.

God, the first time they made love, she and Eliot, he had clung to her like a man dying of hunger. Which he had been, for sure. He had been a man totally starved for affection. The trouble was, now, twelve years later, his hunger had not yet been assuaged. He needs me too much, she thought, not sexually, not anymore. But he always wants me to *be* there.

When she stayed behind these past couple of months, God, he had made her feel so guilty! And for what? It wasn't such a long time, the shuttle worked, didn't it? And surely a grown man with his whole family right there in New York could handle a few weeks' separation. God knows *she* had welcomed the time alone!

Sipping at the lousy coffee—and *liking* it! that was the really terrible part—she took out her papers. She really had to review the lab tests for the patients she would be seeing today. But she couldn't, she just couldn't. Her mind kept circling back to what Janet Rafferty had told her. They really wanted to get rid of maternity. Just like that? But that was crazy! They couldn't do that, or could they? How could Eliot let them keep bringing it up? All he had to do was tell them to forget it! Goddamn it, what was the *matter* with him? Didn't he have any guts at all?

The Eliot she had met, all those years ago, *and* the Eliot she *thought* she knew, would *never* cut back on maternity, would *never* threaten to close down the E.R., would *never* abandon the poor and the disenfranchised—for a profit!

He had seemed to her the epitome of the dedicated doctor. In her he had seen an adoring girl who would become an adoring wife and mother. But they really had misled each other. He got a loudmouthed, workaholic Italian girl, with no respect for men. She got a good boy, too wimpy even to know what he *wanted*! So maybe they were even.

She had twenty minutes before clinic hours began. And, she decided, she couldn't wait one more minute to have it out with the great almighty president! She got up and got out of there, steaming down the hall, full speed ahead. She noticed that people were getting out of her way, and she almost smiled. But damn it. She was *not* going to smile; she was *not* going to enter laughing.

When Toni stormed into Eliot's suite, Betty Cannon was busy typing away. Betty began a smile of greeting but then began to laugh. "You go right in, Dr. Romano," she said. "Better him than me, from the look of you."

Toni gave a bark of sardonic laughter in answer and, knocking just once, let herself into the sanctum sanctorum.

Eliot was standing at the windows, looking down on today's protest marchers. She'd seen them this morning. Who were they? Oh yes, the anti-abortion people, the ones who liked to say they were pro-life but didn't have a clue what they were talking about. There was *another* group she should take on a little tour of the neonatal intensive care unit! Yeah, why not? she thought. Then, she'd ask for people to volunteer to adopt these babies.

"Eliot," she said.

The look of pure delight that lit up his face made her stomach clutch. Oh shit. How could she yell at him if he looked at her like that? Well, she had to!

"Eliot, what's this about cutting back on maternity beds!"

The look on his face changed instantly. Sweetly sarcastic, he said: " 'Well, hello there, Eliot darling. How's it going? I just stopped by because I heard a rumor and I'd like to hear whether or not it's true.' "

"You're not going to sidetrack me, Eliot. It wasn't a rumor; I got it straight from a committee member."

"What? That it's on the agenda? It's always on the agenda and I wish you wouldn't jump to conclusions." He laughed a little. "You have a real short fuse, you know."

Short fuse! Well, goddamn it, he was right about that. But so what? Some things you *should* get enraged about!

"But *why* is it on the agenda? Why haven't you told them once and for all that you're not having any of it!"

He sighed. She hated it when he sighed; she hated his long-suffering patience. "Toni, I understand that you are concerned. So am I. That's right, so am I; you needn't give me that oh-yeah look. I'm fighting the good fight, but come on, I'm not a dictator. I have to go by the rules."

Toni made a rude noise, and he colored with exasperation. She knew that, whatever he said next, he would say it in a particularly condescending tone.

"Dr. Romano," he said in tones of saccharine reasonableness, which made her clench her teeth, "may I remind you that you are not head of OB/GYN; Ken Carlsen is. You should be talking to *him*. I am appreciative of your concerns; as president, I welcome ideas and suggestions from people at every level—"

"The head of my department," she began, matching his even tone with her own, "as you damned well know, is an ineffectual boob! And furthermore," she went on, not caring that her voice was climbing the register with every word, "not only does he never have an idea . . . not only does he refuse to ever make a decision . . . but he *idolizes* Havemayer! Anything the great god Havemayer says, Dr. Carlsen buys, even at the expense of his own department. Eliot, for God's sake—!"

If she was hoping he'd get off his high horse, she was doomed to disappointment. In that same supercilious tone, he said, "Dr. Carlsen is a fine physician; perhaps a bit elderly, a bit old-fashioned, but—"

"He despises women, Eliot, and that's not just my 'usual feminist shit,' either! One of my patients went to him last year, with very heavy periods and a lot of pain; when she told him why she was seeing him, he looked her right in the eye and said, 'We just have to let nature take its course.' What *we*? Since when was *he* having heavy periods? A little elderly you say? A little old-fashioned? A little shit, is what *I* say!"

Eliot sat himself heavily into the big leather chair behind his desk and looked at her. "Damn it, Toni, you, too? Every person in this hospital is on my case, about every damn thing."

"That's your job. The one you love so much."

That stung; his lips tightened. "Look, Dr. Romano, I'm sorry that Dr. Carlsen doesn't measure up to your very high standards. But try to have a little patience. He's only the acting head. Strictly temporary. I'm busting my ass to find a replacement, but, damn it, nobody I want wants to work up here!" Again, he sighed and put his hands out as if to say, Give me a break!

Toni looked at the man behind the desk, the big, white-haired, handsome man whose face and body and voice and moods were so familiar to her. Why could he never stand up and be counted? He had made a life's work out of keeping the lid on *everything*. Had he ever really faced up to *anything*, faced it and fought for it? Had anything ever mattered enough to him?

This marriage is in big trouble. Out of nowhere, it came clanging into her head. She was swept by cold panic. Where had that thought come from? What did it mean? Impulsively, she ran to him and sat on his lap, throwing her arms around him and hugging him fiercely.

"Oh, Eliot, I'm sorry I came barging in here, giving you a hard time. I'm just frustrated by it all."

He hugged her. She kissed his cheek. "I love you," she lied.

5

August

Eliot pushed through the front doors into the lobby of the hospital. Every time he walked in here, he got a lift. It was a lively scene. Everyone seemed in a hurry—on crutches, in wheelchairs, high heels, running shoes, boots, whatever. There were signs posted on every wall, pointing left to the clinic area, right to the emergency room, straight ahead to the elevators, straight ahead and to the right to the Goldstone Pavilion, with the gift shop, manned—womanned, really—by hospital volunteers directly in sight at the back of the lobby. And standing watch over the whole panorama, Sanchez and Brown, the day security guards in their neat gray uniforms. The walls had recently been repainted, gray with burgundy trim, very elegant, the oil paintings of his grandfather Eli and other illustrious founders of the hospital had all been cleaned and their elaborate gilt frames restored. As he always did when he entered the building, Eliot looked up and gave his progenitors a silent salute.

And then he saw, on the other side of the lobby, the familiar stocky build and rumpled seersucker of Dr. Sam Bronstein, known to everyone as Dr. Sam. Brilliant psychiatrist, tennis nut, and most importantly, Eliot's oldest and dearest friend. Sam had come to live with the Wolfes when Eliot was twelve, changing his life forever. He and Sam knew each other better than anyone else in the world.

Even though he was very aware that Lillian would never approve, he yelled. "Sam! Hey! *Sam!*"

Sam turned, and Eliot waved at him, grinning. Sam reminded Eliot of the old gladiator at the Metropolitan Museum. Short, thick, muscular, but with a lot of hair: on his head, on his arms,

56

on his chest, and—lately—on his upper lip. Eliot still couldn't get used to the mustache. "Don't blame me!" Sam had said yesterday at lunch. "It's all Irene's idea. She thinks facial hair is sexy." He waggled his heavy eyebrows and smoothed the new growth with the back of a finger. "You know, a kiss without a mustache is like meat without salt."

Sam turned his head now, and Eliot thought their eyes met, but there was no answering smile, just a blank stare, and Sam continued walking, disappearing around the corner.

For a moment, Eliot stood where he was, feeling off balance. And then he reminded himself that Sam was the most absent-minded person on the entire East Coast. It was a joke to everyone, even to him. A favorite story around the hospital was that one day a new resident stopped him in the hall, and when their conversation ended, Sam had said, "Which way was I going?" The resident told him, and he smiled and said, "Good. Then I've *had* lunch."

There were those who thought the story was an exaggeration, but Eliot knew better. When he got into the office, he was going to call Sam's answering machine and needle the hell out of him!

He hurried down the hall and into his office. "Okay, Betty," he said, passing by her desk, "any messages?" Then he stopped and gave her a second look. Her whole face was smiling, although she was trying hard to look cool and efficient.

"What is it, Betty? You look like the cat that swallowed the cream."

Now a big smile spread over her face. "I'm pregnant, Dr. Wolfe! Pregnant!"

His first thought was, Oh, hell, now he was going to lose her. But that was unworthy of him. Furthermore, it was selfish and childish. He smiled at her.

"I gather from the look on your face that this is a planned pregnancy."

"Planned and prayed for!"

"Well, congratulations. I'm ashamed to admit I never noticed—"

Betty laughed. "Oh, Dr. Wolfe, you *couldn't* notice! I just found out this morning; did one of those drugstore tests. So I'm probably pregnant only about ten minutes."

"Well, don't waste time getting a good obstetrician."

"I already have one in mind, and her name is Dr. Romano."

"And maybe you'd better stop coming in so early and staying so late, Betty."

He was rewarded with a pleased grin. "Thanks, Dr. Wolfe, but I'm tough. And having a baby isn't a disease, it's a natural thing. No need for you to worry."

"Well, just take care of yourself, okay? And now, you want to tell me what I'm going to be doing for the rest of the day?"

She giggled. "First you better call Dr. Havemayer. He sounded real uptight—"

"When doesn't he? I never said that, Betty. Okay, the rest of the list can keep until I see how long this takes."

Looking through the telephone messages she had placed neatly on his desk, he saw that Conrad Havemayer had called *several* times, and each time it was marked URGENT. Everything with Havemayer was urgent. Well, Havemayer considered himself a very important person. And here was a reminder that he had an appointment in ten minutes with Janet Rafferty, head of nursing. What did she want that couldn't wait for their regular meeting? He hoped it wasn't trouble. They had enough trouble with the shortage of nurses without something new.

Havemayer answered, himself, and wasted no time getting to the point.

"Dr. Wolfe, I am not happy with my task today. I do not like hospital gossip; normally, I would not repeat stories, not about anyone. However . . ." There was a delicate pause.

"However," Eliot prompted. What now?

"I understand that you and Sam Bronstein are friends."

More like brothers! But all he said was, "We're good friends."

"In fact . . . I'm afraid . . . no, let me put this another way. Are you aware of any . . . difficulties in Sam's life? Any stresses?"

"No. But that doesn't mean there aren't any."

There was a kind of sigh on the other end. "Sam has been . . . forgetful lately."

Was *that* all? "Sam has *always* been forgetful." He laughed.

"Not at my ethics committee meetings, Dr. Wolfe. He is always prompt and prepared. But he has been late and . . . a bit scattered. Preoccupied, perhaps. This morning, he didn't show up at all."

"You're right to be concerned. Thank you for calling me. I assume you haven't mentioned this to anyone else?"

"Of course not!"

"I will look into it."

"And there have been— No, never mind. I hate gossip. I put this problem into your capable hands, Dr. Wolfe, with every expectation that it will be dealt with, swiftly and competently."

Eliot put the receiver down and made a face at it. Conrad had "every expectation"? What a pain in the ass! Come on, Eliot scolded himself, this is like killing the bearer of bad news. He should be grateful that Havemayer had called *him*. Maybe Sam *was* having a problem. Maybe something with his lady friend. Maybe, Eliot mused, Irene was in the hospital again for more plastic surgery. He knew it made Sam crazy. "No matter how many times I tell her she's beautiful, she doesn't hear it!"

He'd take Sam to dinner, and they'd talk—about Irene, if necessary. They hadn't been living together very long, and in his opinion, Sam really wanted to marry her and was uneasy with this casual arrangement. Eliot had never been terribly fond of Sam's late wife, Eva, who was big and blond and bovine. But every once in a while, he missed her, especially since Sam had taken up with Irene Moore, glamour queen of the fifties, who was *always* "on," and very busy trying to stay young forever. She was enough to give *any* man stress.

The buzzer went off at his elbow.

"Ms. Rafferty is here," Betty's voice announced.

"Send her in." Mentally, he reviewed what Betty had told him about her. In her mid-thirties, the widow of a city fireman, two kids "sent off to live with their grandparents." The look on Betty's face told him that she did *not* approve. Other than that, he knew nothing, nothing personal. Her credentials were impeccable. Head nurse with a background in surgery and in psychiatry.

She came striding in, a tall woman, much more curvaceous than he remembered. She was wearing a blue silk shirt tucked neatly into a plaid skirt, her dark red hair pulled back from a long oval face with high cheekbones and wide-set eyes. He found his eyes drawn to her mouth, which was full, almost pouting, the soft lower lip a bit moist. Her impact was such that he didn't know whether he wanted to move back or get closer. *Wow* was the word that immediately came to mind. Funny, he didn't remember her this way at all. And then he saw that she was angry.

"I don't want to waste your time," she blazed, "so let me get right to the point. I sent you a memo three weeks ago about one of my nurses being sexually harrassed. And I have heard nothing!"

"I'm sorry. I can't imagine how I let . . . Let me look for it. But, meanwhile, refresh my memory."

"It's about Norma Bennett, she's in the neonatal ICU, and that bastard, this isn't the first time—!"

"Slow down, slow down. Who are we talking about?"

"We're talking about Richard R. Stillman, Dr. Wolfe."

"Dick Stillman?" A bright young surgeon, highly thought of.

"That's right. He's come on to every single nurse and candystriper on that floor. The nurses won't testify, because they're afraid for their jobs—all but Norma. Norma's got guts and besides, she's fed up. It took so much courage for her to agree to speak out against a doctor and now, weeks have gone by, and nothing is happening! Meanwhile, she's still fighting him off.

"When is the administration of this hospital going to pay attention to the nurses who work themselves into exhaustion and then are abused by smart-ass doctors who think they can do any damn thing they feel like to anyone who happens to be female! And if you do confront him, he'll be bewildered. What did he *do*? Flirt a little? Pay a couple of compliments? So he patted a rear end here and there. He'll probably tell you the nurses and the secretaries all expect it. He'll probably tell you they *like* it."

When she paused for a breath, Eliot said, "Please. Just slow down a minute. Have a seat. No? Okay. Let me ask you a difficult question." He hesitated, searching for the right words. "I hope," he finally began in his most even tone, "that you aren't telling me that *all* my doctors harrass the women on staff."

"And *I* hope, Dr. Wolfe, that you aren't going to tell me I'm being hysterical. No, that's not fair. I'm sorry. It's just—" She stopped, her voice shaking a little, and visibly brought herself under control. "It's just that there are doctors in this hospital who still think nurses are handmaidens! And if you think this is only a feminist issue, think again. There's a nursing shortage in this town!"

The color had climbed in her face, and she was breathing

hard with her emotion. God, what a gorgeous woman! And then he thought, shocked at himself, What are you thinking of? Her looks have nothing to do with this!

"Ms. Rafferty, please. Take it easy." It occurred to him that it was easier to deal with Conrad Havemayer. Nothing was going to stop her; she was on a roll.

"This sexual harrassment is appalling. It *must* be stopped *now*! Not tomorrow, not someday, but right *now*!"

Eliot stood, putting his hands out in supplication. "Okay, Ms. Rafferty. Right now." His own words took him by surprise.

They regarded each other. He didn't know many women whose eyes were level with his, but hers were. They were hazel, a mix of brown and gold and green, fringed with thick black lashes, intently fixed on him.

He was glad she decided to speak just then; he wasn't sure he could.

"Oh, Dr. Wolfe, I'm so sorry. I don't mean to yell at *you*. It's just that . . . well, it's terrible. And how am I expected to keep nurses here, if this sort of thing is allowed to continue?"

"No need to apologize. In fact, I agree with you."

"Huh?" She hadn't been prepared for *that*. He had to fight his smile.

"I said, I agree with you. This sort of thing cannot continue. I'm very glad you brought it to my attention, and I intend to deal with it immediately."

The buzzer interrupted. "Well, in another minute." They both laughed, and he turned to the console on his desk, punching the green speaker button. "Yes, Betty?"

"Hamilton Pierce on line two."

"You tell Mr. Pierce I'm in a meeting, and I'll call him later. Oh, and Betty. Get ahold of Dr. Stillman and have him down here ASAP. Preferably before lunch." He broke the connection and looked over, catching a grimace on Janet Rafferty's face. "Is there another problem, Ms. Rafferty?"

At her bewilderment, he added, "I thought you wanted me to set the doctor straight. You looked . . . disturbed."

She thought a moment. "Oh. No, if I seem disturbed, it's about Ham Pierce." She looked as if she might say more and then clamped her lips shut.

"You have an opinion on Mr. Pierce? No, don't hesitate. Everyone has one."

"I hate him."

"Well, at least that's unambivalent."

"Oh, I liked him in the beginning. But he betrayed my trust. I'll tell you about it sometime."

"I'd be interested in hearing it. I came in after the movie started, as you know, and it seems to me that Mr. Pierce has too much access to the hospital."

"If you want to know what *I* think," Janet Rafferty said, "I think Ham Pierce has snitches all over the place."

"If he does, believe me, they will be fired the minute I find out who they are."

"Excuse me for saying so, Dr. Wolfe, but I doubt very much whether even *you* will be able to find out who they are."

"Maybe not. But I'm certainly going to give it a shot. Nobody will give a second thought to my asking questions. I'm always poking my nose into everything here . . . even the boiler room. Did you know the head of maintenance gave our boiler room an award during the oil shortage?"

"An award? How wonderful!"

"They're very proud of it. It's up on the wall, the first thing you see when you walk in. Listen, try to run a hospital without heat!"

"You're right. Of course you're right. We do tend to take support staff for granted, don't we? Like my nurses!" She slid a glance over to him, her lips curling in a sly smile.

"Absolutely." He smiled back. It was a pleasure to be with a woman who was trying hard to be nice to him. "You know, I think you could be very helpful to me. About Pierce, for instance, and also about what's going on upstairs. Perhaps lunch sometime?"

"I'd like that." He must be imagining he heard something inviting in her voice. He was a man with a preoccupied wife, that's all it was, that and an overactive imagination. But he could smell her perfume, he realized suddenly. What *was* that perfume? Opium. Now he recognized the scent; it was what Toni wore, but only when they were in bed together. Was that why he was finding this woman so disturbing?

"Now I can tell Norma something will finally be done about it. I can't thank you enough for taking this seriously."

"Of course I take it seriously."

"You'd be surprised how many men in this hospital just

wouldn't get it. A couple of days ago, Dr. Voorhees said to me, 'When rape's inevitable, relax and enjoy it.' Do you believe it? He *laughed*! How can anyone *joke* about rape, in this day and age! The man's a throwback!''

Eliot couldn't help thinking of that old line from the movies: You know, you're beautiful when you're angry.

Luckily, his buzzer went off again. Betty told him that Dr. Stillman would be in his office promptly at two o'clock. Janet, of course, could hear this; they grinned at each other conspiratorially. She had a deep dimple in one cheek, just above her mouth.

"We make a good team," she said. "Well, I've got to get back. Oh, you've just made my day!"

She continued chatting for a moment, but only half of his brain was attending to what she was saying. The other half was elsewhere, in a fantasy featuring satin sheets and creamy skin and a tumble of red hair. He'd better tie Toni down tonight. Christ, he was a happily married man! And, anyway, he was old enough to be Janet Rafferty's father.

After she left, he gave himself a stern lecture and in a minute had convinced himself that it had been nothing at all but the natural normal response of a man who was missing sex. He should know better, but damn it, facts were facts, and he was horny!

All three lines on the console lit up at once. Betty buzzed again. This time her voice had a certain tone he had come to recognize as her storm warning: "Dr. Voorhees to see you, Dr. Wolfe."

He glanced down at his desk calendar. Voorhees was two minutes early for his appointment; he was glad now that he hadn't lingered with Janet Rafferty. Dr. Warren Voorhees, head of sports medicine, was a precise and prompt person, almost robotic.

"Shall I send him in?"

"Absolutely." It pleased him to hear her low chuckle.

A moment later, Warren Voorhees was striding in the door, looking for all the world like a runner. Which of course he was. Of medium height, he was very thin, so thin he looked tall: thin body, thin hair, thin lips, thin lapels, thin ties, long thin hands with long thin fingers and long thin feet with, undoubtedly, long thin toes. It was well-known and often repeated around the hospital that his nurse always told new patients to "bring your running shoes and a major credit card."

Eliot got up and shook hands, preparing himself to listen to something he already had heard, over and over. Voorhees wanted his own sports medicine complex—"Its what the kids call *hot*," he was saying. "Everybody wants sports medicine specialists these days, even little-old-lady joggers. Is that funny, Dr. Wolfe?"

Eliot shook his head, apologizing for the interruption.

"Sports medicine," Voorhees went on, his lips even thinner—if that was possible. "A new center would be a wonderful investment for this hospital, a big money-maker. Need I add that Harmony Hill badly *needs* a big money-maker."

No, you needn't, Eliot thought, but you will and you do, ad nauseam. Still, Eliot was willing to keep his mouth shut, for the moment anyway. Voorhees had attracted some of the country's best young orthopedic surgeons to Harmony Hill—even though everyone knew *nobody* wanted to live in New York City, and nobody's wife did, either. Harmony Hill was becoming an acknowledged major center for the treatment of sports injuries. Eliot had been a bit amused to find that the entire New York Bullets football team was "a patient" of Dr. Voorhees, as well as everyone in the New York Runners' Club, and apparently, everyone on the Upper West Side who ever put on a pair of sneakers, including Lillian.

At his welcoming reception, Eliot had been introduced to Warren Voorhees by his mother, who had gushed that he was "a wonderful doctor, Eliot, he saved my knees." In spite of this, Eliot had disliked the man instantly. First of all, Voorhees didn't find saving Lillian Wolfe's knees even a little bit funny. Lillian did; she had slipped Eliot a wink. And, as Eliot discovered, Voorhees could go on and on and on about his pet project.

At this moment, Voorhees was holding up a beautifully drawn and colored chart. But wait a minute! What was he *saying*? This new sports medicine complex could "take the place of that money-eating emergency room that we don't really *need*."

"Excuse me," Eliot interrupted. "What do you mean, we don't *need* an emergency room. The whole damn city needs an emergency room; the whole damn city *is* an emergency!"

"Crackheads! Violence! Pregnant teenagers, whose parents

just don't give a damn! Dropouts! Gang members! Scum!'' He
gave a little shudder. ''Those people!''

''Those people?'' Eliot said, with forced calm. ''Just who do
you mean?''

Voorhees flushed. ''You know who I mean. They're hopeless.
Look at all the services we've provided for them, to lift them
up, and none of it has made the least little bit of difference. They
want to live like that.''

''Oh. And I suppose they're born with rhythm in their feet.''

Two bright splotches of red appeared on Warren Voorhees's
prominent cheekbones. ''I resent that. I treat many blacks—
athletes, dancers . . .'' A delicate pause, a tiny smile. ''There's
an adequate emergency room at Harlem Hospital. Let the nonpaying riffraff go there.''

''Where they belong? Careful, Dr. Voorhees. In any case,''
he went on briskly, ''there is no way our Board of Trustees
would ever allow us to close the emergency room. And that is
not negotiable.''

Voorhees leaned back, his lips curled in a tight, satisfied
smile. ''Cutting down on our losses *is* negotiable . . . and a
primary priority of the board.''

''Bring your running shoes and a major credit card?'' Eliot
murmured.

''I beg your pardon!''

''Nothing, nothing. As I have already told you, we *will* find
or make space for you. But it cannot be done now, not until I
have thoroughly examined *all* our needs. Until then, I cannot
allocate the funds for anyone's pet project.''

Voorhees stiffened. '' 'Pet project' is hardly the term I would
have chosen. I, of course, bend to your will, but I was *promised*
by Dr. Delafield himself—''

Eliot stifled a sigh. ''Dr. Delafield made a great many promises . . . particularly after lunch.'' He held a hand to ward off
the angry words he could see all but trembling on the other
man's thin lips. ''I will do my very best for you, and I apologize
for 'pet project'; it was a poor choice of words. But—''

''But. But. But. No more excuses, if you please. I make a
profit for this hospital and get no gratitude, but there's money
enough to hire your wife, Dr. Wolfe, to baby-sit a bunch of
irresponsible sex-crazed teenagers who want to have their babies
at our expense!'' He got to his feet, angry. ''I have only to say

the word, and I will be welcomed across Central Park at Mount Sinai—not only myself, but my entire staff!''

Eliot held his temper and his tongue. He really despised this man. But damn it, it was all true. It would be a mistake of major proportions to lose Voorhees simply because the man got on his nerves. Worse, it would be stupid.

"Dr. Voorhees, you are very high on my list of priorities."

"I would certainly hope so.'' That satisfied little smile, again. Christ, he was insufferable. "May I hope to see, ah, concrete evidence of this, quite soon?''

You may hope, Eliot thought, to see concrete shoes upon your feet. "We'll put it on the agenda for the next committee meeting.''

He gave Eliot an icy smile and stalked to the door, where he turned and added in a voice loaded with menace: "I am considered preeminent in my field, whereas you . . . If I were you, Dr. Wolfe, I wouldn't depend on my family name to keep my job.''

Eliot sat very still, looking at the slammed door. "Shit!'' he said, softly. In the course of ten minutes, Voorhees had managed to insult him, the hospital, Toni, his family name, and the entire African-American population of New York City. What in hell was *wrong* with the man? There was no way around it: Warren Voorhees was either reckless or weird, and he sat on that damned committee. He had *power*. Eliot was going to have to figure out how to handle him. Well, he thought, at least Voorhees had done *one* good deed. He had erased all thought of Janet Rafferty and her soft, curvaceous body. Ha!

6

September

Eliot reached out for his cup and sipped cold coffee. It tasted terrible, but he had to stay alert. He was having trouble listening to Warren Voorhees. Voorhees liked to bulldoze his ideas through at these meetings, by repeating the same thought over and over and over again until he wore you down. Betty Cannon's pencil flew across her steno pad, but Eliot just couldn't keep his mind on the muted, droning voice. Dr. Voorhees, as usual, was putting him to sleep, which was dangerous.

The administration committee was the bane of Eliot's existence—especially the three top dogs, two doctors and a multimillionaire. They were the real power on the committee, the *real* authority that made the *real* decisions.

The only way to keep his sanity was to try to find them amusing, but it wasn't easy. There were so many bitter resentments underneath the polite smiles. There were so many hidden agendas and histories. For instance, the renowned surgeon, tightass, and bore, Warren Voorhees, had expected to be named president himself. For instance, Conrad Havemayer, pediatric surgeon, chief of staff and head of the ethics committee, felt that he and he alone was entitled to decide all moral issues. For instance, Barney Goldstone, the hospital's largest contributor, board member and big mouth, was married to Eliot's ex-wife, Arlene; and Barney really enjoyed undermining him at every opportunity.

The Board of Trustees was no help; they tended to rubber-stamp whatever the committee decided. *That* was going to change, but not right away. So he *had* to pay attention to everything that was said today and to all the silent messages, as well.

67

The committee members looked civilized and businesslike, but he knew that some of them were out for blood—*his* blood.

He looked around the table at today's group. Drs. Voorhees, Havemayer, and Harrison; Janet Rafferty; Dave Spellman, the comptroller; the hospital's recently hired fund-raising expert, Cyril Cedarbaum; and Lou Coughlin, head of security. And Barney Goldstone, of course. The other two from the board, Irv Brickman and Suzanne Schlesinger, were absent today. Irv and his wife were on a trip to India, and as for Mrs. Schlesinger, it had been confided to him this morning—by his mother, who else?—that Mrs. Schlesinger was *not* attending a family reunion in Palm Springs but was really at the Betty Ford Center, recovering. He was sorry to hear it, sorry both for her recurring battles with alcoholism—Lillian knew exactly how many times she had been sent to dry out—and for her absence. She was the one member of this committee he could count on to say, "Whatever Dr. Wolfe wants, that's what *I* want."

Quite a collection today, he thought, and all of them would love to see him take a fall. Well, not really all. Not Dave Spellman, of course. Not the fund raiser, not the security chief. And not Janet, looking elegant in something soft and silky and red. With that body, she shouldn't wear clinging things to work . . . but all thoughts of Janet, however seductive, had to be put firmly away.

He had to pay attention to Voorhees, Havemayer, and Goldstone. Especially Barney Goldstone, rumpled, freckled, and fair and looking more like a country bumpkin than the shark he really was.

It hadn't taken Eliot long to catch on to the reason they had hired him. First, the Wolfe name, which still had clout in this city. And his mild manner had misled them into thinking they'd bought themselves another rubber stamp like Delafield. That may have been what they expected; what they got was very different, and they did not like it.

They'd had a free hand for a long time, under Don Delafield's vague and vacant presidency. It was sad, how even his signature had deteriorated from a firm, single flourish of the pen to a shaky, printed "Don." An amiable drunk with connections, that had been President Delafield. And President Wolfe? He was more than they had bargained for . . . at least, he hoped so.

The big topic on the agenda today was the budget, and he

was determined not to let them railroad deep cuts in crucial services to the poor. Which, of course, they were determined to do.

Voorhees was haranguing Dave Spellman, a small, balding man of notoriously short patience, who was holding himself in check but couldn't stop the tense tapping of his pen against the table.

"So, Mr. Spellman, is it fair to say that you, the comptroller, have just told us our deficit will be devastating this year; and that we must, A, expand those areas that are profitable; and, B, cut the fat from the budget."

Dave Spellman did not bother to disguise his exasperation. "For the third time, Dr. Voorhees, yes, that is correct!"

You'd think that Voorhees would take the hint and yield the floor to someone else, but, of course, he never did. He began once more at the beginning, listing those clinics that were unprofitable. His *own* clinics, of course, were making money.

Next to him, Betty, still taking down every golden word, moaned a little.

His mind drifted back to Janet. It was crazy: a man of his age, a married man, a *happily* married man, mooning over a woman like some lovesick adolescent! What was *with* him, anyway? It was ludicrous.

But at the same time, he couldn't help remembering. Just a few days ago, he had stayed late in the office, catching up on paperwork, knowing that Toni wouldn't be home until midnight—if then. And when he had finally left at nine, there she was, in the lobby: Janet Rafferty, all alone, gazing out into the night, her image reflected in the window. When their eyes met in the glass, she turned, her face lighting up.

"Dr. Wolfe! What a lovely surprise!"

He felt suddenly excited. She was always friendly, always pleasant, always cordial. But there was something different about the way she was looking at him, something inviting. And when he got close to her and she put a hand lightly on his arm while they talked, he was sure her touch lingered. He could not keep his mind on what she was saying.

He found himself inviting her for a drink. "It's been a very long day," he added, somewhat lamely, thinking to himself, Idiot! Stop babbling. You're only asking the woman to have a glass of wine, not to bed.

There was a little bar near the hospital, too expensive for the medical students. They were nearly alone in the place. Three men watched a ball game on a huge television set mounted above the bar, with the sound turned off. He and Janet took a tiny round table in the far corner. A little candle was flickering inside a glass shade, glinting off the wine glasses and lighting Janet's face with its warm glow.

They were almost touching; her nearness was disturbing and exciting. She was oblivious to his agitation, sitting calmly, gazing at him from under thick, dark lashes, talking of her plans for the nursing staff at Harmony Hill. And he, in turn, told her what he wanted for the hospital, how he planned to combine certain clinics, enlarge others, put new ideas into action. They talked and talked. He loved her enthusiasm; she was a woman who really cared about the important things. He loved her intelligence. God, it had been so long since he'd had such an understanding ear. And while they were chatting, her hand came to rest on top of his, and he could feel heat coursing all through him.

"It's so good to talk with you, Dr. Wolfe. Dr. Delafield . . . you have no idea. We couldn't do *anything*. But you . . . you're a ball of fire!"

He felt himself blushing. "I appreciate your kind words."

She smiled and squeezed his hand, just a little. "They're not kind, Dr. Wolfe, just the truth."

"Eliot. Please."

She lowered her eyes, and the candlelight cast long feathery shadows of her incredible eyelashes along the curve of her cheek. "All right . . . Eliot." She opened her eyes wide. She had beautiful eyes. "Then you must call me Janet."

"Janet. Yes, I will."

A hint of a smile. "But not in the hospital," she said.

What did she mean? Could she mean . . . ? His mind was gibbering. "Then, where?" he ventured.

"Well, now that I've discovered how to get a few quiet minutes alone with you, I intend to take advantage of it."

Dry-mouthed, Eliot nodded. What was going on here? He wanted to ask her when; Christ, he wanted to make a *date*! But, instead, he pushed himself up and signaled for the check. This was loony; he couldn't believe where his imagination was leading him. Nothing was happening; nothing had happened; nothing was going to happen.

And then he looked down and met her soft, alluring glance and was no longer so sure. When he handed her into a cab, a few minutes later, he found himself fighting the urge to kiss her. If she had any idea what he was thinking—!

He brought himself back to the meeting. It was one thing to lie in his bed, imagining her melting into his arms, but quite another to let such thoughts interfere with his work. Here, especially, he had to watch himself, had to remain vigilant, or the troika would run roughshod over him.

While he had been lost in his fantasies, Voorhees had started in again on maternity beds, and his cohorts were smiling and nodding, while Janet frowned and folded her arms tightly across her chest.

"This will limit the number of indigent patients . . ." He paused, sliding a look at Eliot, doubtless expecting him to protest. He was right.

"And what do you suggest these women do, when they're in labor, Dr. Voorhees? Give birth on the street?"

"Let them go to Harlem Hospital, where they—"

"Where they *belong*?" Janet leaped to her feet, glaring fiercely. "Is that what you're about to say, Dr. Voorhees?"

"No need to get hysterical, Ms. Rafferty." That was Ron Harrison, the plastic surgeon.

Hysterical! Of all the stupid things to say! Even *he* knew it was guaranteed to make any woman furious.

Janet leaned over the table and in a deceptively sweet and mild tone, asked, "Why maternity beds, Dr. Harrison? How about cutting down on the number of beds for, say, breast augmentation or tummy tucks . . . or face lifts?"

Eliot watched the color flood Ron Harrison's face. Good for her!

Janet smiled at Dr. Harrison, silently daring *him* to get hysterical. Harrison bent his head, thumbing through his file folders, neatly stacked on the table in front of him, pretending to look for something, as he always did whenever he was challenged.

Eliot cleared his throat. "Now may we get on to the business of cutting beds—and, ladies and gentlemen—let's all be realistic. As much as I don't like the idea, I must agree that we are going to have do so. However, I don't think we should begin with maternity, particularly after we have had a suggestion from Dr. Havemayer that the hospital needs . . . let's see . . . a pediatric burn unit.'' He pretended to turn pages in his notes. ''And, from Dr. Harrison, a new surgical unit for neonatology.''

There was a murmur around the table, and Havemayer shifted grumpily in his chair. It would have to be a trade-off, instead of a rout, and Havemayer hated compromise. What Havemayer liked was very simple: his own way. But Eliot was not about to displace poor patients for a few very rare and hideously expensive cases. If they couldn't compromise, those maternity beds would be history.

''Let me speak plainly, ladies and gentlemen,'' Eliot said. ''If this hospital does not have the space for crack babies and AIDS babies and babies with fetal alcohol syndrome, then certainly this hospital cannot make the space for flashier, more 'interesting' birth defects.''

''It's not a matter of one or the other, Dr. Wolfe.'' Dr. Havemayer was sitting very erect in his chair. ''All deserve to live.''

Havemayer was a great favorite with the board and with his colleagues. He was handsome, and he knew it, broad, muscular, with a large leonine head, and thick, wavy gray hair brushed straight back. He was considered brilliant. But to Eliot, Havemayer's views about preserving life were narrow, rigid, and emotional, perhaps because he was a survivor of Auschwitz, and he had lost most of his family to the Nazis. Understandably but regrettably, his history governed his every thought and act. There were no gray areas. He wanted *everyone* kept alive, by *any* means available, no matter what anyone else wanted: patient, patient's family, the hospital itself.

In his own specialty, he insisted upon saving even those preemies who would never really be able to function. He always talked about ''salvaging'' them. Eliot found that word so coldblooded. You didn't salvage human life, the way you pieced together a worn-out toaster!

''I beg to differ,'' Eliot went on. ''We *must* make choices. We have a crisis in this catchment area. Too many newborns are dying. Too many mothers are malnourished. Too many babies are born addicted. First things first, Dr. Havemayer.''

From the far end of the table, a booming voice: "Well, then how about drug treatment? What the hell do they *do*, anyway?" Barney Goldstone. "We've had it going for seven years. And do we have less addicts in this city? Hell, no! We got more! I say the hell with them!

"Or, Ellie, how about some of those other ding-a-ling programs?" Barney went on. "The obesity clinic, the parenting program, and how about that Woman's Health Center uptown! They don't do a thing up there that we don't do right here." He pounded his index finger on the table. "Right here in Harmony Hill. Oh, excuse me, Dr. Wolfe, I forgot that a couple of those programs are headed by members of your family." The hell he forgot, Eliot thought, watching the self-satisfied gleam in Barney's beady little eyes.

"All right, then, we'll leave out the Women's Health Center for now. Yeah, and that parenting thing, too. For now," Barney said, a tight little smile curling his lips.

What balls! He had brought up Toni's clinic and Carolyn's program and then offered to drop them from his hit list to give the impression that Eliot could be bought. There was no way he could deny it without sounding as if he, like the lady in Shakespeare's play, was protesting too much. It was a little message to him, about how vulnerable he was.

Quickly, Eliot glanced at his list. The next item read EMS. "While we're on the subject of budget, may we discuss our needs for a moment? In spite of the fact that we're operating at a deficit, there are critical requirements. For instance, we should have two more ambulances—"

"Now you're on the ball, Ellie!" Goldstone was grinning. "Our response time is crappy, and you know why? Because three ambulances aren't enough. We're the only hospital in New York City where the ambulances are manned—oh, excuse me, ladies—staffed one hundred percent with paramedics. Not just EMTs who can take your blood pressure and pray, but *paramedics*, who can save lives. My own sister, last year . . . never mind, we're not here to tell personal stories. But, personally, I vote we buy two more of the things." He leaned back looking very satisfied with himself.

"Two more!" Havemayer protested. "Do you realize the cost of an ambulance! We could have . . ."

Eliot stopped listening. He knew what Havemayer was going to say we could have instead.

". . . at least with burns, we know what to do. Unlike the parenting program, for instance, which is just guesswork."

"Guesswork, Doctor?" Janet had jumped to her feet again, her cheeks stained pink. "Why do you say that? Because it's a program for women, run by women, and nondoctors, at that? For your information, the parenting program has a very good success rate. It's the kind of early intervention that ultimately makes a difference in people's lives. *People!*"

"Those people," Ron Harrison sneered, "are never compliant anyway! It's just throwing good money after bad!"

"We accept state and federal money," Eliot said. "We are required to serve our entire catchment area. Now, as we all know, our area includes a substantial population of poor Hispanics and blacks. So, Dr. Harrison, let us hear: how many of those patients are in *your* beds?" He only wished Toni could be here; then maybe she'd stop accusing him of not caring for the poor and would understand the tricky balancing act he had to do.

"Plenty! Plenty of those . . . the disadvantaged—"

"Not according to the statistics *I've* been looking at."

"Well, Dr. Wolfe, you know plastic surgery leaves scars on black skin, which is why African-Americans do not elect cosmetic surgery and—"

"Bullshit!" Goldstone exclaimed, and a fist pounded down, rattling coffee cups. Barney was a 1960s liberal and still talked about a cocktail party he had given twenty years ago, to which he had invited ten Black Panthers. "My ass is numb, pardon my French! Jesus, if I ran my business the way you run this hospital. Lemme tell you something, there wouldn't be a Goldstone Pavilion. Hell, there wouldn't be a Goldstone pot to piss in!" He threw his head back and gave a shout of laughter.

"Tell you what," he went on, in a serious tone. "Number one, the obesity clinic has gotta go; there's Weight Watchers everywhere; a regular doctor can put a person on a diet—my doctor does it to me every six months." Again, he laughed, and patted his paunch. "Anyway, I've read the reports, and the recidivism rate in that clinic is higher than in the criminal justice system. So if it doesn't help, get rid of it. Number two. The new sickle-cell clinic. Forget it! They already got one at Harlem

Hospital, and the start-up costs are out of sight. And then you make every department cut back by . . . I figure, about two percent . . . and then we'll only be broke, ladies and gentlemen. But at least we won't be in the toilet!''

Barney Goldstone, Eliot thought, not for the first time, was a blustering egomaniac, but he certainly knew how to turn a phrase. People listened to him; people always tended to pay attention to the very rich. And to be fair, the man had brains. In fact, as Eliot watched him maneuver, Goldstone got the rest of them to agree to his proposal. Now it would go to the full Board of Trustees and, as usual, pass without much comment. The obesity clinic was not going to be happy, but it couldn't be helped. He himself was not too happy that he now owed Barney Goldstone.

Moving on, he said, ''We have some good news for a change.'' As he watched, everyone at the table relaxed, almost in unison. ''We have been bequeathed the Bachelor Brownstones.''

Everyone began talking at once, their voices crisscrossing. ''The Abraham houses! What a windfall!''

''I say gut them and make a modern facility.''

''Gut them! Are you mad? They're magnificent. Anyway, the Landmarks Commission will put you on their hit list.''

''Sports medicine, Dr. Wolfe—''

''Facial anomalies, Dr. Wolfe—''

''Dr. Wolfe . . . critical care . . . and we'd treat kids, too.''

''Right. Dr. Wolfe, we badly need a new critical care facility, and—''

Eliot held up his hand. ''You didn't let me finish. This is a most generous bequest. However, it's a restricted gift.'' As he spoke, Betty handed out copies. He gave them a few minutes to take it in and when face after face lifted, wearing an identical look of stunned disbelief, spoke again.

''Yes, ladies and gentlemen, there it is in black and white. Lester Abraham, the last surviving bachelor brother, added a codicil to his will, stating very clearly that 'the three brownstone buildings on West 92nd Street, known popularly as the Bachelor Brownstones,' are left to Harmony Hill Hospital, provided they are used as an AIDS hospice—'for those who are near death, threatened by death, or unable to care for themselves in any way, shape, or form,' as Mr. Abraham put it.''

"AIDS!" Four or five horrified voices.

"Yes, AIDS," he said, in a voice that came out much grimmer than he had intended. "Here at Harmony Hill, we cannot hide from this disease, much as we might like to—"

Voorhees spoke up. "You misunderstand, Dr. Wolfe. Nobody's hiding. But those beautiful buildings, used for doomed patients, who probably don't know or care *where* they are."

"Right now, we have thirty-five AIDS patients. Yesterday, we had thirty-seven. Most of them are readmissions. Believe me, Dr. Voorhees, they know and they care where they are. The point is: none of them are going to recover. We cannot throw them away and leave them to die alone. With this—"

"Hold on a minute!" It was Barney Goldstone, who had turned a very unhealthy shade of plum. He jumped to his feet, overturning his chair, which fell with a thump to the carpeted floor.

"Barney?"

"Jesus Christ! I can't stomach another minute of this bullshit! This may be a godsend to you, Wolfe, but do you realize that my new house—the one that cost me two point five million and another two point five mil to restore—my house is directly across the street from the Bachelor Brownstones? Directly!" He was so agitated, he was finding it difficult to breathe. "I mean, my living room windows face those houses!"

Oh shit, Eliot thought. "Surely, Barney, a man of your humanitarian reputation will not object to having this facility—"

"But goddamn it, those people are faggots, drug addicts, prostitutes, for Christ's sake! Their scummy friends will be hanging out in front of the place! Their drug pushers! Their . . . their . . . their *boyfriends*, goddamn it! No, goddamn it, I won't have it! Lemme tell you, Lester Abraham was eighty-seven years old, and he had waddayacallit, senile dementia. The guy I bought the house from told me old Lester used to come out at night in his pajamas and wander up the street until his man missed him and came running out to get him."

He stopped, reached for a glass of water, gulped it down, belched. "That will could be broken, Dr. Wolfe."

"Don't be too sure." That was Havemayer. "My colleague, Dr. Hays of the Mulberry Clinic—that's in Pennsylvania—tells me that a fortune was left to his hospital and, even though the will was followed to the last period, it was contested. By the time the whole affair was over, the lawyers were wealthy men, and the hospital?'' Havemayer gave a shrug and held up his thumb and forefinger in an O. ''The hospital got nothing. So, I repeat, Barney, you can't be sure of ever breaking a will.''

''I hope not,'' Eliot said. ''No matter what names you want to call them, these are very sick people we're talking about. And our commitment is to sick people. We should be ashamed to even *think* about breaking this will,'' he said, locking eyes with Goldstone.

''Well, then, the hell with you!'' Barney snarled. He got to his feet and slammed out of the room, leaving behind a ringing silence.

Eliot looked around the table. He hoped he looked calm; he certainly did not feel it. The hospital's largest contributor had just stormed out, furious. Barney Goldstone was notorious for getting what he wanted. He was likely to do anything. He could tie up the property in litigation for years. He could get the board behind him. Hell, he could have Eliot fired.

Every face around the table, except Janet's, was set and scowling. Was nobody on his side? Apparently not. Nobody would meet his eyes . . . except Janet. ''Can we have some other comments on this matter?'' Silence. He had a sudden cold feeling in the pit of his stomach that they had all known of the Abraham bequest ahead of time, that they had already met and decided they would oppose it. ''Nobody has anything to add?'' Nothing.

''Well then, this meeting is adjourned.''

They all filed out. There was no chatter. He assumed talk would begin the moment they were out of earshot. Damn! Well, he wasn't going to back down on anything this important.

Of course, he was not a totally disinterested party where AIDS was concerned. There was his own son, Eric. As he always did when he thought of Eric, Eliot closed his eyes against the hurt. Eric had come home a year ago for a visit and announced that he was gay and out of the closet. It still made Eliot sad. Eric would never have children. And it frightened him too—all the gay bashing that was going on these days. And AIDS . . .

Quickly putting that thought out of his mind, Eliot went into his office. He closed his door and, instead of sitting at the desk, drifted over to the wall of windows that looked south and west, over the Hudson River and downtown, to the Manhattan of the movies; the Manhattan of skyscrapers and nightclubs, ablaze at night with bright lights; the glamorous Manhattan of luxury stores, theaters, restaurants, and museums. Harmony Hill was not part of that fantasy picture.

At 100th Street and Riverside Drive, two worlds met and collided. They got every kind of patient at Harmony Hill Hospital: the very rich, the very poor, students from Columbia University, the homeless, drug addicts, and celebrities. The Upper Upper West Side, they were calling it now, as if by giving it a name, they could turn it into a cohesive neighborhood. A house divided was more like it!

Eliot pressed his knuckles to his temples, as if that might ease his headache. It was going to be an uphill battle to save this hospital. Somehow, somewhere, he had to find the way.

Jesus, he was tired—more than tired, worn out. He needed . . . he didn't know what he needed. But he felt empty and depleted. He sat, slumped, for a minute or two, not moving, not looking at anything in particular. Then, he watched his hands as, almost reluctantly, he picked up the phone and tapped out Janet Rafferty's extension.

7

The same day

Softly now, very, very gently, Betty lowered the receiver back
into its cradle, holding her breath as she did so. Done. So . . .
the head doctor invites the head nurse out for a drink . . . very
interesting. She pulled open her middle desk drawer, got her
mirror, and put on fresh lipstick before going home. Were they
getting it off? she wondered; immediately she answered herself:
No way, not him. She couldn't see the elegant Dr. Wolfe going
for someone like Janet Rafferty, no way. He wasn't that kind of
guy, not like some others she could name around here, who
were always sniffing around, looking to get lucky. It was probably hospital business.

She pushed herself up, stretching her back. She patted her
belly lovingly. Nice baby. She still couldn't quite believe she
was pregnant. Thirty-nine years old and pregnant for the first
time; it was kind of a joke . . . but not to her and George. They
were so happy about it!

She'd always wanted a husband and a baby, but for a while
there, it looked like it wouldn't happen. First of all, she was no
raving beauty. Her mama told her, early on, looking her over,
"Betty, honey, you better make sure you can make your own
way in this world. You're way too smart for most of the men
around here." She knew what that meant: no man was going to
ever want her.

She was twenty years old, fresh out of secretary school and
working her first job here at the hospital, when Mama died. It
was the big C, and in a way, it was a relief when she finally
passed. But it meant that Betty had to raise up the two kids:
Daniel, fourteen, and Deedra, who was only eleven. No man

was going to marry Betty Strong, not with two teenagers in the house! So that was that. Until George. Just thinking about her big, strong, good-natured husband made her smile.

She looked around her office, satisfied. The plants in the window were doing nicely, everything was neat, and the cleaning people would vacuum tonight. Okay. Time to go home and see about some supper.

She saw the light on his line go off, so he was off the phone. She knocked gently on his door, put her head in, and said good night.

"Good night, Betty. Take it easy; it's very hot and humid out there. Walk slowly. This is your doctor talking. Your doctor's *husband*, anyway."

He really was a sweet guy, Betty thought, as she walked toward the front entrance. And a good boss; he didn't expect her to be his slave—that was a nice change—and, for a miracle, he even thanked her for her hard work. No, she decided, if Eliot Wolfe and Janet Rafferty were meeting for a drink after work, it was hospital business, for sure. Still, she'd tuck this little item away in the back of her head, just in case.

When she pushed through the big front door, the soggy heat of the day pushed down on her like a wet wool blanket. Out front, they were walking around in a large circle, blocking the whole sidewalk. Someone was always demonstrating about something or other in front of this hospital. As if the hospital never did anything right! She'd be the first to admit there were problems, big problems. But fair was fair. Dr. Delafield was gone now, and they weren't giving Dr. Wolfe even half a chance to turn this place around.

She walked down the wide, stone steps. Some young nurses and doctors, taking a break, were lounging on one side, their faces turned up to the sun. Betty shook her head. Some folks were just young and dumb! She paused at the bottom, regarding the marchers. They were hot and tired, kind of shuffling along, every once in a while shouting out a slogan. Their placards said LOCAL 1099, HOSPITAL WORKERS OF AMERICA and WE WANT A FAIR WAGE and HARD WORK . . . NO MONEY and, the same thought in Spanish, MUCHO TRABAJO . . . POCO DINERO. A couple of very young cops—they seemed to get younger every year—sweating in their blues and caps, stood in front of the blue wooden police barriers, looking bored and weary. Hell, every-one looked weary on a day like this.

Well, was she going to walk through the line of marchers or avoid the whole thing and get across the street?

Her mind was made up *for* her, when someone spotted her. She knew most of them; she'd been at the hospital nearly twenty years.

"Sellout!" someone shouted. Oh Lord, that again! "You should be marching with us, Betty!"

She walked up to them and shouted back, "I'm not a member of the union."

A tall man with a wispy goatee and a flattop came over to her, standing right in front of her so she couldn't move. She knew him; he was supposed to be vacuuming her office, right this minute.

"Why you workin' for whitey, sister, lickin' his boots and makin' his coffee every morning!"

"Get out of my face, Clifton Jackson. At least I do an honest day's work. And I don't make coffee for any man but my hus-band!" *Sister!* I ain't no sister of yours, she longed to tell him. She didn't like him; she wished they'd pick themselves a differ-ent leader. He was too angry and belligerent. Why was he wast-ing his time attacking her? She'd worked damned hard to get where she was; she worked damn hard for her money and then went home and worked hard for her community, too! "I tell you why I work for whitey. Because whitey's got the money, that's why! So move your bones, Jackson."

He stood his ground, glaring down at her from his six feet four. "Don't you think there's something wrong 'bout that? How come whitey's got the bread, while all of us—" He half turned to include all of them. "—all of us go hungry!"

"You sound just like a Communist, you know that?"

"Never mind what *I* sound like! We're talkin' about what *you* are, and you're a traitor. You gone and deserted your own!"

"Fool! I'm on my way home right now to fight for my own!"

A woman in the crowd behind him spoke up. "Let her be, Clifton. Betty Cannon does her share, and you *know* that!"

"Yeah, Cliff, let up!"

Finally, Jackson backed away from her, throwing his hands up. But she wasn't going to let him get away so easy! He'd made her good and mad!

"You listen to me now, Cliff Jackson. If it wasn't for me, your kids couldn't walk to school without some pusher sneaking up to them, sweet-talking them about 'how *good* they gonna feel, how *cool* it be to get high.' Drugs are killing our children! They already got my little brother Danny; drugs put him in his grave, and him no more than twenty-three years old!"

When she paused to take a breath, Jackson held his hands up in surrender. "Okay, okay, back off, Mama. You free to go!"

"I don't need your permission. You listen up, Jackson! You go and do your thing and leave me to do mine. And don't mess with me *no more*!"

From the crowd, hoots and hollers, someone yelling "Ay-MEN!" and then laughter. No way he could keep a straight face, and as a matter of fact, as she marched herself away toward Amsterdam Avenue and her bus, she was smiling, too. He meant to do good; it was just that he went about it all wrong. He thought you had to beat people over the head. She knew better. What you had to do was bide your time, pay attention to every damn thing, and wait until you had enough ammunition. Then you attacked.

She'd been coming to work here for all of her adult life. All those years, sitting in offices, taking notes, typing memos, taking messages, and she was still invisible. As far as they were concerned, Betty Cannon didn't exist! The things, over the years, she'd heard them say about her people! She knew who they meant: the folks who were lazy and no good and only wanted a good time on Saturday night and liked being on Welfare and cheated on their food stamps and all that other garbage! How did they think that made *her* feel? Well, of course, if she was invisible, she wasn't there; and if she wasn't there, her feelings couldn't get hurt, could they?

She had her own ways of fighting back. Snide comments weren't the *only* things she heard. She heard important things, sometimes. In the four years she'd been secretary to the president, first Dr. Delafield and now Dr. Wolfe, she knew about every plan and every scheme long before either the committee or the board. That was the *good* part of being invisible. And she didn't blab everything she heard to everyone she saw. She kept it to herself and only passed on information when and where it would do some good.

God, it was hot and oppressive! By the time she got to the

bus stop, she was feeling wrung out. The sidewalks were shimmering with heat. She went into a Korean grocery store on the corner, bought herself an ice-cold can of club soda, and rubbed its frosty surface all over her face. It was ten minutes before a bus came; but at least its air conditioning was working. By the time she got out, on the corner of 123rd Street, she was feeling a little more human.

She crossed the street, putting a little spring into her step—almost home, almost home! She gave a nod of approval to the Women's Health Center on the corner as she made her way down to 122nd Street, her block. Someone had given the outside of the storefront a fresh coat of shiny black paint. Much better than the old peeling green that had been there for about a hundred years. She wasn't supposed to know it, but Dr. Toni Romano had paid for the paint and the brushes out of her own pocket. "They won't give us a penny to fix this place up!" Dee had told her. So Toni had taken matters into her own hands.

Since Toni Romano had started running the clinic, Betty thought, it had been shaping up nicely. Now the big plate-glass windows were sparkling clean, and there were plants and a couple of bookcases inside, in addition to the mismatched plastic chairs.

Dee claimed that Toni Romano was the best doctor in the hospital. Maybe. Maybe not. Dr. Romano was her teacher, and Dee looked up to her. More than that, really. Dee was like someone in love. Betty tried to tell her to take it easy, to save her devotion until she knew Dr. Romano better. But that only made Dee mad. Betty was very proud and protective of her brilliant little sister—a doctor in the family! Who would have dreamed of it?

It always made Betty feel good, coming home at night. Everyone on the block knew her, and as she made her way to her building, people were calling out to her: "Evenin', Betty!" "How ya doin', Betty?" "Hot enough for you, Betty?" The block was full of life, as it always was in warm weather. Little boys played stoopball or stickball. Little girls practiced Double Dutch. Funny, how little kids never seemed to feel the heat, never even seemed to sweat.

We might be poor, but this block looks pretty damn good, Betty thought proudly. Only two empty buildings, covered with graffiti, boarded up against addicts and street people. And that miserable boarding house, where old men, dejected and solitary, sat all day on the stoop or on folding chairs in front of the steps, drinking out of bottles hidden in paper bags. Every time she saw that building, she got madder at the landlord, whoever *that* was. You couldn't get a human being. The owner of record was a corporation with one of those mean-nothing names. Jobar Buildings, Inc. They never returned her calls, never came around. The rest of the sidewalks were swept at least once a day. There, it was littered and filthy.

When she reached her own building, Clarence Carter was sitting on his stoop, right next door. As soon as he saw her, he put down his beer can and stood. Clarence was one of her regulars on night patrol, in spite of the fact that he weighed about 270 pounds and waddled like a duck. But the pushers had found that those big flat feet could cover a lot of ground, real fast, and when he came after you, you better move!

"See you tonight, Betty?" he asked.

"Not tonight, Clarence. I took last night for Juanita, *and* the night before, so Juanita's on tonight. How about the others?"

"All set. I already got ahold of everyone."

"I don't know how I did it, before you took over the schedule, Clarence." He grinned shyly, like a little boy. "All I know is, I *had* to do it," she said, "and I *had* to get everyone else to do it with me."

Clarence chuckled. "You sure did, Betty. You sure did."

"And now I get to have me a night off. Think I'll start it right now," she said, with a smile and wave.

It was ten years since she had had to go to the morgue and identify the body of her brother. All the way there, heart pounding in her throat, she had prayed that it wouldn't be Danny. But she knew. He hadn't been home for ten days, not even to steal. O.D.'ed on heroin. Danny! The serious, sweet little boy who had promised his sick mama that he'd be the man in the family, he'd take care of the girls. Oh Lord! It made her heart ache, even after all this time.

But at least she was saving other kids from the same fate, she and her neighbors marching up one street and down the other, patrolling this block, from Amsterdam to Broadway, dusk to dawn, year-round, back and forth and back and forth. They scared the pushers away, and then they went after the couriers. Little boys, no more than eight or nine years old! It made her blood run cold. Those low-life bastards! Ruining the life of a child before it hardly had a chance to begin!

She never passed a group of kids, if they were just hanging, without stopping and checking out the situation. By this time, she had a sixth sense about it. Tonight, she saw a bunch of kids jumping in and out of the spray from an opened fire hydrant. That wasn't quite legal, but it was a helluva lot better than dealing drugs.

Well, Betty thought, time to get supper going. Before she mounted the steps, she cast an experienced eye around her building, making sure the pots of begonias weren't too dry and there was no trash on the steps or the sidewalk.

She loved her house. It really *was* hers—theirs, hers and George's. She'd always lived here, in the front apartment on the first floor, but she never dreamed she could ever *own* it. That was George's idea.

"I got some money saved," he said. "Against my old age. But hell, I'd rather get us our own brownstone. Don't say no, now, Betty. If it's *ours*, no one can ever throw us out; we get the rents; and we get us a decent landlord for a change." How he laughed at that. "A decent landlord, yes, it'll be nice to have a landlord who cares about the property!"

It was a brownstone over a hundred years old, once very elegant, with a front garden, carved doors, and bronze lamps on either side. Over the years, as the neighborhood went down, it had been vandalized and abandoned, then spruced up and modernized. All that was left of its former glory was an elaborate stone railing leading up the front steps.

She took the steps slowly; and as she opened the front door, she stopped, smiling to herself, putting her hand on her belly, thinking of the new life inside her. A wave of pure joy washed over her. Baby, she said silently, no child will ever be as wanted or as welcomed or as loved as you're going to be.

As she moved into the dim cool of the front hall, she heard a familiar voice yelling, "Yo! Wait!"

It was Dee, trotting up the steps—where did the girl find all her energy in this heat? "I was in the bus right behind you, but we got stuck down on 105th Street by a fire engine. No air conditioning, of course. So I got out and ran."

"Ran! You're crazy, girl! Get right in here, and I'll give you a nice cool drink."

Betty watched as her sister moved gracefully around the kitchen. Deedra got all the looks . . . and most of the brains, come to that. But hey, you didn't do so bad, she scolded herself. You managed to raise the two of them all by yourself.

Dee poured them both ice water from a bottle in the refrigerator and plunked the glasses down on the painted kitchen table. "Come sit with me and tell me all the gossip."

"No gossip," Betty lied. She certainly would never let Dee know anything about Dr. Wolfe, especially since he was married to Dr. Romano. "Just a big committee meeting." She rolled her eyes, and Dee laughed.

"Well, you know what they say about committees: a committee invented the elephant! Anything new that the staff should know about?"

"Dee, you know I'm not supposed to tell what I hear in those meetings. But I will say that Harmony Hill's going to have to cut back."

"Oh shit. What are they closing now? Besides maternity."

Betty smiled. "I'm happy to tell you that maternity isn't going to close up so fast."

"Well, three cheers for Dr. Wolfe!"

"I didn't say it was Dr. Wolfe," Betty said. They eyed each other, amused. "Now, did I?"

"It has to be him. I know who the others are." She made a little face.

"Well, yes, he's a nice man," Betty said. "Almost *too* nice, if you ask me. He seems to be on our side, but if it ever comes to a real brawl with those others, I'm not so sure he can win. I know that if there were a few people of color on that committee, this community would get its fair share, for sure!"

"Well, why *aren't* there any of us on that committee? I'll tell you why! Because we have a habit of whining about how unfairly we've been treated, instead of taking action, educating our children, and making sure *they* get into positions of power!"

"Shame on you, Deedra!"

"Well, it's true . . . partly true, anyway." She gave Betty a sheepish smile. "I'm sorry. I'm starting to sound like Jesse Jackson. Or Ham Pierce."

"What's wrong with Hamilton Pierce? He's only trying to do exactly what you're talking about: he's taking action instead of complaining."

"I know it. But he takes unfair advantage, sticking it to the hospital about all kinds of dumb things. Or repeating a rumor like it's gospel. Like he just interviewed one of the anesthesiologists, a Jamaican who was accusing the hospital of keeping good jobs from him because he's black—"

"You think that doesn't happen? I can tell you—"

"Hey, Betty, I'm black, right? *And* female. Don't you think I *know*? But this particular doctor is a son of a bitch with an attitude. Everyone hates him, me included. I don't know why Pierce would listen to him. Unless, of course, he's one of Pierce's moles."

"Pierce's *what*?" Betty got up and began to pull plates and glasses from the cupboard.

"Mole. You know, like in the spy novels. Someone working at the hospital who's secretly a snitch and tells Pierce what's going on."

"Oh. Oh, I doubt that, but I guess he has his ways," Betty said vaguely, then abruptly changed the subject. "Guess who called here looking for you late last night?"

"Yuck. I think I know. How late and how drunk?"

"Now stop it, Deedra! Why do you carry on about Ernie Newton that way? He's such a nice boy, and he's crazy about you!"

"He's not such a nice boy, Betty. Maybe I should've told you before. Remember when he was talking marriage? Well, at the same time, he was sleeping with somebody else. I've told him twenty times—no, make that forty—I'm not interested in patching it up."

Betty shook her head sadly. "Oh, that's terrible. But just because one accountant disappointed you, that's no reason to always be going for motorcycle freaks or out-of-work actors!"

Dee stood, looking exasperated, and then suddenly she grinned and said, "How long did it take you to find George, huh? You didn't get married until last year. Seems like pickiness runs in this family!"

"It's just that . . . well, when you two were a steady thing there for a while, I thought, well, at last I can stop worrying about my little sister."

"Betty, sugar, let me remind you that I don't have to ever get married. I can support myself."

"Getting supported is not the point," Betty began. Then she

laughed and gave up. "Are you going to have supper with us? There's a big chicken salad in the fridge, and I bought some of those Italian plums you love."

Dee shook her head. "Sorry. No supper tonight. I'm on at the health center, and I want to get my run in first. I'll grab something later."

"It's so hot, Deedra. You shouldn't be running. What if you faint or something?"

"If I do, chances are very good there'll be a doctor around to pick me up."

"What do you mean?"

"A lot of people from the hospital are joggers. That's right, I'm not the only crazy one. Dr. Romano runs; sometimes I see her. And Dr. Voorhees is a runner. Every once in a while we'll run together. And would you believe . . . Dr. Wolfe's mother? Her, I see mornings."

"Mrs. Dr. Philip *jogs*?" Betty turned, incredulous. "She must be seventy-five years old!"

Dee put her head back and laughed. "No, she doesn't jog. She fast-walks!"

"All I can say is, I hope to heaven I'm able to walk at all when I'm seventy-five."

"You? You'll be running the world by the time *you're* seventy-five!" Dee got up from the table. "I'd better get going."

"You gonna be all alone over there at the center?"

"Now, Betty, I'm not twelve anymore. The social worker will be there with me . . . most of the time."

Sternly: "And what time will you be closing up?"

"Nine, ten, somewhere around there. *Betty.* Stop that. You go marching up and down the street most nights until midnight!"

"Well, I'm different."

"You sure are. You're pregnant. Oh . . . ." She came over to Betty and kissed her on the cheek. "I know, you just can't help worrying about me. But if I'd taken my residency out of town, you wouldn't have a *clue* what I was doing, at any hour."

"That may be true, but I still wish you didn't have to take that duty at night."

"Toni does, and she's a lot smaller than me."

"Toni! How come you call her Toni?"

Laughing, "That's her name."

"She's Dr. Romano."

"Oh Betty, don't worry, I haven't forgotten all your lectures about proper respect. But she *asked* us to call her Toni. Around the hospital, she's known as Dr. Toni. Hell, I've heard *you* refer to her as Dr. Toni."

"Well, then, if *I* do it, it must be all right."

They both laughed.

"Ohmygod! I'm late!" Dee said suddenly. "And I'm outa here!"

Betty watched her racing up the block from her kitchen window. Then she checked the clock on the wall: six-fifteen. George probably wouldn't be home for another ten or fifteen minutes. She wiped her hands on a dish towel, went to the wall phone, and quickly dialed. A familiar, brisk female voice answered. Betty announced herself and said, "Ham Pierce, please. He's expecting my call. I'll wait."

8

October

King Crawford listened with half an ear to the radio squawk from the front of the ambulance as it hurtled, with its lights and siren going, down Broadway toward the hospital. The noise didn't interfere with his work. He was good at doing two or three things at once—like listening to the radio, talking to his partner, and still taking care of his patient. This one was a woman—a very young girl, actually—in labor. He was timing her contractions. About four minutes apart right now; not much different from when they picked her up.

She was a little, bitty thing, and she looked even smaller lying there surrounded by the Digi-Trol suction catheters and the Lifepak defibrillators and the Pulmanex resuscitators.

"Arrest!" the radio announced in its mechanical voice: "Forty-five West one-one-five." Someone had stopped breathing, up on 115th Street. They couldn't take this one, but getting called to an arrest was what paramedics liked. It was a challenge, and that made it interesting; that made it a *good job*. What paramedics called a good job was what the rest of the world would consider disgusting and difficult. But the more difficult it was, the more King liked dealing with it. King liked cheating death.

"Heart attack," his partner Mike remarked from the driver's seat.

"Or pneumonia," King said. "Or some other goddamn thing." Some old people just became scared of dying and began to hyperventilate. They saw a lot of that. Mike grunted and hung a sudden right, around a triple-parked van, cursing good-naturedly.

They'd seen a lot of pneumonia lately. Between AIDS and the huge population of elderly people, it was like an epidemic. When he was thirteen, he'd hardly heard of pneumonia. Then, he got it. He remembered it was like having the flu, a little uncomfortable but nothing to worry about. But his parents explained to him that, before antibiotics, pneumonia used to be a killer. Well, here it was, long after antibiotics, and it was a killer again.

The next call was someone in Riverside Park with chest pains . . . probably a skell. The park was full of them: homeless people, schizophrenics, alcoholics, addicts . . . street people. So many of them. It was getting so that parts of New York reminded him of pictures of Calcutta, a city where people lived out their whole lives on the streets! A city where the police went around every morning to hose dead bodies into the gutters, and then threw the corpses onto a wagon, one on top of another, to be dumped like so much garbage! It was unbelievable. It seemed so inhuman. How could rich people in Calcutta see this horror every day and do nothing?

Well, now it was happening right here, in the Big Apple, the greatest city in the world, right? The richest! The best! And every day, he watched people in expensive business suits walk by men sleeping on cardboard, or women huddled with their shopping bags, and not even give them a glance. Hell, *nobody* seemed to care.

King felt sorry for the homeless, and he always tried to be kind to them. But he had to admit, skells could be a real pain; they would call for nothing. They used the city's emergency service as if it were a car service. A lot of the time they just wanted a bed for the night, or a place to warm up in.

The girl in labor made a little moan. Another contraction. He looked at his watch: three minutes apart. He was holding her hand to comfort her. He didn't have to do much. She was a gutsy little thing, smiling and making conversation and apologizing every time she tensed up against the pain. She had told him she was about six months pregnant: much too soon for this baby to be born. But it was getting born, whether it was too soon or not. She was scared, he could tell, but she wasn't letting herself show it.

"You ever been pregnant before?" he asked her. She looked

like a child herself, small and skinny, her hair all cornrowed
with little gold beads dangling off the ends.

"You kidding me? Look at me, do I look like someone who's
stupid enough to be pregnant the second time?"

He laughed. She's a sharp one, he thought.

"Is it getting born, Doc?"

King smiled at her. "I'm not a doctor; I'm a paramedic."
Saying "paramedic" always made him feel good. He had started
out as an emergency medical technician—a mule—but he soon
got bored with that. Lift and carry, that's all you could do, really,
when you were an EMT. Dad had always told him a man should
love his work and not settle. So he didn't settle; he went back
to school for paramedic training. And now his mom kept saying
that maybe he ought to think about applying to medical school.

Maybe she was right, but he wasn't ready for that kind of
commitment. Six, maybe eight years? That was a long, long
time: he got antsy if he had to sit through a goddamn movie or
plan more than a few days ahead! On the other hand, now that
he was a paramedic, he *did* love his work. And he *had* started
to think about thinking about medical school. Not that he'd tell
his mom. She was a nice lady, but boy, once she got on your
case—!

The girl cried out. "What's wrong?" he said quickly.

"It's a different kind of pain . . . ow . . . kinda sharp."

King put his hand on her abdomen and felt the tightening
under his hand. "That's just a strong contraction," he told her.

"Doc, you ever deliver a baby?" the girl said.

"Sure, lots of them," he assured her. He'd done eight since
he started with Harmony Hill. "There are five little Martins out
there in the world. Named after me."

"Martin's your name, huh?"

"Martin Luther King Crawford. What's yours?"

"Charmaine."

"That's a pretty name."

She started to say thank you; then she gave a little gasp and
bit her lower lip, closing her eyes tightly against the contraction.

He didn't have the heart to tell her that she might be going
through all this pain for nothing. You couldn't count on a six-
month fetus surviving, especially if they didn't make it to the
hospital in time.

Traffic! Driving around this town was a real nightmare. There was no more rush hour; every hour was rush hour. And nobody pulled over to let an ambulance get by!

God, last night when they were trying to get that old movie star who had O.D.'ed on Halcion to the hospital, there had been a big accident on the Henry Hudson, so every goddamn car in New York was on Broadway. They'd had to go crosstown, all the way over to Central Park West. Michael was a good driver, so she survived. What was her name? She'd been written up in the paper a lot, and he'd seen her in old movies on TV.

Charmaine yelped suddenly, then apologized. She wasn't like most of the pregnant girls he'd had in the ambulance. She had a lot more control. Usually they were yelling for Mama. She was probably a lot smarter than most of them. She certainly talked better and behaved better, and he could tell she didn't do heavy drugs. So how in hell had she let herself get into this mess?

"How old are you?" he asked.

"Twenty."

"In your dreams!" King said, and smiled at her, to let her know he was just kidding. She smiled back. Girls were always telling him he had an irresistible smile; girls were always telling him he was so handsome. He couldn't see it, himself. But if women wanted to think he was something special . . . hey! Who was he to argue?

"Come on, how old, Charmaine? The truth."

She grinned up at him. She was really sweating now, and he once again blotted her face with a towel. "Fifteen. Old enough for you, Doc."

"I'm twenty-five. And you should be in school today. You're smart. Too smart to get pregnant at fifteen."

A wan smile. "You know how it is. I had a boyfriend. He said if I loved him, I should prove it."

"By having his baby," King finished. He'd heard *that* story plenty of times.

"You got it. Only trouble is, *I'm* having his baby, and *he's* history."

He'd heard *that* one, too. "That sucks," he said.

"Tell me about it!" But she was trying to smile again. "So, Martin—"

"Everybody calls me King."

"King, huh? Not bad. So, King, you black, or what."

"Black and what," he answered. She gave him a wavery

smile and closed her eyes. Her labor was wearing her down; maybe it was a breech. He had thought for sure it would be born by now. He rubbed Charmaine's forehead gently. "Just close your eyes and try to get some rest, Charmaine."

"Black and what," she murmured. "Cute."

Yeah, yeah, cute. But it was true. Black and Jewish and black and Italian, that was him. His own birth was a mystery. He had been adopted when he was two days old by his mom and dad. She was Jewish and a lawyer, he was black and a professor of black studies; and baby King was just perfect for them. That's what Mom always told him, right from the beginning.

"We wanted a baby so badly, and there you were. See, your natural mother was Italian, but white, like me, and your natural father was black, like Daddy." He never got tired, when he was little, of hearing the whole story over and over again: the trip to the hospital; the first sight of the beautiful little boy, coffee-colored, big light eyes, lots of curly black hair; the excitement; the blue blanket they wrapped him in when they came to get him to bring him home.

"You're special, King, because we didn't have to have you, we *picked* you out of all the babies in the world."

It wasn't until years later that it occurred to him to ask why, if he was so special, his real mother had given him away. His parents were really great. Any question he ever had, including that one, they answered. They never gave him bullshit, and they never said be quiet and stop asking so many questions. So when he asked them, they told him everything they knew.

Which wasn't much. His birth mother was a nurse, and his father was a doctor. They couldn't get married, and she was too poor to keep a baby, and they both wanted their baby to have the best home in the world, where his mom and dad would love him and take care of him and give him the things he needed.

Mom and Dad *had* been good parents; they had been wonderful parents. They still *were*. It was just that, lately, it had started to bug him. He didn't know who he was, really. He found himself staring at his reflection, wondering who he took after, whether he had brothers and sisters. All of a sudden, he needed to know where he came from, where he *really* came from. He needed to know what had happened between them, his real parents. Why couldn't they get married? Why couldn't they keep him? He needed to know why his mother gave him away. There was a law now in New York that said adopted kids had a right to know. One of these days, he was going to find out. One of these days.

Just then, Charmaine tensed up and gave a pitiful whimper. When he lifted up the sheet to check, sure enough, the baby's head had crowned. At least it wasn't a breech. "Hey, Mike, can you speed it up? We got a preemie coming, and he's in a hurry!" To the girl, he said, "Listen to me, Charmaine. Try to take in deep breaths. Steady now. See if you can get on top of that pain and breathe." He demonstrated. "Breathe in . . . and out . . . in . . . and out . . ."

The girl visibly pulled herself together and tried to copy him. She gave him a hint of a smile. "What do you mean, *he*? It's a girl."

"Gridlock!" Michael called back. "But it looks like it's starting to move! Hang on! We're almost there!"

Shit! He didn't want this kid born yet. What could he do here? Not much. They didn't have the kind of equipment you needed to take care of a preemie. It would have to be rushed to the neonatal ICU, right away. Please baby, he begged silently, hold off for a few minutes.

"King?"

"Yeah."

"What's going to happen with this baby?"

He hesitated, then said it straight: "You know this is very risky, Charmaine. You're so young, and the baby's coming too early. We just have to hope for the best."

She sighed and closed her eyes.

Finally, with a lurch, the siren blaring, the ambulance took off; five minutes later, 31 Willy Zebra pulled up at the emergency room entrance of Harmony Hill Hospital.

The nurses were waiting when they pushed the gurney in. King shook his head silently. He hoped that if Charmaine's baby, like so many preemies, wasn't really normal, it wouldn't survive. She deserved a chance to make a life for herself; what kind of chance would she have with a handicapped kid to take care of, all by herself, and maybe for the rest of her life?

This was their last call today. Tomorrow, when he came to the hospital to visit "his" patients—he often did that—he'd make sure he saw her. He'd check in at the neonatal nursery, just to see if this one made it; then, he'd have a look at the Rodriguez baby, even though it always made him feel bad. He knew the parents really wanted to believe their baby was okay, but hell, it had been a couple of months now, and there wasn't any change. Those poor people were really gonna suffer when that baby finally died—which he was gonna do.

Well, no matter what happened to Charmaine's baby, he was going to tell her about the Women's Health Center up on 123rd Street. The word was out, on the street, that the new doctor was really good. The girls all respected and liked her. It would be good for Charmaine if she went up there and got some birth control—and maybe some self-esteem.

By the time the nurses came back, he and Michael had cleaned the ambulance. They didn't have to call in an eight-one; their shift was over. It had been three long days, seven to seven, and when they came back into the E.R. with their Pepsis, Mike stretched and yawned. "It's gonna be nice to see my wife," he said.

King went over to the two nurses and asked how Charmaine was doing. Lois shook her head. "Stillbirth," she said.

"Tough. How's she taking it?"

"Crying but okay. She's better off. How old is she anyway, thirteen?"

"Fifteen."

The nurses rolled their eyes. "So she says. Anyway, I hope she's learned something from this."

"I figure I'll tell her about the clinic on 123rd," King said.

"Women's Health Center? Yeah, that's a good idea. Since Dr. Romano took over, it's gotten a very good rep. You think this one will go?"

"I think so. She's . . . I don't know . . . different. Anyway, I gotta give it a try."

"Old bleeding heart," Michael laughed. "Spends all his spare time checking back on our cases! Why don't you act like a human being and go out on a date!"

King laughed. "Why, you got someone new for me? Your neighbor's wife's sister-in-law's cousin, maybe?" He turned to Lois. "This guy thinks everyone should be married!"

Linda, the younger nurse, a real cute P.R., gave him the eye. "Hey, *I'm* available, King," she said. "And I don't want to get married."

"I'll take you up on that one of these days." And he might, he just might. She was a fox.

"You oughta be a doctor, King," Lois said.

"You and my mother!"

"No, really. At least you care about the patients. And that's more than you can say about a lot of the M.D.s around here!"

"Yeah, King, you're always hanging around after you bring patients in."

Mike laughed. "It's his way of making time with all you gorgeous nurses!"

"Yeah, sure. Why do you hang, King?" Lois asked.

"I want to know what happens to them," he said. It seemed obvious.

"Why?"

He thought for a minute. "I want to know did I make a difference."

"Just like me." Linda smiled at him. Yes, he was definitely going to have to do something about her.

"Speaking of which, Florence Nightingale," Lois said, "we better get back to work."

"Yeah. Lucky us," Michael said, stretching. "We get to go home."

"Never mind, you deserve it."

King walked Michael to his subway, on 96th and Central Park West, and then decided to keep on walking. His shoulders ached; they'd carried a big fat guy down five flights of stairs this morning. At the time, he hadn't felt it, but now . . . Christ! Maybe he should go to the gym. Maybe he should go to the Y and take a swim. No, he'd go home and put on his running shoes and do a couple of miles around the reservoir. Or maybe he'd call Joan, the girl he'd met last week at the Silver Streak. She had a very interesting body, if he remembered correctly, and she had made some very interesting insinuations. If he could remember where he put her phone number . . .

And then, he began to laugh out loud. It had been a very long three days; he had had very goddamn little sleep. And all he could think of was more ways to keep going! What was he, weird? Christ, he had four days off ahead of him. He'd get laid sooner or later. No big deal. He quickened his pace and headed home—for pizza, beer, and bed.

9

Mid-October

The lights in studio 3 at WSUN, Channel 14, were very bright and very hot. Ham had noticed the sweat building up on the brow of the director of *All Tied Up*, a controversial film about sexual bondage. Now it was beginning to trickle down the side of her face, and she was in a quandary over what in hell to do about it. To reach up and wipe at it would make her look foolish, and here she was, trying to convince the babe from Women Against Violence Everywhere that artistic freedom—freedom of speech, according to her—was more important than some super-sensitive viewer's feelings of outrage.

"But this film shows the sadistic use of a woman, beyond all bounds of decency—!"

"These things really happen; and to not tell the story, in all its horrible detail, is to deny that!"

The woman from WAVE looked disgusted. "And you've got to know that some men watching this film will imitate it. This sort of behavior, so denigrating to all women, should be disavowed, not glorified!"

"We're not glorifying. Anyone with a brain could see that."

"Are you suggesting . . ."

It hadn't been the greatest show he ever did. He had wished the entire time that one of them would say something really interesting. Now it looked like maybe it was starting to happen, except that they were both stiffs. Ms. WAVE just kept using bigger and bigger words that meant less and less; and Ms. Director . . . Christ, she was sweating so damned much, he could hardly bear to sit next to her.

"This is a legitimate attempt to shock with a satirical view of sadism."

"Sadism is not a fit subject for satire." Ms. WAVE was spluttering. "And your film . . . it's filthy, it's evil, it's . . . it's an encyclopedia of torture. Women have enough problems, Miss Random—"

"*Ms.* Random, if you don't mind."

"Up yours!" Ms. WAVE picked herself up, giving the camera the finger, and walked right off the cozy living room set and out of there. Ham couldn't believe it. But she had really done it, and if she hadn't left the building, he was going to give her a great big smooch after the show. In a minute, that switchboard was gonna light up like Rockefeller Center at Christmastime! Thank you, Lord, for making women so high-strung!

Smoothly, he continued, hoping to God he didn't look *too* pleased. "I can see why you feel this sort of film is important, Ms. Random. It certainly can arouse strong emotions, as we have just witnessed. But, to be honest with you, I tried to watch your film, and it made me sick. I turned it off after ten minutes."

She smirked. "That's what happens when you produce important and controversial art, Mr. Pierce."

"But there *is* the threat of copycatting."

Now Ms. Random did wipe away the sweat rolling down her cheek. "Oh come now, Mr. Pierce, you can't believe that . . ."

He stopped listening, although his eyes remained fastened on her face. He'd got her going; she'd be good until the wrap. Swiftly, almost invisibly, he glanced up at the booth, where his director held up two fingers. Two minutes. She could go for a minute and a half and then . . .

"Thank you so much, Ms. Random. And thanks also to the absent Ms. Wershansky. This has been the 'Voice of the City,' speaking out and speaking up. Until Monday, same time, same channel . . . this is Ham Pierce, saying keep the faith." He held up both hands, fingers vee'd for victory, smiling. He kept the smile in place even after the director gave the cut signaling the end.

It took him a few minutes to get the lady filmmaker out of there; she wanted to keep talking. But finally, she left, and Dave came down onto the floor, clipboard in hand, and said his usual "Good show."

"Well, good end. But most of the time, it was dead on its feet."

"All right, it wasn't your greatest. But now we'll get calls and mail . . . plenty of calls and mail. And anyway, your viewers are *devoted*." He rolled his eyes. "So, Monday is, what? Dinkins?"

"Yup." Ham shook his head. "I hate like hell to come down on him, but damn it . . ."

"I know, I know. Save it for Monday. And Tuesday, I see we're doing Harlem Hospital. No more Harmony Hill? Isn't it about time for an update on that baby? The one they're keeping alive?"

"I don't know. Isn't that old news?"

"Not if something new happens."

"Okay, Dave. You're right. Lemme look into it. It's been a while . . . but, wait, there's a story going around that the mother's losing it . . . hearing voices, that kind of thing."

"I don't know where you get all your inside info." Dave shook his head in admiration.

"I have ways, my man, I have ways."

"Which reminds me, we gotta do something about Wershansky."

"Like what? She decided to get up and leave." He paused, remembering, and laughed. "She decided to give us all the finger! She should apologize to *me*. Okay, okay, I'll call her. I'll charm, I'll grovel, I'll be a goddamn saint."

It took balls to be a good newsman, and Dave didn't have balls. He was always worrying about the subjects' feelings. Well, Ham knew damn well what their major feeling was: Wow, I'm gonna be on TV! It wasn't until later that some of them had second thoughts. But hey, nobody forced them.

The studio emptied out; he liked it with nobody else there, just him. He'd look around, like he was doing now, and feel that satisfaction just fill him up. He was making it! Goddamn it, everybody in New York City recognized Ham Pierce. He loved it when he walked down the street and people did double takes. He loved the admiring looks. He loved when a cabbie leaned out of his car and yelled, "Yo, Ham, give it to them!" Yeah! That's who he was: the guy who gave it to them, five nights a week, six-thirty to seven!

Too bad his father was dead and couldn't see what a celebrity his son had become. Then maybe he'd take back all those bitter words he'd said when Ham gave up practicing law. "After all my sacrifices . . . and your mother's sacrifices . . . on a whim, on a childish fantasy. As far as I'm concerned, you are no longer my son."

Ham shook his head, to get free of it, of that memory. It still made him mad as hell; it still hurt. His father's dream for him was that he would be a lawyer. And that dream became an obsession, so powerful that the young Ham could not resist. He went to college, he got his A's, and then he went to law school at Duke on a full scholarship—ah, *then* his father was proud, or so his mother told him—and graduated at the top of his class. He was a lawyer for six months and was bored every minute of it.

Then he handled a case that got into the news—the hit-and-run death of a child. He was interviewed for local television, and after that, the courthouse reporters waited for him, hanging on to his every word. When he watched himself on TV, he couldn't believe how good he was, how smooth. No awkward pauses, no searching around for the right word, he just talked and goddamn it, it came out sounding intelligent! Fan letters began coming into the station. When they offered him a job, he didn't even have to think. He jumped at it. And his father turned his back on him forever.

Well, the Reverend Pierce would be preaching a different sermon now! His father had always admired charisma. Of course, that's not what he called it, but he sure as hell *had* it. His parishoners worshipped him. He could tell them any goddamn thing, and they'd believe it. He called it leadership. Ham knew it was more than that; it was closer to mind control. But call it whatever you liked; Reverend Pierce's little boy Ham had plenty of it! All Ham had to do was a five-minute exposé on the show, and the next day, it was front-page news, and everyone in the city was talking about it. He looked good and sounded good, too; but he had something extra. He was smart.

It was *real* smart, recruiting the president's secretary at Harmony Hill. She knew every important move, way ahead of time. Of course, she had a nasty habit of getting up on her high horse about loyalty and confidentiality and trust and all that shit. Jesus, didn't she realize what he could *do*? He talked to millions of people, every goddamn night . . . . and they listened! If only she would come across the way he wanted, he could make things happen, he could put people on the spot. He even had the power to get rid of the president of the hospital. Hell, he'd already done it once—as she damn well knew!

He stretched and got up from his chair, giving it a twirl with his hand as he walked out. He'd give Betty a call over the weekend to see if that story about the Rodriguez woman going bananas was for real. What was her name? Nancy? No, something else like that. Alice, that was it. He and Alice had got along just fine. In fact, he could thank Alice Rodriguez, and her pitiful little baby, for saving his ass. His ratings had been slipping back then, and he had been scared shitless. Then he had covered the Rodriguez story, and that did it. Since then, Harmony Hill had been his favorite Tuesday night subject. And his audience ate it up with a spoon! Everyone hated doctors these days! Including him!

Well, now that he thought of it, not quite *all* doctors. That sexy little Dr. Romano . . . now, she was something else. She was older than him, but who cared? There was something about her that really turned him on.

And hey—wasn't she Alice's obstetrician? Yeah, of course she was. He could interview her. He could ask four different doctors how they felt about this case—should the baby be kept alive or allowed to die peacefully, that kind of thing—and she'd be one of them. She couldn't object to *that*. And then he could lay on the charm and with any luck at all, she'd get to trust him. He smiled a little. And once there was trust, who knew what could happen?

Women were always looking him over, giving him the eye, hell, coming after him. At the hospital, he could have his pick. As a matter of fact, he'd taken one or two of them up on their offers. The head nurse was hot, and he'd considered it—hey, she could be a great source—but she had a rep, and he was a careful man. Thank God he'd never had to make it with Betty Cannon; big, ugly women definitely did not appeal to him. He always did like them little and dark and dynamic. Like Toni Romano. He kept coming back to her. Yeah, she was for him. She didn't know it, but she was going to get to know Hamilton Pierce a hell of a lot better.

He stopped himself. What the hell was he thinking? If he wanted to be a hero to Dr. Romano, he couldn't do a number on the hospital. If he didn't do a number on the hospital, his viewers would turn to Channel 5.

This story could be played too many ways to let it go. If they let the baby die, he could come down on them for being heartless. He could see himself interviewing the mother. Jesus, it could be great, maybe in her apartment, yeah, with a crucifix on the wall behind her. And if they kept the baby on life support. . . ? Easy. Why is this hospital spending thousands of dollars on a hopeless case, while other babies, black babies, mostly, were dying every day.

Yeah! He couldn't lose on this one. But he had to watch himself and not let his gonads rule his brain. It would be dangerous to let himself get really involved with the adorable Dr. Romano.

He let himself out of the studio into the darkening city street, glistening with rain and reflecting the neon sign of the tavern down the block. There was a phone booth right in front of him. He knew someone who right now was hoping he'd give her a call and make this her lucky night. He just might do that, he decided, digging into his pocket for a quarter. He'd get laid, and she'd be grateful, and no problems the next day. Toni Romano could keep until another time.

10

Late October

Toni paid the cabbie and then hesitated over the tip. She generally overtipped . . . or so Eliot said, but Eliot had never been poor. Eliot didn't know what it felt like to be down to your last couple of bucks. Well, *she* did; her father had driven a cab in Brooklyn. Almost defiantly, she added another single.

He had pulled up right in front of her Women's Health Center—after asking her if she was sure this was what she wanted. She couldn't blame him; the block looked like a war zone. But not her clinic. It looked great, all spruced up and clean. The chairs were mismatched, and the bookcases were all painted different colors, but to the women who came in here, this was pure luxury. No rats, no bugs, no dirt, no grease, no cracks in the walls.

She got out of the cab and stood for a moment, taking in a deep breath before going in. She was beat. Her day had started almost twelve hours ago, at six A.M., delivering a baby born drug-addicted, underweight, and shaking with tremors. Crack. She spanked him into life and looked at him with despair. What chance did he have, poor little thing? Many crack babies were developmentally damaged, and they grew up unable to concentrate or learn, prone to fits of violence, unable to connect to other people.

When she tried to get these girls to stop taking drugs and to stop drinking when they were pregnant, most of them just looked at her with blank eyes, turning her off. They had no sense of any kind of future. Instead, they waited for life to happen to them. Unfortunately, the life around here was full of danger. Sometimes she wondered why she bothered.

Oh hell. If *she* got discouraged, what hope was there for *them*? She'd better go in. She had a birth-control group to talk to first; then she'd begin her regular examining hours.

Even before her hand was on the doorknob, she could see that there were only four girls waiting for her. Shit! Only four! They had started with twelve; last week, there had been seven. How the hell was she supposed to help them if they evaporated into thin air!

Imogene was among the missing. She thought she'd gotten through to Imogene, but you just couldn't ever tell. Toni wondered what the excuse was; she got all kinds.

"My mother needed me to go down to Welfare." "My sister made me stay with the kids." "I was late so I thought you wouldn't want me to come." "I was so tired, I just stayed in bed." At six o'clock in the evening!

One of the girls inside was new. Well, that was good, but what use was it to get new girls in, if the old ones kept dropping out? If she didn't watch out, this center was going to vanish from the face of the Earth. Most of her teenage patients had been born to teenage mothers. If only she could get some of these young women to break out of their vicious cycle.

Well, four was better than none. She put a smile on her face and marched in. She was immediately surrounded by three excited young women, all squealing at once and calling her name: "Dr. Toni! Dr. Toni! You're famous! You're famous! Will you autograph mine? And mine? And mine?"

They were all jumping up and down, waving magazines in the air and trying to touch her. Even the new girl, hanging back a bit, had a big grin on her face. Of course. They were all carrying copies of *Gotham* magazine. She had her own copy of it tucked into her bag; she'd try to make the time later to read it. But she *had* taken a good look at the cover before she raced up here.

Twelve photos: doctors, in their white coats, stethoscopes around their necks. She had objected strenuously to the stethoscope—it was so hackneyed and kind of self-congratulatory—but the photographer shook his head. "Sorry, Doc. It's a visual symbol, it says on the editorial sheet. We gotta have it." So there she was, in the second row, looking—if she did say so herself—very goddamn good. In spite of the stethoscope. But why was she the only one smiling? Did she look goofy? To hell

with it! It was a catchy cover. Including the big headline: GOTH-
AM'S DOZEN: THE BEST IN NYC.

When she first saw it, her heart began to race. She, little Toni
Romano, one of the dozen best doctors in New York City? Well,
it was damned nice to get recognition. Wait till Eliot saw it!

It was much more than she had expected. Oh, she knew she
was going to be in an article. A nice young man had come to
interview her a few weeks ago. "Why me?" she asked him.
"I'm a new girl in town."

"Yeah, well, you've made quite an impression, it seems.
Everyone's worried about the problems you deal with. And when
we checked back at John Quincy Adams, they said you did much
the same kind of thing down there. Wasn't it you who started
the pregnancy van program?"

She admitted she had. It had been a good idea: a social
worker, going around the poorer neighborhoods in a van painted
pink, stopping to talk to every pregnant woman, asking, "Are
you getting prenatal care?" If the woman said no, the social
worker would offer to take her right then and there into the
clinic. It had been very successful.

"And now," the young man went on, "I understand you've
started the only clinic for teenage girls uptown."

Modesty made her tell the truth. "Not the only one . . . and
it was there before I got there. I just gave it . . . an emergency
transfusion, I guess you'd call it."

He scribbled away, as fast as she could talk. When he was
finished, he told her he wasn't quite sure when it would appear.
"They don't tell us wage slaves anything." She figured that
maybe she'd be in the article and maybe she wouldn't. And then
she just didn't think about it again.

No way did she ever expect it to be the cover story and to find
her face grinning out from every newsstand in New York. But
now that it had happened, she had to admit she liked it; hell,
she *loved* it! In fact, her bad mood had dissolved.

"Okay, okay, I'll autograph all of them. *After* our meeting."
She laughed at their faces and quickly added, "We have a new-
comer, I see. Hello." She put out her hand. "I'm Dr. Toni."

The girl's hand was tiny, but her handshake was firm and
adult. She wasn't much more than five feet and weighed, Toni
figured, maybe ninety pounds. Maybe. She was neatly dressed
in jeans and a long-sleeved T-shirt. Her shoulder-length hair was

cornrowed and decorated with shiny glass beads. "Hi, Dr. Toni. I'm Charmaine Johnson." She had a nice smile; in fact, she was a very pretty girl.

"Pleased to see you here, Charmaine. How did you find us? One of your girlfriends?"

"No, ma'am." There was a twinkle in her dark eyes. "A guy. Hey, not mine! But I sure wish he was; he was a hunk!" The other girls laughed appreciatively. "He's a paramedic from Harmony Hill. He told me that a terrific lady doctor was running a terrific program, and I was dumb if I didn't try it. Well, I ain't dumb, so here I am."

The girl was looking at her very carefully, as if deciding whether or not she believed this was such a terrific doctor she was talking to. Obviously she didn't care what anyone claimed. This young lady was going to make up her own mind. Toni liked that in a person, and she already liked this girl.

"We're very glad you're here. And *I'm* very glad one of our paramedics is talking this place up. Where did you meet him?"

A little smile. "In the ambulance. I had a baby, but it died."

"I'm so sorry, Charmaine. That's tough."

"Yeah. Well, it was probably for the best. I'm too young to go having a baby. That's why I want to know all about birth control." Another one of those wispy smiles. "I'm only fifteen."

So she really was as young as she looked. But smart. And this paramedic knew enough to send her for help. Maybe all her leaflets and reminders and announcements to hospital staff were finally working! Now that she thought of it, some other girls had been sent by a Harmony Hill paramedic. The same one? she wondered. She had a feeling it was. They had all said what a fox he was.

"Well, you're here now, among friends, Charmaine. This is a great group. Am I right, ladies?" There was a chorus of agreement. "Okay, I guess it's time to start. Just give me a minute to check with Valerie."

Valerie Gomez was the social worker assigned to this clinic, to walk the kids through all the myriad city and state agencies and their paperwork. Oh God, yes, their paperwork, tons of it! It was enough to frighten a strong man, never mind a young woman who already felt lost in the system. Valerie also tried to make sure they stayed in school. She was the one who always opened the office at three. Today, luckily, there had been no ardent boyfriends bursting through the plate-glass window, no baby left on the doorstep, not even one temper tantrum.

"You must be bored to death," Toni said.

Valerie laughed. "I kinda miss my usual afternoon migraine!" she said. "Didn't you notice anything different here?"

Toni turned to examine the big square room. It looked the same to her. A mixed bag of chairs, all donated. Three rag rugs, also contributions. Three different tables, carefully polished by the clientele. Racks filled with health brochures, many of them in comic-book format, and their small library of tattered romances and horror stories. "Different? No."

"Dr. Toni, shame on you! Look on the wall."

Oh God! Of course! There was the *Gotham* cover, neatly taped onto the wall. And then she started to laugh. Her colleagues, one and all, had been X'ed out, and her photograph stood out in solitary splendor.

She stared at her face in wonderment. When she was a kid running around on the streets of Brooklyn, could she have dreamed that one day she'd be a doctor and a cover girl as well? Never!

She still remembered being so in awe of doctors when she was a brand-new nurse. She was working at John Quincy Adams Hospital in D.C., and that's where she first met Eliot. He seemed like a god to her, but hell, back then, *every* doctor was God.

It turned out, with her and Eliot, to be more than that. They thought alike; they did things the same way. She realized the first time they worked together with a patient. It was wonderful. They needed almost no words; they seemed to read each other's minds.

He was the only doctor at the hospital who bothered to praise her. In a way, she hadn't really expected much praise, but now that it was happening, she realized how badly she had missed it. She knew how good she was; why the hell couldn't they say it every once in a while!

Eliot became her mentor, her guru, as well as her friend. He took her seriously. It was Eliot who first suggested she go to medical school. Hell, it was Eliot who *paid* for it, no strings attached. He was everything a man should be, everything her father had never been. She had adored him then, absolutely adored him.

Well, then was then, and now was the Women's Health Center. She had work to do. She turned to gather her group together and glanced out of the big front windows. What she saw wiped the laughter from her lips. There on the street was someone who was supposed to be here now, Janine Jeters, age seventeen, mother of a three-month-old daughter, Kenya. She should have been happy to see Janine, her baby wrapped in a pink blanket with a little ruffled bonnet peeking over the top. But she wasn't. Because while she held her infant in one arm, with the other hand Janine was making a buy from that bastard Boots.

That was all the name Toni knew; it was all the name anybody knew. Boots. Damn him to hell. Toni hated that pusher, *hated* him. She hated them all, but he was the worst. He was ubiquitous, always hanging around outside, sweet-talking the girls as they walked in and out. He was disgusting! He wore a knitted cap, no matter what the weather, and at least half a dozen heavy gold chains, one with a giant gold BOOTS hanging from it. He was always smiling, showing off his gold capped teeth, and his bright red BMW was always parked nearby. Nobody ever touched it, of course. Nobody would dare.

Boots was a power in this neighborhood, a major power and a wealthy man. He was sixteen. What kind of a lousy society turned an uneducated child into a vulture who preyed upon other children!

One day, she had gotten up the nerve to confront him. She went outside and asked him to move away from the center and leave her patients alone. He never even blinked, just kept on smiling.

"Hey, Mama, who *you*, tellin' Boots to leave? Ain't this a free country, or what? This here *my* sidewalk, too. Yo! This here the ghetto, and I be black, and you be white, so this here *my* turf. Tell you what. You don't like me? *You* leave."

She called the cops that day, and they said, sure, Doctor, they'd come over and chase him away . . . but he'd only be back. "Why don't you watch him make a sale and let him go to prison?" she had asked; the sergeant laughed, and said, "Doctor, haven't you heard that our jails are overcrowded? He'll get probation. And *then* he'll be back." It made her so damn mad!

Just one of those vulgar gold chains could pay for another social
worker—which they badly needed.

If a rival pusher came along and shot Boots out there in the
street, and left him bleeding, would she, as a physician, run out
to tend to him? Christ, what *would* she do? She'd want to let
him die. Of course, she couldn't do that, but she *could* walk
very slowly.

She didn't expect Janine to have the gall to come in, but she
was wrong. In she sashayed, displaying her baby proudly for the
other girls. Toni marched over to her and said, "I can't believe
you're still smoking crack, Janine."

"But Dr. Toni, I was good. I did what you said. I didn't do
crack at all the day Kenya was being born. And look at her;
she's fine, the baby doctor says so."

Oh sweet Jesus, Toni thought, a wave of fatigue washing over
her. What good was she doing here? She rounded on Janine.
"Don't you realize how lucky you were? If you keep doing
drugs—" And then she stopped. The girl was no longer listening. Just how the hell, Toni thought angrily, does the fucking
Board of Trustees think I can make out a Success Chart? *Success
Chart!* Of all the goddamn stupid ideas! How do I explain what
goes on up here with columns of figures? Could she cure poor
teenage girls of wanting to get pregnant? Could she treat an
epidemic of incest? How did they expect her to immunize against
poverty, for Christ's sake! If it weren't so stupid, it would be
hilarious. What idiot had this idea, anyway? She thought she
knew. Voorhees. Dr. Tightass.

And when she had screamed about it to Eliot, he acted as
though it was an idea with merit. "Hey, it's not perfect," he
told her, "but at least it's a start. Look, Toni. We *have* to cut
back somewhere; that's the reality. And so we *have* to know
what's going on. And everyone's going to be doing it." Did he
think that following "everyone," like a goddamn sheep, was
going to appeal to *her*?

"If you think for one minute," she'd said in voice made of
ice, "that you're going to cut one penny of my pittance . . . a
pittance with which I strive very hard to save a few girls from a
lifetime of misery and despair, not to mention their babies—!"

He got that look on his face that said, Here we go again. The
look that meant he had turned off. Anyone at that hospital who

thought she was getting special attention because she was married to the president . . .

Goddamn it, she wasn't going to go home and change into a cocktail dress and drag herself to a stupid party at the Schlesingers' duplex on Sutton Place and make small talk. What a waste . . . a waste of her time and her talents. No, she wanted to do something that counted for something. And in a flash, it came to her. She was going to patrol with TACK, Together Against Crack Kids, Betty Cannon's bunch. They were right nearby, and maybe she'd feel a little cleaner after doing something worthwhile.

She was late leaving the center—someone came in off the street, in labor, and had to be sent down to the hospital—but it didn't matter what time it was. The TACK people patrolled all night long. She realized she looked a bit strange, with her silk dress, walking shoes, and briefcase. But who the hell cared? She trotted the one block to 122nd Street and joined them as they came to the corner, turning to go back again.

She got a couple of startled looks, and then Betty said, "This is Dr. Romano, remember I told you about her and the center around the corner." They all greeted her warmly.

They walked up the street in a clump, and Betty explained to her in a quiet voice that usually they split up and patrolled in pairs, but the past couple of nights, a large gang had been harassing whoever got this route, and they had decided that they would all stick together for safety. "And besides, George wouldn't have let me come out tonight unless there was a whole crowd of us." She chuckled. "He made me swear on a stack of Bibles that I wouldn't do anything risky without him here!"

"Where is he?"

"They put him on the night shift this week." She rolled her eyes.

As they walked, some people talked to each other in low voices. There was a feeling that this was serious, but, to Toni's surprise, it wasn't at all tense. It seemed . . . peaceful.

And then they appeared: a large group of men, young for the most part—so young! Fourteen or fifteen at the most, she thought—some black and some not, but all cocky and tough and very sure of themselves. They spread out across the entire width of the street, shoulder to shoulder, walking backward, matching their steps to those of the TACK group.

"Stop, everyone!" Betty shouted, and her group all came to a halt.

The boys started yelling, the voices crossing, but Toni could make out some of what they shouted. "You dudes, you hiding behind a woman!" "You pussy-whipped!" "Yeah, man, you tell 'im!" "Come on, Betty baby, Betty bitch, come on! We dare you!"

Toni's heart began to race, and she wished she knew someone well enough to hold on to. Betty and her neighbors did this every night! She had known that, but she hadn't realized just how scary it was. These were just boys, but they looked as if they had nothing to lose and didn't give a damn if they lost it anyway. They looked dangerous, and she was frightened.

"Come on, Betty bitch!"

"Come on, scare us off!" They all hooted with raucous laughter.

"You scared, Betty? Huh? You scared, old Mama?"

Betty stepped out of the protection of the group and began to walk right toward them. What was she *doing*? Didn't she realize how close to the edge they were? Toni had the feeling that the gang was just looking for an excuse to explode into violence. She became suddenly aware that she was the only white person here. She would make a wonderful target. She licked dry lips.

She was scared, yes, but if Betty took one more step, she was going out there with her. Betty was pregnant. It was poignant, that short, stocky body, outlined in the light, advancing on those creeps.

"Here I am, and here I come!" Betty spat. This was not the same woman who sat in front of Eliot's office, calm and pleasant and soft-spoken. It couldn't be. This was a warrior woman, indomitable, unstoppable. Betty kept on walking, and just as Toni was stepping forward to join her, suddenly the boys broke ranks, turned deliberately, and sauntered off, laughing.

It wasn't until they were out of sight around the corner that Toni turned and realized the patrol was being covered by TV cameras. There it was: the all-too-familiar paraphernalia—the van with the rooster, the woman with the hand-held camera. Ham Pierce. The man was *everywhere*! Just last night he'd been underground, talking to the hundreds of homeless men who lived in an abandoned railroad tunnel . . . not too far from Harmony Hill, in fact. And now he was here.

As Pierce's camerawoman came close to the patrol, panning her camera slowly, it suddenly occurred to Toni that maybe it wasn't such a hot idea to be on television. Caesar's wife had to be beyond reproach. And then she thought, To hell with that! She was who she was, and she believed what she believed, and she could damn well go and take sides with whomever she damn well pleased!

A moment later, Ham Pierce was right in front of her, talking smoothly toward the camera right next to him, which was aimed at his handsome profile and at *her*! Aw, shit! But it was too late to do anything about it.

She expected to have to answer some sort of embarrassing question. But he surprised her. He stopped the camera, handed his mike to a flunky, and said to her, in a low voice, "You think El Presidente would go for this?"

Defiantly: "Go for what?"

"Go for your being here with a group that a lot of people consider vigilantes."

"He doesn't tell me what I can and cannot do."

He raised an eyebrow. "Look. I'm sure Betty Cannon appreciates your gesture, Dr. Romano, but you are very, very conspicuous here . . . too visible for your own good. I'd hate like hell to see you get hurt." She would die before she admitted to him how frightened she had been a moment ago. On the other hand, he was probably right. She had not thought this out first and now, truthfully, she wasn't so sure it had been such a hot idea. Maybe she felt better, putting herself on the line, but had she helped TACK? She doubted it.

"Perhaps you didn't realize just what goes on up here after it gets dark," he said, as if he could read her mind. "It's a different world. I think it might be a good idea for you to go home now."

She was all set to tell him to mind his own business, when it occurred to her that he was right, and she told him so. "They don't need me," she admitted. "I wouldn't have had the guts to face those guys."

"Yeah, well, there aren't too many like Betty."

"I just wish . . . oh, well, I guess I'll be on my way," Toni said, and turned to walk to Broadway.

"Whoa!" He put a hand on her arm. "You don't want to do that alone, Dr. Romano."

"I came alone."

"Well, I'm here to tell you you're not walking this block back to Broadway alone. I'm coming with you."

Together they started off, down the middle of the street. She found herself almost jogging, trying to match his long-legged stride. When he noticed, he threw his head back and laughed, apologizing. This was a Ham Pierce she had never seen, or was it just that she had some preconceived notions about him?

He looked down at her. "What brought you up here tonight, Dr. Romano?"

She hesitated. She certainly didn't want to find herself quoted all over. On the other hand . . . "What brought me here was my patients." She told him about the pushers and the boyfriends hanging out in front of the center, waiting for their clients, their women, to go in, to come out, waiting to sell them something, to ask for something, to taunt them for even going into the center. "I just got tired of it, suddenly, that's all. It just got to me. Damn, my girls have enough to deal with, without those damned leeches sucking the life out of them!"

"You sound like Betty. In fact, Dr. Romano, you sound like me!"

Her first reaction was irritation. That was pretty egotistical. But when she thought about it, well, he wasn't far from wrong. He was always talking about the death of a whole generation and the waste and the shame of it.

"I beg your pardon. I sound like *me*."

Again, that deep rumble of laughter. "Keep that up, Dr. Romano, and you know what? We'll actually be getting along!"

It was too dark, even under the streetlight, to read his expression. She decided not to answer him. They stood on the corner together, and he hailed a cab that came by, and then another. Neither pulled over. And then he laughed ruefully and said, "I'm stupid! I'm no help to you here!"

"What do you mean?"

"Hey. Dr. Romano. Look at me. If you saw a big, tall guy up in this nabe late at night, and you were driving a cab, would you stop and pick him up?"

"But every cab driver in New York must know *you*!" Toni blurted.

"Doesn't matter much after dark. Look. I'll hang back, and *you* signal the next one. You'll see."

And he was right. The very next taxi responded to her upraised arm, pulling over with a screech of his tires. She got in, feeling sad. She gave her address to the cabbie and then, on an impulse, just as they were pulling away, she rolled down the window and peered out into the darkness. Where was he? A large bulky shadow separated itself from the other shadows, and she saw him. "Ham! Ham Pierce!" He lifted an arm. "Thanks! But you still can't do a story on my center!"

She could hear his laughter, loud and rich, as the taxi took off, roaring down Broadway.

11

The same night

Eliot sat hunched forward in his chair, the big leather lounger he was supposed to relax in, and stared at the television screen. Betty hadn't said a word about TACK being covered. And there was Mr. Pierce. Of course. Betty knew that Pierce was after the hospital, and that meant he was after every single one of them! Why had she kept it a secret? What other things was she doing behind his back? And then he scolded himself for being a typical New York paranoid, suspicious of everyone. Well, it was making him crazy, that somebody in the hospital was giving Pierce confidential information.

But who? Seven times a day, he wanted to ask Betty who she thought it was. And seven times a day, he had to remind himself that—goddamn it, he hated thinking it—but he had to remind himself that it could be her. Hell, it could be *anyone*.

His attention was drawn back to the television screen. It was an interesting segment, full of tension and drama—those damned punks, cursing at her that way!—and when she marched forward, very grim and determined, and the creeps slunk away, he wanted to applaud. It was a Ham Pierce story, and yes, there he was, close up, talking very earnestly to the watching audience. In the background, people moved around a little. Among them was a white woman. She really stuck out in this crowd. No white woman would live in that neighborhood; so what in hell—

He rose to his feet, he was so shocked. It was Toni, for Christ's sake. What the hell was his wife doing on West 122nd Street for the whole world to see!

He was beside himself, almost unable to see, he was so angry. The message she left him on the machine said she'd be working

116

late. Nothing about risking her life in a drug-infested neighborhood, marching around with a group of vigilantes, a walking target! Jesus Christ, and she wasn't home yet! Agitated, he looked at his watch, then checked the clock on the wall, even though he knew perfectly well what time it was: ten after eleven. Damn it!

He paced back and forth in front of the TV set, watching for her, but she never appeared again, and then they switched to a burning tenement in the Bronx, so that was that. Infuriated and, yes, a little frightened, he switched the set off with a vicious swat. What was she trying to *do* to him? That damned magazine article was more than enough! He had thrown it across the room earlier, after he had read it through. Now he retrieved it and, like a person searching out the sore tooth with his tongue, looked at it once more.

There she was on the cover, right in the middle, Dr. Toni Romano, head tipped to one side, smiling broadly, looking very young and very energetic and very, very sure of herself. He hated that cover, that picture, that smile on her face! It was all false. She had lied to him; she had withheld from him; she had made a goddamn fool out of him in the pages of a national magazine. He still couldn't believe she would be so two-faced. And now this appearance on television, and on Ham Pierce's story, to boot! He couldn't remember the last time he'd been so angry. He slammed out of the library, down the hall to the living room. He was surprised not to see smoke coming out of his ears, in his reflection.

This morning, Betty had come running into his office with that magazine in her hand, breathless with excitement. "Look, look, Dr. Wolfe! Isn't it wonderful? Dr. Toni is *famous*! Oh why didn't you *tell* us about this?" He had stared at it for a moment, while behind him, Betty's voice went on and on about how, if anyone deserved it, Dr. Romano did, how Deedra loved her, couldn't say enough good things about her. He kept nodding, making noises of agreement, trying hard to hide a sudden, nasty, unexpected surge of jealousy.

Then he took himself in hand. There she was, his wife, on the cover of the city's most popular magazine, looking fabulous, getting recognition for being special. And he was the one who had first spotted her potential!

"She did mention something about this," he answered one

of Betty's questions. "But her interview was weeks ago, and as far as I know, she had no idea when it would appear." Finally, he managed to meet her eyes. "It's very nice," he said lamely.

Betty didn't notice; she was so excited by the whole thing. "I'll get her on the phone for you," and she disappeared out the door. But Dr. Romano was delivering a baby, it seemed. He chided himself for being childish and left a warm and loving message for her. Then he took the magazine to his desk to read, planning a little celebration later this evening, when they were ready for bed . . . a bottle of champagne and, yes, maybe a dozen roses. Why not, for one of *Gotham* magazine's dozen best doctors.

Of course, he never did any of it—not after he'd finished reading the article. He was too damn mad. He paced back and forth in his office, planning what he was going to say to her. Should he face her before they went to the Schlesingers'? No, it would probably put a damper on the whole evening. Suzanne had invited two investment bankers looking for a worthwhile cause; Arnold Halevi, the Pita Bread Prince, would be there, too, and very anxious, Suzanne reported, to meet the new president of the hospital and his lovely wife. He was going to have to shine like a bright and gleaming star tonight. So . . . no arguments before leaving. Also, he didn't want to give Toni the opportunity to say she wouldn't go. No, much better to wait until after the party.

And then, damn it, when he got home, no Toni . . . just a message. Once again, he was going to have to make excuses for his quote lovely wife unquote! He took a cold shower, trying to cool off. As he got into his formal dress and started struggling with the tie, he thought it would be very satisfying if it were her neck instead of his. He took a long, stiff drink before he left, and then, at the Schlesingers', he visited the bar much more than usual. It didn't seem to affect him at all; he was probably burning off every ounce of alcohol before it had a chance to get near his brain.

Thank God Sam was there. He and Sam had always made a good team; together, they charmed the living daylights out of the Pita Bread Prince, the two investment bankers, and then, just for the fun of it, Suzanne's ninety-year-old aunt Bryna. Somewhere in there, probably while Sam was making tears come to the eyes of the Pita Bread Prince with his jokes, it occurred to Eliot that there wasn't a damn thing wrong with Sam Bronstein. He was the same as always, funny and witty and, yes, goddamn it, winsome. Well, at least he didn't have to worry about *that* anymore; the next time someone came to him with a story about Sam's forgetfulness, he'd just tell them, "That's Sam."

He purposely stayed later than usual. Let *her* see how it felt to sit home waiting! He even managed to enjoy himself, but the moment he got back and she *still* wasn't there, he got even angrier. And then, to top it all, that goddamn TV news!

When she finally came home, he was sitting in the big easy chair in the living room, so he could hear her the moment she came in. He pretended to be engrossed in *The Russia House*, but the moment he heard her key enter the lock, his head came up, book forgotten; later, he realized he couldn't remember a damn thing he had read.

"Toni!" he called.

She came racing into the living room, her face alight, and flung herself into his lap. "I got your message; it was my first. Thank you, darling, thank you, thank you . . . especially thank you for telling me I could go to medical school and become a doctor." She was kissing him all over his face, laughing. "One of the twelve best! Aren't you proud of me? Admit it, admit you're proud of me!" She had her fingers deep in his hair, and playfully, she pulled his head up to look into his face. What she saw there stopped her cold.

"Eliot!" It was a totally different tone. "What's the matter? Are you all right? Has anything happened to anybody?" After a moment, she slid off his lap and stood by the chair. "What *is* it?"

"I suppose now that you've been featured on the cover of *Gotham*, I'll *never* know where you are or what you're up to!"

"Eliot!"

Coldly: "I've read the article."

"Oh my God, what does it *say*? What did they say about me? All we talked about was the program! Oh shit, everyone warned me they always misquote you. . . ." Her voice faded as she regarded him.

"You mean you haven't read it yet?" Eliot said, wishing he could get rid of the cold lump of anger that sat in the pit of his stomach.

"No! I never had a minute!"

"But not too busy to get yourself on television," he muttered. When she asked him to repeat it, he held his hand up and said coldly, "Let me read to you . . ." He picked up his copy of the magazine, which opened to the right page. " 'Toni Romano had made herself indispensible at John Quincy Adams Hospital in Washington, D.C., where she won three major awards and was, last year, honored at a dinner sponsored by the National Organization for Women. What could have made her leave for the colder climes of New York City? Says one of her former colleagues, at John Q: "We didn't want to lose her. In fact, she was asked to head up her department. But she felt that being with her husband [Dr. Eliot Wolfe, the new president of Harmony Hill Hospital in New York] was more important." ' "

He stopped reading, carefully closed the magazine, and lifted his eyes to her. "Well?"

"What do you mean, *well*? You're using a tone on me I haven't heard since I was in parochial school and Sister Mary Immaculate accused me of wearing lipstick on the sly!"

"Don't make jokes, Toni. Not this time. I'm too goddamn mad!"

"I can *see* that. What I don't get is why. What was wrong with what you just read to me? It's true. They offered me the job, and I turned it down. I wanted to come to New York to be with my husband because I thought it was more important than any promotion."

"I'm sorry I held you back."

"Eliot!" She grabbed two handfuls of her own hair, something she did when she was frustrated. "What are you talking about? That's what I wanted, and I'm glad I did it! So, come on, okay, let's kiss and make up and go to bed. I'm beat."

"No kissing and making up this time, Toni. I have been betrayed," he said in a very remote tone.

"You have . . . *what*?" She put her hands on her hips and glared at him. "Eliot, I've had enough of this bullshit. Either you spit out what's bothering you, or fuck off!"

Eliot ground his teeth. She knew he hated it when she used language like that. Is this how she intended to kiss and make up? "You told *Gotham* magazine and the whole world that you were offered a big promotion at John Q., but you neglected to tell one person, namely, *me*. Remember me? That husband you always said was your best friend."

She took in a deep breath and let it out noisily. "All right. All right. I didn't tell you, that's true. I didn't tell you because . . . well, you were so hurt by them passing *you* over . . . as you had a perfect right to be . . . I just couldn't make you feel worse, especially since I had no intention of taking the job anyway."

"Furthermore, you promised to be with me at the party tonight, and you copped out. *Again!* Your message said you were working late, but you weren't working. Another lie. You were on 122nd Street, where you had no business being, playing vigilante!"

"Jesus Christ, Eliot, I don't believe what's coming out of your mouth. First of all, I *didn't* leave a message that I was working late. I left a message that I would *be* late. A small difference, but a significant one. And secondly, I wasn't playing at anything; I was trying to do something helpful. Maybe I didn't, but at least I tried.

"Just look at yourself!" she continued. "You're pouting like a child. You know what I think? I don't think this is about 'betrayal' or lies or 'playing vigilante.' I don't even think it's about my not being at your side at the Schlesingers' tonight. I think this is all about my being on the cover of a big-time magazine being called one of the twelve best doctors in New York City; when it's *you* who's *the* Dr. Wolfe. That kind of honor is supposed to be reserved for you."

He sprang to his feet, his heart hammering. "What a shitty thing to say to me! *I* was the one who sent you to medical school and encouraged you every step of the way." He could not believe the weight and the iciness of the fury that possessed him. Even his head felt cold and heavy, as he stomped past her, down the hall to the study, slamming the door behind him.

12

November

At seven-thirty, all the lights were ablaze on the ground floor of the modern, year-old Abe and Sarah Goldstone Pavilion, a glass-sheathed dome connected by a glassed-in walkway to the original Harmony Hill building. Anyone walking on Riverside Drive could clearly see a parade of elegant couples in formal dress streaming toward the central atrium as if carried by a current, only to come to a standstill, clustering in one spot.

This traffic jam was caused by the presence of a huge television set in the waiting room, which was turned on and alive with scenes of Harmony Hill: the people walking in and out the big front entrance, nurses clustering around a bassinet, a mother coming out in a wheelchair, her newborn held proudly in her arms.

And then, the scene changed to a living room, painted bright pink, a crucifix on the wall behind the pretty young woman who sat, tears streaming down her face, trying to talk.

"I . . . I don't understand. I'm the mother . . . he's my baby. Why does the hospital want him to die. . . ?"

Then her voice faded. The camera lingered on her stricken face with its swollen eyes and wet cheeks, but now it was the voice of Hamilton Pierce that came over the set.

"Alice and Joe Rodriguez had a dream. Not a great big dream, just the dream of having a child, their own child. After many pregnancies and many miscarriages, they thought their dream had come true. And it had . . . *almost*." The images now changed rapidly as he went on: "Their son was born prematurely and kept alive in a respirator, until he might grow and be strong enough to make it on his own. But the president of Har-

122

mony Hill Hospital has other priorities. Dr. Eliot Wolfe says it costs too much to keep little Steven Rodriguez alive. Pull the plug.''

The mellifluous voice lowered, intimately. ''Dr. Conrad Havemayer, Harmony Hill's renowned pediatric surgeon, who has performed two miracle operations already on this tiny baby, has asked the court to appoint him guardian of Steven Rodriguez to save his life. What will happen? Which side will triumph?''

The camera turned once more to the weeping woman. ''Harmony Hill Hospital doesn't care about us,'' she said.

Another woman's voice from the center of the group standing in a loose circle around the set called out, ''That's the thanks we get!''

What a stupid thing to say, Lillian Wolfe thought. And who was this ''we'' she was talking about? Was she on the staff of the hospital? No, she was just one of the guests at tonight's $500-a-plate dinner. *We*, indeed! Whoever she was, she should only know the agonizing choices Eliot had to make every day!

She turned, irritated, to see who the speaker was. She didn't recognize the voice, which surprised her. She thought she knew everyone attending tonight's dinner, but she didn't know *this* young woman: ultra thin, Bill Blass strapless—last year's—the latest short haircut with very nice sunstreaking, a professional job. And then she realized, of course, this was Adolph Zimmer's new wife. He had never given emeralds like that to Edna! Really, these old men could be disgusting; the woman wasn't a day over thirty-five, and Adolph must be, well, he was much older than Eliot, well into his sixties, too old to start in with a young woman and break his wife's heart. And emeralds were not good for blondes, anyway, not even bleached blondes.

Lillian sent a rather chilly smile in the direction of the second—or was it the third?—Mrs. Zimmer. ''I don't believe we've met,'' she said. ''I'm Lillian Wolfe, Philip's wife.'' She felt she had to add that last bit; after all, tonight's affair was in his honor.

''Oh, Mrs. Wolfe, I've heard so much about you . . . so thrilled to meet you. I'm Bunny Zimmer, Dolph's wife, and I'm so looking forward to hearing your husband speak! I understand he's marvelously eloquent!''

Well, the new Mrs. Zimmer at least had good manners; but . . . *Bunny! Really!* They shook hands and then Adolph came to claim his prize. He and Lillian greeted each other warmly, with a hug, and then he said, "Isn't it awful, what that Pierce fellow is doing to the good name of the hospital. That man ought to be taken off the air!"

Lillian smiled. "I believe we have something called freedom of speech in this country, Adolph."

"Bah! So nincompoops like Pierce can malign a perfectly marvelous institution. By God, we've probably had *him* as a patient! We're the ones who are responsible for the health care of that whole neighborhood up there!" He made a vague gesture in the general direction of uptown and exited with a snort at the television set.

"All of New York weeps tonight for Alice and Joe Rodriguez . . . and for little Steven, too, now, it seems, doomed by the will of the hospital's administration." The man *was* maddening. Freedom of speech, yes, but, really, sometimes Mr. Pierce went too far. He did hold your attention, though. She had come out here, into the lounge, intending to turn it off, and here she was still, ten minutes later, unable to turn away—and God knows she had plenty to do inside, greeting people, reminding Philip of everyone's name, and introducing Eliot to people he hadn't met yet.

She glanced over at the TV, but this time she was not going to get sucked in. Why did something like this have to go on the air right in the middle of Philip's dinner? It was not right; it was *the* topic of conversation, you couldn't get people to change the subject. Arguments were breaking out. It was just too bad there had to be this controversy tonight, of all nights!

Well, it was nearly eight o'clock, time for her to get back and circulate. But as she turned, she could hear Pierce's aggrieved voice.

"The president of the hospital seems to think that Mr. and Mrs. Rodriguez are incapable of making an informed and intelligent decision. Is this Eliot Wolfe playing the Great *White* Father again?"

Who did he think he was? And he didn't even have the courage to say it to Eliot's face, so Eliot could tell him off. Now he *had* gone too far! Turning on her three-inch heels, she marched smartly back to the television set and turned it off, right in the middle of a sentence. She didn't care! She put on a bright smile for the dozen or so people who had been watching the program and who now stared at her, startled. "Dinner time!" she caroled. "Everything will get cold."

So saying, in she marched, searching automatically for Philip's white head, towering above most others. But he was already sitting down at the head table, holding court. His hip had been bothering him again; she was glad he had decided to get off his feet.

Then she spotted Eliot, chatting with the Lerner twins, Herbert and Marvin. Big contributors, big, big money. How they got it was something she didn't quite understand: something like the stock market, only different. She didn't know exactly what: junk bonds, LBOs, hostile takeovers? Who knew? Who could understand that talk? It didn't sound like business, it sounded like war! But who cared, as long as "Herbie" and "Marv"—grown men going by little-boy nicknames!—kept giving a lot of it to Harmony Hill. The three of them were grinning and smiling at one another in a way she recognized. Money was about to change hands . . . in a manner of speaking.

Well, Harmony Hill deserved whatever they had to give, maybe more. Twelve years ago, Dr. Conrad Havemayer had saved the life of Herbert's firstborn, a son. He had operated when the baby was only ten days old, closing a hole in his heart. And the boy had lived; in fact, he was now a big, strapping boy about to be Bar Mitzvahed. In those days, to save such a baby was considered a miracle. And then, the next year—could you believe!—Marvin also had a son and that child was born with the same defect. It ran in the family, apparently. Needless to say, Conrad saved that one, too.

If you listened to Herbert and Marvin Lerner, there was no finer surgeon than Conrad Havemayer; there was no finer physician than Philip Wolfe, who had referred them via Herbert's mother-in-law, their dear friend, Phyllis Brickman.

Oh, and speak of the devil, there was Phyllis, coming in right now. What a shock! She'd let her hair go gray, after all those years of being a redhead.

Lillian hurried over to Phyllis and embraced her, whispering, "I love your hair. It looks gorgeous."

"Never mind my hair, Lillian, if you'll forgive me for interrupting you. I'm so aggravated! The nerve of that Ham Pierce! After all you people did for our Stuart and our Jason! Irv and I

are just sick over it! These people never appreciate what's done
for them!''

"Now, Phyllis. Take it easy. Get yourself a drink—Wellman's
has done such a beautiful bar—and calm yourself.'' Face it, she
told herself, Phyllis Brickman is more than a bit of a bigot, and
you're not going to change her tonight. ''Come, we could both
use a little champagne,'' she said, and she walked Phyllis into
the big room.

Irv Brickman was there, looking for his wife, and after the
usual effusive greetings, took her away, leaving Lillian to work
the room, as she always did at these functions. Much as she
considered him a cold fish, she headed for Warren Voorhees,
who was standing all alone, ramrod straight, looking bored.
What was the matter with him? He should be greeting people
himself; sports medicine was a very popular specialty, and his
clinic always made a profit. There were plenty of people here—
plenty—who had reason to be grateful to Dr. Voorhees.

Sue Milkman, for instance, wouldn't be spending half her life
at the tennis club, if it weren't for him. Why wasn't he by *her*
side, charming her? She had more money than God, especially
since Arthur died! She could well afford to give the hospital a
little extra.

But Lillian was fated never to get to either Dr. Voorhees or
Sue Milkman. Someone grabbed her arm and said, ''Grandma!
Just the lady I'm looking for!''

Lillian turned and opened her arms. ''David! Oh my God,
it's so good to see you!'' She held him close. Although she loved
all three, he was her very first and very special grandchild. He
was so skinny; she could feel every rib. She shook her head
ruefully. ''Such a wonderful thing, to be doctor to all those poor
dying children in Ethiopia. But, David, do *you* have to be so
thin?''

He laughed, but it never reached his eyes. *That* made her sad.
''Will you join me in a drink, David?'' she joked with him,
hoping to see a little spark in his eyes.

''You think we'll both fit?'' He smiled. It was an old joke
between them, one he'd brought back from Boy Scout camp. A
moment later, he added, ''Of course I want a drink. I *need* a
drink. How else could I be expected to get through a hospital
fund raiser?'' The same old David.

But her other one! She didn't know *what* to think about Eric.

Eric was closer to his grandfather than he was to his own father. It was true. By the time Eric had been born, the marriage was already shaky. Eliot had made himself very busy with his practice. Didn't he once, in a weak moment, say to her, "Lillian, I hate to go home." And as for Arlene, well . . . having the three kids just seemed to make her worse than ever. Lillian had always tried, in little ways, to make it up to Eric, the baby, the forgotten one.

She had told him she'd pay his airfare from San Francisco so he could be here tonight. "Eric, honey, listen, how many times does a man get honored?" And of course, Eric came right back with a smart answer. "You talking about Grandpa? About every two weeks. Listen, of course I want to come. But would you want me to break a contract? With the Evil Eye? Don't get upset; it's the name of a comedy club, I *think*!" The tone of his voice made her laugh; he always could make her laugh. He went on, talking, talking, talking. But in the end she knew nothing except he wouldn't be here tonight.

But she couldn't stand around like a zombie, worrying about her grandson. Tonight was Philip's night. He was eighty-three, even though he didn't look it, and who knew what tomorrow might bring? Thank God they both had their health. A little arthritis, but who their age didn't have some arthritis? They were lucky. They had always been lucky.

She, especially, was the lucky one. It was fifty-five years ago, now. She could hardly believe it. She had taken one look at the tall, handsome, shy young doctor and said, "That's for me." She was already considered an old maid—twenty-five years old and still looking around!—but she didn't care. Her family was poor; they lived in an ugly apartment with shabby furniture, and she hated it. She wasn't going to marry a boy from the neighborhood and end up like that, never!

And so, she hadn't. She'd stuck to her guns, and she had escaped her fate. She had married Philip and with him she had married money, position, respect . . . all the things she had always longed for. But Philip had done well for himself by getting *her*, if she said so herself, who shouldn't. Sweet, easygoing, placid Philip: what would he have done without her to protect him? If it weren't for her, he'd have been eaten alive by all the people who put demands on him.

"Lillian! Lillian Wolfe!"

She turned to the familiar theatrical voice, smiling and holding out her hands. She always became a little more dramatic in her gestures whenever she was with Irene Moore; it was fun, really. Wherever Irene Moore went, she created her own theater, and everyone responded to it. But if Irene was here, that meant Sam was here also. These days, they were everywhere together. It was so nice for poor Sam; Eva had been a good wife, but . . . well, a bit boring. And Irene Moore? Anything but! "Irene, darling! How wonderful you look!" Lillian couldn't help thinking that she certainly ought to look wonderful; she had recently had her third face-lift, and either she had found herself a miracle-working bra or Dr. Harrison had also done a little breast work while he had her in the O.R. "I love your dress!" It was gorgeous; a Scaasi white-silk column with a sunburst picked out on the bosom in gold sequins. Lillian had seen it in Bendel's when she was looking for a dress to wear to the Lerner Bar Mitzvah. It wasn't for *her*; you had to be tall to carry it off.

Irene smiled and twirled gracefully and put a hand on her Grecian-style hairdo. She had a habit of checking herself this way, touching first one part of her body, and then another. "Isn't it gorgeous? It cost the earth, Lillian; even a legend in her own time could hardly afford it!" She laughed good-naturedly and added, "But nobody could expect me to walk by Henri Bendel's twice and not go in. And once in Bendel's . . . well!" She rolled her eyes as if to say that everyone in the world had four or five thousand dollars they were compelled to spend in a dress shop.

"That's why I try to stay away," Lillian said dryly.

"I know, I know, it's absolutely too horribly self-indulgent of me. But, you know, actually this dress was a gift from Charles." Charles Wentworth had been Irene Moore's third husband; he hadn't stayed long but had left behind a substantial amount of cash. Irene Moore leaned close and Lillian could smell the sweet scent of Poison. "Take it from me, darling, it pays to marry many times! Except, of course, if you're lucky enough to find the perfect man—such as your own magnificent Philip!"

They exchanged wide smiles, and Lillian thought, *You think I don't know about the passes you made at the magnificent Philip, all those years ago? My dear Irene. . . !* "Or your own wonderful Sam!" she countered.

"But, of course, I haven't married him—not yet! And perhaps

I won't; it's a lot more fun this way . . . just the hint of sin! Oh and here's my drink, at last! Ronald, darling, you are a wonderful doctor!''

Ronald, darling, was Dr. Ronald Harrison, chief of plastic surgery and Irene's own personal fountain of youth. Since the beginning of her career in the movies—much longer ago than she liked to admit—she had been considered one of the world's sexiest women. She still was by some—yes, even at her age— and, thanks to Harrison's talented scalpel, didn't look a day over forty-five. Maybe forty-six, but certainly not her real age.

Lillian did not particularly like Ronald Harrison. He was an undercooked Robert Redford, in her opinion: not quite blond, not quite handsome, not quite sexy. He played a good game of tennis, a good game of golf, he knew good wine, and he regularly went to Arthur Murray to brush up on all the latest dance steps. Very ordinary. But you could take him anywhere, Lillian thought.

Without looking away from them, Irene suddenly announced, ''Here comes my favorite shrink.''

The woman had eyes all over her body, Lillian thought, particularly for spotting men.

Which was more than you could say for Sam, who proceeded to walk right by them. Lillian had to laugh. He was the most absentminded man she had ever known, and she should know. He had come to them to live when his parents were both killed in a plane crash, just past his Bar Mitzvah, poor little thing; so she knew him as well as she knew her own son. He *was* a son to her—almost as dear to her as Eliot!

Look at him, what a cutie pie, a year older than Eliot, but still without one gray hair. The mustache . . . now that was a different matter. It was almost completely white. Sam was shorter than Eliot and broader, and he had a tendency to put on weight. Just like his father, may he rest in peace. When he was a boy, poor Sam, he had to wear such thick glasses, like Coke bottles, it was a *shandah*. He had such beautiful dark eyes, and those glasses made them look beady. But thank God for contact lenses!

''Yoohoo, Dr. Bronstein,'' she called, still laughing. ''Remember me? Mrs. Wolfe?''

Sam turned with that look she recognized, a million miles away; then it went away, and he grinned. ''Hi, Mrs. Wolfe,

darling, good to see you." He came over. "Harrison, good to
see you. Irene, you're looking lovelier than ever!"

"Since five minutes ago? Well, Ronald keeps me young!"
She gave a devilish smile and patted Dr. Harrison's rear end;
Sam hooted.

"You are incorrigible, Irene!"

"I do hope so! I went through a slow period for a while, but
I'm getting my second wind! As a matter of fact, you'll love
this, Lillian, this is very interesting. I have me a Fan, I mean a
capital 'F' Fan, like in the old days, when I was a star."

"What do you mean, capital F?" Lillian said.

"Some nut," Sam said. "I've told her a thousand times, it
isn't amusing and it isn't cute. I think she should report him to
the police."

"Whatever for, darling? All he does is write me letters about
how he loves every one of my pictures. He takes them out, in
videos, you know, and he watches them over and over. Now,
Sam, stop laughing, I think it's rather wonderful. You can't
imagine how it boosts a girl's morale! I do believe you're jealous!"

"I don't see anything to report," Lillian said to Sam.

"He seems to be escalating his attentions. Tell her, Irene."

"Well, lately, I've been noticing a young man, very pale
and poetic-looking, leaning against the building across the
street, looking up toward my windows. Seems like he's *always* there—"

"Doesn't he work?" Lillian said, somewhat sharply.

"Now that I think about it, Lillian, it's usually in the evening. So he does go to work . . . or school . . . or *something*.
Well, last Saturday, when I came out to go shopping in the
afternoon, he was right next to the front door and, what do
you think, he handed me a long-stemmed rose, one perfect
rose!"

Lillian noticed that the two doctors exchanged a swift, indul-
gent smile. Irene did have a tendency to . . . dramatize, you
might say. Or you might say she made things up.

"I thought it was very sweet!" Irene went on. "I asked him
his name, and he just ran off! Isn't that wild?"

"He's a fan with a capital F, all right. Look, Irene, I know
it's flattering, and I know it's appealing . . . but just remember,

you've had other experiences with fans, and they're not always good, are they?''

She shrugged. "Did you have to remind me?''

"Yes I did. Am I not your favorite shrink?'' And he laughed.

"Oh Sam. Yes, you are, but you're not being fun tonight, and I am going to go play with somebody else. Ronald, darling? Let's hit the buffet before the vultures pick it clean.'' And away she went, back straight, on an undeviating course, like a ship in full sail, with Dr. Harrison bobbing along in her wake.

Lillian put a hand on Sam's arm. "Well, at least *you're* not talking my ear off about the Rodriguez case!''

"Who?''

"Sam! The baby in the hospital, the one Eliot wants taken off the respirator!''

"Modern medicine! It's created more problems than it's solved!''

"Well, it's not easy to just let people *die*, Sam!''

"We used to, in the good old days, and with a lot less suffering . . . for the patient *and* the family. As far as I'm concerned, it was much better that way.''

"You've never liked Conrad Havemayer, that's the problem!''

"Lillian, dear, my feelings about Conrad Havemayer have nothing to do with it.''

"Did I hear you taking my name in vain, Bronstein?'' Havemayer said as he walked up to join them.

"I was just saying,'' Sam said, "that, if it were up to me, I'd take that baby off the respirator.''

"There's brain stem activity.'' Havemayer's voice was tight with annoyance.

"Come on, Conrad, you know if you took him off, he'd die within hours.''

"I know nothing of the kind. . . .''

Lillian knew Conrad Havemayer was supposed to be outstanding, but she wasn't so sure. She found him self-righteous and self-serving.

"Well, I really should go to Philip,'' she said to make her exit and save herself from this little altercation. "He doesn't like to eat alone.'' Philip wasn't alone, of course; he was surrounded by people. They were standing in line next to his chair at the head table, waiting to have a word with him.

The buffet had been ravaged—you could always count on this

crowd to be ravenous—and the caterers were busy replenishing the platters. Not for *her*, she was very careful about what she ate. The men behind the buffet all greeted her; after all these years of doing hospital functions, not to mention Eliot's Bar Mitzvah and all of her big parties, they knew her. They knew her, and they had very good reason to love her; God knows she had sent enough business their way. She paid well, and she tipped well.

When she finally made her way to Philip, he was talking with Barney Goldstone . . . well, actually, he was listening to Barney. And there was Arlene, of course. Inwardly, Lillian groaned.

"Arlene. Haven't seen you in ages!" They kissed the air between them.

"Have you seen David, Lillian? He said he'd see me here, but he hasn't bothered to find me." Arlene's voice was aggrieved, as always.

"Oh, Arlene, I'm sure he looked for you."

"You'd think, after almost three years of being half a world away, he'd want to see his mother."

Oh, spare me, Lillian thought, and like an echo of her thought, Barney turned and said, "Oh, God, Arlene, spare me! You'll see your son. I'll hunt him down. Later. Or, better yet, go find him yourself, how about that?"

"I shouldn't have to . . . but I will."

"Women!" Barney said, through a mouthful.

Lillian turned her head, so she would not have to look at him. The man had no polish! He was soft and fat and not as smart as he thought. He must drive Arlene crazy; she was fastidious to a fault. Talk about your "odd couple"! Of course, the Goldstones had more money than God; last year, in the *New York Times*, hadn't there been a big picture of a crane Barney hired to lift their twenty-five-foot Christmas tree into their penthouse? A Christmas tree! Okay, she and Philip had a little greenery, a few pine boughs, a bouquet of holly, maybe, for the holiday season. But her little bit of decoration was a far cry from a tree nearly as big as the one in Rockefeller Center!

Barney was still going on—about *his* atrium, *his* trees, *his* pavilion. If he said *his* hospital, she was going to crown him! But that was Barney for you; he thought the whole city belonged to him. Every piece of real estate he owned—and there was plenty of it!—had his name on it. The Goldstone Palace . . . the

Goldstone Arcade . . . the Goldstone Building . . . the Goldstone Tower . . . the Goldstone Fountain. She detested the man.
She shouldn't, really; when it came to giving money to the hospital, you couldn't ask for better. But of all the people for Philip
to have saved!

Barney was already a college student, very heavy, very tired
all the time, when his father had brought him to Philip. Philip
took one look and had known: diabetes. He gave him all the
tests and, of course, he was 110 percent right. One, two, three,
he had him on a diet and insulin, and Barney Goldstone was a
different person! He always said Philip had saved his life.

Now here he was, all grown up, pushing food into his face,
and acting like a boor. In a minute, his plate scraped cleaner
than even a dishwasher could get it, he excused himself to get
some more.

As soon as he had gone, Eliot appeared, put his arm around
her, and gave her a kiss. "The most beautiful woman in the
room," he said.

"Let me tell you something," she said lightly. "Everyone in
this room had their life saved in this hospital. It occurs to me,
if Philip hadn't saved so many lives, I could be home watching
'thirtysomething.' " She waited for her laugh, and she got it.
Then she said, "So where is your beautiful wife?"

He gave her one of his wry smiles. "If I only knew . . .
Somewhere in this hospital. We were out the front door when
her beeper went off. I'm sure at some point, our paths will
cross."

"I'm sure. And I'm sure it's just a coincidence that Arlene
was here and left and Barney was here and left and now that
they're both gone, you appear."

Again, the smile. "Do you ever miss anything? Barney's okay,
but I'd rather not be with Arlene."

"Antonia is better," Lillian said, and Eliot laughed. At their
wedding reception, years ago, in her living room on Central
Park West, he had lifted his glass of champagne and said,
"Somehow, in the last year, I've learned how to laugh again.
So . . . to laughter and to love." Lillian would never forget
it; it was so touching. And for once, Antonia did not have a
smart remark; in fact, her eyes had actually filled, and she had
blushed. Well, it was beautiful!

Now her daughter-in-law came running up, a bit breathless,

to give her a kiss. Then she turned to Eliot and lifted her face. He looked so happy to see her; hadn't he said that Antonia was working all hours at that clinic? How were they going to make a marriage if they were both working too hard? Lillian could tell them, from experience, it wasn't so easy with only *one* doctor in the family.

Just then Carolyn came over, beautiful as always. Tonight she was wearing red—a color that really suited her—a short dress that showed off her beautiful legs and her beautiful new figure. For a while, she had gotten a bit heavy, but now, you'd never know this was the same young woman who used to wear men's sweaters so she could hide her body. What a problem she used to be! And look at her now, poised and confident. It saddened Lillian that, once again, she was without an escort. When was she going to get herself a boyfriend? They must be after her all the time, a pretty girl like that, with brains and money in the family, too, not to be sneezed at!

"Sorry I'm late. Grandpa didn't talk yet, did he? Hi, Dad. Hi, Toni." Lightly she kissed all of them, then reached down and picked a slice of carrot from Lillian's plate. "Mmmm, I'm starving!"

"Go, darling," Lillian ordered. "Wellman's has outdone themselves. They have the poached salmon you love so much and a new dill sauce."

Before Carolyn could go, however, the chairman, Dr. George Noble, rapped on his glass and tested the microphone. "Will all members of Dr. Philip Wolfe's family please gather in the waiting room for some family pictures," he announced.

Taking Philip by the arm, Lillian headed for the lounge, and who was there but Eric! She could hardly believe her eyes. He was just taking off his old overcoat, the one that reached to his ankles. When he turned, he saw them and came right over.

"Eric, sweetheart. Where did you come from?"

He was laughing; he didn't look so good, a little too thin . . . like his brother, as a matter of fact.

"You're just in time, darling. We're going to take a family photograph."

"Great!"

Now she had her whole family with her, all of them. Content, she watched Philip and Eric walk together, talking animatedly.

Eric was good for Philip; they had always had a special relationship.

The photographer was running around, a young woman in a long aquamarine dress, with a peplum, yet! Did that dress bring back memories! Lillian had worn a dress very like that for a Wolfe family photograph . . . it must have been 1936, soon after they were married, and she was considered a member of the family. How excited she had been, to have her picture taken as a Wolfe.

Eli and Bettina, Philip's parents, had still been alive, of course, and as usual, they had been at the center of everything, including the picture. Her Philip was the only son left; his brother David had been killed in an automobile accident when he was only sixteen years old. So it was Dr. Eli, in his fifties, tall and handsome, a commanding presence, like Philip. Like Eliot. In fact, Eliot looked a lot like his grandfather. And next to Eli, Bettina, also tall, buxom, not a beautiful woman, but a face full of character, and a heart full of warmth.

They had been so good to her, a girl from a poor family, a family of nobodies. The Wolfes weren't like most of the German Jews in New York: big snobs, and if they found out your family came from Russia, to hell with you!

Lillian blinked away the tears that crowded under her lids. So long ago, so long ago . . . She watched her clan gather around her own dear Philip, and her heart was full. She was still proud to be a Wolfe.

Philip smiled at her and motioned for her to come to him. She walked straight over into the shelter of his arm, to the place where she belonged.

When the picture taking was finally over and they were set free, Eliot looked for Eric, but Eric was deep in conversation with his grandfather. When he and Arlene had been divorced, Eric chose to stay with his mother. It had bothered Eliot then, and it still did. He had missed so much of Eric's growing up; they'd never had the chance to become close. It had all happened a long time ago, but it still made him sad, sometimes.

He watched the two of them, his father and his son, walk away, and he sighed. A voice at his elbow offered a penny for his thoughts—"unless they're really raunchy, in which case I might up the ante to a nickel!"

Sam. Of course, Sam. Eliot turned, and as always, his heart warmed at the sight of his old friend. Next to Toni . . . oh, and his children, of course, and maybe his parents . . . Sam was his favorite person in the world. But maybe Sam *should* go to the top of that list, because there was nothing, nothing at all, he couldn't tell Sam. There was nothing they couldn't tell each other. In which case, he scolded himself, why had he avoided telling Sam that he and Toni were having problems? Never mind. Starting tonight, he and Toni were going to make a fresh start.

"Sam, old buddy," he said, "don't take this the wrong way, but I have a suggestion about your tux."

Sam balled his fists and took a fighter's stance. In fact, he had done some boxing in college before they told him he might hurt his head. "Love me, love my dinner jacket," he growled. "It's a dear, old friend."

"*I'm* a dear, old friend; that getup is just old."

Sam threw an arm around Eliot's shoulder and laughed. "Anyone else but you said that to me, I'd punch them in the nose."

They both grinned, very goddamned pleased to be with each other. Damn it, Eliot thought, he had missed Sam during those years in Washington. He had missed them *all*. In fact, he had missed the entire city of New York. Why in hell had he thought he had to run away from everything he knew and loved? He'd been a stubborn kid, just like his mother had said at the time.

The babble of the crowd was like a wall of sound, but Irene Moore's trained voice had no trouble penetrating the din. "Darling! I'm over here!"

Eliot spotted her, standing by the bar, on tiptoe and waving as only Irene Moore could wave—with her entire body, dramatically. He would have guessed there was no way to ignore her, but Sam kept right on talking. Maybe she did this too often, and he didn't like it.

"Over here! *Sammy!*"

Now Sam turned, and his face lit up. It occurred to Eliot, not for the first time, that this was the woman Sam had always needed. His marriage . . . well, his marriage had not been *bad*, exactly; it was just . . . ordinary. Eva had adored her husband and had dedicated her life to taking care of him. But she wasn't what you would call exciting.

"Sammy! Get over here! I'm lonesome!"

"My master's voice," Sam said, then added, "I should say, my *mistress's* voice." He cackled evilly, making Eliot laugh, and hurried to her side. They kissed and stood smooching a little and holding hands. Sam and Irene were always holding hands; some people found it funny. Eliot had always thought it wonderful. So what if she was a flirt? She made Sam happy.

A waft of delicious and familiar perfume made him turn. Here was *his* happiness. Toni had come up behind him. She smiled and murmured, "Private joke?"

"Something like that."

"How's Sam?"

"That's a strange question! You've seen him! So you tell *me*: how's Sam?"

She paused, nibbling on her lower lip. "I'm worried about him, Eliot. There's something . . . I don't know. I just don't know. There's something not quite right." She paused again, obviously reluctant to say what she was thinking.

"Go on."

"Do you think he might be . . . on drugs?"

"Sam? No. Not a chance."

"If you say so; you certainly know him. But there's something. . . ."

He wished she wouldn't harp on it. She really didn't know Sam. And then it struck him. "Hey! I think Sam's having the best sex of his life, and that's all he can think about. Like somebody else I could mention," he added in a different tone. He reached out and pulled her into a quick, close hug.

"Eliot! Not here!" She softened this with a light kiss on his mouth. "Later." And she was gone in a rustle of black taffeta.

Eliot watched as she walked away, in that stilted, sexy way women had when they were wearing very high heels. Her hips swayed invitingly. It was a very nice dress, with a short puffy skirt and a low-cut front. She had pushed a velvety rose into the space between her breasts, and she was wearing the ruby earrings he had given her five years ago. She looked . . . edible. He had kept his distance from her for too long, and now he was paying for it. He was melting away. He could hardly wait to take her in his arms and make up for lost time.

Funny how things happened, sometimes. He had still been angry at her, earlier this evening, had still felt cold as ice. Then, when they were together in their bedroom, getting ready for the party, discussing what needed to be done and who would do what, it struck him what a good fit they were. What the hell had he been thinking of? What had he been *doing*? Being a self-righteous prick, that's what!

He found himself studying her movements as she chose her lingerie. She shed her terry bathrobe and stood by the dresser, naked. Her belly was rounder and fuller than when he had first seen her without clothes, but her waist was still narrow and her buttocks still firm. She hated her thighs, but he didn't. Oh Lord, no. They looked smooth and creamy to him. Her breasts were small but shapely, and he could no longer resist. He walked over to her, just as she was pulling out something black and lacy from the drawer and, standing behind her, cupped a breast in each hand.

She gave a little gasp of surprise and leaned back against him. He was instantly erect, and she felt it because she gave a throaty laugh.

"I've been such a fool," he mumbled, bending his lips to her soft shoulder and giving her a love bite.

"So what else is new?" She turned to face him, putting her arms around his neck. "Only kidding, only kidding."

Eliot gazed down into her eyes. "But not really."

"But not really," she agreed.

"I'm so sorry, Toni. Can we kiss and make up?"

Her answer was to move in closer to him, pushing her hips into his. He gave an involuntary little groan, and she laughed. "Later," she promised. "It's a date."

It was one date he was going to keep, come hell, high water, or beeper. He cast his eyes around the room, looking to see if anyone important needed his attention. Earlier, one of the security guards had come to whisper in his ear that Mrs. Schlesinger had had a bit too much to drink and was singing "The Bell Song" from *Lakmé* at the top of her lungs . . . in the men's room. Eliot had been amused. It took a while before he asked himself how a security guard with only a high school education came to recognize an esoteric operatic aria.

Everyone seemed busy. Maybe he could get ahold of Eric for a few minutes. He spotted his mother, standing at table one, holding aloft a champagne bottle and trying to get his attention. Toni was with her and so, as a matter of fact, was Eric. By the time he made his way over, the whole family had clustered around Lillian.

"Champagne time!" Lillian warbled, gesturing everyone to the table, now lined with crystal champagne flutes. "A toast to Philip . . . come here, darling, and be toasted by your family. Will you do the honors?"

His father knew how to make a small gesture grand. He examined the bottle, smiled approvingly at the label, held it out in display for all to see, unwrapped the gold foil with practiced, dramatic movements, and then, deftly, pushed at the cork with his thumbs. It took a moment and then, suddenly, with a loud pop, the cork flew into the air, and everyone applauded.

"Looks just like me when I'm coming!" Sam shouted, laughing.

There was a stunned silence. Nobody knew what to say. Eliot stared in disbelief at his old friend.

And then, Sam added, "The cork looks like me, too! A little on the small side, but hard!" He laughed uproariously.

Nobody could look at anybody else. Time seemed to stand still. Eliot cast wildly about in his head for something, *anything*, to say. But all he could think was, *Who else had heard?* Christ! And now, suddenly, a lot of little memories flashed through his mind: Sam missing meetings, Sam forgetting appointments, Sam walking away from conversations. As a matter of fact, he *had* asked Sam, months ago, to give him a call and make a date for dinner. And then they had both promptly forgotten about it. Or maybe both of them hadn't "forgotten." Maybe one of them was in trouble and the other was into denial!

"Sam Bronstein," Lillian said into the pool of silence, in a tone that belied anything being seriously wrong, "what a thing to say! You were always such a *good* boy!"

Everyone was relieved to be able to laugh, so they all laughed and lifted their glasses high and drank and began to talk a mile a minute. Eliot could see that the incident was going to be purposely forgotten. It was going to become a non-event. Except not for him. Not this time.

13

End of November

The neonatal nursery was ablaze with light and alive with musical chirps and bleeps and beeps from all the monitors. Up front, at the desk, were a couple of plastic jack-o-lanterns left over from Halloween, and cardboard cutouts of turkeys and pilgrims were tacked all over the walls. The three nurses on duty busily bent over the tiny occupants in the clear plastic bassinets, checking tubes, adjusting medications, crisp in their pastel uniforms, always moving, always on the alert.

The mournful figure seated by one of the bassinets seemed alien in the midst of this activity. Dressed all in white, a lace shawl draped over her head, Alice Rodriguez sat, absolutely still except for her hands, the fingers automatically counting out the beads on her ivory and silver rosary. She was seated on a turquoise plastic chair from the cafeteria, her feet crossed at the ankle, and she was leaning a bit to the right to rest her shoulder against the Plexiglas side of the bassinet with its brave signs of welcome to THE LONG-AWAITED STEVEN DAVID. Her face was thin and without expression, and her eyes looked nowhere.

This sad picture was the first thing Eliot saw as he came into the nursery. What was he going to say to her? What *could* he say to her? He turned away, relieved that Conrad Havemayer had just appeared at the doorway. Good, he could use the support. The two of them could tell her together. He raised his hand as Havemayer's eyes met his, beginning to smile in greeting.

But there was no answering smile; in fact, Havemayer's lips tightened. Without a pause, he turned on his heel and marched away. Oh God, Eliot thought. Havemayer was still furious that the judge had refused to make him the baby's guardian. Ever since the Baby Doe case, the courts were refusing to do it. Now he was doubly angry because Joe had signed an order to "stop all aggressive treatment" of his son.

Eliot turned back to Alice. He was going to have to talk to her about Joe's decision and convince her that it was the right thing to do. It was a lonely prospect. A little moan escaped him.

Marie Campbell, the head nurse, bustled up. "She looks dreadful, doesn't she? We're very worried about her. Isn't there something the hospital can do?"

"There's only one thing Mrs. Rodriguez wants, Ms. Campbell, and that's impossible to give her."

The nurse nodded, her brown eyes filled with sadness. "I feel so sorry for her. But, you know, she's demoralizing the other parents. I mean, she sits there night and day, never moving, never speaking, just praying and praying, looking like Death. If my nurses didn't insist, she'd *never* eat."

That's all we'd need, he thought, Alice starving herself to death in the hospital! He regarded the pathetic figure, slumped on the chair. How to get her to see that he *had* to remove her baby from the life-support system. Today Steven was running another high fever. What next? Another operation? Not if Eliot could help it! Damn! What had happened to Alice's years as a nurse in St. Vincent's? How could she keep on hoping in the face of what she must know! She was on the edge, anyone could see that, and he would have to tread carefully. But damn it, this couldn't go on!

To the nurse, he remarked, "She's supposed to make an informed decision, but what the hell is informed? She's a nurse, and still, she isn't capable of that—"

"I know, Doctor."

Of course she knew; and, thanks to Hamilton Pierce, everyone else in New York City knew, also. "I'm sorry, Marie. I don't mean to repeat the obvious, but this is a tough one."

Gently, she said, "It's always tough. We all hate it, even when we know it's the only thing to do. And . . . well, Alice isn't thinking like a nurse anymore; she's thinking like a mother."

Eliot nodded and put his hand briefly on her shoulder. "Well, today's the day. I can't keep putting it off."

He sucked in breath, squared his shoulders, and went to Alice. She didn't look up or indicate in any way that she was aware of his presence. Damn it, he wished Toni could be here with

him! She was so much better at this sort of thing. The cozy
bedside manner had never been his long suit, and he was growing more and more uneasy every moment.

The signed order had been in his hands for several days and
he'd been unable to move on it. He came upstairs at least three
times a day, to look at Alice, to see if maybe by some miracle,
something had changed; to see if maybe by some miracle, she
had given up and was ready to face reality. But, of course, nothing had changed. It looked as if he and Alice were *both* looking
for miracles.

During last night's "Voice of the City," Pierce had opened
the phone lines for calls about the Rodriguez baby. Several call-
ers said, "Pull the plug, for God's sake, just pull the plug."
Eliot had turned it off in disgust. Pull the plug, like it was a
toaster!

Still, Eliot was convinced that letting the baby die was the
best thing he could do for Alice. This obsession was killing her.
It had already estranged her from her husband. Once this thing
was ended, she would be free. She could get on with her life.

"Alice," he said. His voice came out too loud, too brusque.
He felt his stomach beginning to knot up. "Alice," he repeated
in a softer tone. "I have to talk to you . . . about taking the baby
off the life-support system. There's no hope, Alice. We have to
do it."

He waited a moment, cursing inwardly. If only there were a
better way to do this. Then, she turned her head and looked up
at him and began to talk in a flood of Spanish.

"Alice, please speak in English."

She shook her head. *"No comprendo ingles,"* she said. Her
eyes were blank, but he knew damned well she was only stonewalling, pretending not to understand him.

"Alice . . ." There was nothing he could do to ease her pain,
to make it easier. "I'm sorry," he said at last, "but Steven is
not going to get better." She had already turned away from him,
focused once more on her rosary. "If we keep him on the machines, he'll always be like this." He paused, then added, *"Exactly* like this . . . for his whole life. Sooner or later, Alice, you
will have to face reality. You can do it, I know you can." She
never so much as blinked.

They might have to go to court, he thought, as he strode down
the hallway. He hoped not, but this was not helping anyone.

Sooner or later, they would let this baby go, with or without her consent. And it was the right thing to do, he was sure of that. In which case, why was he feeling so awful?

It was just past one o'clock when Toni walked into the nursery, grabbing a smock and scrubbing her hands quickly. She had wanted to come up this morning, but there had been one emergency after the other, and she had never had a minute. Marie had called her, alarmed. She felt Alice was becoming more and more depressed. Toni had to agree. Yesterday, when she had come up to see her, it had struck her how much Alice looked like the photos of war victims: starved, exhausted, overwhelmed. She had been sitting there next to her baby twenty-four hours a day, praying. It had been ten days now.

In the beginning, she'd been so rational—well, why not? She was an R.N. and a damned good one, by all accounts. The morning he was born, she had looked at the baby and the charts quite professionally, even while the tears rolled down her cheeks, and had agreed, "If he can't breathe on his own, don't do heroics."

But by that evening, she had already given consent for the first operation. After that, she got more and more adamant, insisting that everything possible be done. And after *that* . . . well, she just let loose of all her training. And here was the sad result.

God, what a tragic business! Toni thought. There were days she wished all these technological advances had never been invented.

She glanced at her watch and decided that, today, she'd see Alice first, then talk with the nurses and try to decide what steps should be taken. Joe Rodriguez had refused to come to the nursery; he believed his wife's mind had been poisoned by Havemayer, whom he referred to as "that damn butcher."

But Alice was not *quite* alone, Toni found as she entered the nursery. A young man in a cream-colored Aran sweater and tan corduroy pants had drawn another chair up next to Alice and was bent toward her, talking earnestly. You couldn't miss seeing him; his hair was bright red. It was Father O'Donnell, the hospital's Catholic chaplain, nice young man, very up to date. Maybe Alice was taking a turn for the better.

But when she got closer and could hear them, her heart sank.

Alice was *not* taking a turn for anything. Alice was still the same broken record, saying over and over, "They can't kill my baby, God will save him."

Father O'Donnell put his big broad hand over Alice's, and for a moment, the constant telling of the beads ceased. "Come home, Alice. I'll take you. Joe needs you; he's lonely. Joe is suffering too, you know."

"Joe has turned on me," Alice said in a monotone. "He won't even pray." And then she went right back to her litany: "God will save my baby. . . ."

Toni touched the priest's shoulder gently, and when he turned, she said in a low voice, "Let me sit with Alice for a while, Father. Maybe we can talk this over."

The priest shrugged as if to say there was no chance of talking anything over. She already knew that; she had watched Alice's deterioration since the beginning of this fiasco. She had tried and tried to comfort Alice. She had talked until she was blue in the face. She was exhausted; she didn't know if she had anything left to give. Damn Havemayer! Where was he now that Alice so obviously needed help? He didn't give a damn about Alice, only that once again the great Conrad Havemayer had kept an infant from death.

The murmuring sounds of the monitors were suddenly drowned out by a long, drawn-out *bleeeep*, the signal that somewhere in this room a tiny baby had stopped breathing. There was a quiet but immediate hustle over to one of the bassinets, and she could hear the nurse saying, "Come on, Penny, atta girl . . . way to go!" The infant had started breathing again.

Alice was oblivious to everything. That was one sound that should have brought her instantly to attention. "Alice," Toni murmured, sitting close to the young woman, "have you eaten? You should eat. You need your strength." No response. Nothing. "Alice, please listen to me. I know you're there." She took Alice's hand; it felt so small and frail. At her touch, Alice gripped her fingers, clinging like a child.

Toni glanced at the chart and what she saw made her even sadder. "Steven has a new infection, Alice. His temp is a hundred and four."

Alice shook her head. "He's getting antibiotics," she said. "He'll get better."

"Alice, I don't think so."

"He will." It was the only strength she had left, this obstinacy. "He looked at me today. I swear to God, he opened his eyes and looked at me." Triumphantly: "He knows I'm his mother."

Toni's heart sank. She was out of arguments, out of pleas, out of words. She had never felt so helpless in her life.

And then, from behind her, a familiar deep voice. "Now, Alice, didn't we talk this over yesterday? Didn't we decide little Steven can't *really* see you?"

Toni turned, startled. It was Ham Pierce. "What are *you* doing here?" Who the hell had let him in? Come to that, who the hell had let him in yesterday?

She got to her feet, but of course he still towered over her. She wished he wouldn't stand so close to her. Every time she saw him lately, she was aware of a strange kind of electricity between them and it made her uneasy. Not that he had ever done anything or said anything, but it was there, all right. She wished there were some way she could step back without stumbling over the chair.

He smiled down at her, his voice quiet. "I was invited. Alice likes to talk to me. It seems to help her."

Oh, sure, Toni thought. Mr. Wonderful thinks everyone likes to talk to him. But I know what he's up to, and it's not helping Alice. She gave him what she hoped was a pleasant smile and said, "Well, I'll just hang out with you, if you don't mind."

Mind! Ham thought. No, I don't mind. He wondered how she would react if she could *read* his mind. Well, no matter how shocked she might be, she couldn't be more staggered than *he* was to find his thoughts constantly turning to her, even after he'd set himself up to fight this whole damn hospital! Not only that, but she was opinionated and stubborn and aggressive, everything he most hated in a woman. Nevertheless, he found himself loving the thick dark hair she was always running her fingers through, and the big round eyes, and the slightly graveled voice.

"Oh, Mr. Pierce, I'm so glad you're here!"

He moved to Alice, feeling a bit guilty. This was a real sad case, and he had no business standing here thinking about sex. He put a hand on her scrawny, little shoulder. Alice Rodriguez must have lost ten pounds in the last couple of weeks alone. She looked pitiful. But the worst part was, her mind was slipping. He couldn't use her on the show; she wasn't sympathetic anymore.

Now everyone was feeling sorry for Joe, the forgotten man, the father of this child, abandoned by his wife, left to suffer by himself. God, if he could just get Joe onto the show, they could keep the story going for another week. Damn! He should have gotten him while the getting was good. But it was no go. Joe was refusing to talk to any reporters.

Oh hell. Face it, Joe was pretty much useless to him, anyway. He'd set up the story as a battle between this heartbroken, Hispanic, upwardly mobile little family and the big, impersonal, imperial, white, uncaring hospital. If it became widely known that the father of the baby wanted it over with, then it would seem like just another domestic quarrel. Which, in a way, it was.

And he was stuck right smack in the middle of it. Every day, if he didn't show up here, one of the nurses called to tell him Mrs. Rodriguez was asking for him. He was beginning to hate Alice's clinging, her helplessness, the beseeching looks she kept giving him. Like he could do anything! He could get people riled up about it, and he had, for sure. But now, no way. This baby was not really alive, as far as he was concerned. He didn't know why the hell they'd put him on all these machines in the first place. He pressed Alice's hand, wishing she would just give up and go home.

"Has anyone called her priest?"

"Father O'Donnell was here. Alice . . . Alice isn't hearing anyone, really."

"I've been talking to God," Alice said. "I told Him, if You can make a miracle, You'll make my baby well."

The woman was a stuck needle in a very long-playing record, Ham thought. Maybe it was time to call the shrinkers and put her into a rubber room.

"You have to trust in God's will, Alice," he said. Christ, he sounded just like his old man. Whenever he heard his father coming out of his mouth, it chilled his blood. He'd run long and hard and far to escape the Reverend Pierce. And then he recalled something else his father liked to say to him: You can run and you can hide, but you can never escape yourself, Hamilton. Jesus, was he just a copy of the old man?

"Yes," Alice said, holding on to his hand with a grip of iron. "God's will." Something in her voice made him look, really look, down at her. The blankness was gone from her eyes, and she had begun to cry without sound. "Mr. Pierce, do you think Jesus wants my little boy to be with Him?"

He found he couldn't answer her; the words stuck in his craw. And then he was saved by the lovely and intelligent Dr. Romano, who knelt in front of Alice, took her free hand, and looked right into her eyes.

"Yes, Alice," she said, "I think Jesus wants your little lamb to come home to Him."

"My little lamb," Alice repeated and she let go of Ham's hand to reach down and tenderly touch the baby's cheek. "Do you want to go home to Jesus, *cariño*?" She turned back to Toni. "He's been baptized. Hasn't he? Didn't we have Steven baptized?"

"Yes, yes you did," Toni assured her.

A strange, dazzled smile spread over Alice's face. "Then he'll go straight to heaven with the angels."

Toni smiled at her and nodded. Please, Alice, she begged silently. Just come back to us. Hear us.

"Will he suffer, Dr. Toni?"

"No, no, I promise you he won't. We'll take all those ugly tubes away, and we'll put him into your arms, and you'll sit in a rocking chair, and he'll just . . . it will be as gentle as falling asleep."

Alice's eyes filled with tears, but she was smiling. She looked down into the bassinet. "I'll miss you so much, baby. But I'll see you again, in heaven." She turned and said to both of them, her smile radiant, "Now I'll be able to hold him at last."

None of them said a word for a few moments. Then, Alice let go of Toni's hand and stood up. "I better go find Joe," she said briskly, and out she went, walking fast.

Ham was totally taken by surprise; two minutes ago, she'd been in a daze, and now, suddenly, she had come to life. What the hell had happened?

Toni got up from her knees and looked over at him with a little smile of relief. "Well . . ." she said and stopped and let out a big sigh.

"Yes. Well, you did it, Dr. Toni."

"I think *you* did it."

"Okay. *We* did it. Do we make a good team, or what?"

She slid him a look. "Or what," she said, and walked quickly away.

14

Thanksgiving Day

The doorbell chimed, and Sam went, brushing past the hired help, to let in Lillian and Philip, both resplendent; he in his new alpaca coat, she in her favorite fur, mink, and her favorite diamonds, large.

"Lillian, Lillian," Sam laughed. "It's only a *hamish* Thanksgiving with the family, not an opening at the opera."

"And these are my *hamish* diamonds, darling," she retorted, giving him a swift kiss on his cheek.

Eliot hurried over to greet his parents. As soon as Carolyn and David arrived, they would all be here. He eyed the huge, gaily wrapped and beribboned package Lillian had pushed ahead of her into the hallway. It was large, and it was flat. If it was what he thought it was, he did not want it: that painting Uncle Leonard had done during his "artistic period," sometime in the thirties. It was a street scene in Paris. Eliot *hated* that painting; there was something slightly wrong with the perspective so that the houses seemed to tilt in different directions. As a boy, Eliot had named it—silently, of course, because Uncle Leonard was his mother's favorite brother—*Paris Falling Down*.

God, how many times had his mother, thinking for some reason that it was a particular favorite of his, said, "One of these days, Eliot, I'm going to be willing to give up Uncle Leonard's painting of Paris! And then it will be yours!"

He kissed his mother and put out his hand to his father.

His father eyed him. "I've been watching these reports on TV, son, and I must say I'm bothered. What seems to be the trouble?"

"*What* reports?" Eliot countered. "I hope you don't mean 'Voice of the City,' Dad."

"Yes, I think that's what it's called."

"Ham Pierce is not friendly to Harmony Hill, and his reports are slanted. You know it's tough in the hospital business these days—"

"Eliot, I think it's very important for you to maintain a certain . . . *image* as president of the hospital. These television commentators carry a great deal of weight in some quarters." He got a look on his face that Eliot remembered very well . . . remembered and hated. "It could be dangerous to make an enemy. You can pull it off. After all, you're a Wolfe."

Eliot found himself wanting to give several different responses, none of them terribly polite. At his age, did he need his father telling him how to behave? But he only nodded and grunted and handed his parents' coats to a young woman hired for the occasion, and they continued into the living room. He was sorry to see that Lillian was shlepping her present along with her.

"I'm quite satisfied with my leadership," he finally said to Philip. Well, he *was*, he told himself defensively. He was very satisfied—except for a few minor details like the flap over the Rodriguez baby, like his mostly hostile hospital administration committee, like the number of sexual harassment cases coming up, like the constant picketing in front of the hospital, and like the ubiquitous presence of Ham Pierce. Other than that, his incumbency was damned near perfect.

His marriage, though, was *far* from perfect, but at least it was getting back on track. Toni had saved his ass the other day. Talked Alice Rodriguez into giving her consent. He'd asked her how the hell she had done it—"She wouldn't even speak English to *me*," he had admitted—and she hesitated and then said, "I'm not sure that I did it. Ham Pierce was there, too, and to tell you the truth, I got the impression she was listening to him more than to me."

That's all he had to hear! He lost it, blew up at her, demanding to know what the hell Pierce was doing in the neonatal unit, and how come she hadn't thrown him the hell out when she found him up there.

Yelling at her was a mistake. It just made her mad. Her face had gone all stiff and cold, as had her voice. "For your information, Mr. Pierce was invited to the neonatal unit by Mrs. Rodriguez, and to tell you the truth, he dealt with her much better than any of the rest of us. If it weren't for him, Alice would still be up there, sitting and moaning and creating a major problem for you."

Okay, okay, he thought, and then said all the right things to make up with her. He didn't want any more fighting. What did he care, anyway? It was done, and it was no longer an issue, thank God. In fact, he and Toni had gone to Steven's funeral together.

The coffin was unbelievably tiny, and it was surrounded by floral offerings that made it look even smaller. It sat out in the middle of the aisle, dwarfed by the soaring Gothic arches and huge stained-glass windows.

There had been only a small group of mourners, huddled in the front pews; the priest's voice had echoed a bit in the vast spaces of the church. Candles flickered, casting strange shadows over Alice, who was all in black. She sobbed pitifully from the first moment to the last. Joe, tight-lipped and pale, sat close to her, but she never acknowledged his presence.

Eliot didn't remember too much about the service; he was focused on Alice, who suddenly seemed much more . . . human, here in her church, with her friends and family. He realized with a pang that he had seen her only as a problem to be solved, to be got rid of. In that little white box, dead, lay her child, her baby boy. He suddenly remembered seeing his own children as newborns, gazing at them, dreaming about what they might become, who they might be. But for Alice and Joe, it struck him, the future had ended on his say-so.

He was gripped with anguish so intense that his stomach turned. Swallowing, he sat in the pew and made himself become calm. He reminded himself that Steven Rodriguez had never been really alive; there had been no future right from the start. It wasn't anyone's fault.

"Little Steven is with the angels," the priest said, and for some reason, it was more than Eliot could take; he'd had to blink back tears. Toni, sitting next to him, apparently concentrating on the service, had looked over at him and had taken his hand. The feeling that she was there for him was like a balm on his troubled spirit. So now she understood how tough it was for him, too.

But enough of funerals and sadness. His family was here for Thanksgiving. He was *not* going to think about the hospital, not even for one more minute. There was a linen-clad table presided over by two young men in white jackets, and in the kitchen was enough food to feed a small country.

Putting on an enthusiastic smile, he asked Lillian, "Is that by any chance Uncle Leonard's Paris picture?"

Lillian drew back and gave him her best disdainful look. "You hate that painting. Why should I give it to you?"

"But you always promised—"

Now she threw her head back and laughed. "Not promised, darling. Threatened. Eliot, Eliot. It was a *joke*. Philip, I thought you raised your son to have a sense of humor."

"Honor, my dear Lillian, not humor." His father rarely laughed aloud, but he had a way of twinkling when he was amused. And right now, he twinkled. "Humor's *your* department."

Eliot, gazing upon his parents, thought once again what a lucky man he was. He was a friend to his parents, and so was Toni. And so were his children; look at the way Eric leaped up to greet them! And he *meant* it! So tight a knitting between generations was something that very few families enjoyed.

Toni's family, for instance, was always feuding about some damn thing or other and refusing to talk to one another. He couldn't understand how people who shared blood and history could cut themselves off from each other so easily, so casually. Of course, maybe he was prejudiced, being an only child. Before Sam came, he had always fantasized brothers and sisters. He had a few cousins, but the Wolfe family gatherings always seemed so piddling, so . . . minimal.

When he first met Toni and heard about her dozens of cousins and numerous aunts and uncles and honorary relatives as well, he had said to her, "I love big, warm Italian families. When I was a kid, that's what I always longed for. Now, I can belong to yours."

She shrieked with laughter. "What big, warm Italian family are you talking about?" she demanded. "Forget it! We all hate each other; I couldn't wait to get away! You'll see. Nobody from my family will come to the wedding except my cousin Teresa, my sisters—*maybe* my sisters—and my mother; and my mother will cry and sniffle through the whole ceremony."

He must have looked totally nonplussed. "Dummy!" she went on, squeezing his hand to show she was kidding. "Not only are you not Catholic, but even worse, you're Jewish. And even worse than that, you're divorced. And even worse than *that*, you're much older than me, and I'll be a young widow and have to wear black the rest of my life." She made the sign that would ward off the evil eye and laughed. "Only *I*," she added with a passionate kiss, "will know how lucky I am."

When had she stopped considering herself lucky to have him? He was feeling so off balance with her these days, and no matter what he did to straighten things out between them, it never seemed to last long. He'd even gone to Sam about it. Well, that wasn't quite fair because he'd made an appointment with his old friend, half to talk about his marriage, yes, but also half to see if he could spot anything amiss with Sam.

The meeting had started out just fine. Eliot got a lot off his chest, about Toni and that damned magazine piece and her center and never seeing her anymore, and about becoming more and more turned off. At that point, just as he was about to tell him about Janet, Sam held up a hand. "Save it, would you?" he said. "I gotta take a leak in the worst way!"

He was gone just a minute or two and when he came back, he looked surprised. "What're *you* doing here?" he said. "Not that I mind . . ."

Eliot felt chilled. "Sam, come off it, okay? This isn't funny. We've been talking for an hour. If my problems make you uneasy, just say so, and I'll go to a different shrink."

A flash of something crossed Sam's face and was instantly gone. "A different shrink? What are you, crazy? So I have a lousy sense of humor! Sorry. Let's continue." He busied himself with some papers, and Eliot couldn't read his eyes. "Go on, my man. I'm all ears."

But Eliot couldn't quite bring himself to talk. There was something disturbing about all this. Then Sam lifted his head and looked straight at him. "You were saying, about Toni?" he said.

A wave of relief swept over him. It was all right, then. It was just the usual. It was very typical of Sam to go pee, get lost in thought while contemplating the bathroom wall, and forget what he had been doing. But now, Eliot found he couldn't tell him about Janet. The moment had passed. It hadn't been such a good idea anyway.

Eliot's eyes were still fixed on Lillian's surprise package. "If not Uncle Leonard's painting, what is it?"

"It's for Toni. Yoohoo, Toni! Come here, darling, we've brought something for you!" She turned to Eliot. "Where are the other children?"

"On their way, I assume. They're—would you believe—at the Wollman Rink, ice-skating."

"Ah," Lillian said, lighting up. "The Wollman Rink. So why aren't you with them, Eric? You were always the best . . . oh, I can still see you doing those twirls!"

"I wanted to be here when you got here, Grandma."

"Oh really? Or was it that you wanted to sleep late?"

"Caught me again!" he laughed. "But don't worry, Grandma, I won't forget your skating lessons. Toni and Dad and I have a date to go skating."

"Your *father*?"

"Excuse me," Eliot said. "I manage to creak around okay!"

Toni came bustling in from the kitchen, kissing them, and said, "Who creaks around? Nobody in *this* room!"

Lillian pushed the awkward package toward Toni. "We have a little surprise for you, Antonia."

"For me? How lovely." She ripped off the fancy paper and tossed it aside. Turning the large, framed artwork around to see the front, she stopped and gave a little gasp. "Oh, dear! My face again! Oh Lillian, it's really marvelous! But where in the world can I put it? I can't be looking at myself all the time!"

"Well, darling, of course it's meant for over the couch in the study! I chose the matte to coordinate with your color scheme, see?"

Even before he moved around to see what it was, Eliot knew. It was that damned magazine cover. And he was right. There it was again, blown up to monstrous proportions, mounted and framed so it would last forever. Nevertheless, he managed to murmur something appropriate as he gave it the hairy eyeball.

Thinking back on the way he had behaved the day the magazine came out, he was not proud of himself. He was not a man given to rages, and it embarrassed him to think of himself acting like that. He took the huge poster from Toni, walked with it into the middle of the living room, and leaned it against the mirrored wall where everyone could see and admire it.

The phone rang, and he tensed a little, alert. He hoped to God it wasn't for him. And it better not be for Toni, either. At least for the family, she should stay here!

It was a wrong number, and Toni gave a huge sigh of relief. "I have three, count 'em, three patients about to go into labor," she explained.

"That's why I would never choose OB/GYN," Sam called from across the room. "Women are sex fiends."

"You wish!" Irene retorted. Every once in a while, she got off a zinger and made Eliot wonder just exactly how dumb she *was*.

"What about the bad old days, before group practice?" he said to Sam. "You didn't have to be an obstetrician to be called away from every dinner party you ever attended."

"*I* remember the bad old days," Lillian commented, and everyone laughed.

Eliot stood for a moment, regarding Sam. A few days ago, he had called an old medical school chum, now head of neurology at Mount Sinai, and asked about a "cousin" who was showing certain symptoms.

"Come on, Eliot," the old school chum had said, "you know as well as I do, it could be any one of a number of things. I could guess, but then, so could you, and I wouldn't take any bets who would be right. Send him in for a complete neurological work-up; at least then some things can be eliminated."

There was a certain note in his voice that let Eliot know: the guy was certain he was talking about himself. "Oh, God, Sid, it's not *me*! Scout's honor!" And they both had a good laugh. But when he hung up, the laughter stopped. Of course, Sam should go in for a work-up; the problem was how to get him to do it. Could he just say it, right out? "Sam, I think there's something wrong with you, mentally." Oh, Christ! How could he? Just the thought of doing something like that made him feel anxious.

He glanced over at Lillian's little surprise. No doubt about it, he was still miffed. He knew it was stupid and childish, but Toni should have told him about her job offer, damn it. If she'd only been honest with him, this thing with Janet would never have started. While he ruminated, Irene came over to him. "Larger than life," she commented. "Aren't you proud?"

"Of course I'm proud." He was proud of *himself*, that he was finally able to say it and carry it off.

From nearby came Toni's laughing voice. "Eliot absolutely hated me being a cover girl, Irene!"

"Oh Eliot, shame on you!" Irene said with a big smile.

Eliot went cold with anger. "I did not hate Toni being on the cover of a magazine," he said, hoping his voice sounded normal.

"Oh, Eliot, how can you *say* that with a straight face?" Toni came over to him, putting a hand on his arm. He badly wanted to shake it off but restrained himself. "You sulked for a month, darling!"

Eliot did not trust himself to speak. She'd done it again—and this time, in front of his family! Luckily, at that moment, in came David and Carolyn, flushed from exercise and the cold.

There was a great deal of laughter, as Carolyn and David halted in front of the giant poster and bowed to it. He had better put a smile on his face, Eliot told himself, and keep it there for the duration.

Carolyn turned to him. "Hey, Dad, does this mean Toni gets a promotion?"

"Antonia doesn't need a promotion, Carolyn, darling," said her grandmother, forcefully. "She's already the best as far as we're concerned."

Everyone applauded this. Eliot joined in. Hadn't he just promised himself to behave?

Carolyn came over. "You must be very proud of her. Only a few months in town and already she's famous—"

"Proud of you, too, kiddo. You're doing a great job. I heard it through the grapevine," he added, when she gave him a look of disbelief.

"Really, Dad? And I heard that the parenting program was slated for—" She made a slashing motion across her throat.

"Why does everyone at that hospital get hold of every goddamn rumor that floats down the corridor?" Eliot said. "I'm not letting them cut out your program, Carolyn. I think it's a good one, and I'm fighting for it."

He eyed her fondly. Carolyn was small and dark and petite, unlike the rest of the Wolfes. She was also smart and interesting and funny. Why wasn't she married, at the age of twenty-eight? She liked men, he knew that. Yet, he never saw her with a date.

Eliot put an arm around his daughter's shoulders and gave her a squeeze. "So tell me, sweetie, anyone special in your life?"

"Oh, Dad! I don't believe you said that!" She laughed at what must have been a very sheepish expression on his face. "Don't worry about me, Dad; I date. I beat them off with sticks!"

"I didn't mean—" he began, when David called to his sister from across the room. "Come here, Caro, I need you to settle an argument!" he yelled, and she was gone like a shot. She was glad to escape him, Eliot realized. Well, he probably shouldn't ask her about her love life. She was a grown woman. She'd tell him if there was anything he should know.

Soon, everyone was singing around the piano, songs like "Happy Days Are Here Again," and "I'll Be Seeing You," even "Danny Boy," one of Philip's favorites. And then, the phone rang again. Now what?

This time, it *was* for Dr. Wolfe, and immediately, all three of them—David, Philip, and Eliot—started for the phone. Then they all stopped, grinning at each other.

"Which Dr. Wolfe?" Eliot asked; not for the first time, he felt a swell of pride. By God, they were all physicians, all care givers, unto the fourth generation, and it was splendid. For the first time in his life, he understood why his father had so badly wanted him to follow the family tradition.

"Dr. *Eliot* Wolfe. They say it's an emergency."

Eliot ran for the phone. The voice on the other end was thick with urgency. "Douglas Doyle here, Dr. Wolfe, night security supervisor. There's been an . . . accident."

Accident? They wouldn't call him for just *any* accident. This was something serious, and "accident" was just a euphemism for disaster. "What happened?"

"It's a doctor, I'm afraid. Ethan Green."

Eliot quickly ran through his mental catalog. The name was vaguely familiar. Wasn't he an emergency medicine resident? "What about him?"

Doyle cleared his throat, hesitant, apparently, to give the bad news.

"For God's sake, man, tell me!"

"I went to the can, and I found him. On the floor. Dead . . ." Again, that embarrassed pause. "O.D.'ed."

"Christ!"

"Yes, sir. I'm about to call the police."

"Good. I'm on my way."

Eliot hung up. "Sorry everyone. Emergency." He paused, wondering whether he ought to tell anyone, and then decided, why not? Tersely he told them what had happened.

"Dead!" Lillian echoed, with a shudder. "How horrible."

"Damn!" David said angrily. "That guy should have been weeded out long ago! I've seen too many doctors too damn weak to face life without drugs!"

"But doctors are under much more stress than ordinary people—" Philip said.

"Bullshit! Excuse me, Grandpa, but bullshit. Being under stress doesn't give you the right to mess up your brain and screw up your patients—maybe kill them! Any physician who's on drugs should be thrown out!"

"David," Lillian interjected. "I don't think your grandfather was justifying drug addiction, darling."

"I didn't think he was. Look. Ethan Green worked in the E.R. with me. He made a lot of mistakes; he was careless and sloppy, and everyone knew it. We all had a feeling he was on something."

"So why didn't anyone blow the whistle?" Toni said.

"I did, and was thanked very politely and very politely given the brush-off!"

Eliot put a hand on his son's arm. "You weren't given the brush-off, David. I was informed, and we were dealing with it."

"Well, okay, but I wish I had been told that," David said, in a somewhat mollified tone.

Philip cleared his throat, and Eliot knew he was about to make the closest he ever got to a speech. "David, there's a very important thing called trust. Doctors must have the public's absolute trust; otherwise . . . chaos. At Harmony Hill, we have never covered up for one another, but such matters are handled with . . . discretion. Believe me, son, we are aware and we *do* weed out those who are not trustworthy." His voice remained mild, but, Eliot noted, his face had turned quite pink. His father was not normally one of the world's great pontificators.

"Now, now, Philip, it's not good for you to get excited. We'll discuss this another time. Go along, Eliot, dear. I'm sure they're anxious to see you at the hospital. We'll save you something to eat."

Eliot realized he had been stalling. He had to get to the hospital and deal with Ethan Green's suicide—because that's what they were going to call it. He wished he could talk this over with someone who would understand the weight of his responsibilities. He needed to have someone, goddamn it, who would give him a little support. His father and his son had their own agendas. His wife? Out of the question. And as for Sam . . . well, he couldn't be sure about Sam anymore.

And then suddenly he knew what he would do. As soon as he was finished at the hospital he'd make a phone call. Just the thought of her lifted his spirits.

"Don't save me anything," he said to his mother. "This might take quite a while."

15

December

The neon light filtering in through the half-closed blinds made glowing bars of gold across Eliot's chest and shoulders. He looked like a beautiful tiger to her, sleek and strong, poised above her on taut arms. His eyes were closed, and his skin glistened with sweat as he drove himself into her, moving faster and faster. He had pulled his lips tight; he always did just before he came, his hips moving faster and faster. She held on to him, moaning, one hand on each taut buttock. Now his cock was tightening, swelling, getting so big. She thrust her hips up, close into him, meeting each thrust, whispering, "Yes, yes, yes, yes." She could feel him getting close, and then he threw his head back, pumping into her, groaning in pleasure. He collapsed over her, kissing her throat, her ears, her hair, her shoulder, whatever he could reach.

"Oh, God, how sweet, how sweet that was, darling," Janet breathed into his ear, holding him tightly. He grunted—all he could manage right now. Fondly, she chuckled and gave him a little squeeze. He did just fine for a man of his age. Not that she'd ever *say* that, of course not! She would never bring up the age difference between them, never. She knew how to treat a man, make him feel . . . manly . . . sexy. Even though he had relaxed so completely that his entire weight was pressing on her chest, she would never, ever push him away. She wanted him to know that she loved having him inside her, even after it was over.

After a few minutes, though, he moaned and rolled off her and sprawled next to her, spread-eagled, one arm flung across her belly. "What you do to me, Janet!" he managed, after a minute. "It's criminal; you should be outlawed!" He moved his head to look at her and grinned, his eyes already starting to close.

This was only their third time together, but she already knew him so well. Now he'd pull her close to him and, wrapping his arms around her, would be fast asleep in a matter of seconds. And he would smile as he slept.

Sure enough, he reached out for her, pulled her into his embrace, and fell asleep. She was jubilant. She had him! Oh, he didn't know it yet; he never said anything that committed him to a damn thing . . . not even to another date. He could be as careful and cautious as he pleased. It didn't matter. It was going to happen, she knew it! He was already half in love with her.

She'd give him time; she was good at waiting, especially when the payoff was becoming the next Mrs. Eliot Wolfe. He was a plum ripe for the plucking, just hanging on the tree, waiting for some smart woman to reach up and grab him.

Everyone in the hospital knew he wasn't getting along with Dr. Toni. She *never* appeared at any of the hospital social functions with him, never. And all the most powerful people didn't like it. It was the topic of a lot of gossip.

That last time she'd seen Conrad, they'd just had a drink— well, *he* did; she was still on the wagon. She wasn't going to bed with him anymore; he was never going to leave May, no matter *what* he said! But he'd told her all about it. The trustees were mad as hell that the president's wife could never seem to fit a hospital function into her schedule. What made her work so much more important than all the other doctors? Dr. Toni wasn't even the head of a department!

Well! She wasn't about to let him get away with *that*! "For God's sake, Conrad, you of all people should understand why Toni Romano is so busy! She's an obstetrician! And a damned good one, too, according to my nurses!"

"I didn't say *I* object to Dr. Romano's absences, Janet, dear. I said the trustees find it . . . eccentric, even insulting. Of course, I do think the wife of the president should readjust her priorities and *make* time to be at her husband's side. You know what they're saying, Janet. They're saying, 'What kind of a man can hope to manage a huge hospital, if he can't even manage his wife!' "

Could you believe it? Supposedly sophisticated people in the

1990s still talking about men managing their wives? Well, she wanted to laugh in Conrad's face; he really was an old fart! She was glad she was finished with him. But, bless him, the great boring Dr. Havemayer was the one who had put her on the track about Eliot. He had verified what she had already guessed for herself.

The first time she saw Eliot Wolfe, she thought to herself, *This one is hungry, he'll be easy.* But he hardly even glanced her way, so she put him on the back burner. Then, when that horny idiot, Richard Stillman, hit on another one of her nurses, it gave her a golden opportunity. She went into the ladies' room and carefully tousled her hair and put on a little extra blush so she'd look prettily agitated. It generally worked with these old guys who still believed in chivalry of all the damn things. Nothing worked like a little helplessness! Not too much, of course, because then they wouldn't think you were good at your job. Just the slightest trace.

So when she charged in, she let her bosom heave a little, widening her eyes. She knew how to maintain that delicate balance between assertiveness and femininity.

It had worked. She could tell by the look on his face that he'd like to try it, but was too well behaved to do anything about it. But look how eager he had been to keep talking! She could feel the tension in his body. He had been holding his breath, poor baby! She was awfully glad, at that moment, that she had squirted a little perfume between her breasts before she went down to his office.

She noted every one of his moves that time and made herself a promise that, one day soon, she'd see what was doing with him. But she knew his wife was still in Washington. She wasn't interested in being a convenient substitute while wifey delivered babies out of town. Janet Rafferty might be a lot of things, but she was *not* any married man's one-night stand.

Her own career was very important to her, so she couldn't fault Toni Romano. She admired everything Toni stood for: Toni was totally honest, dedicated, and didn't push her patients, or the nurses, around! But, hey, if Dr. Romano didn't want her handsome, wealthy, powerful husband anymore, if she was going to throw him away, far be it from Janet Lois Rafferty to let him go to waste!

Next to her on the bed, Eliot stirred, ready to wake up. She kissed him softly on his big, strong jaw, and his eyes opened.

"Hi there, kiddo. How're we doing?" He always said the same thing.

"Do you say that to Toni when you wake up?"

"Huh?" He blinked, startled, then laughed and eased himself to a sitting position.

"Do you say, 'Hi there, kiddo,' to Toni when you wake up?"

"She's usually gone when I wake up."

"Eliot, don't make fun of me!"

Oh dear. That had come out sounding petulant. Wrong, wrong, wrong, Janet, she scolded herself. She wriggled over, close to him, murmuring, "You're so far away, and I'm so lonesome!" He immediately reached out for her and pulled her against him, rubbing her back and burying his face in her neck.

"You were wonderful, last night, on Ham Pierce's show," she said. "You've single-handedly changed the whole image of the hospital."

"Really?"

Men were such babies! They believed anything a woman said to them, just so long as it was a compliment.

She put on a sonorous tone of voice and quoted what he had said on TV: " 'The life and death of Steven Rodriguez is a tragedy, but it is a personal tragedy, Mr. Pierce, a family tragedy. It would not be appropriate for me—' "

"But that's exactly what I said!" He pulled back a little so he could look at her, smiling, a little embarrased but very pleased.

Janet laughed out loud. "Of course! And the look on Ham Pierce's face! It's the first time I've ever seen *him* at a loss for words!"

"I have to admit, it felt pretty damn good. And I have to admit, *you* feel pretty damn good."

She knew she felt good to most men. She'd discovered that when she was in her teens. Felt good and looked good. Even now, she worked out plenty to keep it that way.

He gave her a light kiss. "You know, I called you on Thanksgiving."

"You called me?"

"Yeah. I had to leave the family gathering to go to the hospital, and I thought, maybe, while I had a good excuse . . ."

Oh, shit, and there she was, at her mother's, being bored to death by her relatives. She felt a pang of regret, but really, she had told him she'd be away, and how was she to know he'd suddenly be free on Thanksgiving Day?

"I hate to leave," Eliot said, stretching. "Just look at it out there." He gestured past the foot of the bed to the uncurtained window overlooking Columbus Avenue and the Tex-Mex restaurant across the street, with its blinking sign of the desert sun with wavy rays coming out of it. And tonight, just to make everything that much more delightful, a mix of snow and sleet was hissing against the windowpane. "But it's so warm and cozy and nice here," he added, giving her another kiss. This one, she knew, was his farewell. "It's nine-thirty, and I really have to go . . . but, damn it, I wish I never had to leave!"

She hid her smile as she watched him get dressed. He was right. Seeing the wind and the snow and the cold out there only made her little Art Nouveau bedroom, in the glow of its stained-glass wisteria lamp, seem all the more seductive and soft and luscious.

He put on his overcoat and picked up his thick muffler, looking at her with such sad eyes. "God, I hate to leave," he said. Now she did smile, holding her arms out for a good-bye embrace, letting the quilt drop away from her bare breasts. The look on his face was something to see! Yes, he was coming along quite nicely.

Toni glanced up from her charts and swore. What a filthy night! She was using the reception desk in the main room of the center. It felt a little creepy in the back, in her office. There, she had only the desk light on, and there were deep, unfamiliar shadows in the corners. She was all alone, and it was too damn quiet for her taste.

Here, at least, she could turn on all the overhead lights. In their glare maybe she could stop running the tape of the Rodriguez funeral through her head. She kept thinking there was something she could have done, or said, that would have made it all easier on Alice. But she had to stop that. She was only Alice's doctor, not her mother.

And to think she had chosen ob/gyn because it was "the happy service." Because on the maternity floor, life began. She remembered one of her professors glowing as he told her there was nothing better in this world than delivering babies. Of course, back then, there weren't any crack babies, and most newborns with severe birth defects died.

She pulled in a deep breath. She really had to stop thinking about this; she had other patients, other problems. She bent once more to the papers on the desk. Damn that committee for their damned success reports! They didn't even know what success *was*, around here!

Every time she thought about Eliot on Ham's program last night, she got mad. Oh, it was smart to stonewall, and, if she was really honest with herself, what he said wasn't a lie. It *was* a family tragedy, and it *was* a personal tragedy. But, damn, it was a Harmony Hill tragedy, too. Conrad Havemayer with his "sanctity of human life" and his glamorous reputation had too much power by far. She could just picture him, the handsome head bent over Alice's bed, the distinguished brow drawn into serious lines, the rich voice assuring her that he, and he alone, could keep her baby alive. Alice and Joe had been in shock, and he had taken advantage of them. And Eliot had done nothing to stop him.

He was lucky Ham Pierce had had the good sense not to make a big deal out of the funeral. Ham could have pilloried the hospital. There might even have been a state investigation! But it hadn't happened. Ham had soft-pedaled the whole story in the end, and the press had moved on to the next, newest tragedy.

She looked at her wristwatch, but she didn't really have to. She knew what time it was: way past 9:30. The car service was late again, *if* they hadn't forgotten her completely. She had to get up, close the ledgers, pick up her bag, put on her coat, and go out into that shit and go home. The sleet and the snow were slamming against the front windows like bullets; she could just imagine the wind-chill factor out there!

Well, lucky her, with her nice, warm, down coat and her lined boots. Lucky her, not to be caught in the poverty trap—like most of her girls . . . her *patients*, her *woman* patients, she corrected herself, though she couldn't help thinking of them as girls. So many of them were still kids—much too young to be pregnant, much too young to have to think about raising children without enough money, without enough space, without enough clothing, without enough *anything*. It was a trap, and they had almost no hope of ever getting free.

She, on the other hand, was here by choice. She got to leave,

if the car service ever came. Impatient, she reached over and
punched the REDIAL button again. Still busy. Well, car service
or no car service, she didn't have to stay in this neighborhood
and face the grinding poverty that wore you down and wore you
out.

On Thanksgiving Day, she had looked at the table, crammed
with enough food, and had felt slightly nauseated. Why did they
have to have so *much*? They didn't need it, and it was excessive.
So many of her girls at the center were undernourished. Some
of them didn't even know what good food was! The amount of
leftovers here! Her mother-in-law was ready to tell the caterer
to get rid of it.

"No, don't, Lillian. I'll take it up to the Women's Health
Center. We can use it."

You had to give Lillian credit. As soon as Toni spoke, she
was all for it. "Of course, of course. How stupid of me." She
immediately began wrapping it up herself, chattering about her
own poor girlhood. "I should never forget. But I do. Shame on
me!"

Lillian was a good person, really. It was so sweet of her to
make that poster of the magazine cover . . . and typical. Of
course, Eliot loathed, hated, and despised it. He had behaved
well—when did Eliot *not* behave well?—but she could tell he
was seething. He just didn't know what to do with her success.
He had been so damned wonderful about her going to med
school—encouraging, supportive, understanding, uncompeti-
tive. In fact, he had been terrific, so long as he was in control.

Well, she was out of his control, way out, and he did *not* like
it. He had loved being her mentor, her guide; he hated being
her equal. On Thanksgiving Day, she noticed, really noticed for
the first time, how Lillian's eye was always on Philip, how she
was always anticipating his every need. His cup was refilled with
coffee before he realized he wanted it. A little frown between
his brows brought Lillian with a glass of water and two aspirin.
It was quite wondrous, this mind-reading act, but it wasn't for
Toni Romano.

Had Eliot wanted that kind of room service from Arlene? He
didn't like talking about his first marriage. But Toni had gathered, from little bits and pieces, that, under Arlene, the Eliot
Wolfe household had looked perfect . . . even the kids. Yeah,
yeah, Toni thought, but once those kids were grown! All you

had to do was look at them now. David, the depressed workaholic. Carolyn, hostile as hell. And Eric, the comedian, the
gay activist. Suddenly, after years spent clear across the country,
he was back, staying in their apartment, watching TV day and
night.

Not so perfect now, were they? Toni roused herself, got up
from the desk, walked to the window, and looked outside. Nothing had changed. Still no car to take her home. She went back
to the desk; maybe she could do some work while she waited.
But she really knew better. Her mind was too active to set her
free.

She had known for a long time what was wrong with Arlene.
She had pieced it together from Eliot's anecdotes. One, in particular, had rung a bell in her head. It was about a dinner party
they were giving, Arlene and Eliot. . . .

"And it always takes Arlene a couple of hours, no exaggeration, to get ready for anything!" she remembered Eliot saying.
They were sitting crosslegged, the both of them, on her bed,
eating Chinese food out of those little white boxes.

"The guests were already there," Eliot said, "and Arlene
wasn't downstairs yet. There were plenty of jokes about her
not finding exactly the right jewelry for her dress, and everyone laughed. But time kept passing, and she still wasn't
downstairs. So I went up. And there she was, sitting on the
floor sobbing, surrounded by—I don't know—maybe every
dress she owned. Everything just strewn around everywhere,
shoes, too. She told me she just couldn't go downstairs. None
of her clothes fit her. She had put on two pounds, she was
fat, she was ugly, she just couldn't face anyone. Isn't that
funny?"

He had laughed, but Toni remembered thinking, No, it's not
so funny. It's weird and strange and sad. But she said nothing;
she was only the Other Woman. God, that had been a long time
ago, a very long time ago. She had felt so smug when she and
Eliot got married years later; she had thought, Well, he certainly
got himself a different kind of woman *this* time. But had he?
She obsessed over her work as much as Arlene had ever obsessed
over her wardrobe. Did she really care about anything—or anybody, for that matter—as much as she cared about her work?
What family did she have? The Romanos? She'd cut herself free
of *them* long ago. The Wolfes? She wasn't really part of them.

No. She was on her own, alone, attached to nothing, attached to no one. She hadn't even had time, in New York, to make women friends, and she missed the closeness, she missed the giggling and the confiding and the sharing of thoughts.

Christ, the bad weather was making her morbid! She shook her thoughts away and massaged the back of her neck. She was tired, that's all. She looked again out the window at a white world, empty of people, empty of traffic, empty period. Well, shit. She'd been sitting here, getting maudlin, while the storm outside was getting worse. The car service was obviously never going to show.

She jabbed at the REDIAL button . . . give them one last shot. The phone bleeped out the number, then burped that damned busy signal. What was *wrong* with them? Stupid question. She knew what was wrong. There had been a rash of murders, always at night, always uptown, of *course* uptown. Somebody would get into the car, put a gun to the driver's head, take his money, and shoot him dead. So there was a shortage of guys willing to drive at night, especially in certain neighborhoods. Like this one.

She had asked them twice, just to make sure: "I'm at 123rd and Amsterdam. Can you pick me up there or would you rather I walk over to Central Park West?" She had been assured, in a heavy, but cheerful, Hispanic accent, that there was *no problema*. Well, maybe not for them, but Toni Romano was having a great big *problema*.

Why was she so unnerved tonight? She'd been alone in the center before, and nothing had happened. So far. And, anyway, it was stupid, getting scared just because it was cold and dark and stormy. There weren't any people walking around or hanging out, like they usually did. It was childish and unreasonable. It was neurotic. It was, goddamn it, typically *female*!

She suddenly got to her feet and shoved her papers into her bag. She was getting out of here before she got snowed in permanently. She bustled about, getting her stuff together, putting on her boots and her coat, pulling a knitted hat down over her ears. And then came the moment of truth, when she turned out all the lights and there she was, alone in the dark, about to go out, essentially blind, into the stormy night, for Christ's sake!

She ordered herself to stop being a baby, opened the door to a frigid blast of air, and quickly stepped out. When she turned to lock up, she thought she heard footsteps squeaking on the snow, coming toward her. Her spine froze with fear. The keys trembled in her hand, but she forced herself to keep locking the door.

What should she do? Move, that's what; get out of there. She turned and started to walk, away from the footsteps, hefting the heavy briefcase in her hand, prepared to smash it into whoever was coming after her. Her heart was thumping like crazy.

"Dr. Romano!" She sucked in air. It was someone who knew her, but she didn't recognize the voice. "Dr. Romano!" he called again. It could be one of the boyfriends, one of the husbands, one of the many men who came around, pissed with her for interfering with their women. Well, in that case, she could talk herself out of trouble. They were mad at her, but in awe of her, too.

Suddenly resolute, she halted and turned to face the unknown. Now the wind blew snow into her face, and she ducked her head a little. She called out, "Who is it?" The steps continued toward her. *"Who is it?"* she repeated, an edge to her voice.

"Dr. Romano! Don't be scared. I'm one of the paramedics from the hospital." Now she could discern his shape through the swirling, stinging needles of snow. He was big; well, he'd just better be one of the paramedics from the hospital, she thought, lifting the case just a little, getting ready.

"What's your name?" she demanded.

"King Crawford."

She couldn't place him, but she really didn't know them by name. Every once in a while, she'd see paramedics upstairs with an emergency patient, but they were usually too busy for small talk or introductions. By this time, he had come quite close and she could see his face. He was part black and good-looking. His gloved hands were spread out flat in front of him to show he meant no harm. She had a momentary pang.

"What are you doing here, King?"

"Waiting for you."

Waiting for her? "Why?"

"I . . . I wanted to talk to you. And then, when it really started to snow hard, I figured you probably could use a ride home."

"Talk to me? About what?" He was a *very* good-looking

boy, tall and strong. And worried. Or something. His face was
tense and somber. "Talk to me. Go ahead. I'm listening."

He licked his lips. "Dr. Romano." He paused, drew in a
breath. Blew it out noisily. "Dr. Romano . . ." he began again.
"Dr. Romano . . ." And then he blurted it out. "I'm your
son."

16

End of December

Delivery room two was buzzing with activity at three-thirty in the afternoon. A bed, propelled by two nurses, had just rolled in; Deedra Strong, in her green scrubs, her mask, gloves, and booties, followed it. The woman on the bed, in the last throes of labor, was demanding painkiller at the top of her voice.

Also there were Dr. Toni Romano; a pediatric resident named Iris Rothman; and obstetrical nurse Lorraine D'Angelo. Dee bent over her patient; the baby's head was crowning.

"Dr. Strong, you gotta gimme something! I'm dying!"

"No time, Yolanda, sorry. The baby's almost here." This was going to be an easy birth. Good. She'd already delivered four babies since she came on duty, one of them from high-risk room two. The mother was Rh negative, and she had come in with her ankles swollen to twice their normal size, a bad sign. It was a boy, and he was now in an isolette, waiting to be taken to the neonatal ICU so they could keep an eye on him.

He was doing fine, but his mother and father were terrified. This was their first son, and because they were Turkish, a male was of premier importance. She hated that whole way of thinking, but so many of her patients felt that way: Asians, Hispanics, Orthodox Jews . . . almost everyone in the world, it seemed, preferred boys. Often she wanted to say, "If males are the only valuable human beings, then how can you put your life into *my* hands?" Of course, she never did.

"Push, Yolanda, come on, help us," the nurse said. But Yolanda would not push and would not help. Yolanda did not give a flying fuck. Dee wasn't surprised. She made all the first evaluations for every patient up here, private and public. She knew that Yolanda hadn't even come in for prenatal care until the ninth month, and that almost every piece of advice was greeted with a shrug. She just didn't care. Maybe after it was born . . .

Yolanda now screamed, and the baby's head came out into Dee's waiting hands. She bent and quickly suctioned out the nose and mouth. Another cry from Yolanda, and the shoulders emerged; then, in a matter of seconds, the baby was born and was already wailing.

Dee handed the infant over to Dr. Rothman, who said, "You have a fine baby boy, Ms. David." Yolanda turned her head away from the doctor's voice, saying nothing. Iris Rothman exchanged a look with Dee, who then glanced over at Dr. Toni. They were all thinking the same thing, she knew it. What should be the most exciting moment in a woman's life was an empty one for this girl.

Dr. Rothman put the baby under the warming lights and examined him. "Perfect," she said in a few minutes. Again, no response from the mother. The pediatrician wrapped him in a cotton swaddling blanket and laid him on his mother's belly.

"Take it away," Yolanda said. "Take it away."

Dee longed to shake the woman until her teeth rattled. But that would hardly be professional. She picked up the baby and gave him a kiss on his forehead. Poor little unwanted thing. He was going to have enough trouble in life; he obviously had a white father. Mixed kids were mixed-up kids. But at least he could have a decent mother; then he might have a chance!

Now Toni tried. She took the infant and hunkered down, so that the tiny bundle was at Yolanda's eye level. "Just *look* at him, Yolanda," she pleaded. "He's your son. He's beautiful. At least give him a name."

Yolanda stared stubbornly at the ceiling, her mouth set. Toni sighed, straightened, and handed him to one of the nurses. "I think she'll be sorry one day," she said in a weary voice.

"Not this one," Dee said, once they were outside the delivery room. "This one doesn't care." She stripped off her gloves and mask and, turning to Toni, exploded. "You know what's going to happen. She'll disappear some time today or tomorrow, and we'll never see *her* again! Instead, we'll have another sad little boarder baby! He'll probably end up being shoved from one foster home to another, never feeling loved, never feeling security. Another black baby doomed to a life that leads to prison, the streets, or death!'' She stopped, breathing hard.

Then, again, she stormed, "What is the matter with these women! It makes me ashamed to be black! One step forward, three steps backward! What do we think we're doing up there in the Women's Health Center, anyway? Are we going to help even one of them? Are they *ever* going to learn? Would you like to guess the odds?

"You know what the big problem is? 'She's Gotta Have It!' That's the problem! If I see one more patient who kinda grins and tells me she just can't *do* without a man, I'm going to commit murder!''

Toni put her hand on Dee's shoulder. "Race isn't the issue, Dee. The issue is poverty, and what it does to people—black, white, red, or green. It robs them of hope; it takes away their future. If we persevere, they'll learn. Already, we're making a difference—''

Dee put a hand out, and gave Toni a wry smile. "Don't worry. It's okay. It just burns me, that's all.'' She sighed. "And I'm tired.''

A nurse stuck her head into the room. "Dr. Strong, Mrs. Chen is ready to go!''

Dee immediately perked up. "I'm outa here!'' She disappeared to scrub.

And I'm outa here, too, Toni thought. She went to her office, gathered her gear, took her messages—all on automatic pilot. What was spinning around in her brain was a plan. If Yolanda David *was* going to disappear herself and leave her little boy here, it needn't be a total tragedy. Alice could take him. Would she? Could she accept a child not of her body? Latinos could feel very strongly about that. Except that Joe was open-minded. It seemed to her that he tried to talk about adoption one day in her office . . . what had happened? How did the subject get dropped? She couldn't remember.

Yolanda's baby was a beautiful, healthy boy. Of course, Alice had to go through the whole bereavement process. Toni would have to convince Alice that the baby needed *her*, not the other way around. And the beauty of that approach was, it was absolutely true.

She had it all planned out in her head and was feeling pretty good about it by the time she got into a cab in front of the hospital. And she was still thinking about it when she got out at the center.

As always, she looked first through the big plate-glass window to see what was going on before she walked in. What she saw made her smile. The Orchids were here in full force today—seven black and Hispanic girls aged eleven to eighteen—all of them proudly wearing their lavender sweats, the shirts imprinted with a big purple orchid, the name in flowing script underneath.

Funny, that it had been Ham Pierce's idea to call the different groups clubs. He had been doing a story on 122nd Street—"The Block That Will Not Die," a whole series of vignettes showing the renovations of the buildings and the determination of the people to bring their block back to life—so naturally he dropped into the center whenever he was around, trying to talk her into letting him interview the girls. No matter how many times she refused, he refused to give up.

Of course, he tried to ingratiate himself by bringing in pizzas or bunches of flowers, and once, a case of soda which she insisted he take away. "I'm trying to teach these young women how to eat right!" she told him. So he left with it and came back with a case of apple juice. The girls thought he was Santa Claus; half of them had crushes on him. But Toni was determined not to let him use her girls.

He hung out at the center, anyway, while he was doing the 122nd Street saga. And one day, he drifted over to her and said, "When I was a kid, we loved being members of a gang, any kind of gang, good, bad, indifferent, sports, church, you name it. And you wanna know why? Because of the club jacket, the club shirt, the club hat, the club insignia. It proved you belonged, you were In, you were Somebody."

"You think it would work here?"

"Why not?"

"Aren't gangs always boys?"

He began to laugh. "Oh, Dr. Romano, for shame! A feminist like you, thinking that way. Hey, what if they were? This is the 1990s! Women are as good as men, right?"

She gave him a look, but she had to admit to him that she liked the idea. And when she broached it with the girls, they loved it. So now there were four clubs: the Orchids, formerly Monday's sex education group; the Lilies, formerly Tuesday's

Prenatal group; the Passion Flowers, formerly the young unmarried mothers' group; and the Gladiolas (the girls loved that Toni called the flowers 'glads'; they thought it was very cute), formerly Thursday's sex education group.

Of course, there had been zip in the budget for club "uniforms." Forget jackets; the simplest one cost sixty dollars, and that was without any insignia at all. Forget anything; when she asked Eliot what he thought of the idea, he said, "Are you really suggesting that this is something your department should spend *money* on?" So she knew it was counterproductive to even speak to her department chief. She bought the sweats with her own money. The girls didn't have to know. Nobody knew.

Or so she thought, until one noon, Ham materialized by the side of her table in the cafeteria and stuck a check under her plate. "No reason you should have to foot the bill. You're already doing enough for them." The check was written to her, and it was for a lot of money. She gave it back to him; he put it back under her plate; she gave it back; and he put it back again.

"You can't buy your way into my good graces, Mr. Pierce. The answer is still 'No.' No interviews in my health center."

"You think I'm doing this so you'll let me have a story? You really think that?"

She was flustered. The truth was, she didn't know what to think. But she said "Yes!" in a very sure tone.

He bent down so his face was very close to hers, and he whispered, "You're wrong, Dr. Toni. I'm not trying to buy my way into your good graces for a story. I'm trying to buy my way into your good graces for . . . more personal reasons."

Alarmed, she felt the blush rising in her face. To cover up, she took his check and ripped it into little pieces. His face, so close to hers, immediately froze, and with an intake of breath, he straightened up and walked away. For a moment, she thought she would call him back, but then she asked herself why. It would only encourage him. Nonetheless, she felt she had behaved badly.

There were moments, she thought now, going in the front door of the center, when she wished she hadn't torn up that check. There was never enough money, never, not when the patients were all so needy. What was wrong with her, anyway? Pierce had done an awful lot of good around here—except for his damned interviews! He wasn't such a bad guy, and he did his damnedest to help people.

As soon as she was inside the door, the Orchids rose up, en masse, and clustered around her, all of them trying to talk at once. While fielding their questions and giving hugs, she managed to look around to see how things were going. Charmaine was at the reception desk. Good. She was delighted with the way Charmaine was coming along. She answered the phone, handed out vitamins, kept the girls in a cohesive group, ran errands, went shopping, made sure the center had enough soap, toilet paper, and paper cups—made herself useful in all kinds of ways.

Charmaine was a natural, so quick to catch on. Toni didn't have to explain birth control more than once; she chose the Pill, saying, "That way, no man can sweet-talk me out of it."

Toni gave her a wave and a smile. She came almost every day after school, to help out—"to set the sisters straight," she liked to say. She mingled with the patients, the unofficial welcomer, often giving pep talks.

She was a great help, with her ever-present smile and her unflappable good humor. It had occurred to Toni more than once—as it did now—that when school was out, she'd love to hire Charmaine, at least part-time. It would reinforce her hard-won self-esteem.

But there was no room in the budget for that, not even that. And Toni knew better than to ask El Presidente for it. He had no idea what went on up here; he'd never even come to look at her center! He was so proud of his reputation, as the president who had been to every nook and cranny of Harmony Hill, from the boiler room to the laundry to medical records to the computer center. Oh yeah, his eye was on the sparrow . . . but not on the Women's Health Center! He said he trusted her completely, he didn't *have* to check up on something she was running, but that wasn't the point. Oh hell, if she wanted to give Charmaine a job, she'd have to pay for it herself. And she would.

Wasn't King smart to bring Charmaine here! Yes, he was. The more she saw of him, the better he looked to her. He was smart and perceptive and caring. Well, he was her boy. There was something to the theory of genetic transmission of character traits! She really loved him; she really did. Every time she thought about him, she got the sweet feeling of a delicious secret. And she wished it didn't have to be a secret; he was such a lovely young man. Eliot was sure to like him . . . well, maybe not, but he could certainly *try*. Of course, he couldn't try if he didn't know, and he couldn't know until she got up the guts to tell him.

The phone rang, and Charmaine picked it up, answering with her musical, "Women's Health, how can I help you?" She put her hand over the mouthpiece and motioned to Toni. As Toni took the phone, Charmaine got up to hand out the vitamins, and added, "It's a man."

Toni stood a moment by the desk, holding the receiver away from her. She'd have to remind Charmaine again to always ask who was calling. She hated being unprepared.

"Yes!" she barked into the phone.

"Hi, sweetheart. Am I interrupting? Not that I have to ask; I'm always interrupting, when you're up there."

Eliot? At this hour? And calling her *sweetheart*? "No, I have a minute or two."

"Good. Then let's discuss the DeMayo party. It's tonight, in case you've forgotten, and I'm sure you have."

"Roseanne DeMayo is a bore when she's sober and a horror when she's drinking."

"You promised."

Shit. So she had. She was too damn tired to argue anymore, too damn busy. Why couldn't he stop pressing her? That was stupid; because he was a man, that was why. And then, sitting there, running her fingers through her hair, trying to figure very quickly what she should do about tonight's party—be good and go, or be comfortable and beg off—she saw a familiar figure walking by the center.

Alice Rodriguez! God, she looked *awful*! She'd been trying to get Alice on the phone for days now. She'd left dozens of messages. No answer. She must talk to her. Joe was so worried about her. "Dr. Toni, I never see her eat, I swear." She hadn't been in good shape since the baby's funeral, drifting around like a ghost, crying constantly, seemingly unable to hear anyone.

She had to catch her. "Eliot, gotta go! Emergency. Alice just walked by."

She didn't wait for his answer, just hung up and ran out. In the busy street, she looked up the block. Alice had disappeared. She must have gone around the far corner . . . or into one of the stores. Or maybe, it *wasn't* Alice she saw? But you couldn't mistake those bowed shoulders, that madonnalike hairdo. She knew Alice Rodriguez when she saw her!

She first ran around the corner. No Alice. Then she ran back, peering into the dim interior of each business: the laundromat, the beauty shop, the bodega, even OTB. But that was crazy; Alice was not going to be betting on horses!

Finally, she had to give up. She had patients to see, a lecture on birth control to give. And she was out of breath. And she was freezing to death, running around like a lunatic without her coat. She wished she had been faster. She wished she had found Alice. She wished she didn't always have to do it all herself. Damn. She wished Ham Pierce was here. He always seemed to know how to find people. He always seemed to know what to do.

When she let herself back into the warmth of the center, Charmaine told her that a lady had just called, ''and she didn't sound so good.''

''Did you write down her name?''

''I don't have to write down names. I got a good memory. Alice Rodriguez.''

''Oh, shit! Sorry, Charmaine, but I was just outside chasing after her. Did she say where she was calling from?''

''Nope. Just 'tell Dr. Toni that Alice Rodriguez called.' And then she hung up. I didn't get a chance to ask her anything. I'm sorry.''

''Not your fault, not your fault.'' Whose fault? she wondered; then she shook off the thought. Alice needed attention, but what she needed would take a sizable block of time. She'd call Alice later, she decided. No. Tomorrow. She *had* to go to that theater party with Eliot tonight. Her marriage needed some attention, too. Alice would just have to wait; tomorrow would be soon enough.

17

January

Janet Rafferty sat at the desk in her cheerful office, with its yellow walls, its windowsill full of plants, and its bright posters from the Metropolitan Museum. But she looked at none of them; instead, she stared out the window at nothing. It was dark outside, and she was up on the eighth floor; there was nothing to see. She had been waiting over an hour for Eliot to call—he'd said Wednesday—but the phone stood stubbornly mute. She was damned if she was ever going to call him again. Not this lady! She looked at her wristwatch: seven-fifteen. Seven-fucking-fifteen. Obviously he wasn't *going* to call her. The bastard! He could go to hell!

She banged her fists on the desk, completely frustrated. Now what was she going to do with the long, cold evening ahead? Damn him! She knew what she needed. She needed a drink. Ice-cold Finlandia vodka on the rocks, a big, beautiful glass, tinkling as you lifted it, with perfect little drops running down the side, making crystal tracks in the frost. She took a deep breath, imagining the taste of it, the bite at the back of her tongue, the easing at the back of her mind.

She pushed herself up from the chair. Oh God, she had to stop thinking this way. After all her years with AA, after all her struggles, she *couldn't*! Biting her lips, she marched back and forth in front of the desk. She could call Nancy. But no. She'd call Eliot; he was probably still in his office. She'd call him and turn him on, and she'd get laid. An hour of sex, an hour of oblivion, that would get her through this.

But why the hell should she call him, when he obviously considered her nothing but a convenience! It was beginning to piss her off. When they were in bed, he was so romantic, so intent, he couldn't get enough of her; he'd kiss her all over and tell her how much he needed her, how good he felt with her. And then, he'd leave and forget about it! She was beginning to think that all thoughts of her went totally out of his mind the minute he put his foot outside her door. He never called just to talk, only to make arrangements for them to go to bed.

He was always so eager when he was with her, he acted like a man in love, he *must* be in love with her. But she was getting tired of waiting. A couple of weekends ago—actually the week before Christmas—his wife went away to a gynecology meeting in Seattle. He never even mentioned it, never tried to spend extra time with her. Just Friday evening. That was it. And she had been so pleased about that Friday date; it was the first time she'd ever seen him on a weekend night. She'd thought this was the beginning of a new phase.

God, it was depressing. And how about New Year's Eve? She hadn't had a real date for New Year's Eve in so long, she couldn't even remember! Not since Jim died! No fancy dress, no dancing, no champagne, no kissing at midnight, not for Janet Rafferty! No, she was in her mother's cramped split-level in Yorktown Heights, sipping ginger ale with her mom and dad and her kids.

It was nice to see them, of course it was. She loved her boys. She only wished she could have them with her all the time. But they needed a stable home, with a man in it. They loved it up there; they had a big yard to play in, and lots of little friends on the block, and she didn't have to worry about them. She hated their living apart, but that's how it was.

When Jim was killed, it felt like the end of her life. She couldn't stop crying, she couldn't see anything ahead of her but blackness. She started drinking just to get through the day. And then, one horrible day, she woke up in a hospital bed, with no memory of how she had got there, or even what day it was.

Somehow, in the midst of her bender, she had called her parents to come get the boys. And they had come alone to see her in the hospital. They said her children were not safe with her, not while she was drinking. She had to agree. And she had to face the fact: she was an alcoholic.

She lay in her hospital bed, weeping for her lost life, her lost self. And then a nurse came in one afternoon. "Your parents gave me your room number," she said. "I'm here to help you. My name is Nancy, and I'm an alcoholic."

She was stunned. This vibrant, cheerful woman, who seemed so together—an alcoholic? Yes, she was, but she had been sober for six years. She was a member of AA, a Twelve Stepper, someone who intervened to help alcoholics in crisis.

And that was the end of her drinking days. God, but right now, she wished it hadn't been. She could use a drink, really use it. She could call Nancy; Nancy was her sponsor and would talk with her as long as she needed. But no. She didn't need that anymore. I am strong, she whispered to herself. I am sober. One day at a time, she reminded herself fiercely, one day at a time. And this day was nearly over.

There was a loud and hurried knocking on her office door. It was Phyllis Kraven, one of the night nurses in the neonatal ICU. Phyllis was out of breath, her face bright pink.

"Am I glad you're here! What a mess. Come on, we need you!"

They were both heading out the door.

"What?"

"Alice Rodriguez."

"Oh Lord! Again?"

Alice had been inconsolable since Steven's funeral. Janet didn't understand it. Alice herself had decided that Steven's heart and liver and kidneys should go to the sick babies who needed them. "That way," she had said, "Steven will never really die." And then, a few days after the funeral, suddenly she reappeared in the nursery in the middle of the night, looking wild, wearing a trenchcoat over her nightgown, demanding her baby. When she was reminded that Steven wasn't there anymore, she just stood, screaming, until they got her sister to come to get her.

Janet and the nurse took the stairs down the two flights.

"She's really flipped. Remember when she thought we were *hiding* her baby? Well, now she's screaming that we've murdered him. She was running up and down the hallway, accusing everyone she saw. We lured her into the scrub room. When I called you, your line was busy—"

Her line busy? Maybe Eliot *had* been trying to call her, after all. "Shit!"

"Exactly!" Phyllis said fervently.

They pushed open the door to the sixth floor, and immediately Janet could hear the commotion. It sounded like a dozen people, all yelling at one another. She broke into a run, sorry she had worn high heels to work this morning—high heels for her date.

Two orderlies were guarding the door to the ICU. One of them recognized her and stepped aside. Inside, it was bedlam. Everyone trying to tell everyone else what to do. Every baby in the place was wailing. Three nurses were holding Alice still, or at least were trying to. She wriggled and struggled and kicked, shrieking at the six or seven people surrounding her. "Get away from me! Get away from me! I want my baby! I'm his *mother*; you can't keep him from me!"

Alice looked horrible. She had put on jeans and a thin T-shirt and leather jacket—for January! Her hair was hanging loose halfway down her back; it looked as if it hadn't seen a brush for a week. Her eyes were feral.

Janet pushed her way through everyone and stood directly in front of Alice, trying to look her in the eye. But Alice was incapable of seeing anything or anyone. "My baby! My Steven! Let me have my baby! Call the police!"

One of the nurses said, "If you don't calm down, Alice, that's exactly what we're going to do."

"She can't hear you; don't waste your breath," Janet said. Stepping close to the agitated young woman, she grasped her upper arms firmly. "Alice!" she said loudly. "You're very angry!"

Alice stopped her struggling. "Yes, I am. I'm mad as hell!"

"You miss your baby!"

"My baby!" she whimpered. "Give me my baby!" The struggles began again.

"Alice, your baby is with Jesus!"

"No, he's in there. I saw him! He's there. Honest." She was trying so hard to be reasonable. "I saw him. In the bassinet. I just want to take him home!" Tears began to leak from the corners of her eyes.

"It's the McCreedy baby. A little girl," one of the nurses said dryly; then she grunted as Alice poked her in the ribs with an elbow. "You little—!"

"All right, all right, let's settle down."

Janet turned, surprised and pleased to see Toni Romano striding in the door.

"Alice!" Toni called, as if she had come for a cup of tea. "How are you? I've been calling you and calling you."

"Dr. Toni, make them give me my baby!"

"Alice, dear . . ." Her voice softened, as did her expression. "You know nobody can bring Steven back to you."

To Janet's surprise, Alice's face crumpled . . . her whole body seemed to cave in . . . and she began to cry, loudly, her mouth wide open, like a small child. Toni held out her arms, and Alice walked into them without argument. Toni turned and said to Janet, "Come with us, will you? I could use your help."

Alice gave up the fight and allowed herself to be led into the elevator and taken downstairs into the lobby, sobbing quietly the whole time. Each of them had one of her hands, and she held on with fierce strength. When they came into the lobby and she let go of Janet's hand, it tingled.

The lobby was very quiet. Toni picked a couch in the far corner, motioning to Janet that she should sit on Alice's other side. "Now, Alice, you know that Ms. Rafferty and I are here to help you."

A nod.

"Alice, dear, you know that little Steven is gone."

"No—" But it wasn't shouted, this time, it was hesitant.

"Yes, Alice. Remember the beautiful mass in the church? The white roses? All those white roses. You said Steven would be looking down and loving all those beautiful flowers. Remember?"

Another nod, more tears, sniffling. But no more frenzy. It was amazing, Janet thought, how suddenly it had all changed. She had been certain they'd have to either call security or admit Alice into the psychiatric unit. And now look at her: as peaceful as a lamb, miserably unhappy but no longer ready to kill.

"That little baby in the bassinet, Alice. That little baby is a girl, a little black girl. You must not have looked too carefully."

Alice nodded. "I forgot. I forgot that Steven—"

"Shhh, no need to talk about it if it makes you unhappy . . ." Toni's arm was tightly around Alice's shoulders, and now Alice turned and buried her head in Toni's bosom. Over her head, Toni said to Janet, "Why don't you call Alice's mother. Somebody from the family should come to get her."

"She's been staying with her sister. I'll call her."

When Janet came back from the telephone, yet another transformation had taken place. Alice was sitting up, dabbing at her face with a handkerchief, while Toni braided her long tangled hair. Alice was actually smiling; still, something about her was not quite right. She looked pleasant enough, but . . . vacant, somehow.

They had to wait only ten minutes before Alice's brother-in-law came to collect her, apologizing profusely for all the trouble. "I don't know how this happen! We watch her, the whole family watch her. But my wife, she went to the baby and boom! Alice is gone. I don't know!" He shook his head. "Look how she goes out! Twenty-two degrees, and look how she goes out!" Still clucking and shaking his head, he took Alice by the arm, and she went with him, completely subdued, not even turning for a good-bye.

In the sudden release from tension, Janet realized how tightly she had been holding herself together. It had really gotten to her, seeing Alice in that condition. She had deteriorated so badly!

"She needs some therapy, and quick," she said, sitting down heavily next to Toni. "And so do I!"

They laughed. "I'm awfully glad you were here, Janet. She's like a powder keg; you don't know what's going to set her off."

"Well, you handled her beautifully. She calmed right down."

"Yeah, well, sometimes it works."

"Don't put yourself down, Toni. You were terrific."

"Thanks." She yawned and stretched. "God, it really takes it out of you, doesn't it? You know what we need? We need a good stiff drink."

Janet smiled a little. "Maybe *you* do, Toni, but a drink is exactly what I don't need." Toni raised one eyebrow in question. "I'm a recovering alcoholic."

"I'm surprised."

"Really? Why?"

"I know I shouldn't be. But . . . I don't . . . you don't seem the type."

"Not the type. Well, I didn't think so either. Jim and I—my late husband—Jim and I did a lot of social drinking. We'd get looped together. You know, sometimes I'd wake up in the morning, knowing we had made love, but not able to remember a single detail."

"Mmmm. . . ?"

"Of course, we didn't think it was a problem. We went to

work, we went to church, we were good citizens.'' She laughed briefly. ''After Jim died . . . in a fire . . . I fell apart. I drank and I slept around. A couple of times I woke up in bed with a guy I couldn't even remember meeting. But it wasn't *really* a problem. Hey, I went to work every day, cooked dinner for my kids—'' She stopped. ''Sorry. This is boring. So, no drink; but I'm up for a cup of coffee. If we can find a place.''

As soon as she suggested it, she realized how badly she wanted company this evening. She and Toni were feeling close, and she could see that neither of them was ready to disconnect, not yet. But, this was crazy! She'd just been agonizing, waiting for this woman's husband to call her, to come to her apartment, to fuck her brains out! And here she sat, confessing to her!

They ended up in Toni's office, of all the damn places. It was a cute little room, with a coffeepot and two mugs and even a box of Fig Newtons—''My favorite since the age of four,'' Toni said with a laugh; and Janet said, ''Mine, too!'' though it wasn't really true. Yes, a nice little office, but she realized, as she looked around, it was crammed with reminders that she was an intruder here, the *Other Woman*.

One wall was covered with photos of Toni and Eliot together. Toni and Eliot on the beach; Toni and Eliot in Paris; Toni and Eliot in wedding regalia; Toni and Eliot and the rest of the Wolfes, all in evening clothes, all grinning at the camera.

She looked away from the pictures. They were making her so damn miserable. She was never going to get him! She was just an easy lay! How come other people got to have lives filled with happiness and success and comfort, while she had to struggle with alcoholism and depression and a growing feeling that her entire life was a waste? It wasn't fair! It just wasn't fair! She blinked away tears, hoping to hell that Toni wouldn't notice, and quickly turned to look at something else, anything else. There was the usual wall of diplomas and honors. And damned if that wasn't a nursing school diploma! Oh, it couldn't be. She walked over to look at it carefully. And it was. Antonia Romano had graduated John Quincy Adams Nursing School in Washington, D.C.

''You were a nurse?''

''Until Eliot sent me to medical school.''

Christ. Oh Christ. She'd never be able to fight all of *this*! He had sent her to medical school. Then he married her. Now they were doctors together, husband and wife. He'd never leave Toni, never, never, never.

"Those were the good old days," Toni added dryly. Janet could hear the sound of the mugs being set down on the desk. She turned to discover a funny look on Toni's face. Janet made a noncommittal sound. Toni gestured for her to sit in one of the chairs as she took a sip of coffee. She made a face. "Terrible. But better than the cafeteria's." There was a moment of silence, and then she said, "It's not easy for Eliot, being married to me. I'm not good wife material. My work has always been just too important."

"You don't have children, that's why."

Toni paused, took another sip. "Actually . . ." she said, looking away. Then she looked back, directly into Janet's eyes, and said, "This is a secret." Janet nodded, eager to hear what was coming next.

"I did have a child. A long time ago. I was in nursing school, and I put him up for adoption." She put her cup down and wrapped her arms tightly around herself. Then she smiled a dazzling smile that made her almost beautiful. "He's just found me. My baby found me. Nobody else knows, not yet. He's wonderful. He's handsome and bright, a lovely boy.

"I never saw him, you know. In those days, if you were giving up your baby, they didn't let you. I understand why; they didn't want any last-minute hysterics . . . most of us were so terribly young. God! When I think of it . . . I did pray, though, that somebody really wonderful would take him. And then I pushed the whole thing way into the back of my mind, where I didn't ever have to look at it. But I always wondered, of course, and worried, and my dreams—!"

Janet wanted to say, I've had to give up my sons, too. But she thought better of it. It was the same, sort of. But it was different. Instead, she said, "How wonderful that you have him now."

"Yes. Yes. I'm so thrilled, it surprises me. He never stopped wondering about *me*, either." She sat for a moment, then shook her head impatiently and in an entirely different tone, said, "Here I go again, breaking my promises! Eliot is supposed to have his wife with him at all these hospital functions . . . don't ask me why. I don't really see what I have to do with it. But apparently it's a rule. Where the king is, there his consort must be, by his side. Eliot always says he *needs* me; you know men!

I hardly ever go to these things, but I know it's not fair of me.''
She glanced at the clock on the wall. ''It's only half over; I can
get there in time for the Viennese table.'' She rolled her eyes
dramatically and laughed.

They walked out together, still companionable, still chatting.
But inside, Janet felt that old, familiar pain. She hoped she was
keeping a smile on her face. She guessed she was because Toni
never asked her if anything was the matter, not at all. When the
elevator came and Janet said she needed to get some papers from
her office, Toni gave her a big grin and said, ''I've been missing
my women friends. Let's do this again.''

''I'd love that,'' Janet said. The doors wheezed open, disgorging a mass of visitors with baby presents and flowers and
books. Everyone in the world had a family, everyone in the
world had *someone*. Janet turned, hurrying up the stairs to her
office, fighting back tears.

In her office, she slammed the door shut and leaned against
it, letting herself weep. She had been sitting around half the day,
waiting for him to call her! And the whole time, he'd already
had plans! For a party! With his wife, of course! Of course, with
his wife! *What made me think I had a chance? He doesn't know
I exist!*

What had happened to her life, what had happened to all the
promise it had once held? What had happened to *her*?

She suddenly made up her mind. She was finished fighting
and struggling and conniving and always losing. No more! Never
again.

She knew exactly where to go. Brenda, the nursing office
secretary, kept a whole bunch of them in her file cabinet. She
had joked about it: ''Under *B* for booze!''

Janet went to the letter *B* in the file drawer, looked down, and
drew in a sharp breath. She was smiling. There were twenty or
thirty little bottles in the drawer, the kind they sold you on the
airplane, all different kinds: gin, vodka, brandy, Scotch, everything! She reached down, scrabbling in the pile, searching for
vodka. Two, three, and there were two more, over in the corner.
So many! Brenda would never miss just a few!

18

February

The ambulance went screaming and hooting around the corner of Brockman Place onto Broadway, heading downtown. King looked at the woman lying on the stretcher. He knew her; they'd had her in the bus at least twice before. She was a celeb, a famous old movie star, he kept forgetting her name. And then it came back to him: Irene Moore. There was nothing really wrong with her; there never was. She was always throwing fits and making herself faint. Probably took a lot of pills and then drank on top of it, probably didn't eat enough.

Of course, this time she wasn't talking, for a change. She was either out cold, or pretending—probably pretending. He was right; her eyelids fluttered open, and then a slow flirtatious smile spread across her face.

"The dark angel!" she said in her husky voice. "I was hoping I'd get you. Has anyone ever told you you should be in the movies?" She laughed.

"Hello, Miss Moore."

She opened her eyes wide. "He remembers me. How sweet. But the last time, you held my hand."

"Last time, you were real sick, remember?" And anyway, last time, he didn't hold her hand, she had grabbed his and held on like she was drowning.

"Oh, it would make me feel so much better. . . ."

These old babes! He had to admit she looked good for her age. The word was, she went into the hospital once or twice a year, just to keep everything in place. She'd had a breast job and a hip job and a tushie job and a thigh job and a nose job and a face-lift—at *least* one, Michael had said, maybe two.

"I just went all woozy, and the next thing I knew, you were bending over me. They couldn't find Sam . . . my escort, my gentleman friend. He has a way of wandering off. I hope somebody tells him what happened to me. Did they tell *you* what happened?"

He couldn't repeat what had been said. So he lied. "It was pretty warm in there—"

She laughed. "You mean they didn't tell you I'd had too much to drink? I can't believe that!"

"Well, as a matter of fact . . ." he said, feeling uncomfortable. She smiled at him and squeezed his hand and said, "You're sweet," and closed her eyes again. "I'm feeling *much* better already."

Of course she was; there was nothing wrong with her to begin with. Her blood pressure was fine, her pulse was fine, everything was okay. "If you like, we could send you home in a taxi."

"No, no! Take me to the hospital!"

"Sure thing. Why don't you just close your eyes now and relax?"

To his surprise, she obeyed. He didn't want to deal with her anymore. She wasn't sick. She was famous, so she thought the whole world had to pay attention to her. They could be missing a good job while they schlepped her into the E.R. What a waste of their time!

Well, anyway, there was talk they'd soon have two more ambulances at Harmony Hill. He'd seen Dr. Wolfe on television, saying straight out that their area needed more paramedics and more emergency vehicles. Right on! Finally, a hospital president who had some sympathy for poor people. He'd never met him, but they were related, kind of. Dr. Wolfe was married to . . . *her*. His birth mother.

His birth mother. God, it was weird to say that, after all those years of wondering: what was she like, what did she look like, what would she do or say if he turned up on her doorstep, would she even *like* him? Nobody knew but them; they had agreed it had to be a secret, for a while.

He'd never forget walking toward her that night, sweating bullets and sick to his stomach. What if it wasn't really her? But it was, he *knew* it was. On the birth certificate, it had her name: Antonia Romano.

Mom had always told him his birth mother was a nurse. Once

he got into his head that he wanted to find her, that's where he started. He couldn't find her on the Nurses' Register, or in the New York phone books. So he figured she wasn't in New York. She had probably got married a long time ago and had a different name . . . maybe even kids. Sure she did. Christ, what was he doing, anyway, looking for her? She probably didn't want to see him. If she'd wanted to, wouldn't she have come looking for *him*?

Then one night he went out for some takeout Chinese and on his way home, he bought himself *Sports Illustrated, People*, and then, just for the hell of it because they had doctors on the cover and he was always interested in medical stuff, a copy of *Gotham*. He leafed through it while he waited for the light to change.

Jesus! The name leaped out off the page. It felt like someone had punched him. The light changed back to red and back to green and back to red again, and he couldn't move.

It had to be her. It had to be. Dr. Antonia Romano . . . who figured her for a doctor? Yeah, and there in the story, it said she had been a nurse! He scanned the article quickly. She was married, and of all the goddamn things, she was married to the president of Harmony Hill! And Christ, *she* worked there, too! He thought his heart was just going to stop, just stop dead, right on the corner of Broadway and 92nd Street. Some old Jewish guy even stopped and asked him was he okay.

He picked up the phone a hundred times after one of the nurses gave him Dr. Wolfe's number. He thought about going to her office in the hospital, or to that center she ran uptown. In the end, he didn't have the balls to do anything until one night, after he'd had a couple of beers, suddenly it seemed like a terrific idea to just go over to her Women's Health Center and get it over with.

He knew it was her when she locked up. He expected her to walk toward him, and when she didn't, he started to walk after her. It wasn't until she turned to go in the opposite direction that he said to himself, Shit, she thinks I'm a mugger or something. So he called out to her. He wanted to run away, but he couldn't. It was too late.

When he told her he was her son, she didn't do any of the things he had imagined. She didn't faint; she didn't scream or run away. She didn't say or do anything at all for a minute, and then she looked up at him, very serious, very calm, and said, "You look like your father."

He got such a chill down his spine. His father. Jesus, his father. He'd never thought about his birth *father*; that was pretty strange.

"My father," he managed to say. His voice was a little shaky, but then, so was hers. "Was he really a doctor?"

"He was really a doctor. How did you find me? Wait. Before we get into all that, tell me one thing: do you have wonderful parents? I made them promise to find you wonderful parents."

"They're great."

"I'm so glad." She made a little move toward him. Was she going to hug him? He didn't know if he wanted her to do that. But she stopped, and said, "Do you understand why I couldn't keep you? Did they tell you?"

"Because he was black? My . . . father?"

"Good God, no! I would have married him. But, unfortunately, he was already married. Two little kids. I was crazy about him; we were crazy about each other. I don't know if that makes you feel good, or not."

"I'm sorry I scared you, before. I should've written or called or something, but . . . well, tonight I finally had the courage."

"Don't be sorry. I'm glad you found me. I'm gladder than you can ever know. I've thought of you so often."

Anger rose up in his throat so quickly, he didn't know how it got there. He was having trouble swallowing. Thought of him so often! Then why in hell hadn't she ever looked for him? Why in hell had she given him away? He wanted to cry, he wanted to scream, he wanted to hit her. *Hit her!* His own mother! He had looked for her; he had hoped he would find her; he had fantasized that she would be happy to see him . . . and it was all happening, just like he'd imagined! Jesus, what was the matter with him?

"I've always wondered," he said. "If you didn't want to keep me, why didn't you get an abortion?"

She gave him a sad little smile. "In 1964, King . . . that's your name, right? King? Anyway, back then, abortion wasn't legal. And in any case, I was still in nursing school, and I had seen the results of botched abortions." She shuddered. "But I don't think I could have done it anyway. I was brought up Catholic. Your family—?"

"One Black, one Jewish."

Suddenly she smiled, and he couldn't help but smile back. Then they both began to cry at the same time. No loud sobs, just tears pouring down. And then she came over and put her arms around him, and he put his arms around her, and they stood like that for he couldn't tell how long.

Irene Moore was tugging at his hand. "And I want to see a doctor right away, and I'd prefer it to be Dr. Harrison—"

He interrupted her. "Sorry, Miss Moore. When we get there, which is in about two minutes, you'll be triaged, and they'll take care of you as soon as possible."

Just then, Michael called back. "Yo, King! On the police radio! Trouble at the Women's Health Center. Assault."

King's stomach took a sickening turn. It could be his m— Toni. Would she be there this late? Of course she could; it had been almost this late the night he went looking for her. "A woman?"

"Yes. A woman doctor. They're bringing her in."

"She all right?" King was astounded by the way his heart began to race. A couple of weeks ago, he didn't know who his mother was or even if she was still alive. And now, all of a sudden, he was terrified something had happened to her; he wanted to run and protect her.

"Don't know." The ambulance pulled up to the emergency entrance and stopped halfway up the drive. One of the other buses was already there. He could hardly wait to get Miss Moore inside and find out what was going on.

"Why are we stopping? Are we there?" Irene Moore sat right up. There was nothing wrong with her.

"We have to wait just a minute; another ambulance got here before us. As soon as it moves . . ."

Irene Moore immediately began to fuss over herself, pulling her dress, patting her hair, looking around for her belongings. "My rose! My rose! Didn't I bring it? I thought it was tucked in my bag!"

King looked down. What the hell—? He could understand it if she wanted her purse . . . but a *flower*?

"Sorry, Miss Moore. No rose."

"Oh, dear. And he managed to be at the front door when I got out of the limo. It was so sweet. You see, I have an admirer, a young man who follows me everywhere. I don't know how he

does it. Tonight, there he was at Tavern on the Green, holding
a perfect red rose, and as I approached, he handed it to me.''

He never had to comment, because then they got very busy
getting her admitted into the E.R.

The minute they walked in, King was looking for Toni, and
to his relief, there she was, talking to Dr. Chu, head of the E.R.
Toni looked mad as hell and strung out, but she was on her feet,
talking a mile a minute. Obviously, she wasn't the victim. He
asked one of the nurses, ''What happened at the Women's Center?''

''Rape.''

''Jesus Christ.''

''One of our own residents, too. Damn it, we go into those
crappy neighborhoods to help those people, and this is how they
repay us! I don't know if I can work at this hospital anymore.
I'm sick to my stomach all the time! I mean, King, you ought
to *see* her! Face full of bruises! God! Isn't it enough that they
rape us? Do they have to beat up on us, too?'' Her eyes filled.

King sat on the edge of the desk and put an arm around her
shoulder. She'd been in the E.R. as long as he'd been working
at Harmony Hill; maybe it was time she took a break. This job
could really get to some people. Not him; he loved it; he considered it a challenge. But some people took it too much to
heart. ''Hey, Debbie, take it easy. Maybe you should transfer
outa here?''

She looked up at him, startled. ''Hell, no! This is what I want
to do. But I'm allowed to *kvetch*, aren't I? *Bitch*, that means.''

''Hey, I know what it means. I'm only half a goy,'' he said.
That made her smile, so that was good. He patted her shoulder
a few times and then looked around for his mother. Toni. But
she was gone; and standing with Dr. Chu, notebook in hand,
was Hamilton Pierce.

Toni sat by the side of the hospital bed in cubicle B, looking at
Deedra Strong, holding one of Dee's hands with both of hers,
and feeling sick. Dee was her responsibility, and she hadn't been
able to protect her! She should never have let any of the young
women take the night shift. She wanted to cry, but she couldn't
do that here. She couldn't do that to Dee. It would reveal too
precisely just how dreadful she found the girl's appearance.

Dee's mouth was swollen, and there were blue marks just

beginning, made by fingers gripping tightly, on the sides of her face. She had complained that her left shoulder was throbbing. Jim Chu said it was probably sprained from being twisted behind her, although he couldn't be sure. She wouldn't tell him a goddamn thing, he told Toni, just shook her head and turned away from him.

She took one of Deedra's hands and said softly, "Dee. Will you talk to *me*?" Dee shrugged, and her eyes opened. She looked exceptionally calm, expressionless, really. Rape trauma syndrome, Toni thought. It often fooled the cops, the courts, the medical staff—even the family. The woman often was able to tell the whole horrible tale without a tear or a tremor, so that everyone assumed that nothing much had happened and she was perfectly all right. But sooner or later . . .

"We need to know what happened," Toni said, keeping her voice very quiet and calm.

Deedra took in a ragged breath but said nothing. She shook her head.

"Dee. Come on. You, of all people, you know how important it is to talk about it."

"He came up behind me. When I was closing up. His arm around my throat," she recited, looking up at the ceiling. "Made me open the door. Pushed me into the back and—" She stopped, swallowed noisily, and then went on, still in that mechanical way.

"In the back room. Where nobody could see. He . . . he . . . he . . ." She closed her eyes and clamped her lips together. "I was stupid. I was stupid! I should have known better!" Her eyes flew open, and she looked straight at Toni. "I did know better; I should have stayed inside until the car service came. And when I saw him—"

Saw him! But she had said he came up behind her! Toni hesitated, unable to decide whether Dee was just confused or— could it be?—lying for some reason.

Gently, she said, "I thought you never saw him. I thought he came up behind you."

There was a long silence. Then, Dee turned, wincing a little as she tried to prop herself up on one elbow. "I lied to the police, Dr. Toni."

"You what? But why?"

"I told them it was a stranger; I told them I couldn't see him, that it was dark in the back. . . . Not true. It was . . ."

"Go on, Dee. It was. . . ?"

"It was . . . someone I knew. A doctor. A doctor at Harmony Hill."

"Jesus, Mary, and Joseph! A doctor! *Who?*" It was all she could do not to shake the name out of Dee. *"Who?"*

Dee fell back onto the bed. Now tears oozed out of her eyes. "Please. I can't. I have to think."

"Think about *what*? A doctor rapes you, and you have to *think* about naming him? I want to know, Dee, and I want to know now!"

"I can't! I can't! He . . . he'll deny it!"

"Tough shit! He *hurt* you, Dee. Dee, listen to me, you've got to name him!"

"Nobody will believe me! Oh, God, I'm so ashamed!"

"You have nothing to be ashamed of! The bastard! No man has a right to force himself upon a woman, to use his cock as a weapon!"

A very small smile appeared on Dee's face. "I've given the same lecture. But now I know how it makes same feel. . . . So filthy, so violated!" She shuddered. "Ugh! I can't stand to think about it . . . the look on his face . . . ugh!"

"You've got to tell us." Toni's voice was shaking with her tension.

"I can't. He'll just deny it. What's my word against a doctor, who's the—" She stopped abruptly.

"Who's the . . . ?"

"I can't. He'll get me! My career will be over before it even starts!" She turned her head to look directly at Toni, and as she did so, her face crumpled and tears came pouring out of her eyes. "I didn't kick him, Dr. Toni, I didn't even scream! I didn't do *anything*! I froze! After all my training!"

"You didn't 'freeze,' Dee. You did what you had to do to protect yourself."

"I could've screamed."

"And it could've been the last thing you ever did. A man who's that desperate might do anything. None of this is your fault. You did nothing; *he* did it. For God's sake, don't make the victim guilty!" Toni leaned over and kissed her on the forehead. "You did what you had to do, Dee. Look. Enough. Betty will be here any minute. I'll be back to see you in a little while. But right now, I think you should try to rest.''

Like a child who's been given permission, Deedra closed her eyes, sighed deeply, and seemed to fall asleep.

Toni stayed by her side, still holding her hand, for a few minutes. Her mind was racing. It was *her* fault; she should never have let Dee take that night duty. It was too damned dangerous. She had *told* Eliot they needed better security up there. Not enough money in the budget! There wasn't enough money in the *world* to make up for this!

Gently, she loosened Dee's grip on her hand. Let her sleep. Feeling very goddamn tired and disgusted and discouraged and depressed and guilty and enraged, she tiptoed out.

Betty was coming toward her, her face ashen, her lips tight. What could she say to make her feel better. *Feel better!* What a concept; how could any woman feel anything but grief and pain under these circumstances!

"How is she? Did he . . . ?" Betty said. Her eyes were glittering with anger.

Toni nodded.

"I'll kill him! I swear, if I ever get ahold of him, I'll make sure he *can't* do this to another woman!"

"I feel the same."

"I want to see her!"

"Betty, she has a couple of bruises on her face. Apparently, when he put his hand over her mouth, he really held on. It's not bad," she quickly added as a spasm of pain crossed the other woman's face. "She's mostly upset, thinks she didn't do enough to save herself—"

"Women do blame themselves for every goddamn thing men do to them, don't they! But I thought I taught Deedra better than that!"

"I'm sure you did. Hell, Betty, she's counseled rape victims, herself. She knows how it is. But now she knows something new . . . unfortunately." A wave of guilt washed over her. "I blame myself."

"None of us is to blame, Dr. Toni. The man that did it, *he's* to blame. Oh Jesus—" Without another word, they fell into each others' arms, and at last, Toni let herself cry.

After a minute or two, she managed to say, "You should go to her." They pulled apart, two women sniffling and trying to be brave through their tears. She wanted to tell Betty that the rapist was a doctor at the hospital; she wanted to share her outrage and her anger. But she couldn't; Dee had to be the one.

It suddenly struck her, Dee was going to have to tell Eliot. He had to know. A doctor, maybe someone she worked with. Which one, though? Somebody pretty high up, Toni would guess, since Dee was so afraid of him. But who? It was horrible! He was a threat to every woman in the place!

She couldn't say anything, not now, not yet. She reached out and put a hand on Betty's shoulder. The other woman turned and went to cubicle B, pausing, head bowed. Then she took in a deep breath, squared her shoulders, and visibly made herself look calm. And then, she walked in.

Suddenly, to Toni's horror, a memory was there in front of her: her mother's face, twisted with her grief; her father's, tight with righteousness.

"You're no longer my daughter," he was snarling. "No daughter of mine gets knocked up! No daughter of mine is a goddamn whore!" And, like counterpoint, weaving around his ice-cold voice, her mother's entreaty: "Paulie, please, no, please Paulie, please don't. . . ." But her mother never stood up to him and said, "She's my child, too, and I say she doesn't leave." She just stood there, wringing her hands, helpless and ineffectual.

Toni shook off the recollection, like a bad dream, putting her mind back on the present. Let her talk to Jim Chu, if he wasn't too busy. It was a zoo tonight in the E.R. Every chair was taken, and there were people leaning against every wall. Lots of coughing, lots of moaning, children crying, babies wailing. One man, bearded and filthy, railed on and on in gibberish.

As she stood there, the team of women paramedics came in wheeling a gurney which held a man, his head wrapped in a turban of blood-soaked bandage. Probably another shooting, she guessed; it was a goddamn epidemic in this city. The waiting patients didn't even look up. By this time, they were dulled to the continual parade of horror; every one of them looked exhausted. And wasn't that Irene Moore, in a wheelchair over at the other side of the room, arguing with one of the nurses?

Toni went around the corner, looking for Jim. For a change, he was standing still. "God, is the whole world in here tonight?" she asked him.

"Could be!" He rolled his eyes. "It must be a full moon; every full moon, they go crazy."

"Jim! You can't believe that."

"I don't but, believe me, it happens every time. The nurses put in extra supplies every month when the moon's going to be full; they know. And it never fails."

"Where are the cops?"

"For Dee? Over there." He looked in the direction of two young, uniformed officers, one of them female, lounging against the coffee machine.

"At least he didn't beat her," Jim said.

"Yeah, he only bruised her and twisted her arm and scared her to death and gave her a nightmare she'll never forget." She felt the rage rise up in her throat again, but Jim looked so weary, so drained, she didn't have the heart to harangue him.

Instead, she patted him on his arm. "How you do this day after day, night after night, and still stay sane, I do not know."

"Who says I'm sane?" He grinned a tired grin. And then a nurse came up to him with a pile of X rays and they were gone, down the hall.

The big clock on the wall read ten thirty-four. She realized she was bone tired. Every muscle was aching, and behind her eyes was a burning sensation. She really ought to get out of here and go home and get some sleep. She had rounds tomorrow morning at eight o'clock. All of a sudden, the din in the waiting room got on her nerves. God, it was bedlam in here! And the stench! She knew she was going to be sick if she didn't get outside, into the air, immediately. She ran for the door.

Outside, in the chill damp night, alone in the dim light beyond the ambulance entrance, she took in gulps of fresh air. Much better. No reason she couldn't handle this; she'd been through worse. So, of course, the minute she thought it, she began to cry—not a slow seepage of tears, but a burst of heavy sobs that felt like they were being ripped out of her. Damn it, she couldn't even be certain *what* she crying about, but she couldn't stop.

She felt a hand on her shoulder, gentle but sure; when she looked up, of all the goddamn people, it was Ham Pierce. "Oh, God, I can't stand these awful things happening to people! I'm sorry, I'm sorry!"

In the next minute, she was wrapped tightly in his embrace, her face buried in his chest, weeping as if her heart would break.

"Shhhh, take it easy. Just go ahead and cry it out. We'll get this guy, I promise you that."

It was astonishing. She believed him and felt comforted. She clung to him, letting herself lament, letting all her pain out. Finally, the sobs subsided into little hiccups. It felt so good to be held, to be comforted, to feel someone else's strength holding *her* together, for a change.

And then she said to herself, Toni, for God's sake, you're standing here in the arms of Hamilton Pierce, the man who bedevils your hospital, who goads your husband relentlessly, and who may simply be coming on to you! Quickly, she pulled away from him, but swayed without his support. He reached out to hold her arm, his eyes never leaving her face. There was something in his gaze, something tender and caring that made her feel like crying again.

Defiantly, she said, "I suppose we'll all be seeing this on your program tomorrow."

And then she regretted her thoughtlessness. Just a few moments ago, he had been murmuring sweet, soothing words into her hair like a mother to a hurt child. And she had felt comforted, had clung to him. What was wrong with her? "I'm sorry," she said. "That was uncalled for. I'm . . . upset." She laughed a little. "As you may have noticed."

"Toni, I—"

A sound made her turn, and she saw her son standing in the light by the E.R. entrance, staring at her. Had he been watching the whole time; had he seen *everything*? She didn't want him to think she was weak or helpless. She wanted him to be proud of her.

"Toni . . . you okay? Shall I take you home?" Ham asked.

She looked at him and felt confused. She had to pull herself together. Take her home? Just because he caught her at a weak moment!

"I'm not going home just yet. But thanks for aiding and comforting the enemy."

He smiled. "I don't think of us as enemies anymore."

Sure, sure. And I'm the queen of Romania, Toni thought. For Hamilton Pierce, she was sure, the story was not the main thing, it was the *only* thing. "Sure, sure," she said.

"Adversaries, maybe. And maybe something else."

She didn't have time for this. King was still standing there.

He was waiting for her, trying not to look as if he were. She smiled to herself. That was her kid. She only wished she could tell Ham Pierce. *That* would be one helluva story, wouldn't it!

"Excuse me, I really have to go," she said, and she walked toward her son. How proud she was of him. She should be able to say to Ham Pierce, "Excuse me, my son is waiting for me." She should be claiming him as her son to the whole goddamn world. It wasn't fair to him.

And at the same moment, she thought, I haven't been fair to Eliot, either. I haven't been honest.

Well, now the time had come. She was going to *have* to tell Eliot about her child, and she was going to do it tonight.

19

Late January

Wollman Rink was crowded. Of course it was crowded, Toni thought. Today was one of those crystal-clear, sparkling, blue-sky-white-snow winter days that are rare in New York City and feel like a miracle. It was especially welcome since the past week had been unremittingly gray, damp, and gloomy—the kind of weather when the very light coming in the window looks dirty. Today, however, was glorious, glorious!

And, she discovered, she could still ice-skate—a little wobbly and not too sure how to stop, but she was moving right along, her arm around Eliot's back, his arm around hers—propping her up, if the truth be told. It felt nice . . . friendly, cozy . . . loving. Yes, that's what it felt like: intimacy. Something she'd been missing ever since she came up here. Between the sunshine and the happy throng and the crisp, clean air and her husband's arm steadying her, Toni was feeling quite cheerful. Except for maybe one little knot of anxiety, but that was pushed far down into the depths of her stomach. To get rid of it altogether, she began to whistle—the dwarfs' working song from *Snow White*. Well, she felt like a little kid!

Eliot laughed. "One of my fondest memories," he said, "is of Lillian, teaching my kids how to skate. I wasn't supposed to be there; this was *her* thing. But I snuck over and watched from a safe distance. I remember it vividly: she laced on her skates and then theirs: Eric's, then David's, then Caro's. She took them out onto the ice, one at a time, talking very loudly, telling them not to be nervous, she had them, they were fine, they were doing just fine. She taught them all to skate that day." He paused and laughed.

"That's such a wonderful story. What's so funny?"

"You don't know just how wonderful it was. See, Lillian had never in her life been on ice skates before that day!" Now he really laughed, throwing his head back. "God, what nerve! My mother!"

"But if Lillian had never been on skates, how did *you* learn?"

"Sam taught me." He laughed again. "Everything I know, I learned from Sam!"

She slid him a smoky look. "Everything?" she murmured.

His arm tightened around her. "Well, *some* things I learned from *you*, darling." He leaned over and gave her a kiss on the cheek and then, suddenly, let go and whooped: "I'll race you to the snack bar!" And he was gone.

"You no-good!" Toni called, stumbling after him as best she could. She stopped this time by letting herself crash into him as he stood waiting by the barricade. "No fair!" she panted. "I haven't skated in a zillion years, I have lousy ankles, and anyway, I'm a girl!"

"You sure are!" He put his arms around her and pulled her close into him. For a few minutes they stood there, embracing, until the sound of girlish giggles behind them reminded Toni that they were in a public place—a public place that was full of kids.

"Speaking of my weak ankles," she said. "How about it? Can we sit down and have something to eat? Some nice hot coffee would go pretty good right now, too."

He sat her down at a little round table and stumped away to get them some lunch. As soon as she was alone, it came popping up: today was the day she was going to tell Eliot about King. She'd been putting it off all day, waiting for the perfect moment. There would never be a perfect moment, she realized that now. As soon as they had eaten, she would tell him.

Thoughts of King had dominated her waking and sleeping hours ever since their encounter in front of the center. She'd made herself a promise a week ago that she'd tell Eliot that very night; then she had chickened out. Her *son* . . . the words almost didn't make sense. She'd never seen him, never. And suddenly, here he was, all grown up, beautiful, bright, a lovely boy. Just thinking about him made her eyes sting with unshed tears. It was amazing: she'd never known her son, but as soon as she found out who he was, she loved him—no ifs, ands, or buts. All of a sudden, all at once. Love just flooded through her, unlimited, unquestioning, unconditional. It didn't make any sense; but there it was, and what could she do? He was now a part of her life; she was never going to let him go, never, not now that she had found him! Correction, she admonished herself, now that *he* had found *her*. Every time she reminded herself how thoroughly she had put him out of her life, her heart squeezed up in her chest. They had a date for supper, Tuesday night, two days from now; she was determined that she'd be able to tell him that it was all out in the open.

A bunch of children, some of them tramping around on double runners, some practicing intricate pirouettes, skated back and forth in front of her. She watched them for a moment, fighting tears, thinking how she had missed all of this, *everything,* with her own child.

She quickly shifted her gaze, concentrating on two couples on the ice, beautifully costumed in rich shades of velvet: burgundy, royal blue, forest green. One couple was quite elderly; they glided by in large, swooping arcs, managing to avoid all the kids. Music sang out of the loudspeakers; sun glittered on the ice; uniformed city workers pushed scrapers out onto the ice, looking dreamy. In the background, the fashionable apartment houses on Fifth Avenue rose behind the bare branches of the trees. Where in this city was her son, at this moment?

And there was Eliot, hobbling back, loaded down with those flimsy cardboard trays. She smiled brightly as he reached her. "What a beautiful day," she said. "Aren't you glad I forced you out into the fresh air?"

Eliot laughed, putting down his burden, and sat down. "I always did say you were the smartest woman I ever knew."

"Only the smartest *woman*?" she teased. "Never mind, never mind. Just hand over a hot dog."

They were silent for a while, both wolfing down their franks as if they hadn't eaten in a week. Eliot looked so contented, and she was going to spoil it. There was a feeling of dread in her chest, and it was growing by the moment.

Finally, she decided she just had to say it. "Eliot."

"Yes?"

She swallowed. "Eliot, I have something to tell you, something really important."

He put down his paper cup, folded his hands, leaned forward and nodded. "I'm listening."

Eliot arranged his features very carefully. She was still very upset about Deedra, he knew that. She had talked about it endlessly for the first few days after it happened; he would have thought she had talked herself out. But, a few days ago, she had started again, conjecturing who it could have been, trying to figure out how she could get Deedra to tell her, working herself up into a tearful rage. He didn't get it. If it was so painful, why keep dragging it up? It was like probing a sore spot, he guessed: hurtful but irresistible. Everyone had tried with Deedra, himself included. She wouldn't talk. Toni had to stop berating herself about it.

But okay. If she needed to go over it one more time, he was prepared to sit and listen patiently. And when she finished, he was going to tell her what he thought.

Then, to his amazement, she began to talk about her *father*! Her childhood! How her old man had been cold and rigid and strict, and how he'd never given her any slack, never showed her any affection or approval, how much she had always longed for him just to ruffle her hair or praise her.

He waited to see if there was a point to all this, but she just rambled on. As gently as possible, he interrupted, putting a hand over hers to show her he meant to be kind. "Toni? I know about your father. You've told me all of this before."

She frowned a little. "I know that. Can't you be patient? This is very difficult for me, and I need you to let me tell you in my own way."

"Okay, okay. I'm listening." He still didn't see the point. He just hoped his eyes wouldn't glaze over; she hated that. But there were times he couldn't help it; his mind just drifted. So he made an immense effort.

"And so then, when I was in nursing school, I was there all on my own. My father was against it; he said all nurses were sluts. 'There's only one reason a girl wants to live away from her family!' he always said. I knew what he meant. ... ."

He'd heard all of this before, too. What was going on? She was talking about some other guy. He didn't care, at this stage, who the hell she had slept with in her youth!

"Toni, forgive me, but I thought you said this was important."

Uh-oh, he'd done it again. Her lips tightened. "It *is* important, more important than you can possibly know. And you needn't get that look on your face; I'm not dramatizing."

"Sorry, sorry, for whatever look you think was on my face. Look, Toni, I just don't understand what all this ancient history has to do with . . . well, with me. Can you just get to the point, maybe?"

"Okay. I'll get to the point." He should have been forewarned by the icy edge on her voice. But there he sat, like an idiot, and when he heard the words, he couldn't even make sense out of them, they were so unexpected, so unreal.

"Excuse me, would you mind repeating that?"

"I said, 'When I was a nursing student, I had a baby that I gave up for adoption.' "

He found himself swallowing, hard. "You . . . *what?*"

"I had a baby when I was a nursing student, and I gave him up for adoption, and now he's found me, and I want him to be a part of our lives."

"You've got to be crazy!"

"Crazy, to want my own child?"

"No, goddamn it. To think you can just suddenly dump this news on me this way and expect me to respond by saying, 'Yes, yes, let's have him move into the apartment and be our own little boy!' "

"I didn't expect anything from you except maybe a little common decency. I don't want him moving in with us. He has a family, a mother and a father. He's an adult, for God's sake. In fact—" She stopped abruptly.

"In fact, what?"

She drew in a deep audible breath, then let it out. She reached across the table, taking his hands in hers. He really wanted to pull them away. He was so angry at her, he didn't want her touching him. And it amazed him that she was ignorant of this simple fact. "Look, Eliot. I'm sorry. I'm rushing. I'm allowing my nervousness to get the better of me. You can't imagine what it's like, giving up your child . . . and then finding him again. I'm probably a little overemotional . . . all right, maybe very overemotional. But he's lovely; he really is. He's a nice young man, and he's been looking for me for a long time. He only wants to get to know me. And I only want for it not to be a secret anymore.''

''Not a secret! Oh, wonderful! And just what are we supposed to tell people? 'Please meet Toni's illegitimate son whom she had in secret and gave away for adoption and kept the whole thing a secret from her husband and would have kept it a secret forever if the kid hadn't shown up and—' '' He hated her phony calm voice, all sweet reasonableness, all an act.

''Eliot, I know this is very difficult for you, and it hasn't made me happy to keep it a secret. But I couldn't see any other way to handle it. . . .''

''When you first met me, okay, maybe that's understandable. But how about when we got married? You could marry me, but you couldn't trust me with this?''

''Oh, Eliot—''

''And stop looking at me as if I were a wounded bird, goddamn it! I'm not hurt. I'm goddamn furious!''

''Eliot, please. He's a sweet kid. He's a paramedic . . . at Harmony Hill—''

''At Harmony Hill! You mean, he's running around my hospital, blabbing his great news?''

Sharply: ''Don't be ridiculous. He's very intelligent and, unlike most men I know, tuned in to other peoples' feelings.''

He got up abruptly, towering over her. ''Is there any other little detail you'd like to share with me in this rare moment of honesty?''

She stood, too, color blazing in her cheeks like two burn marks. ''As a matter of fact, there is one other little detail. His father was black.''

He hadn't thought he could get much angrier, but he was wrong. Who did she think he was?

''Is that supposed to horrify me, Toni? Don't you know me better than that? I don't give a shit what color his father was. What burns *my* tail is that you didn't love me enough to tell me, and you didn't love me enough to have *my* child!''

To his dismay, tears burned at his eyes, but he managed to blink them back. He managed *not* to cry. But when he looked at his wife, trying to see if she understood what hell he was going through, he could see only a blur.

20

Valentine's Day

Steven wasn't there, in his bassinet. Where had they taken him? "Where have you taken him? Just tell me where?"

They were holding her, two of them, huge, strong, two nurses, holding and squeezing. They said she had to get out of here. "I want my baby! What have you done to my baby? Tell me, tell me, tell me!" She was in a nightmare; her voice would not come out of her throat. The two women kept talking, talking, but she could not make out any words. It was like barking, a lot of noise. She had to get out of here.

"I have to get out of here!"

"Yes, Alice, we'll help you. Come on . . ."

Alice was surprised. Suddenly she knew what they were saying. But they had taken her baby away from her!

They were tricky, but she was trickier. She made herself slump, and they let loose of her. And she ran.

"Alice, wait! Let us call your husband!"

She ran; she ran like a leaf in the wind, so light. . . . Her husband. Joe. Joe didn't really love her. He never had sex with her anymore. He made them kill her baby. Kill . . . the word reverberated in her head.

She stopped running, stood very still, looking around. She did not know where she was. In the hospital, but where? Now she remembered the little white coffin heaped with flowers, so pretty, so small, and the church and the cemetery, oh sweet Jesus, they put him in the ground!

The tears came again. There were always tears; there was no end to them. She just let them come. Her baby was dead. Steven was dead. She was dead inside. She saw an open door and, without even thinking, walked in. It was a small room, with just a table and three straight chairs. She sat down in one of the chairs and let her head down onto her arms, folded on the table.

Inside, she was hurting so much, like her insides were one big bruise. It was an ache that never went away. It would never go away. It was so awful. Sometimes she saw her own face in the mirror, and she remembered that she couldn't eat. She looked in the mirror how she felt inside, like nothing, like dead.

If she was dead, there would be no more hurting. If she was dead, no more pain. Dr. Toni wanted her to take another woman's baby . . . she shuddered. Another baby! What good was that? Would it make Steven come back? She could see his face, his sweet little face, and now he was gone! She couldn't bear it, she just couldn't bear it! What good was her life? What good was she? What was the use of living anymore?

Some romantic lunch! Eliot bit into his corned beef sandwich—the one corned beef sandwich per year he was allowing himself—and chewed hard. If he concentrated on chewing, maybe he could forget he was annoyed.

But it didn't work. He was annoyed. He was annoyed at his wife, for openers. It was Valentine's Day, and he had hoped to use the occasion to make peace with Toni. But she was not eating the nice lunch he had ordered, not looking at the vase of roses he had bought for the occasion, not smiling at him with love. Instead, she was haranguing him about her Women's Health Center. Again.

As if he wasn't reminded of her center every moment of the day, by the mob of women—some of them mere children, who damn well ought to be in school instead of protesting things they couldn't possibly understand—parading up and down the sidewalk, right under his windows, hollering at the top of their lungs that women were not safe at Harmony Hill Hospital. They were hoisting placards, printed in amateur capital letters: "HARMONY HILL . . . OUT OF TUNE!" "NO MORE RAPE!" "PROTECT OUR CENTER!" "THE HOSPITAL THAT DOESN'T CARE!"

They'd been out there for two weeks, in every kind of weather! Were they never going to get tired of it? It wasn't as if he didn't care; it wasn't as if he hadn't done anything about it. He had done all that he could. And he cared, of course he cared. Dee was one of his residents, for Christ's sake! She was Betty's sister! How could he *not* be involved? Of course he was involved.

And so was Betty, damn it. At this very moment, she was out there with the rest of them, marching, yelling, brandishing her clenched fist, instead of sitting at her desk where she belonged. He was feeling very ambivalent about Betty right now. On the one hand, he damn well should fire her for demonstrating against the hospital. But on the other, he couldn't; it would be so heart-less. And, in any case, he'd miss her.

They'd sent him a substitute, a girl from medical records. She could type, and that was it. She hadn't yet figured out all the buttons on her telephone; twice this morning, she had cut off very important people and had put through several calls he really didn't want to take. Like Ham Pierce. Betty knew how to screen his calls. Betty knew *him*. What did she think she was doing, seven months pregnant, marching around in the freezing cold!

"Toni, darling." He interrupted her, keeping his voice as even as he could. "I have half a dozen satellite clinics to think about. Yours is not the only one."

"No! No, damn it! Don't give me that line again! You're *always* shortchanging us! Who cares about a bunch of poor, black, teenage kids, right? The whole damn world is willing to waste them, so why should I be surprised!"

"I have the advisory committee to answer to, Toni—as you well know."

"I'm sick and tired of your lousy committee, Eliot! You're the president; if they're giving you such a hard time, get rid of them! The issue here is rape! *Rape!* Do you have any idea how horrible it is to always have it in the back of your mind: the fear that some man, some time, is going to do it!

"Why the hell do you think I leave the center with my keys sticking out of my fist if it's dark? Because of *rape*, Eliot! Do *you* have to make sure you're armed every time you go out at night?" She made a gesture of dismissal, turning away from him. "Forget it! There's no way any man in this world can understand the horror of rape!"

Oh, for Christ's sake. He sighed heavily. "Could you just lay off the feminist propaganda, for a change?"

"I'm going to try to forget you said that." She started to say something else, then composed herself, taking in a deep breath and turning to look out the window.

He craned his neck to see out. There were several dozen women down there, a couple pushing strollers, some of them shaking their fists at the window. He wouldn't be the least bit surprised if Toni had told them exactly where his office was located. She was really mad at him. Well, too bad. He was mad at *her*. He couldn't believe that she really had expected him to remain calm while she exploded her bombshell all over him. Every time he allowed the thought to rise to the surface, it stabbed at him. Like right now. So he pushed it right back down.

In her sweet-reasonableness voice, the tone he could hardly stand, Toni said, "Okay. I'm off my soapbox. Let's talk about what you *can* do for us."

Scowling, he took another bite out of his sandwich and chewed vigorously. What was he *supposed* to do? Personally escort every woman who used the center at night? That neighborhood was terrible; everyone knew it; that's why the center was *there*. It was impossible to be one hundred percent safe anywhere, damn it. What did they *want* from him? And if any of the community leaders got a whiff of the board's talk of closing the center—! Then the women out there would really make trouble!

Oh, hell. He shouldn't be angry at them; they were innocent dupes. Ham Pierce had engineered the whole thing. He hadn't wasted a minute in using Dee's ordeal for his own purposes. He'd gone straight to the center the next morning, bright and early, pushing a mike in front of every single female he could find—in the center, in front of the center, hell, walking *by* the center! And every woman he stopped was hit with a barrage of leading questions. How did she feel about what happened to the young doctor who was attacked? How did she feel about a hospital that wouldn't hire guards to protect vulnerable women? Shouldn't the president of Harmony Hill be made to answer? Shouldn't he be accountable? Was she planning to join her sisters in raising their voices until the president of Harmony Hill could hear them?

It still bugged Eliot. The very next day the demonstrators had appeared, and there they still were. He was pretty damn sure that his wife had encouraged Pierce, as well as the protesters, although she denied it. She was absolutely obsessed with that center of hers. It came before everyone and everything.

She turned back to him now. "If Irene Moore wants a gym

so she can keep her carefully sculptured body in shape, that's top priority!'' she spat. ''But if I want a few hours of night security on 123rd Street . . . that's a priority of a different color!''

''Irene Moore isn't getting a gym. The hospital is getting a sports medicine facility. And the whole thing is a trade-off. Voorhees gets sports medicine; I get to keep your center open.''

''What are you talking about: you get to keep my center open?''

''The board was all for shutting it down. It loses money, as you well know; and the hospital deficit grows daily, as you also know. Sports medicine will pay for the Women's Health Center, and that's the bottom line.''

''Oh, the famous bottom line again! I'm sick and tired of the bottom line! Your board should come to 123rd Street and see what I see every goddamn day. *That's* the bottom line!''

There was no talking to her, not about this. Why was she allowing herself to become such a fanatic? In his most moderate tone of voice, he said, ''Toni, look, the reality is, I *have* saved your center, and I *have* given you more security.''

''You gave us two hours more—from five to seven. Hell, the creeps don't start to crawl out of the cracks in the sidewalk until after dark!''

She was yelling, and he hated it. ''Then close the center *before* it gets dark. Damn it, we haven't got the money for all that overtime, Toni!''

''And when we *have* to stay late?''

''Don't stay late!''

''That's no answer and you know it! It's—''

The buzzer on his desk went off. He didn't want to interrupt, but to hell with it. He was president of this hospital, and if he wanted to pick up his phone, he damn well would.

''Yes?''

''Mr. Pierce. Says it's important.''

Oh, Christ, now what? But if he didn't take the call, Pierce would just keep saying on his show that Dr. Wolfe had no comment and wasn't that interesting, folks? ''Put him through.''

Ham Pierce's voice, mellifluous, rich, heavy with irony. He never said hello, just started to talk. As he did, this time. ''I just heard a rumor, Dr. Wolfe, a disturbing rumor. . . .''

''I can't be expected to deal with every rumor that starts about this hospital.''

"But this one is *especially* interesting, Dr. Wolfe. I hear that Harmony Hill is planning to move its maternity service downtown."

Thank God it really *was* only a rumor—awfully damn close to the truth, but no cigar—and he could honestly deny it. "No truth to it at all. You have my word."

"Not even . . . *partly* true, Dr. Wolfe?" Damn the man!

"The maternity unit is not moving anywhere. It's staying right here on 100th Street and Riverside Drive."

"Hmmmm." A very unconvinced sound. And now, Pierce would dig and dig like a ferret until he found out more. And then there would be yet another chapter of "Voice of the City" on every television set in town, and yet another throng crying for blood—*his* blood!—outside his office. He wished to God he could catch the lousy informer who was giving Pierce his inside information.

He put the receiver down and turned his attention back to Toni. "Where were we?"

"*We* were about to say closing the center early is no answer at all. If we close early, we won't be there for working women, or for night people. We won't reach those most desperately in need."

"Toni, what can I tell you? I gave you a guard until seven o'clock; it's the best I can do."

Toni picked up her untouched sandwich and then put it down again. "Well, you can take your best, and you know what you can do with it!" She jumped to her feet and gritted out through her teeth: "Was your best good enough for Dee?"

"I know what happened to Dee was horrible, but I wish you would stop bringing it up, as if it were *my* fault!"

Eliot stared at her angry face and wondered how they had come to this. He had planned a nice peaceful lunch here in his office; there was a little box sitting in his desk drawer, a little box with a diamond heart on a gold chain. There was also a little bottle of champagne in the little refrigerator in the corner. But forget Valentine's Day, forget love, forget celebration. Forget anything but her Women's Health Center! Obviously, she cared more about her hookers and addicts and assorted misfits than she did about him!

He'd sent her to medical school, for Christ's sake! Arlene had made his life a living hell when she found out, and he *still* had done it. Toni could have a little gratitude, goddamn it. If it weren't for him . . .

Aloud, he said, "Sometimes I wish you were still a nurse; at least then you'd have a regular shift, and I'd see you every once in a while! Maybe even in bed, from time to time," he added, after a slight pause.

Last night, all of a sudden at two A.M., he had awakened with a hard-on, wanting her for the first time in a long time. He turned, curling spoon fashion around her back, kissing her neck, reaching around to cup her breasts, whispering her name. At first, she had made little moans of pleasure that aroused him even more, and she wiggled her buttocks back against him. And then, as he started to push himself into her, she wriggled in an irritated way, trying to shake him off. In another minute, she was asleep again; he knew, because she began to snore softly. And there he was, totally fired up, feeling frustrated and foolish. It had been stupid even to try with her! No wonder he was fucking another woman!

Toni remembered last night, too. She flushed a little. "I'm sorry. I already told you I was sorry." As she spoke, her voice changed from apologetic to aggressive. "I didn't fall asleep on purpose, for God's sake. Give me a break! I'm tired! I work hard!"

"You don't have to work so hard, Toni. You *make* work for yourself."

He pretended to start eating again, as she stared past him, her mouth set in a grim line. Well, he didn't have much of an appetite, either! Every day there was another conflict. If it wasn't her hours, it was his attitude, and if it wasn't his position, it was her son. *Her son*.

A knife went right through his guts. He just couldn't put it out of his mind. She had been his wife for twelve years and all those years, not a word, not one word. If that wasn't betrayal, what was? Living a lie, then springing it on him, all of a sudden! Get me a cup of coffee, please, and by the way, I have a son, he's twenty-five, he's half-black, and I'd like him to be a part of the family!

She strode over to the windows and stood, her arms tightly crossed, pretending to look out. After a moment, she wheeled to him, and said, "You know what? I've had just about enough of you!"

"Oh, really? Well, I've had *more* than enough of you!"

She stared at him in surprise. Well, he had surprised himself!
Then she turned on her heel and marched out, pausing just long
enough in the doorway to give him the finger. She slammed the
door behind her so hard that his diplomas on the wall quivered
and shook.

Pasting on a smile, Toni sailed by the secretary's desk; they'd
replaced Betty for the duration, and the substitute was a scared-
looking kid with bitten fingernails. She wondered if the girl had
heard any of their quarrel . . . wondered if she, too, thought
Dr. Wolfe was a wonderful, calm, understanding man, like Betty
did. It was clear, every time she talked about "Dr. Wolfe," that
Betty was very enamored, almost reverent.

"There aren't many like him!" Betty had burbled to her, the
day after Dee's ordeal. Eliot was giving her time off to be with
Dee; he was so sensitive, so unusual.

Not many like him, indeed! Toni seethed, marching down
the hall. She could attest to that! She ought to tell Betty he didn't
have the *balls* to fire her! She ought to tell Betty that he had
been passed over, back at John Q., that he was jealous of his
wife, that he was acting these days like he was King Shit!

She was furious with him; no, she was more than furious.
She was disgusted! He had turned into the perfect bureaucrat,
no thought or feeling for people, for individuals and their problems. He sat in his office, far behind the front lines, making
pronouncements. Where was the man she had married? "We're
doing the best we can." What was that "we," anyway? The
royal we? Did he think he was Queen Victoria, or what?

Enough, she told herself. Don't waste your time thinking
about him. She glanced at her watch—one thirty-five. Clinic
didn't start until two o'clock. She'd see if she could get ahold of
Alice Rodriguez. She'd called a hundred times; no answer. Alice badly needed help to get over this. She needed to be taken
by the hand and led to the Neonatal Bereavement Group.

So she'd call for the 101st time. There were phone booths at
the end of every hall. She went into one and dialed. Shit. No
answer. She dialed again, just in case she'd done it wrong. No
answer. She'd call her again right after clinic hours. Damn Eliot
for getting to her! He was such an asshole lately!

His whole reaction to King, for instance. He demanded to

know why she had waited until now to tell him. When else *could* she have told him? When she first met him? Before the wedding? On their honeymoon? And anyway, it had happened long before she met him, and her past was *her* business!

But once she met King, there was no way she could keep him a secret forever. He was her son; she was his birth mother; she wanted to have a relationship. Today was his birthday. For years, she'd had to think about him secretly and sadly on Valentine's Day, and cry alone where nobody might ask her what was the matter. No more, no more. Today, she was meeting him for a drink, and she had a present for him in her desk drawer: a great little portable CD player that she knew he had been longing for.

She had really wanted to send him a card, but she thought better of it. He had told his parents already, but although they were happy for him, they weren't quite ready to meet her face-to-face. Well, she could understand that.

But Eliot's response was off the wall! He had reacted as if she had told him she was a murderer—or was having an affair . . . which, by the way, was beginning to have its appeal. He had stared at her, and then, without a word, he stripped off his skates and left. Without a word! She'd actually gone *after* him, begging him to listen, just try to have a little compassion for her!

And when he finally stopped, outside the rink, and allowed his eyes to meet hers, what did he say? "You have betrayed me!" Pretty heavy-duty for a Sunday afternoon! And that didn't sound much like Betty's sensitive and understanding Dr. Wolfe, did it? Toni tossed her head impatiently, as if to shake off her thoughts.

"I hope it's not me you're mad at," a familiar voice said. "I'd hate to face you in a temper." A hand descended onto her shoulder, and she turned, startled.

Then she smiled. "You don't know the half of it!" she said. It was funny, how she and Ham Pierce had hit it off. She had been so sure she'd hate him forever. They began to walk together quite naturally toward the cafeteria, and she pretended not to notice that his hand stayed on her shoulder. It didn't mean anything. Ham, as she had discovered from a couple of cafeteria lunches, and a number of chance encounters, was a hands-on guy. Not that he had ever taken advantage of her boo-hooing all over him on the night Dee was attacked. He hadn't *mentioned* it, even.

"Toni, I gotta talk to you. Maybe I'll get some answers. Your

husband . . . well, he's President Stonewall. I just tried talking
to him a few minutes ago and—''

"I know." It made her smile, to see how he tried to hide his
astonishment. Laughing, she intoned, in her best fake Russian
accent, "I haf my spies everywhere."

"In the spirit of *glasnost*, let's have lunch together?" They
were at the cafeteria entrance, and he made a mock bow, ush-
ering her in past the potted palms and stacks of orange plastic
trays. "And you can tell me what you think of the latest plan to
move maternity downtown, where it's nice and safe and where
none of the poor people who live up here will be able to use it."

"Ouch." She knew this had been discussed at a committee
meeting because Eliot had mentioned it to her. But how had
Ham heard about it? And furthermore, it suddenly occurred to
her, was Mr. Pierce using her, pretending to be friendly? The
thought disturbed her, and she stopped mid-step.

"Second thoughts?" he said. "The renowned Dr. Toni, I
hear, always knows exactly what she wants."

She regarded him for a moment. She decided no, he was not
using her. And anyway, she was too smart to be used. "I'm
stubborn, you mean."

"No. Not stubborn; that's a negative word, and you are a
positive woman."

Toni slid him a sideways glance. "And you are a charmer.
Has anyone ever told you that?"

"What do you mean?"

"Ham, we have a saying where I come from. Don't kid a
kidder. You know damn well what I mean."

"You have found me out. Yes, I'm told I have charm. They
mean I tell pretty lies. I never tell pretty lies. I tell what I see,
what I feel. I tell the truth. Especially to you."

She took in a breath. He was *definitely* flirting with her and
she was liking it. But why was she liking it so much?

They moved on into the main dining room and were immediately assaulted by noise. There were people in scrubs and
people in dress-for-success suits, people in jeans and sweaters,
and people in white; and they all seemed to be talking at the
tops of their voices, all at once. What looked like the entire first-
year class of nursing students was crowded around one of the
large rectangular tables, loudly singing "Happy Birthday" to a

blushing redheaded guy. The usual mid-day Harmony Hill cafeteria crowd, blowing off steam and taking a little R and R.

They threaded their way past the crowded tables, past the extra chairs pulled up into the middle of the aisles. Pausing to let a wheelchair get by, he grinned down at her. "Don't you agree that you're positive? Assured? Confident? Optimistic?" A small pause. "And very attractive?"

Toni paid close attention to the red Jell-O mold she had grabbed. It was quivering on its bed of shredded lettuce, nestling against its scoop of cottage cheese. She *hated* Jell-O and didn't think much of cottage cheese, either. What the *hell* was going on? She very carefully did not look at him.

And then it suddenly occurred to her: she had let him lead her into the cafeteria, and she was about to have lunch with him. She had just finished "having lunch" with her husband, and why hadn't she told him so? She didn't want to know the answer. She was a married woman, and this man was coming on to her, and by all rights, she should be discouraging him. Actually, she scolded herself, she should have said Hello Ham and Good-bye Ham and gone upstairs as she had planned.

But there she was. And she told herself rather belligerently, she had actually eaten nothing in Eliot's office, and she was hungry. Furthermore, she was going to have a long, tough clinic, and she needed to eat. And even furthermore, she liked talking to Ham Pierce, and she wasn't doing anything wrong!

They finally spotted a little table squashed into the far corner, out of the way, and ran to get it.

"So, Toni," he said suddenly. "Who're you so mad at? Not me, I hope."

"What makes you think I'm angry?"

He shrugged his massive shoulders. "I don't know. Maybe because you're scowling?"

"It's nothing." Why in hell didn't she say, My husband and I had an argument? She was behaving like an idiot! "It will pass. So tell me . . ."

He put his hand over hers on the table, causing her heart to take a little jump. "Listen. I think you should come to dinner with me. How about the Four Seasons?" He laughed. "Dr. Pierce's prescription."

"If you give that prescription to every angry woman you meet, you're going to be one busy man!"

"I'll just take *you*, if you don't mind." His eyes bored into hers; she didn't know where to look. This was ridiculous; this was stupid. But this was so nice. Eliot had been so distant and self-righteous lately. He didn't even come near her for ages, turned his back in bed, didn't even say good night, just acted as if she weren't even there. Until last night, in the middle of the *night*, for Christ's sake, when she was sound asleep, and so now he was in a snit!

"Will you, Toni?"

"Will I what?"

Ham shook his head and smiled at her. His eyes crinkled when he smiled. "Will you come to dinner with me?"

She regarded him carefully. A very cute guy. Too cute. Too cute by far. This was dangerous. But, come on, he hadn't invited her to his apartment, for God's sake! He'd only asked her to have dinner with him!

"Okay," she said, making up her mind quite suddenly.

"Great." He sat back and smiled at her. "When? You say. Any time."

As a matter of fact, Eliot was going to some dumb convention in Los Angeles for five days, without a thought for *her*. He hadn't discussed it with her, just announced it.

"This Saturday, then."

"You're on. I'll—" He stopped talking, as his eyes moved past her, and he frowned.

Toni turned. There *was* a strange sound behind her. Now she saw that it was all the chairs, scraping back, as every person in the cafeteria got up, all at once. And everybody streamed out, heading in the same direction. What was going on?

"Let's go." Ham was up, out of his chair, and already taking long strides after the crowd. She had to run to keep up with him. They caught up with a group of nurses and Toni said, "What's happening?"

"Someone's sitting on a ledge up on the sixth floor—"

"Threatening to jump—"

"Who?"

"Don't know. A woman, they said."

Oh God. One of the mental patients?

Ham reached out and gave her hand a quick squeeze. "I've got to get out there. I'll call you." And he was off like a shot, racing down the hallway. Watching him, Toni was reminded that he had been an athlete; she wondered how old he was. And then she, too, began to run.

Outside, it was bright sunshine but cold, cold, cold. Most of the people crowded across the street, all looking up, were coatless and hatless, but nobody moved to get back into the warmth. The Channel 14 van was already there, and she saw Ham's usual camerawoman pushing through the crowd.

Toni ran out into the street and, shielding her eyes from the glare with one hand, peered up. A small figure sat huddled on a window ledge. The nurses were right; it was a woman, gesticulating with one arm and shouting, although it was impossible to hear words down here. It was horrible, to think that anyone could feel so desperate that the only way out was to jump from a building in front of a crowd of strangers. She didn't understand it. She herself had always responded to adversity with anger, not with hopelessness.

As she stared upward, she suddenly knew who it was; the minute she realized, she was running back into the hospital. Alice! Jesus, Mary, and Joseph, it was Alice! She had to get upstairs to Alice. What had they said . . . ? Sixth floor.

The elevator would not come, so she took the stairs, two at a time. By the time she got to the sixth floor landing, her chest burned, and she could hardly breathe. She pushed the heavy door open, wondering which way, praying she wasn't too late.

Down to the left, at the end of the corridor, dozens of people swarmed around a doorway. She ran, yelling, "Let me through! I'm her doctor! Let me through!" The mass parted for her.

It was a small office, the window thrown wide open, a freezing cold draft sweeping through. And there was Janet, sitting on the sill, leaning forward, talking earnestly. Toni could see that Alice, thank God, was still sitting there.

She stood inside the door and spoke quietly to Janet. "It's Toni. What can I do?"

Janet spoke calmly without turning her head. "I'm so glad you're here. We're just discussing how Alice can come back inside."

"I don't want to live!" With a sinking heart, Toni heard Alice's shout. "My baby is dead! I want to die!"

"Dr. Toni is here, Alice. You wanted to talk to her."

"She's too late!"

Toni walked to the window and scrunched in tightly next to

Janet. "I'm not too late. You're still here, and now I'm here, too. I came to see what you want, Alice."

"I want to die!"

"But we don't want you to die, Alice. Your family doesn't want you to die. Joe doesn't want you to die."

Should she make a grab for her? No, she thought she remembered that was the worst thing to do. Christ, if she only had some expertise in this!

Murmuring softly, she said to Janet, "Has somebody called the police?"

"Yes. I wish they'd get here; I don't know what to do."

"What are you saying?" Alice's voice sharpened. "I hear you whispering."

"We're saying we'd like it if you'd come in and talk to us. We want to help you, Alice."

"No help for me, no help, no help . . . !" The voice drifted off, and Toni leaned forward a little, her heartbeat accelerating. But Alice was still there, unmoving, her face pinched and stony, her eyes wide but without tears. "Why should I live?" Alice asked of nobody in particular.

"Alice," Toni said, leaning out as far as she could and holding out her hand. "Why don't you take my hand? Please."

Alice's eyes focused for a split second, and her gaze locked with Toni's. Such empty eyes! But her hand came slowly out, and as she moved her arm, she turned her head, looking down, as if suddenly aware how high up she was. Toni held her breath. Come on, Alice, atta girl, come on, just take my hand, she ordered silently, take my hand, and then we can pull you in, come on. . . .

Alice looked at her again. Their hands touched. She smiled. And then she pushed herself away from the wall and let herself fall.

"Jesus Christ! No!" Toni cried. "No!" She could hear Janet's echoing cries. She pulled herself into the room and stood, head bowed, both hands clutching at her hair. No, no. It couldn't be. She couldn't have. It had happened so fast.

"I had her," she said aloud, "I almost had her hand. Almost, almost . . . ! Oh, God, I should have grabbed her!" She felt Janet's hand on her shoulder, and suddenly she was limp with exhaustion. When Janet tugged at her, she fell in a heap, sitting on the floor under the window, her face in her hands, rocking a little. "I should have grabbed her! I let this happen! I didn't see it coming! I can't believe it. I can't believe it!"

Janet was next to her on the floor, talking in a shaky voice. "It's not your fault; it's nobody's fault."

At that moment, a voice above her said, "Police."

Toni lifted her face from her hands to look at him, but Janet spoke first. "It's too late. She jumped. We couldn't stop her."

"Shit!" The policeman looked stricken. He turned and said, "Downstairs. I'll be down in a minute." He held out a hand. "Come on, ladies, let's get you outa here."

Janet scrambled to her feet. Toni felt as if she couldn't move, would never again be able to move. She allowed the young cop to lift her up. He didn't let go, either, but kept tight hold of her, looking at her with sad eyes.

It never gets easier, she thought, not even for people who deal with it all the time. And then, suddenly, she became painfully aware of details: the two young nurses in the doorway, holding each other and crying; the expensive black-leather handbag, put carefully on a chair on top of a neatly folded red coat. Alice's. She'd been so proud of that bag; she'd saved up the money out of her paycheck, and she'd told Toni once that it was the nicest thing she'd ever owned. Toni's eyes filled with tears. Alice was gone. Alice had killed herself. One minute, she was there, alive, her outstretched fingers grazing Toni's; and the next minute, gone. Gone, just like that. Gone. Oh, God . . .

Alice had been so sick, had really been feeling that hopeless, that despondent! She had cried out for help, and her doctor hadn't listened! Her doctor had been too busy feeling sorry for herself! Oh, God! For the first time since she was fifteen years old, Toni Romano found herself praying for forgiveness.

21

February 22

The large main hall of the Hispaniola Social Club was packed with people, most of them sobbing openly. Outside, a bitter wind howled, rattling the windows; but inside, it was almost *too* warm. Eliot was not comfortable.

What's more, he couldn't understand most of what was being said up front. Almost all of the speakers were Hispanic. Right now, a short dark man with a very black mustache was struggling to speak—in Spanish—tears streaming down his face and choking his voice.

There had been no church service. Alice was a suicide and denied a Catholic burial; so the family had arranged for this memorial service, with various relatives, friends, and nursing colleagues standing up to speak, or sing—or pray, for all he knew. He felt very conspicuous. Unlike almost everyone else in the place, he was tall and fair and, with his white hair, he was sure he stood out. He felt that people were staring at him, and not necessarily with kind feelings.

Yes, he felt guilty about Alice's suicide. No, he hadn't done enough to prevent it. But, on the other hand, he argued silently, he hadn't done anything wrong. That baby would never have lived on his own. His "life" was all in Alice's wishful thinking. The state of her mental health was never his responsibility. And he had done his very best; they all had.

Joe wasn't mad at him. Poor Joe. He was in the front of the room, of course, along with the rest of their family. It was a very large family, all wearing black, all crying. Except for Joe; Joe was dry-eyed. He looked like a man who didn't know what had hit him.

On the opposite side of the room, Ham Pierce and his camerawoman conferred, then quietly walked toward the back until
Eliot could no longer see them. A minute later, they had shifted
their position again, to get a better shot. A better shot of *what*?
Of people weeping . . . of the family suffering? Ghouls! It was
outrageous. This was a tragedy, a very personal tragedy, in
Eliot's opinion. And the grief being displayed here today was a
very personal grief, certainly none of the business of the viewers
of Channel 14.

Pierce, it seemed, was determined to get at least one more
show out of this. And when that damned microphone was shoved
in Eliot's face and one more time he was asked for his comment,
he wished he could look the reporter right in the eye and say,
"You have no business here today." Maybe he would!

He shifted on the hard folding chair. How much longer was
this going to last? He glanced at his watch: ten-thirty. He'd been
here an hour already; he'd thought surely it would be over by
this time. He had a meeting at noon, and it would be impossible
for him to leave without looking bad. He was right in the middle
of the row, sitting by himself.

Normally, everyone from the hospital would have come together. But Havemayer and his group were across the room; he
was being hostile. Toni had told him this morning she'd have to
come a little late. He'd put his coat on the chair next to him,
saving it for her, but she had never come to claim it. Surely she
must have arrived by now . . . but there was no way he could
turn around and look for her. Maybe his wife was being hostile,
too.

With an effort of will, he made himself stop thinking about
her. He really had to put his mind on something other than his
messed-up marriage. And like a little devil, a picture popped
into his head: Janet on her knees in front of him, caressing him,
looking up at him with wide, intent eyes before she bent her
head to take him into her mouth. An involuntary shiver went
crawling down his spine.

She had come into the office around seven-thirty last Tuesday,
a big smile on her face. "We have to work late at the office,
Eliot, darling," she had said, and before he could figure out
what she meant, she had locked his office door, turned out the
lights so that only the glow from a streetlight outside was left,

and was taking off her clothes. "Janet! Wait a minute! I have to leave!"

She was already naked from the waist up. "Then I'll have to be very quick," she said. Dropping to her knees, she looked up at him, smiled sweetly, and purred, "But not *too* quick . . ." The next thing he knew . . . *Enough!* he told himself. This was neither the time nor the place for sexual reveries.

He knew Janet was sitting somewhere in this room. "Of course I'll be there," she had told him. "And I'll be with you in my mind, even though we can't sit together." And she had given him one of her soft-mouthed kisses, slow and seductive. Succulent. The taste of her mouth was so sweet. . . .

He felt someone staring at him. Janet? But no, she was thoroughly discreet; it couldn't be her. Slowly he turned and found himself looking into the blank eye of Channel 14's hand-held camera. Carefully, he kept his face composed and, just as carefully, turned away.

Goddamn it. Hadn't last night's attack on Barney been enough to keep Pierce and his producers happy for a while? Any hospital was a microcosm of society, including its evils. Harmony Hill Hospital didn't create the problems; it only tried to heal them. But Pierce could care less about *facts*. Harmony Hill was an easy target. And, hey, it was nothing personal—as Pierce had told him on more than one occasion.

But that's not how Barney took it. He took it very, very personally; even before Pierce had signed off with his annoying v-for-victory sign, and his annoying "keep the faith," the phone on the hall table was shrilling. As Eliot picked up the receiver, he could already hear Barney screaming.

"Goddamn it, Wolfe, somebody talked to that son of a bitch! I'll have his balls for breakfast, that fucking loudmouth nigger lover!"

"Barney, Barney, calm yourself."

"How am I supposed to calm myself when somebody is leaking confidential information, goddamn it . . . leaking it to that fuck!"

"I know we have a problem with leaks, and I'm working on it."

"Look, Wolfe, you're the only one I talked to about going to Landmarks! I was a goddamn *prince* to let you know in advance

. . . and what do I get for thanks? I'm fucked over on TV for the whole city to see!''

"I hope you aren't suggesting that *I'm* Ham Pierce's source."

"Suggesting? I'm *saying* it! Who the hell else could have told him?''

"You have my word that I did not." Even though I would have loved to be the one who did, he thought. Barney had had the goddamn gall to go to a buddy of his on the Landmarks Commission. He wanted to get the interiors of the Bachelor Brownstones declared historic landmarks. Then, of course, they couldn't be changed and would be useless to the hospital. Even if Barney lost, it could take years to get a ruling; meanwhile, the hospital could do nothing. The sleazy part was that Barney had gone behind everybody's back. And he had the nerve to call *Eliot* a sneak!

"As you know, Barney, I've been quietly working on a real-estate switch for Central Manhattan Hospital—''

"Central Mediocre," Barney interjected.

"Whatever! The point is, we could have all been happy, Barney, including you. The Bachelor Buildings would have gone to the bank and the old Central Manhattan facility would have been perfect for us . . . *without* the cost of gutting and renovating. I had already spoken to the executors of the will, and they thought that was a great idea. Now? Who knows!''

"Okay, okay, okay. I shot from the hip. But goddamn it, it was in a private conversation, Eliot; *my* point is, somebody told that son of a bitch! Goddamn it, I've given so much to this city, and that asshole is going to make my name mud! Goddamn it, I'm in the middle of some very delicate negotiations with the Chinks . . . a seaside resort in Hong Kong, when they get it back! If you don't get him to lay off me, it'll be in the toilet! And you'll be in the toilet next, because if that happens, kiss Barney Goldstone and his bucks good-bye!''

If this weren't so important, Eliot had thought, he'd be laughing. Goldstone was such a clown. But a very wealthy clown, he reminded himself. So, he soothed.

"Barney, of course we don't want you or your deal ruined— and we certainly could never do without your support. I promise you one thing: our lawyers will have some very strong words for Mr. Pierce about slander.''

Thinking about this, he turned back to where the camera had

been staring at him. Let him look Pierce straight in the eye and let the guiltier one look away first. But the camerawoman, the camera, and Pierce, had all moved on.

Toni, sitting way in the back row, watched Ham and his camera rove about the room, looking for drama. If he came anywhere near her, she'd kill him! He'd promised! He knew how she felt about Alice, about her own complicity.

She'd made the mistake of talking about this with Ham. Hell, she'd probably made an even bigger mistake by going out with him at all. What had she been thinking of? He was the enemy, no matter how sweetly he looked at her, no matter how sexy his smiles! He was after the hospital, period. And she was an idiot for forgetting that, even for one evening!

It had been so nice, though. He knew an Italian restaurant in Queens, a neighborhood place, no frills, no fancy anything, he had warned her, just the greatest pasta she'd ever eaten. "And they know me. I've been going there for years. We won't be bothered, and there'll be no gossip."

"Going there for years? With ladies?" She had the mixed pleasure of seeing him squirm. So the answer was yes, and for some reason, that bothered her. So stupid! Why should she care what he had done in his free time before she had even known him? She changed the subject, teasing him. "If you think I haven't already had great pasta in my life, then you don't know what kind of ethnic a lady named Romano is."

It was the kind of family Italian restaurant she'd known her whole life. Four booths and six tables, candles in Chianti bottles, just like in the 1960s, a big mahogany bar, and the smell of marinara sauce. They sat in the back booth, taped accordian music playing in the background, and started in on a carafe of red wine. She had drunk much more than she was accustomed to; she had also talked much more than she was accustomed to.

And the horrible part was, the next morning, she couldn't exactly remember everything she had said. She remembered talking about Alice and crying a little, she remembered Ham moving to sit next to her and his holding her hand; and she remembered, sort of, talking about her worries and her problems. Yes, and her husband. She did the unthink-able; she told Ham that she couldn't talk to her husband anymore, and she had cried a little bit then, too. And then he kissed her.

Oh Christ, he kissed her, and she kissed him back. She had gotten such a jolt when his mouth covered hers; and then, she leaned into him and felt his intake of breath, and her heart began to hammer. They kissed and they kissed. . . . Thinking about it now, she wanted to sink into the ground and disappear. Like a sex-starved teenager. Hell, like a sex-starved lady doctor! Now he *knew* it, and she felt so dumb.

And then, there was his program last night. All the stuff Eliot had confided in her—the committee meetings and Barney Goldstone and Barney's friends on the Landmarks Commission and Barney's plans . . . It was all there, pouring out of Ham's mouth. *Had she told him?* That's what was bugging her. Had she told him, in a weak-willed, candlelit, Chianti-soaked moment?

She was so afraid she'd babbled. All right, he was good-looking; all right, he was charming; all right, he was—let's face it—seductive, and he did have an irresistible way of getting people to talk to him. But she should have known better. She, the wife of the president of the hospital, *she* should have been on her guard. Hell, she should have been home, instead of confiding in Hamilton Pierce that her husband was furious with her! Oh God! She hadn't told Ham about *King*, had she? Her blood ran cold at the thought. She couldn't have; no matter what was going on, she couldn't have told *that*. What a mess she was making of things!

She knew she had done it badly telling Eliot about King. She should have been more careful, more gentle, more diplomatic. But goddamn it, he made her so mad! It was next to impossible to get him to listen to her these days. She had tried to tell him in a way that wouldn't come as a terrible shock. But he kept looking impatient, and then finally said, "Will you please get to the point!" in a tone of voice she hated.

Then she had just come out with it, plain and simple, blunt and to the point. And provocative, let's admit it. Still, she found his reaction off the wall. It had happened over twenty years ago, before she even met him. And how about *her* feelings? Didn't *she* count? She knew damn well she wouldn't be responding to Ham if her husband was there for her, if he was loving her.

* * *

Well, look at that, Janet thought. They're not even pretending anymore. Eliot was right in the center of the room, sitting straight and tall. He was a man who stood out, wherever he went. And where was his wife? All by herself, scrunched in a corner, her head bowed. He never once turned around to look for her. Janet knew, because she'd had her eye on him the whole time.

Excitement bubbled up in her chest. It was happening; it was really happening. Just as she had hoped, had dreamed . . . had planned. She studied Toni Romano briefly and decided that no matter how good a doctor she was, no matter how nice a person, she was *not* cut out to be a president's wife. Look at her, sitting there, her hair all messed up, no makeup, wearing a loden coat. A *loden coat!* It was laughable. Nobody wore them anymore, and anyway, it was entirely the wrong color for someone with that sallow Italian skin.

Eliot hardly ever mentioned her anymore when he was confiding little secrets about himself to Janet, little stories about his children and his ex-wife and his childhood. The way he looked at her, lately—! She hardly dared dream of marriage. Still . . . it might happen.

She lovingly fingered the delicate little diamond heart on its gold chain. What a surprise when he'd given it to her on Valentine's Day. She hadn't even planned on seeing him that night; he hadn't said a word. When he had called and asked if she was free, you could've knocked her over with a feather. Well, of course, she had lied; she said she had a date, but if he really wanted to see her, she could probably break it. He hadn't said anything for a minute, and she castigated herself. There you go again, Janet, pushing things too hard! "Oh, it's just an old friend who's thinking about divorce and wants to talk," she added quickly.

And he had said, "Well, in that case . . ." and she could breathe easy.

He grabbed her the minute he was in the door and kissed her so hard, she thought she'd faint. And then he handed her a plain little white box, unwrapped, with no ribbon. "Here, Happy Valentine's Day." She'd known then. A diamond heart on a gold chain was the kind of present a man gave to a woman he was serious about.

She'd had to claw her way up to where she was. Her mother

and father had been alcoholics, both of them, and every cent
went for Irish whiskey. But she'd always longed for all the good
things in life. Thick steaks and diamonds and furs and travel
and chauffered limos and antique furniture. With Dr. Eliot
Wolfe, she could have it all. She, who had never had *anything*,
could have it all!

22

March

"Dr. Wolfe, you coerced Alice Rodriguez—behind my back! *I* was the physician in charge! Your behavior was indefensible, unprincipled, underhanded, unprofessional and—yes, I will say it—immoral!"

The nerve of him! Betty Cannon thought, talking to the president that way! She wished she could speak *her* piece, but of course, she was not allowed to speak, not in this room. This conference room, with its polished rosewood oval table and its thick, pale carpeting, was not for the likes of her.

"You pressured that poor vulnerable woman into giving her consent—with the tragic results we are all too well aware of."

Tight-lipped and obviously angry, Dr. Wolfe glared at Havemayer but spoke quietly. "I did not coerce Mrs. Rodriguez. I spoke to her, yes, I told her the truth. She made up her own mind."

"Someone made it up *for* her."

"It's possible someone talked to her and convinced her . . . who, I do not know. After all, the baby's father was against keeping him on life support. And he said so in writing."

Betty watched Dr. Havemayer, wondering how he was going to answer *that*. Everyone in the hospital had seen that letter; half of New York City had heard it when Ham Pierce read it on his show.

"We don't know who coerced the father, either." Smug little smile. But what did he really know about it?

What did any of them know about it? With every pregnancy, a woman had to live with the fear that her baby might have some terrible birth defect, or be born dead. The infant in her own belly moved and kicked as if responding to her thoughts. Soon, her baby would be born. She'd been so careful: no drinking, no junk food, no medication, not even an aspirin, no hot baths. She'd had amnio, on account of her age, and everything her obstetrician told her, she did.

But anything could happen! God, every time she saw an article about some terribly crippled child, or a picture, she got cold chills. She used to go upstairs in the hospital, sometimes, to help out with children who had birth defects, but no way could she do it now! She was ashamed of herself, but she just couldn't. Sometimes, when she let her mind wander onto what might happen, her heart would stop beating for a minute and a big void would open up in her chest. Then she'd begin to pray. Please, God, let this baby be okay, let this baby be healthy.

They all talked about Alice as if she had been crazy. There was nothing wrong with her except she'd been waiting so long for this baby, and finally, when he was born, he wasn't really alive! Which one of these folks, with all their education and their money and their privileges, could have faced it any better? Poor Alice, it was her last chance to be a mother. Betty knew how that felt; this pregnancy was *her* last chance.

Now Dr. Voorhees was giving Dr. Wolfe a hard time. Betty wrote down his words automatically. He talked like a fag. She'd dealt with him for years, and she didn't like him a bit better now than she had at the beginning. When he had been so sure he was going to be the next president, last year, he had begun to suck up, smiling, giving her phony compliments—"What a pretty dress, Betty!" "My, your notes are impeccable!" That kind of thing. He gave her the creeps.

Oh, it made her laugh to think how, for a while there, he would walk into these meetings like the Lord God himself. Well, he was one shocked doctor when they announced they were hiring Dr. Eliot Wolfe of Washington, D.C. She kept her eye on him *that* day; she had been curious. His face was a study, every feature frozen, every muscle very still and quiet. But she had seen the beads of sweat on his forehead and the two blotches of color high on his cheekbones.

He wasn't the only one who had got pissed off because he didn't get it. The three of them—Voorhees, Havemayer, and Goldstone—used to push everyone around—especially poor old Dr. Delafield with his goofy smile. She remembered meetings that hadn't taken more than ten minutes. They'd come in here and give him his marching orders, and he'd smile and nod and sigh and agree. When he had been president, it was the three of *them* who ran the place, and they couldn't stand that somebody else had been put over them. Dr. Voorhees *still* liked to act as if he was in charge.

Dr. Wolfe, still very quiet, repeated for the fifteenth time, "Alice Rodriguez was *not* coerced or forced in any way."

"Tell us another!" Barney Goldstone gave a nasty laugh. "Sure, she decided for herself, and then she jumped out a window because she was so satisfied with her decision."

Tell him off, Betty thought fiercely, her eyes boring into Eliot's profile. His hands clenched for a minute, but then he flattened them out on the table and said in a pleasant tone, "May we continue now, to the next item on the agenda?"

She was familiar with the agenda; she had typed it, from his dictation. She was very aware of the very last item on the list, the one of least importance, the one that very well might be pushed over to the next meeting. It had been almost an afterthought. Security in the satellite clinics.

Nice and sanitary. Deedra's *rape*, that's what it was! So why not say it? And why in hell *was* it an afterthought? An innocent young woman attacked by one of the doctors! A devil who pounced on her poor little sister—threw her down, threatened her, forced her legs apart, forced himself into her, *forced* her—! Who? Which one?

She'd thought Deedra was safe, with her good upbringing and her good education and her medical degree. Safe from the fate of so many black women: to be abused, used, and thrown away. But there was no safety, not anywhere. Dee was attacked on hospital property, and she was one of their own, one of their best! Yet, today she was on the bottom of the list!

When that young white doctor over at Cadman Memorial was shot last year, outside the hospital, nobody could stop talking about him. Even now, everyone at Cadman dated things by "before Goodman got shot" or "after Goodman got shot." But not at Harmony Hill. Why? Because Dee was black? Because she was only a woman? Because it was only rape?

Deedra had been brutally violated—and right around the corner from where Betty and her group marched up and down every night of the year, keeping their block safe! Safe! They had been fooling themselves! Why were decent black folks forced to live in dangerous, rundown, ugly neighborhoods? It didn't happen if you were white! And if there was a rape in a white neighborhood, you can bet the whole precinct would be out, hunting down the creep that did it.

Last night, she'd cried out to George, "What are we thinking of—bringing a baby into this lousy world! Are we crazy? We have to get out of here, George! But, damn it all, who in the world would buy this house *now*? Nobody, that's who! We're stuck here, George. Stuck forever!"

He had practically run across the room to put his arms around her. "This doesn't sound like you, baby. You've always been a fighter, Betty. You've always had faith!"

"Well, sweetheart, my faith's gone, and my fight's fizzled out. I'm so tired, George, tired of fighting and, mostly, tired of losing." She leaned into the solid strength of him, tears pouring from her eyes.

"We haven't lost yet, baby. Come on, buck up. This isn't you talking."

"It is now!"

And today, here she sat, taking notes like she always did, sitting quiet and peaceful, like always. The invisible woman. Little did they know. She'd had it, right up to *here*! With *all* of them! The only reason she was still here, doing their bidding, was so she'd know what was going on. They'd better deal with what happened to Deedra, or else! She knew a lot; she knew a lot she had never told.

She knew why Mrs. Schlesinger, sitting across the table in her designer clothes and her designer makeup, was absent from so many meetings. She knew which smart-ass doctor had been carrying on with Janet Rafferty, before Dr. Wolfe. She knew all of it. And, if it came to it, she knew exactly how often and for how long Dr. Wolfe and Janet Rafferty spoke on the phone, cooing at each other and making dates.

They were damn lucky she knew how to keep her mouth shut. But if they didn't start getting their priorities straight, she was going to declare war! She knew where she'd start. With that loudmouth Goldstone. He owned some of the worst slums in Harlem. Those buildings were horrible: full of rats and cockroaches, broken windows, and no heat or hot water. Yet, with all those Goldstone This-and-Thats, all over the city, his name on all of them in great big letters, he never put his name on anything he owned in the ghetto. He just took the money and ran.

"I would like to discuss the Bachelor Buildings right now," Dr. Wolfe was saying. At last, her boss was going to give it to that jackass. She could hardly keep from cheering. Goldstone thought he knew how to get around black people, thought he was charming, thought *she* was stupid. Whenever he saw her, he'd always give her the big hello, the big smile, pat her on the shoulder, ask after her family, tell her what a jewel her boss had, and call her "Beverly" the whole time.

Voorhees glared and tapped an imperious finger on the paper in front of him. "Let's stick to the agenda, Dr. Wolfe, if it's not asking too much!"

Warren Voorhees was a man, Eliot thought, totally unable to go with the flow. If you deviated from the printed schedule, it made him crazy. Well, damn it, Dr. Voorhees made *him* crazy. He thought by this time he'd be rid of this pack of hyenas. It was highly irregular anyway, this committee. It had only come into being to fill a vacuum, when Don Delafield had become unable to function. But every time he suggested dissolving it, the board mumbled something about transition. Transition, my foot, he thought, it was torture.

He was ready to fight Barney Goldstone. Barney had his own way too often, and he needed to be taught a lesson. But Voorhees, as irritating as he was, happened to be right. This time. The Bachelor Buildings were number five on the agenda, and they had not yet covered number four.

"I get it," Barney said. "You'd rather talk about me than face the facts about your screwball pal. Sam Bronstein's a looney tune; everyone knows it, and it's high time he was out on his ass!"

Eliot felt all the blood drain out of his face. He clamped his teeth together, afraid of what he might say if he let himself speak.

There was a long embarrassed silence, and then Suzanne Schlesinger broke it. "Barney! We don't call names here! And in my opinion, it is counterproductive to bring personalities into a discussion."

Janet gave her a warm smile and then turned to Barney, speak-

ing quietly. "If we think a doctor is incompetent, Mr. Goldstone, we can request a peer review. We don't dismiss good
doctors arbitrarily."

Eliot looked at her fondly. This was a hell of a lot more
support than he got at home these days! He always came away
from Janet renewed and refreshed. She was very good for his
ego. Janet wasn't the most intelligent woman he'd ever met—
Toni was, by far!—but she'd just scored now, and she had
managed to shut Barney up, for the moment anyway.

In any case, Barney was half right. Eliot *didn't* want to discuss Sam. He had to admit that he hadn't really followed up on
any of the stories he'd heard. He should have. He'd been remiss.
Hell, he'd been denying how troubled he was about Sam. Today's little lapse was a case in point. Ironically, it was just the
sort of "Freudian slip" Sam had always loved. Eliot had managed to skip Sam's name on the agenda because he didn't want
to see it.

"My apologies," Eliot said. "By all means, let us take up
the matter of Dr. Bronstein."

"I have already spoken on several occasions to Dr. Wolfe
regarding Sam Bronstein's erratic behavior," Havemayer said.
"We agree that it is troubling, primarily because it is so unlike
Dr. Bronstein. When it was a matter of missed meetings and
forgotten appointments, one could argue that we are none of us
getting any younger. . . ." There was a little ripple of amuse-
ment at that.

"But I have regretfully come to the conclusion that perhaps
it is more serious than any of us thought." He paused, glancing
over at Eliot apologetically. "I had reason, last week, to see Dr.
Bronstein in his office here in the hospital . . . to consult about
a patient. He was not there when I arrived, but the chief resident
was, and she was very agitated. On rounds that morning, Sam
had excused himself to go to the men's room. The residents and
interns waited patiently and saw him come out of the men's
room and turn in the opposite direction, walking away. They
waited for him to realize what he had done and to turn around,
but he didn't. When he disappeared around the corner, the chief
resident ran after him and hauled him back.

" 'Dr. Bronstein! We're on rounds!' she told him. She reports that he looked blank for a moment and then smiled and
said, 'A little test. I wondered when you guys would realize I

was gone.' Pretending it was a joke. But this young woman assures me that it wasn't a joke. Because, a few minutes later, when they were all gathered around one of the patients, he suddenly broke off in the middle of a sentence, stared off into space, and then walked away. This time, nobody went after him . . . and now, nobody knows what to do.''

Havemayer stopped speaking, folded his hands in front of him, and turned to Eliot, as if to say, What now?

What now, indeed? Sam, the great teacher and lecturer, forgetting what he was saying, right in the middle of a sentence? On rounds, in front of a patient? Impossible. But obviously it wasn't impossible; obviously, it was happening.

"I will see Dr. Bronstein, first thing tomorrow," he said.

"Tomorrow?" said Voorhees. "This matter should have been attended to long ago! It seems to me, Dr. Wolfe, that you *often* wait for this committee to tell you what needs to be done." There was a little gasp from the women, including Betty.

Eliot rose to his feet, leaning forward, his hands braced on the table. He kept his voice even. "I beg your pardon, Dr. Voorhees. Considering I've been here only six months and inherited a five-year-long mess, I'd say there has been much improvement at Harmony Hill."

"Dr. Voorhees, I think you owe Dr. Wolfe an apology." Of all the people, Havemayer. Voorhees inclined his head grudgingly, and Eliot sank back into his seat.

Another skirmish; another victory. Lately, his whole life was a series of the same. He only wished Havemayer would support him more often, instead of always siding with Voorhees. Havemayer was popular. Voorhees was not, but he was powerful. He had a worldwide reputation; he was a favorite of the board; he was asked to teach all over the world. And now, he'd written a book, *How to Run Forever*. His publisher had printed an enormous number and was running big ads in the *Times* and *Gotham* magazine—as Voorhees made sure you knew at every possible opportunity. It had been on the bestseller list for weeks. Right now, Voorhees had more clout in the hospital than the president himself. How could he defuse the man?

It would also be nice if Ham Pierce weren't still nosing around all the time, stirring up trouble. Just yesterday, he had been wandering around the cafeteria, accosting everybody with questions. As soon as Eliot sat down with his lunch at a table way in the back, hoping for a few minutes of peace, there he was, pulling up a chair and sitting closer than was absolutely comfortable.

"So, Dr. Wolfe, my viewers would like to know why a brilliant, talented, young doctor with a fabulous reputation leaves Harmony Hill Hospital so suddenly. Was he fired; was he forced out? Is this about . . . AIDS?"

"Absolutely not. You have my word. Every physician in this hospital has volunteered to be tested for the HIV virus."

"So what's the story?"

"No comment."

"Aw, Dr. Wolfe, come *on*! 'No comment'? You can do better than that!"

"What if I told you it had begun with an affirmative action complaint?"

"Dr. Stillman had a *complaint*?"

Eliot shook his head, savoring the moment. "No, no, Pierce. The complaint was *against* your brilliant talented young doctor." And he looked Pierce in the eye, enjoying the man's obvious bewilderment.

"You're not bullshitting."

"For once, you're one hundred percent correct, Pierce."

"Okay. Okay. But I still want the story. I know you think I'm a one-way bastard, but first and foremost I'm a newsman. If I'm wrong, I'll tell it like it is."

"Sorry. I cannot say more. Why don't you ask Stillman himself?"

Pierce got up swiftly, said that's exactly what he would do, and beat it. Eliot watched him go. What has my life come to, he thought, that besting this pain in the ass can make me feel as if I've conquered the world. He'd love to tell Pierce that Stillman, brilliant as he was, was a sleazeball who couldn't keep his hands off the women he worked with.

When Eliot had called Stillman in and told him that he was about to be brought up on sexual harrassment charges, Stillman had been stunned. He was so sure that nobody could touch him. After all, he was already quite well-known in his field.

"That little girl can't mess with me," he'd said. "All I have to do is call Ham Pierce, and she'll wish she had been born with a sense of humor!"

Eliot set him straight, very sweetly, very quietly; young Dr.

Stillman, quite ashen, decided that he would seek affiliation elsewhere, starting that day.

Five minutes later, Eliot was able to tell Janet the good news. "Dr. Stillman has resigned."

"Really?"

"He has a better offer."

For a moment, she did not respond. Then she said, "Oh, I see, that's the party line. Okay. Is he furious?"

"I would use the word chastened."

"Oh, that's wonderful! You've really handled this effectively. You're really terrific."

"I wish the committee shared your view," he said, but he couldn't help smiling.

"Eliot, you know what I think? You don't promote yourself enough. You do so much, but so subtly and cleverly, nobody ever knows!"

He knew she was flattering him. But he liked it. And besides, he thought to himself with a smile, she was right. "How about a drink after work?" he had said.

She knew what that meant, and her voice changed, softened. "I can hardly wait," she said.

Eliot shook himself mentally and brought himself back to the committee meeting. He called for order.

"I wanna say something about that lousy 'Voice of the City' I'm sure you all saw," Barney said. There was an immediate buzz of indignation. "All right, everybody, keep your pants on! Maybe I should have brought it up here first! But a man's home is his castle, right? And maybe those rooms *are* landmarks! Christ, old Lester never touched a damn thing; I think the original toilets are still there. Maybe the goddamn Bachelor Buildings should be a museum!"

"You know we can't go against the stated intent of the will," Eliot said. "In any case, I'm sure it's illegal."

"I'm gonna fight that will every way I know how. You're not living right across the street; I am."

"You can't do that and still serve on the board," said Dave Spellman. Shut up, Dave, Eliot thought silently. Just shut up.

"The hell I can't. Only a majority vote will get me off the board, and let me tell you something that you should know already, Mr. Spellman. This hospital needs me more than I need it."

Eliot thought fast. "Barney," he said, "this is new business. You're completely out of order. I suggest you call off the Landmarks people until we've all discussed this."

"I know what you're gonna say. Everyone knows you're a bleeding heart. That's why this hospital needs a hard-headed businessman like yours truly."

"And the people in this city," Eliot countered, "need an AIDS facility. We're in the middle of a plague, Barney!"

"Agh!" Barney waved off Eliot's words with a flick of his wrist. "The only reason you care about those people is because of your fag, excuse me, your *gay* son."

There was a strange, strangled gasp around the table; then Suzanne Schlesinger rose majestically. "Mr. Goldstone, you have gone too far. I insist you apologize. Immediately."

"Yeah, yeah, okay. So I was outa line. Eliot knows better than to take it to heart. Eric's a great kid. . . ."

Eliot let a minute go by, pushing the feelings of outrage away. "We're running short of time, ladies and gentlemen," he finally said. "If you don't mind, I'd like to skip to the last item on the agenda. You have undoubtedly all heard by this time that one of our residents, a young woman, was attacked at the Women's Health Center."

Havemayer, without even a pause, began to shake his noble leonine head, making a cut-off gesture with a sweep of his hands.

"What happened to that girl is, of course, tragic and horrible and regrettable. But I've said all along that the Women's Health Center belongs here in the hospital building . . . that if it *must* be made convenient to the neighborhood, it should be closed at night. Anyone who really needs it can come in the daylight hours."

"Hear, hear!" Voorhees put in. "There's been a sad lack of success up there. Now, Dr. Wolfe, please don't take this personally. There were a lot of problems up there even *before* your wife took it over. I'm sure she's doing the best she can, but . . . No, I agree with Dr. Havemayer. I say close up the place if there are so many objections. It's never been profitable anyway."

He got to his feet, glanced at his heavy gold wristwatch, and announced, "I have patients." Looking at Eliot, he said, "Close up that place, Dr. Wolfe. That's my final advice to you." As he strode rapidly out of the room, he magisterially called back, "Feel free to continue without me."

Eliot stared after him for a moment, the metallic taste of futility in his mouth. Voorhees knew the victim was Betty's own sister! What was wrong with the man?

He sensed a change in Betty's posture, and he turned to look at her, amazed at how openly the hatred blazed on her face as she, too, followed Voorhees's exit with her eyes.

23

The next day

It was unseasonably warm for the middle of March, and Eliot walked at a leisurely pace, enjoying the mild warmth of the sun on his face. After a few blocks, he unbuttoned his topcoat, then took it off and carried it over his arm, savoring the promise of spring in the air. Riverside Drive was a grand old street, he thought, with grand old architecture, grand old trees, grand old everything. It curved and meandered, here alongside the park, there next to a wide stretch of path where joggers jogged and starched nannies pushed prams. Every tree was ready to burst into leaf, and there were crocuses poking up through the grass. The hospital seemed very far away. Walking here was like escaping to another time and place.

And that's exactly what he must not do. He had promised to investigate Sam's situation, and he was off to a bad start: strolling along, enjoying the signs of spring, and letting his mind wander. But his mind badly wanted to wander; every time he asked himself, What's wrong with Sam? his heart thumped painfully, and his chest constricted. It could be so many things, and all of them were frightening.

His heart had started banging away this morning, when he lifted the phone and called psychiatry. Lunch, he thought, he'd ask Sam to have lunch, and that would make it seem natural. But Sam wasn't there and wouldn't be.

"This is Dr. Sam's day for private patients," the secretary had told him. "He sees them in his office at home, you know."

"Thank you," he said. "I'll call him there."

"I'll be happy to make an appointment for you, Dr. Wolfe."

"No, no, I'll call him myself."

Eliot had waited until the end of the fifty-minute hour and called at ten fifty-one.

Sam picked up the phone himself. "Hi, old buddy, what's up?"

"You still in a meeting? No? Good. How about lunch at one?"

"One is great! Someone cancelled. I'll make *Samwiches*!" He laughed and Eliot had to smile. Sam loved to construct quadruple-decker sandwiches so thick, you couldn't fit them into your mouth; but a knife and fork were strictly forbidden. He'd made them as far back as Eliot could remember. "And just this once, to hell with your cholesterol! I've got some lean corned beef you wouldn't believe!"

"My mouth's watering already." Eliot sat at his desk, smiling for a few minutes after he hung up, remembering certain *Samwiches* from his teens, concoctions that had made the cleaning woman, Edna, roll her eyes and mutter under her breath about boys' stomachs. They had always had such a good time, he and Sam. And now . . . ? He quickly grabbed a handful of memos left neatly stacked on the side of his desk and bent to them.

But he hadn't been able to concentrate; the words just swam on the page, meaningless. That damned Voorhees! He had demanded a special meeting of the ethics committee to discuss Dr. Samuel Bronstein. Eliot had promised to look into it, and he was doing it! But Voorhees was so intent on discrediting Eliot, he didn't care what he did to Sam. Ethics! Voorhees had all the ethics of a snake! He still wanted Eliot's job.

Sam's apartment building was on the corner, a large, turreted, castlelike affair. Sam always told people that a look at his building could save them a trip up the Rhine. Eliot didn't have to ring; Josie the doorman knew him and flung the door wide open, gesturing him to the elevator. Josie was an elderly man now; he'd been there since Sam and his bride had moved in as newlyweds, which had to be over twenty-five years ago. Josie always wore a vest under his navy blue uniform, usually a bright blue. But every year on the first of December, there would appear a vest of brilliant crimson, which he would wear, in honor of the holiday season, until the end of the month. With the new year, it would be back to the blue. But today—

"Yellow, Josie?"

"My grandson gave it t'me, Dr. Wolfe. Said it was time for

a change. Kinda pretty, ain't it? And it's velvet, like.'' The old man preened for a moment, then came to attention and hurried to open the door for someone else.

Eliot took the elevator to the tenth floor; it was a familiar trip, done countless times without thought. This time, of course, his mind was whirling. When the elevator door slid open, he stood, staring at an unfamiliar hallway with a painting he'd never seen. And then he saw the brass number was not 10 but 11, his parents' floor in their building. Oh, he wasn't *very* anxious about this, not much!

As he finally stepped out on the tenth floor, a voice called out, ''Yoohoo! Hold that for me, would you, darling?'' It was a voice familiar to millions—and to him, as well. Irene Moore, in very high heels and a short, fluffy fur coat, was in the process of locking the front door of the apartment. Sam's office had its own entrance, very near the elevator.

''Hello, Irene,'' he said, walking toward her. If they were going to talk about Sam, he wanted it to be as far from the office door as possible.

''Eliot! How nice! Oh, dear, I see you're carrying your coat. Am I overdressed? Oh, I hope not; I love wearing fox in the spring! It looks . . . I don't know . . . *young*, you know what I mean?''

Eliot had not the slightest clue what she might mean. Where oh where was Lillian when you needed her to interpret? But he smiled and nodded.

''Oh. Dear. Why are you here during working hours? Why aren't you at the hospital? Is something wrong?'' Her voice tightened and sharpened as she spoke, and the brilliant Irene Moore smile was replaced by a worried frown.

''Wrong?'' He tried very hard to look innocent, and obviously he failed, because she said, ''Then you've seen it, too.''

''Seen what?''

She gave him a sharp look, raising one eyebrow. ''That Sam has been having . . . moments when he's . . . not quite himself? Oh God! Eliot, what *is* it? What's wrong with Sam?'' There was real panic in her voice. Eliot reached out and took her hand.

''I'm not sure. Little strokes, maybe?''

Irene flinched. ''Oh, God.''

''Yes, well . . .'' He paused. What would she do if he listed

some of the other possibilities? ''Has he talked to you about
it?''

''No.'' Her lower lip wobbled. ''Oh damn. I mustn't smear
my makeup; there's not enough time to redo it.'' Now her voice
shook, and she stopped, blinking rapidly. ''Once, I said something to him about a checkup, and he blew up at me. Eliot . . .
he . . . he pushed me, he was so mad! He was like a crazy
person! Eliot . . . You don't think Sam's . . . *crazy*, do you?''
He saw fear flickering deep in her eyes, and he squeezed her
hand briefly.

''Lord, no! He's still the sanest person I know.''

She stood, looking at him, half-smiling, and then she said,
''Now I *must* run! Eleanor—my agent—Eleanor will have *kit-
tens* if I'm late again! Here, let me unlock the door for you.''

They walked briskly to Sam's office and she unlocked the
door to the waiting room. She tipped her head up for an air
kiss—she smelled of some heady exotic perfume—and went to
the elevator, pushing the button. ''Oh, Eliot.''

He paused, his hand on the knob. ''Yes?''

''You didn't happen to notice a young man hanging around
downstairs, did you? A rather tall young man, with dark hair
that flops over his forehead and really intense, burning eyes?''

That woman! ''No, Irene. I don't remember seeing anyone
other than Josie in a really intense yellow vest.''

He had a momentary thought that only Irene could be flat-
tered by the attentions of a stranger. And then he let himself in,
ready to march through the empty waiting room, right into Sam's
office, and announce himself starving and ready to eat *anything*,
anything at all, ready then to confront him, arm around his
shoulders, man to man, friend to friend, brother to brother. . . .

But the waiting room wasn't empty. Two pairs of round blue
eyes turned to stare up at him. What the hell—?

He consulted his watch. Five after one. ''Excuse me,'' he
said. ''I have a one o'clock appointment with Dr. Bronstein.''
He forced a little laugh. ''Unless I'm wrong, and I *don't* have a
one o'clock?''

The couple sitting side by side on the tweed sofa, holding
hands, looked amazingly alike: pale blond hair in Dutch boy
haircuts, his a bit shorter; pug noses; freckles. They also looked
amazingly young at first glance, but then you couldn't help but
notice the network of fine lines on both faces, and the wide,

matching gold wedding bands. They were his age! His age, and they dressed like college kids from the fifties. She was even wearing argyle knee socks and saddle shoes. God, he hadn't seen a pair of saddle shoes since he was at Columbia. Something about the couple nagged at him. He was sure he knew them, yet he was equally sure he'd never met them before.

The woman spoke in a high-pitched, childlike voice. "Oh, no, you could have had a one o'clock. *We* had a twelve o'clock."

Eliot looked at her, waiting. "Yes. And—?"

Now the man answered. "Dr. Sam must be running late . . . and it must be pretty deep, or he would have come out and told us we'd have to wait."

Running late? Yes, it could happen. But, then, Sam would never leave somebody waiting *this* long! "Have you tried knocking on his door?"

"Oh, no! We'd never do that! It's very unnerving when someone interrupts you—"

"Especially when it's deep!"

"Yes, of course. But, aren't you concerned? Aren't you annoyed?"

"Oh no!" The woman was almost too girlish. "It's never happened before, and Tim and I believe in patience and fortitude. Oh, hell, I might as well admit it!" She dimpled, and Eliot couldn't help but notice her husband dimpled right along with her. "Dr. Sam made time for us today . . . *squoze* us in, you might say! . . . so we can't complain if we're kept waiting a little bit, can we?"

"A small crisis," her husband added.

"Oh, darling, not really a crisis!" the woman protested.

"Now, Brenda, darling, you *know* you've been just the littlest bit . . . unnerved. You always are, when you have to play Auntie Matilda." To Eliot, he explained, *"The Gingerbread House."* Of course! That's why they looked so familiar! Brenda and Tim O'Connell. God, when he had been in college, they had been the hottest thing on four feet! They and their show. He wrote it, starred in it as the Hero and she had played the ingenue for countless years. Hell, *The Gingerbread House* had run almost forever! In college, Eliot had known all the words to all the songs. Everyone had.

"It's a real pleasure to meet you," he said, and they smiled and blushed simultaneously. "Love your show."

"Then you've seen it!"

"Only six or seven times." Which happened to be true. It was a charming musical fable with hummable tunes. All his kids had loved it. He stood smiling at them, wondering what they'd been doing since it closed, back in the 1980s. So, he asked.

"Oh, we've been *very* busy. We've taken the show all over this country and all over the world."

"And, do you know, Tim still plays the Hero. Audiences just love him!"

The smile was relentless, but her voice gave her away. She was not a happy camper. And then it came to him. Auntie Matilda was one of the characters in *The Gingerbread House*, a chubby elderly woman of unending folk wisdom and forgetfulness. So. Tim got to stay young forever, while she had to take on character roles. Maybe that's why they were here to see Sam.

And, speaking of Sam, what the hell was he doing in there? He couldn't possibly have a patient! Making up his mind all at once, Eliot strode to the door and, accompanied by gasps from Tim and Brenda, knocked loudly. When there was no immediate response from inside, he opened it a crack and stuck his head in.

No patient. No doctor, in fact. Nobody. The office was empty. He stood for a moment, trying to figure out what to say to the O'Connells, how to look deep into those identical round eyes and lie.

"He must have had an emergency at the hospital," he said, turning to them with his best professional smile. "You'll probably find a message waiting for you on your answering machine."

They agreed that probably that's exactly what they would find. But as they left, calling out cheery good-byes, Eliot knew in his heart that they would find nothing from Dr. Sam when they got home.

He walked into the familiar office, dimly lit, wood paneled, with its wall of framed photographs, Sam's collection of pre-Columbian statues, and the inevitable boxes of tissues, strategically placed by each chair. Even the smell was familiar: a mix of leather, lemon oil, and chocolate. Eliot paced in front of the big desk that was never used, then drifted over to the photos. One in particular caught his eye: the twelve-year-old Sam, still terribly thin and looking haunted by his parents' sudden death, standing beside the boy Eliot, whose shoulders were back like his mother had taught him, well-fed, well-dressed, well-behaved.

He remembered that day: that was the day Sam had been rescued from his aunt and uncle in the East New York section of Brooklyn. The uncle was his mother's ne'er-do-well brother, always in businesses that failed, always in some kind of trouble. But, he was the closest relative when Aaron and Ida Bronstein died, leaving their only son an orphan. So, Sam was handed over to Uncle Al and Aunt Myrna.

Although the Wolfes called Sam regularly, he was never allowed onto the telephone and never returned their calls. So after a week or two of this, Lillian decided they'd better get over there to see what was going on. Eliot was told none of the details; when asked, Philip's lips tightened, and his eyes flashed. Lillian, of course, had more to say, but even that had been abbreviated.

"They are terrible people, and they were working that poor child like a slave in the store! Never even told him we called, those *momzers*!" Eliot still remembered it word for word. It was one of the few times he could ever remember his mother using profanity—and in Yiddish! She had made such a horrible face that, if you were eleven years old, you knew you didn't *want* to know any details.

It was Sam, years later, who told Eliot how Lillian had stood there, daring Uncle Al to just *try*, just *try* to throw her out. "He threatened, all right," Sam said. "But he couldn't scare *her*! She stood there, refusing to back off. 'Don't you move even your pinky, Al Feuerstein,' she said, 'because if you do, I'll have the police here in two minutes flat!'

" 'Oh yeah?' Uncle Al said. 'You and what army?'

"And your mother, without turning even, said, 'Philip! Call the cops! Sam! Pack your bag! Al! Go to hell!' " Eliot had been so impressed. He had always known she was strong and tough, but he had no idea she could say "Go to hell!" And the end of the story was, all three of them obeyed her, instantly. "What a moment!" Sam had said, in admiration. "What a woman!"

Eliot pulled himself away from the photographs, away from the memories. Oh God, this was so difficult! How could this be happening to Sam of all people!

Maybe Sam was somewhere in the apartment and had forgotten he had patients waiting. Maybe he was in the kitchen, building Samwiches. Eliot strode to the door that led into the back of the apartment and walked down the hallway. There was no one here; he knew it. Goddamn it.

He found himself, like a child, thinking, Please God, don't let it be true. Don't let anything be wrong with Sam. He was bargaining with the deity, thinking, If Sam can be okay, then I'll . . . I'll be more careful with Toni; I'll give up Janet, and I promise it will never happen again. Foolishness.

He walked into the kitchen, still hoping against hope that he'd find Sam deep in the refrigerator, arms loaded with meats, cheeses, tomatoes, and containers of cole slaw and pickle relish. But no. No Sam, no Samwiches, no nothing.

When Sam had first come to live with them, it had felt like a miracle to a lonely, only child whose parents were very busy and apt to treat their son like another adult. Sam was a dreamer, a planner, and a marathon talker. A year older than Eliot, and much taller back then, he'd seemed godlike. He had not been brought up as if he were a miniature grown-up, and he didn't know any of the rules. He let doors slam; he left lights on; he read in bed after his bedtime; he *ran* through the apartment.

And he talked back. Sam was brave and oblivious at the same time. He didn't seem to catch on that you were supposed to sit quietly at the table, speaking only if addressed directly. He didn't seem to realize that the world revolved around the Doctor and that the Doctor required peace and quiet. Hadn't Lillian taken him aside and explained all that? Apparently not. He chattered, he told moron jokes—and then laughed at them—he ate noisily and enthusiastically, and he talked with his mouth full. And he belched! The first time that had occurred, Eliot couldn't believe it. He waited for the sky to fall in, but Philip only gave Sam a look. "Manners, my boy, are what you are judged by," he'd said gravely.

After Sam came, there appeared on Lillian's armchair table a pile of books: the Gesell Institute book on child development, *You and Your Teenager*, even Dr. Spock. When she caught Eliot gawking at them, she said rather defensively: "Well, before, there was just you, and you're such a good boy. But now, there is . . . there are *children* in this household, and Sam has suffered a great loss."

He never did figure out the logic of that. All he knew was

that things had changed. Sam even dared to disagree with Philip about the formation of the state of Israel, and the Doctor not only allowed this act of insubordination, but actually held a discussion on the subject. Wonder was piling upon wonder, and the young Eliot was wonderstruck.

He particularly remembered one dinner hour—he even recalled that they were having lamb chops—when Sam told the latest Little Willy joke: "Little Willy lit a rocket, put it in his father's pocket. Next he told his Uncle Dan, Daddy is a traveling man!" Eliot had just taken a big swallow of milk, and when he began to laugh, milk came pouring out of his nose and mouth. He shot a quick look at Lillian. She was laughing, too. Trying not to, but laughing. And Philip's lips were twitching! Sam, of course, was shrieking. The real miracle was that he was not reprimanded.

After everyone had calmed down, Lillian regarded Eliot at length. He wasn't sure he liked the way she was looking at him; it made him uneasy. He didn't know what to expect. And still, she managed to surprise him.

"Eliot, darling, do *you* tell these silly jokes?"

His first impulse was to say no. But Sam was always advising him to "tell them what you really think! They won't mind, you'll see! You gotta stand up for yourself!" And now Sam kicked him under the table, reminding him; so, his stomach churning, he admitted that yes, he told those silly jokes.

"Well, well," Lillian said. "And is there anything else you'd like to let us in on?"

Sam kicked him again, hard, and when they looked at each other, they couldn't help it, they started laughing. They had been plotting and planning for weeks—that is, Sam had been plotting and planning. And now Lillian had asked the magic question, without even needing prodding.

"Go on!" Sam said.

"Yes, Eliot," his mother urged. "Go on. What is it?"

Out it came, in one long breath: "Please, we'd like to have a dog, it could be a small dog, only not too small, please, and we'll take care of it, honest. Both of us, we'll take turns, we'll walk it, we'll feed it, and if it gets sick, we'll take it to the vet. Really, we'll train it, we'll make it behave so well, you won't even know it's here, and we'll pay for its food out of our allowances and . . ." He ran out of breath. "And everything."

There was a long silence, a long look exchanged between his parents. Neither of them moved or even nodded, but when Lillian turned back to the two boys, it had apparently been decided. "Okay. But if I find that dog being neglected in any way, out it goes!"

He and Sam leaped up from their chairs, rushing to hug her, to shower her with kisses and thank-yous. She giggled. He could see she was very pleased with their response, but she waved them off, saying, "My hair, my hair." And then, when they sat down again, she smiled and looking heavenward, asked, "Oh, Lord, what have I done?" Then they had all laughed.

If anyone asked him for the single greatest moment of his childhood, Eliot knew that would be it. After that, they had Seamus, an Irish setter of sweet temper and boundless affection. The dog, to Eliot's unending delight, chose to sleep at *his* feet.

Thinking about it now, in Sam's empty, sun-filled kitchen, Eliot realized that Seamus had given him his first real experience of unquestioning love. Or had it been Sam? Sam, the dog, the change in the household—a new world of possibilities had suddenly opened up before him. Sam had taught them all to do life differently. But now, what was happening to him, what horrible thing was draining the very soul out of Sam?

Eliot sat down at the old porcelain-topped kitchen table. He thought he knew what it was. They would have to do all the usual tests, of course. But he was finished with telling himself little fairy tales about Sam. When he added together all the symptoms and all the stories, he kept coming up with the same dreaded diagnosis. And the thought of it—early-onset Alzheimer's—made him put his head down into his hands and weep.

24

March

They walked down the street together, hand in hand. Well, hand in *glove*, anyway. How long had it been since they had held hands, even with gloves on? Gloves were a necessity today; there was a bitter wind blowing down from Canada. It was so bright, and the sky was such a clear blue, that she had been fooled, looking out the window, into thinking it was really spring; and she had put on a coat that was much too light. How long had it been since she had felt this good with Eliot? She felt like skipping, Toni realized. Actually, she felt like *singing*, but she didn't want to scare people off Columbus Avenue, now did she?

She slid a glance up at her husband and found him looking down at her affectionately. They grinned at each other. How long since *that* had happened? Last night, they had made love. How long since *that* had happened? Never mind, never mind. Things were going to get better now.

Last night, still wrapped in each other's arms, he had said, sleepily, "Toni, I've know I've been . . . stupid. I'm going to . . . I think . . . it's going to be fine, tomorrow, with . . . him."

She pushed herself away so she could look at him. "Oh, Eliot, it's so good to hear you say that. You really mean it?"

"I'm actually looking forward to it, in a kind of queasy way." A strange way of putting it, but he laughed, so she laughed, too. And then, they had made love again.

And here they were, on their way to the Greenhouse for brunch. With her son. With King. She had thought it would never happen; she had thought Eliot would stonewall forever.

She was going to ask, last night, what in the world had made
him change his mind, but for once in her life, she knew when
to keep her mouth shut. And anyway, who cared? There, standing in the sunlight in front of the restaurant, was King. She
called his name, simultaneously remembering with a twinge
how Eliot had reacted when she had told him that he had been
named after Martin Luther King. "Martin Luther King *Crawford*?" he said, incredulous, and she had winced at the distaste
in his voice.

What was wrong with that name? What was wrong with *Eliot*? Shut up, Toni, she told herself. Don't make waves. They're
finally meeting each other; just enjoy it, okay?

She beamed with pride and pleasure at the good-looking
young man waiting for them. How could anyone resist him?
Now he turned, and he spotted her, and he was smiling. He was
so adorable, she thought; look at him, how tall and strong he
is, how well built. And look at that sweet smile. Her heart just
melted.

She dropped Eliot's hand and ran the last few feet, so glad to
see King and so glad this was all happening. She expected a big
hug from her son; the last few times they had met privately, they
had hugged. But, although he grasped her arms, he came no
closer, but he bent his head to kiss her cheek. He must be nervous. Then she turned so she could introduce them, and she saw
a certain stiff look on Eliot's face that she knew very well meant
he was none too comfortable, himself. What babies men were!
she thought and then chided herself. It was bound to be a little
awkward in the beginning. *Paziènza!* she scolded herself.

After they were seated by the big window overlooking the
street and had ordered drinks, there was an awkward silence,
which Toni filled by saying brightly, "I wonder why it's okay to
drink at brunch. We'd never have a drink at breakfast, but we
don't think a thing of it, not on a Sunday and not at a brunch."
The two men gave her identical vacant looks.

"So. What are we going to eat?"

That was more of a success. They could discuss the menu for
a minute and a half. And then that same horrible silence fell
once more. Come on, Eliot, she thought; you're the president
at this table. You're able to charm ten thousand little old ladies
at once; how come you're struck dumb at the sight of my child?

"How do you like working for Harmony Hill?" Good, Eliot.

"Much better, now that you're the president." Oh, King! That one gets a gold star!

"Why?"

King laughed. "The hospital just seems to . . . work better. Morale is up; people just seem a lot happier about coming to work. And, it's much more efficient in the E.R."

"My son's in the E.R. Do you know him? Dr. David Wolfe."

What is this, a contest of sons? Toni thought, annoyed. Was he trying to rub it in, that *his* son was an M.D. and *her* son was only a para? And then she chided herself. What are you talking about? Shut up, Toni!

"King's mother wants him to be a doctor," she said. The moment she said "mother," she realized she'd made a mistake. What an awkward thing to bring up! The worst! *She* was King's mother, too, but Eliot didn't particularly want to be reminded of that fact. And maybe King didn't, either. After all, it was Mrs. Crawford whom he called Mom. She was not doing this very well.

But King didn't seem to take it amiss. "Doesn't every Jewish mother want her son to be a doctor?"

Eliot's face changed subtly, and he leaned forward a little toward King. "Your . . . adoptive mother is Jewish?" He actually sounded interested.

"Yeah. So she *says*. We always have a menorah at Hanukkah, along with the Christmas tree; and she fasts on Yom Kippur. But I've never seen the inside of a synagogue." He laughed.

Eliot pulled back. "Then you were raised as a Christian?"

"They flipped a coin, and Jesus won," King said, still laughing. And then he noticed that Eliot was not amused and stopped. "The religion in *our* house is fighting for the underdog," he said.

Toni felt like a soda with all the fizz gone. I give up, she thought. This is not going to be wonderful. The waiter appearing with their food was a welcome sight, and they all dug in as if brunch were a job that had to be done with complete concentration. Toni toyed with her Eggs Benedict and tried to get Eliot to meet her eyes, which he wouldn't. She and King chatted about the Women's Health Center and Charmaine and the science courses he'd have to make up if he wanted to apply for medical school. Eliot finally chimed in—well come on, if a doctor couldn't talk about medical school admissions, who could—but he was withdrawn and too goddamned polite.

You're behaving very badly, Eliot. She stared at him, trying to send her thoughts to him. You're supposed to be the grown-up, Eliot. Why can't you give the kid some *real* responses; he really is planning to apply to med school. You did it for me, she thought. And I'm sorry if you don't like to face the fact that this young man is my child, but he is. He's my son. If you love me, you should at least be able to accept that. So what's the matter with you?

Eliot stared across the table at King Crawford. The kid was really good-looking, and he seemed bright enough. For a few minutes at a time, he could forget and just talk to King; then the thought would hit him again, like a fist in the belly. If he wasn't careful, he'd end up with colitis again.

This was Toni's son. *Toni's son.* The same Toni who never had time to have *his* child. She wanted to bring this young man, this stranger, into their lives—into the Wolfe family, for Christ's sake—just like that! And he was expected to knuckle under and say sure, okay, whatever you say. He was expected to open his arms and accept without reservation.

The young man—he couldn't think of him by his name, just couldn't because it made the whole thing too real—seemed to be decent and intelligent. After all, he was a paramedic and a college graduate, so he wasn't an ignoramus. But Christ, he was half-black. She wanted to *introduce* him as her son, she wanted to acknowledge him. But that meant everyone in the world would know all about her affair! It was like revealing every dirty thing in your past for the whole world to see and judge. And how would they judge her? His wife and her child? Her bastard, which is how everyone else would think of him!

"Is that what you think, Eliot?"

"What? Excuse me, I was woolgathering."

Her voice was tight, a sure sign, as he well knew, of her growing impatience. "Medical schools are looking less at science grades and more at the *person.*"

"They always did, Toni. I had many long interviews . . . and so did you."

"But you and I had to be straight-*A* students."

"I didn't have straight *A*'s."

She regarded him for a moment, much as a scientist might peer at something under his microscope, and then she deliberately turned away and continued talking to her son.

What was *he* supposed to do with this sudden new "son"? Damn it, he had more than enough to contend with, with his own! He needed her to support *him*. She had no right, goddamn it, to pull this stunt on him! This kid didn't need her! He *had* parents; she said he loved them. That wasn't the point, and he knew it. The point was, her son was young and healthy, and his son was under sentence of death.

Eric. Eliot's eyes stung with the threat of tears. But only the threat. God knows he wished he could weep.

Goddamn it, this wasn't supposed to happen to his family. His family was well-to-do, well-educated, well-endowed and well-thought of. Only good things happened to the Wolfes. They were on an upward climb to the summit, next stop Mt. Olympus. Or so they all had thought!

Eric had told him on the goddamn telephone. Well, that was on purpose; he admitted it. "I didn't want a scene," he said. That's why he'd called at the hospital.

He was HIV positive—"But no symptoms. Maybe I'll escape." Eliot couldn't help the groan that was torn out of his throat. There was no escape from this horror, not yet. As usual, Eric was hiding his fear behind a facade of funny comments. All that clowning around: whistling in the dark!

He couldn't just stand by, helplessly. Whatever treatment there was, however questionable, however experimental, wherever in the world it might be, however much it might cost, he would get it for Eric.

Eliot came back to brunch with a jolt. God, he had no idea what they were talking about! It was embarrassing. He felt Toni's gaze, and when he looked she was giving him a look that could freeze fish.

"I'm sorry," he said and tried to laugh. "I seem to keep drifting off. I must be tired."

"Sure," King Crawford said, and his smile didn't look any more sincere than his own apology had been. "Well, I gotta be going. I've got a lot of . . . stuff to do," he said, lamely. A minute later and he was gone.

As soon as King was out the door, Toni said, through clenched teeth, "You sure were America's sweetheart, Eliot. Just a Yankee Doodle Dandy.'' Now she wouldn't look at him. He couldn't win. He said so.

''Eliot,'' she said, in a tone he recognized. ''Eliot, you can't be that stupid! I refuse to believe it!''

He swallowed his angry answer and gestured for the check. They did not speak while he proffered his credit card, waited for the waiter to bring the receipt, and added a tip—hiding it with his hand so she couldn't see how much it was. She always gave him such a hard time about being a lousy tipper! All this time, they sat together without exchanging one word. He snuck a look at her; just as he had feared, she was grim and tight-lipped. Well, *that* did it! The end of what had been a pleasant weekend!

They walked back up Columbus Avenue in cold silence for two or three blocks, and then, finally, she spit it out. ''You know, Eliot, I didn't want very *much* from you today. Just to meet King. *And* to be polite. It seems you couldn't manage that.''

''All *I* ever want from *you* is that you occasionally come with me to a hospital function. *And* to be polite. And you don't seem to manage *that*!''

''Give me a break! It's a very different thing, and you know it.'' Her eyes had filled with tears—if she thought crying was going to soften him up, she was sadly mistaken. He was pissed. He had come today only for her sake. Too bad that wasn't enough. Nothing, goddamn it, was enough for her!

''He's my baby, and you were awful to him!''

''It seems to me, Toni,'' he said, very calm and very much in control, ''that the time to worry about 'your baby' was about twenty-five years ago.''

She gasped. ''Fuck you!'' she yelled at the top of her voice, her face turning purple.

God, look at her! He didn't have to stand here in the middle of the street and take abuse! Didn't she have any sense of pro-priety? Well, maybe *she* didn't, but *he* did! Everyone, goddamn it, was staring at them!

Turning on his heel, he marched away, fully expecting to hear the clicking of her high-heeled boots following him. When he had crossed the street, he stopped and turned to see what she was doing. But she was gone. Just disappeared; he couldn't see her anywhere. To hell with her. He'd take a walk and let her cool off. Maybe he'd call Janet . . . no, he wouldn't. He could go see if Sam was home or, even better, he'd drop in on Lillian and Philip—they'd be so pleased—and read the Sunday *Times* in peace.

Damn that kid for finding her. Why the hell couldn't he mind his own business? Christ, why did that boy have to come into their lives and screw up everything! And then Eliot recalled just how her son had discovered her. On that goddamned magazine cover. That goddamned magazine story was going to haunt them forever.

25

Same day

Toni watched her husband's cowardly retreat for two seconds, and then she turned away in disgust! Why couldn't he stand and fight? He never stood up for himself! Never! *Never* fought back! He was *never* going to change, either! To hell with him!

She steamed crosstown, heading for the apartment, not giving a damn that she probably looked demented, charging along muttering to herself. Eliot had better not be there! And if he was, he'd better steer clear of her!

What if she treated one of *his* kids like that? She'd always been wonderful with them, and they weren't so goddamned perfect, *and* it wasn't so goddamned easy, either! That Carolyn! There was a wildness in her, and it had sure been in evidence when she had been a teenager, living with them. Yeah, how *about* Carolyn as a teenager? Hadn't Toni welcomed her, even though she and Eliot were newlyweds? She'd been a royal pain in the ass, little Carolyn. But had Toni told Eliot to get that kid into a boarding school before she killed her? No, she had not. She had bitten her tongue and kept her mouth shut and suffered, praying that she and Carolyn would live through it! Now that she thought of it, she'd been a goddamned saint!

Not a word of thanks from the father, oh no! And then look what happened the minute David came back from Africa. Invited to live with them . . . without a word to her! Lucky that David didn't want to. Lucky for Eliot, because otherwise she would have been forced to wring his neck. She was supposed to become a mommy at the drop of a hat, and he couldn't even bring himself to show the modicum of courtesy to her son! Oh, it was maddening! Eliot had to know that King was feeling strange and awkward this morning. It was his job to put the younger man at ease.

Well, that made her laugh. Grown up? A man who looked around frantically to see who was watching because his wife just said "fuck" out loud? A man who dodged his own weaknesses by running away? Fuck him! She'd said it before, and she'd say it again.

"Fuck you, Eliot!" she said and then giggled at herself. "Thanks, I needed that!"

She looked up then and saw with surprise that she was home. This was her building, and that was her doorman looking at her with a shocked expression, which he was trying very hard to hide.

She held herself very straight and sailed by him, with a breezy, "Thank you, Frank, have a good one!"

"You, too, Dr. Romano!"

Once inside the apartment, she realized she was still angry and unsettled. She couldn't relax. She couldn't do the *Times* puzzle. She couldn't *think*. She paced back and forth in the living room, fidgety and disgruntled. Damn him! Why wasn't he home so she could yell at him some more? The more she thought about the debacle at the restaurant, the less she could understand Eliot's behavior.

Oh my God, she thought. She'd been home ten minutes and hadn't even thought to call her service. As she went to the phone, her mood began to lift. Maybe she would have something to do, something that would take her mind off her woes.

Two messages. One from Gloria Gomez, saying she might be late tomorrow but she might not. And then one that made her heart precipitously begin knocking against her ribs. "Mr. Pierce, Hamilton Pierce." She took down the phone number and was even able to ask in a normal tone of voice whether or not it was urgent. But she never heard the answer. Her thoughts were spinning.

This could be dangerous. She stared at the phone, at the block letters she had printed, spelling out his name. She could call him tomorrow from her office. She could have the secretary call him. But even as she was thinking these very sensible thoughts, her hand was reaching for the phone. Why would he be calling her on a Sunday? What could it be?

As she dialed, she told herself it must have something to do

with the hospital or the center. She really ought to be worried,
or at least concerned. Instead of that, though, she was remembering that Italian restaurant, the eager mouth on hers, the solid
muscular arms around her, the way the heat had climbed in her.

She licked dry lips and waited to see if he would answer, half
hoping, half dreading. There was a click and then the thin sound
of a recorded message. Her heart plummeted.

"Hi"—only when he said it, it was more like *hey*—"you've
almost reached Ham Pierce." Damn it! Almost was *not* good
enough. But shame on her for feeling this way! Very unprofessional! Very immature! Very quote "feminine" unquote!

And then there was his voice, his *real* voice, yelling over the
message, "Don't go 'way! I'm here! I'm here!" Just that little
touch of Southern drawl that made everything he said sound so
intimate, so appealing . . . to his audience, of course. And then,
the machine clicked off, and he said, "Yes?" in a rather brisk
tone.

She suddenly felt so awkward. Of course this was about the
hospital. She should just say, "Mr. Pierce, this is Dr. Romano,
returning your call." But that was so contrived. Why couldn't
she just be natural? What was the matter with her?

"Hi, Ham. This is Toni." Keep it casual.

"I know your voice, Toni." His intonation had transformed
itself so suddenly to "warm and intimate," it made her a little
light-headed.

She began to talk rapidly. "It must be something important,
or you wouldn't be leaving me messages on a Sunday . . . unless, of course, it's an old message. I can't really remember
when I checked in last, I was in the hospital most of the day
yesterday, and today—"

"Slow down, Toni." She wished he would get that tender
note out of his voice. "Stop talking a minute, and I'll explain."
He paused. "You still there?"

"I'm still here." Where else would she be? "And . . . ?"

"I was thinking about a new series . . . it could be great. I
hope you're not going to turn it down without thinking about
it." He laughed. "Now *I'm* babbling. I haven't even told you
what my idea is. See, I've been looking around this town, and
I've found out that there are some wonderful women who are
making a big difference. One special person can accomplish a

lot, and I'm beginning to see how often that special person is female.

"Let me tell you what I mean. There's a security guard at an elementary school up on Lenox Avenue, a woman, a black woman, about fifty years old, unmarried, who's become the big mama of the entire school. Kids come to her with their problems; parents come to her to ask why a kid is acting up; teachers come to her to talk about kids who are troubled. This one woman, all by herself, has made an enormous difference in that school."

"That sounds exciting, Ham, but I don't understand. What has that got to do with me?"

"Oh. Well, of course, you're one of them."

"Oh, Ham, that's nonsense. No."

"I'm calling the series 'One Woman'; isn't that a great title? You promised you wouldn't turn me down without thinking about it!"

She laughed a little. "I didn't say that. *You* did."

"You. Me. What's the difference, as long as it got said? Oh, come on, Toni, you'd be terrific. You've got a mouth! And I know how much of a change you've made, in several lives. Charmaine Jackson's, for instance. All I want to do is get together with you and talk about it."

"Well . . ."

"I know a place where you can get the best Chinese food in New York."

She knew she should tell him she'd already eaten and was full. But damn Eliot! She was still mad. It would serve him right not to find her at home when he finally decided to come back and face her. "Sounds good to me. Where?"

"A nice little spot called 'my place.' "

"Ham!"

"I'll be a perfect gentleman."

Oh, damn! Oh, damn! But it would serve Eliot right if she was at Ham Pierce's apartment, and he didn't know where to find her!

"Okay," she said.

Her heart began thumping the moment she approached U.N. Plaza, his building, and it kept right on hammering as she crossed the silent lobby to the huge desk, was announced, given

a pass, presented it to the elevator operator, and was—finally—
taken up to the ninth floor. "To your right, ma'am."

She nodded and walked down the hall, telling her heartbeat
to slow down.

He was standing in the open doorway. As she moved past
him, he took her briefcase from her, with a laugh, and handed
her a glass of champagne.

She took it and gulped before she even thought about it.
"What is it with this building?" she demanded. "I thought I'd
never be allowed up here. It's easier to get into the Crown Jewels
. . . and how come champagne? I thought this was business."

He grinned at her and gestured her to the left. She went; she
was in his hands. As soon as she walked into the living room,
she was faced with an entire wall of windows with a breathtaking
view of the East River and the bridges beyond. "Oh my God!"
she said. "How marvelous!"

She walked over to look out, aware that he was right behind
her. "It's beautiful. You feel so close to the water! And didn't
Georgia O'Keefe paint this exact view?" She felt his hand lightly
on her shoulder. Nervously, she moved on. "Oh and what a
beautiful sculpture!" She reached out to touch a large black
wood carving. Only a moment later did she realize that it was a
female figure, very definitely female, with every female attri-
bute emphasized, *definitely* emphasized.

She pulled her hand away as if it were burned. Behind her,
Ham laughed. "She's my fertility goddess! She doesn't bite!"

She took another sip of champagne. Really, she shouldn't be
drinking this early in the day. She could already feel a little buzz
way in the back of her brain, and it made her uneasy. The best
idea was to keep moving, keep talking, look around . . . and
there was plenty to look at. Sculpture, paintings, built-in bookcases, filled with all kinds of books.

"You read all of these?"

"Avidly." That laugh, again.

At that very moment, her eye happened to light on a group
of books: Masters & Johnson; *Intimate History of the United
States*; a *History of Erotica*; and, for God's sake, *Sex and the
Single Girl*. Oh, Christ, he'd caught her looking at them. *Caught
her?* When was the last time she'd had a thought like that? In
parochial school? For God's sake, she was a gynecologist!
Breasts and sex and buttocks didn't embarrass her! She was

never like this, never! She could feel his eyes on the back of her neck. She wished he would stop staring at her.

She moved away again, heading for the white leather couch— no, no, not the couch, one of the chairs!

"Toni, it's not a race! Keep still for a minute and let me refill your glass, at least." She felt his hands on her shoulders, and her glass dropped with a crash to the floor, splintering into a thousand sparkling shards.

"Oh!" she cried, looking down at the mess in dismay. "Oh, God, I'm such a klutz! That beautiful glass. I feel terrible; I—" And then, she was pulled gently back into him. And then, she felt his breath softly on her neck. And then, his lips, his warm caressing lips. She was sure he could hear her heart pounding in her chest. "No," she protested, but even she could hear that her voice didn't mean it. "Don't. Please."

His hands turned her around. She was staring at the middle of his sweatered chest, and she tipped her head back to look at him. And was immediately sorry, because she met blazing green eyes. She didn't know what to do, where to look, what to say. She could only stare at him, like a doe mesmerized by the dazzle of headlights.

He spoke softly, still holding her gently by the shoulders. "Look me in the eyes and tell me no, Toni."

"Ham, this isn't fair! This isn't me! This isn't how I do things!"

"Well, maybe it's time you let somebody else do things, then."

"Ham, I mean it. Please let me go."

Immediately he lifted his hands, freeing her, and she staggered back. Laughing, he took hold of her again, this time pulling her in close to him, bending his head to nuzzle into the soft place where neck meets shoulder. A shudder ran through her, and she heard herself give a quivering little sigh. "No," she said weakly.

"You want me to stop?"

"No." This one burst out of her, and again he laughed deep in his throat. She could feel his delight rumbling in his chest, and she wanted to laugh aloud, too. But she was not given the opportunity. He tipped her head up, smiled at her. She closed her eyes, her lips trembling, and he kissed the tip of her nose.

It had never before occurred to her that a soft little kiss on the tip of the nose could create such havoc below.

Her eyes flew open. God only knew what he saw there, but it made him hold her even closer. "Mmmmmm, nice," he murmured and bent his head again. Toni drew in breath and waited. Her lips longed for his mouth. He kissed her chin and then allowed his lips to slide down into the hollow of her throat. She was burning; she was melting; she was turning liquid. Her knees began to give way, and he wrapped his arms tightly around her.

"Now," he breathed and covered her mouth with his. He tasted of champagne and something else, something sweet. Her body yearned toward his, and she found herself on tiptoe, trying to get closer, closer, closer.

It was a long, lovely, exploring kiss. His mouth was delicious; she couldn't get enough of him. She moved her lips into his, electrified by the hard bulge of his erection. When he lifted his head to smile down into her eyes, there was no resistance left in her, no coherent thought, no hesitation. She wanted him. Now. And he wanted her!

He stepped back a little and let her go, just holding on to her hand with his. "Let me get you a new glass."

Toni stared at him. "You gotta be kidding!" It just blurted right out of her.

Ham threw his head back and laughed. "No, darlin', the way I figure it, we're bound to be thirsty if we keep on this way. You're going to need a new glass; just come with me."

She hardly remembered being led into the small kitchen—so neat, she remembered thinking—and watching him easily reach the top cupboard for another champagne flute. And then she was led down the hall into his bedroom, a dramatic place with black walls and black lacquered furniture and a beautiful Chinese screen of gold with cranes among the water lilies. And, she half noted, there was an open bottle of champagne nestled into an ice bucket on one of the night tables.

"What a beautiful room!"

"You're surprised. Didn't think a crass TV reporter could fall under the spell of lovely things? And yet . . ." He pulled her into his embrace with just the smallest tug of his hand. "And yet . . . *you*."

She had only time to stare at him, thinking, *What?* when he bent to her. This time, there was no play, no teasing. This time, he was avid, thrusting his tongue deep into her mouth, sucking on hers, biting her lips, clutching her so that she could hardly breathe or move.

By the time he began to undress her, she was a moaning, heated, quivering, greedy, unthinking mass of desire. Every part of her was named and praised and kissed ceremoniously. She almost could not believe what was happening to her. When he laid her down onto the creamy sheets and stripped, looking at her the whole time, smiling, watching her face, she thought, *Wait a minute, I'm forty-five years old, I'm sagging, I'm bagging, I'm drooping, I'm waging war against cellulite, and even on my best days I've never been considered a beauty. Fiesty, mouthy, ebullient, strong, tough, powerful . . . yeah. But beautiful?*

This isn't supposed to be happening to me, she thought. *This can't be happening to me.* Nothing like this had ever happened to her before in her life. No man had ever treated her like this. She had always been the aggressor, the hot little Italian number, always in control. That's how she did it. She picked the man she wanted and bowled him over. It had worked with Arch, it had worked with Eliot, and with everybody in between. But this—!

He was naked; he was divine; he was covered with golden hair; he was huge and erect. She held her arms up, and he flung himself down onto her, growling in his throat, nibbling on her belly, sucking on her fingers, running his hands all over her, stroking her thighs and her breasts, her back, her buttocks. She was going out of her mind.

"Please, please," she heard herself begging. She wriggled under him, thrusting her hips up to him.

At last, he entered her, and she exploded. He laughed and held her tighter, and she said, "Oh, you think it's funny, huh? Let's see how long *you* hold out!" Together, they rolled over so that she was on top of him, straddling him, riding him, arching her back, looking down on his face as his eyes widened and his breathing became ragged. Then suddenly, his eyes closed, and his head went back as the cock inside her swelled and tightened. He gritted his teeth and holding on to her buttocks, pushed her rhythmically faster and faster until they were moving as one, merged and melded, one feverish creature searching with wild abandon for release—which they found together, clinging, kissing.

They lay there, spent, both gasping. Ham gave a deep, contented groan and pulled her into his arms. Toni floated into a half sleep, wrapped in his embrace, feeling his warm breath on her brow. Never, never, *never* had any man made her feel this way. Never. Suddenly she heard music playing in the background: a male voice singing, "You were my favorite love. . . ." It was a gorgeous song; she couldn't remember ever having heard it before. This was a glorious bed; she couldn't remember ever having felt quite so comfortable before. . . .

Suddenly she opened her eyes, not knowing where she was. She sat up, trying to look around, but it was dark. The windows were black, and out there in the darkness were little pinpoints of light. "Oh," she said aloud. Ham's apartment, Ham's bed. Oh God! How long had she been asleep? "What time is it?" she wondered aloud, and from the other side of the room, Ham's voice said, "Six-thirty."

"Night . . . or morning?" Panic squeezed her throat.

"Night. Don't worry. I wouldn't let you sleep till morning. You hungry? There's a wonderful Chinese restaurant close by, called Chin Chin. I could order in."

He flicked a switch, and a gentle light in the far corner went on. She was still groggy. She rubbed her eyes and stretched and then, suddenly, remembered. She could feel the heat climbing in her cheeks. Ham laughed that sexy laugh, and she looked up at him. He was lounging in the doorway, a thick white terrycloth robe belted around his waist. His curly, fair hair glistened with tiny droplets of water. He looked good enough to eat.

"I gotta get going. Why did you let me sleep?"

"Sorry. You looked so peaceful, and I figured, hell, any time a doctor can catch a few extra zees . . ."

She scrambled out of bed. "I've really gotta go, Ham. I don't want you to think I'm running . . ."

"But you are."

"But I am."

He shrugged but, even in this halfhearted light, she could see he was hurt. "I'm married," she said, almost like a plea.

"I know you're married."

"I don't *do* this."

"You just did."

"I know that, Ham. I guess what I'm trying to say is I'm . . ."

"Sorry?"

"No, goddamn it; I'm not sorry." She walked over to him, still naked, and stood close to him without touching him. "It was wonderful. Really. But it musn't happen again."

"Why the hell not?" He moved as if to take her in his arms, and she backed away, shaking her head. "Maybe this is the real thing, Toni."

"I have to think. I have to get away from you so I *can* think."

He grinned. "Then it's not a definite no yet?"

"Yes. No. I don't know. I'm confused."

"Good."

She turned from him, suddenly embarrassed because she hadn't a clue where her clothes were. They had been taken from her and she hadn't given a damn where they went to. Not until this moment. As if he could read her mind, he said, "On the chair over there. Neatly folded." And they were. She was aware that he was watching her as she got dressed, and she couldn't believe that it didn't bother her. She felt strangely at ease. Hell, she *liked* him looking at her! And that made her even more determined to get the hell out of there while the getting was good.

She almost made it. Got dressed, got all her stuff together, combed her hair, saw a flushed, pretty, young-looking Toni in the mirror, smiled, chatted—even remembered to pick up her briefcase—and had said a breezy "So long!" when he pulled her in for a good-bye kiss, and her resolve dissolved in a flood of lust.

She wrenched away from him. "Ham, for God's sake, give me some time!" she said.

He let her go, his gaze lingering on her, and as she trotted down the hall to the elevator, he called after her, "I'll be seeing you soon!" The words made her feel so good. She should be ashamed of herself! But she wasn't; she wasn't!

26

Early April

Betty took a look out the front window. A gusty wind was blowing, and the people walking by were all hunched into their clothes. When was spring going to get here? She went to the closet and picked out her nice warm down coat. But it wasn't fitting, suddenly! She looked down at her burgeoning belly and laughed with happiness.

"What's funny?"

"I can't see my feet anymore, George! And my favorite coat won't even go around me!"

"Good! Then you can't go out tonight!"

"Now, George, you going to start that up again? Don't, I'm telling you! I'm going on patrol like I do every Tuesday, and that's that!"

He moved closer to her and put an arm around her shoulder. "I'm worried about you, sugar. So much more violence on the streets lately. You know I love this neighborhood, and I'm with you one hundred and ten percent to make it safe. But I don't know. You're due in less than a month, Betty; nobody expects you to go out there now."

"*I* expect me to go out there now."

"I don't know why I waste my breath on you, Betty Cannon. You're the stubbornest woman I ever knew."

She chuckled. "That's why things get done around here."

He gave a big sigh, but he went to the closet and came out with a big old woolen hunting shirt of his. "Here. If this doesn't fit you, then you gotta stay in and give birth!"

They were still laughing as they came out of the house and down the front steps, where the rest of tonight's patrol was waiting. Loretta, Clarence, Clarence's brother-in-law, Juanita, Lesley, and Roberto. A good group.

"Betty Cannon, what are you *doing* here? Loretta came to take your place!"

"And let a gorgeous creature like her walk alone in the dark with my man?"

There was a lot of laughter at this. Loretta Kingsbury was her best friend; in any case, Loretta had already been married six times and kept saying she had no use for men anymore.

"George, how come you let Betty out when she's so close to her time?"

"You ever know me able to tell this woman what to do?"

More laughter. And then, the business of the evening, which was testing the walkie-talkies, pairing off, trading whatever rumors were going around that night, and assigning areas. Betty and George got the immediate four-block area—"In case Betty's time comes, she can get home in a hurry."

Everyone laughed at that; George didn't. She knew George was concerned about her and the baby. Lately, she had begun to have that duckfooted pregnant-woman walk, the one that made her look like she was bent backward. He probably thought she couldn't take it. But he was wrong. No way was she going to stop, especially not now, not after what happened to Dee! Dee, who was so strong and fast and slippery! If some brute was able to scare Deedra Strong into submission, then what was going to happen to weaker women?

Damn it, every time she thought about it, pictured it happening, she was ready to kill, ready to put her hands around that man's neck, whoever he was, and just squeeze until his face turned blue. Of course, when she had said that to George, he'd just smiled.

"You, Betty? You couldn't do that! You like to *think* you could! You like to think you're the toughest woman in seven states; but you're wrong."

No, *he* was wrong. George was a good man, the best; but, like most men, he didn't have a clue about what made women tick. If she ever was put face-to-face with the man who had raped her little sister, she'd kill him or die trying.

The streets were pretty quiet tonight, Betty thought, as they walked along, alert for anything unusual. One good thing about bad weather of any kind: it kept everyone inside, including the scum of the earth. Tonight was just too blustery for much activity, and she yawned. "I hope I don't get bored to death," she teased George.

But there was no danger of that. She might be big and fat and out of breath, but she was vigilant. If you couldn't go out in your own neighborhood, you were giving the street over to the criminals. "Here, Mr. Mugger, Mr. Drug Dealer, Mr. Rapist, Mr. Pimp, it's all yours. Feel free to do whatever you want!" Oh, no, not for Betty Cannon; not for Betty Cannon *and* her child!

Just then a car went by, all its windows open, blasting music so loudly it echoed off the buildings. But it wasn't the usual rap or heavy metal, Betty realized, it was "I Apologize." Such an old song!

"Listen, George, it's Billy Eckstine!"

He grabbed her and they fox-trotted a few steps, and then she made him stop. "I'm getting out of breath, George!"

"You? Girl, you used to dance me to my knees!"

She sighed and shook her head, as they resumed their patrol, throwing their flashlight beams into dark corners and under stairs. Once they had found a woman huddled behind a garbage can; the EMTs had actually been able to save her life.

"I hate to admit it, George, but this probably *is* my last night out . . . until after the baby is born."

"Yeah, right! And you gave me such a hard time. You knew I was right; you just didn't want to admit it!"

"Maybe . . ."

"No maybe about it!" He reached over and put a gentle hand on her belly. "He kicking around tonight?"

"George, you *know* the amnio said it's a girl!"

"I can't believe any little girl could kick like that! Well, on second thought, seeing as who I'm married to, maybe I can believe it."

She gave him a playful punch on his muscular arm. Again they laughed, and he took her hand briefly, giving it an affectionate squeeze. She was so lucky! Not too many black women had a good man, a loyal and faithful and true man, like her George. Not too many white women, either, come to think of it, judging from what she saw and heard every day at the office. She glanced sideways at her husband, smiling to herself.

He was so good, even about little things. When they found

out the baby was a girl, she had immediately said, "I want her to be Winnie, after my mother. Winifred, she was." And then she had realized suddenly. "Oh, I'm sorry, honey. I didn't even stop to think. Your mama's gone, too. Maybe you want the baby to be named after her?" She took in a deep breath and silently prayed, Oh please, don't let it happen. His mother's name was Beulah. Could she really give an innocent, sweet little baby a name like Beulah? It sounded like a slave name!

But George just laughed. "Name her after my mama? Forget it! My mama was a nasty old woman! No, no, I don't want to have to say her name every day for the rest of my life!"

Bless him, she was a lucky woman. She moved closer to him, glad of his company on this bleak, windy night. Her walkie-talkie sputtered into life and then she heard Loretta's voice saying, "Break-in at the shoemaker's. Cops on the way."

"Roger. Everything quiet here."

Behind them, there was the sound of a car going very, very slowly. Betty turned, her flashlight held down. "I know what this is," she said.

"They probably think we're the local connection."

They stood still and waited for the car to cruise up to them. Jersey plates. Sure, come on across the bridge and ruin *my* neighborhood! she thought angrily.

"They could do us all a favor and blow the George Washington Bridge to kingdom come," George said. He put his flashlight beam directly into the face of the driver.

"Hey, watcha doin'?" the driver yelled out. "I'm only looking for someone. You know a guy called Boots?"

"Boots!" Betty sniffed.

"Watch this," George muttered. He marched up to the car, leaned close, and bellowed: "If you love being alive, just move yo' ass, white bread! And *quick*, you got it?"

The last words weren't even out of his mouth, when the car took off with a squeal and went racing up the block.

"George!" Betty laughed. "Are you *black*?"

She had to laugh as he imitated the open mouth and frightened eyes of the driver. And then, as they started to walk again, George said, "Yo. Number Four fifty-five over there. Isn't that front door always locked?" He flashed his light on one of the buildings owned and abandoned by the city, its windows blanked out with sheet metal. The big front door hung ajar.

"It doesn't look right," Betty agreed. "And I didn't hear anything about it being sold, did you?" She wished someone would buy it and fix it up. There were window boxes up and down her block; soon they'd all be in bloom with geraniums and petunias and impatiens, and it would look so pretty. Then they'd all start digging the community garden. This neighborhood, she thought fiercely, deserved to be *lived* in! "If they're starting another crack house in there—"

"If they are, sugar, they won't be for long. I'm taking a look. Oh, no. You stay right here and wait for me."

"Don't go inside, George."

"I'm not going inside. I just want to see what's what."

Betty watched him as he carefully climbed the front steps; for such a big man, it was amazing how quietly he could move. The baby did a somersault, and Betty gave a little "Oof!" Then she laughed. "You in a hurry, Winifred Cannon? Well, so am I. I can't wait to meet you. But not right now, okay?"

"Betty Cannon! How you doin'?" It was Martha Jones and her two little ones, all dressed up.

"Where *you* going, looking so slick?" Betty said. Martha and her husband Jeffrey were a young couple earning plenty of money, who had decided to come back and buy a house right here, instead of escaping downtown.

"We're just coming back from Open School Night, and these two children have done me proud. . . ."

Betty was vaguely aware that another car had turned into the block—it better not be another piece of trash, trying to make a buy, or she *would* go blow up the bridge! She wished George would hurry up; she didn't like him being up there all alone. Sometimes they got crazy, those crackheads.

"Isn't that great?" she said to Martha Jones, smiling at the two children. One day, it would be her and her Winnie coming back from Open School Night. That car was going awfully fast, she suddenly realized. Kids, probably. She turned, thinking, I'm going to stop them and give them hell, and if they've been drinking, I'm going to give them double hell! The car speeded up. What did they think they were doing? Betty thought; then there was a burst of sound and . . .

King was driving when they heard the report on the police radio. "Report of shots fired at Four fifty-five West One-twenty-three

near Amsterdam.'' Holy shit! He called their dispatcher to say
they were taking the job at 123rd, listening for more details.
One person shot, then it was two, one a child, one a woman.

''Goddamn trigger-happy assholes!'' Michael said. ''Shooting kids!''

Putting on the siren, King burned a U on Broadway and
headed back uptown. In a minute, he was joined by two cop
cars, coming in from different directions. He could hear them
answering the same call. ''Everyone's on their way,'' he said.
He wanted to be first. It was one way the wrong way, but never
mind that. He slowed down a little, warned everyone off with
the siren, and then bulled his way up the block.

He pulled up as close as he could get, considering the size of
the crowd gathered at the scene. They stood all over the street;
they didn't care. They just wanted to look. He pulled up the
hand brake; then he and Mike opened their doors and jumped
out. As soon as he hit the street, he heard all the hollering.
''Save her! Save her! She's pregnant,'' someone was wailing.
Oh Christ. No time to waste.

As he and Mike ran to the back of the ambulance and started
unloading their equipment, two more ambulances pulled up,
one from St. Luke's-Roosevelt, one from St. Anthony's. They
could take care of the others. He and Mike were going for the
pregnant woman. Without having to say a word, they grabbed
the long board, the MAST pants, collar, blanket roll, stretcher,
and oxygen.

They had to force their way through the mob, everyone busy
looking and saying, How awful, How terrible, How gruesome.
Nobody would move . . . hell, that was nothing new; they never
moved, unless you made them. ''Out of the way!'' they hollered, then, ''Out of the fucking way!'' Finally, King bellowed:
''Get the fuck out of our fucking way, goddamn it!''

Finally they got in. King scanned the scene quickly and ex-
pertly. On the stoop, a little girl was bleeding. A woman, probably her mother, was pressing a tissue or handkerchief to the
kid's head. Probably a flesh wound; the kid was sitting up and
blubbering loudly. A boy, looking very scared, hung on to the
woman's sleeve. He didn't look hurt.

He knew who needed the attention; he and Mike turned to
her. She lay on her back, on the sidewalk, sprawled out, looking

like she could be asleep. But, of course, she wasn't. And she was very definitely pregnant.

King knelt next to her and checked her airway. "She's not breathing." He could see one bullet wound, a neat little hole on her skull. Practically no blood. "Give me the BVM." They bagged her, and Mike squeezed the bulb to keep that oxygen moving through her bloodstream; maybe they could save the baby. Brain dead, King figured. He checked her pulse. Good and strong. Deftly, he and Mike did what they had to.

As they were putting the cervical collar on, two cops came up.

"What happened?"

"Gunshot wound. In the head. Right through the brain."

"She gonna make it?"

King shook his head. "No chance."

There was an eerie howl of pain from the crowd; it put shivers down his spine. He glanced up. A big, muscular black guy, being held by two other guys, was standing there, tears streaming down his face. He started to move, and King held up a hand. "No! We're doing all we can!"

The guy backed off, but he kept shaking his head. "Not her, not my wife, she's too damn strong to die. Too damn tough, too damn mad, too damn good! Don't tell me no chance! You gotta save her!"

I wish I could, King thought, but when there was a strong pulse and no breathing, you knew. Brain dead. Next to him, the sound of the bulb being compressed, the air hissing through, inflating her lungs, would keep her going for at least a little while.

The cop behind him said, "Why are you doing all this stuff? I mean, if she's—" Mike answered him. "The *baby*, for Christ's sake. We gotta keep her alive so the baby doesn't die."

King cut her clothes away, only half hearing the man's protests, checking for any other wounds. None. Just that one bullet, but that's all it took. Now they worked very quickly, sliding the board under her, supporting her head, taping it down, picking her up, putting her into the bus.

All the time he was working, he heard the usual cop-and-bystander dialogue.

"Did anyone see anything?"

Silence.

"Come on! Somebody musta seen something!"

Muttering and murmuring. Then: "It was a white Lincoln. I saw it tear-assing onto Broadway."

"I saw it. Four guys. I think."

"Recognize any of them?" Silence. "Come on, you people. I bet you've seen them a hundred times."

Silence.

"I think it was a Continental. Eighty-two, maybe eighty-three, when they put all that chrome all over. But I didn't see no faces!"

She was in. It was time to go. One of the St. Luke's EMTs came to drive. This was going to take both of them in back. A cop climbed in with them while his partner took her husband in the police car. The police car, siren wailing, took off, with 31 Willy Zebra right behind.

"Gotta get her tubed," King said.

"I'll do it." Mike was smaller and slimmer and could squeeze himself into the tight space behind her to get the breathing tube down her throat. The cop sat as far away as he could, getting a little green. King straddled her and got the IVs going. She was an inert lump, not a living person at all, but the baby in her belly was. At the sound of the siren, it had started to kick and flail. The blanket over her belly was jumping around.

The cop had recovered and was watching every procedure. "I thought you said brain dead."

"Yeah."

"So how come you keep taking her pulse and giving her oxygen?"

"Her pulse is fine. Her heart's beating just like normal. It's like the body doesn't know the brain is gone."

"Weird," the cop said.

"Yeah."

They decided to take her to Harmony Hill. She really needed a trauma center, but the nearest one was too damn far away. She was in extremis. They called their dispatcher for a standby at Harmony Hill.

"Three one Willy Zebra," the dispatcher's voice said, "go ahead with your standby."

"Forty-plus-year-old female, respiratory arrest with blood pressure of one fifty over one hundred, pulse rate eighty, respiratory rate zero. She's about eight months pregnant, and we think she's going into labor. We should be there in about two minutes."

"Okay, Three one Willy Zebra, hospital will be notified."

Yeah, King thought, sometimes it actually worked. There might be a miracle tonight.

The ambulance went screaming down the street and into the emergency entrance. Mike kept bagging her while King unhooked the IVs. The EMT had already jumped out of the driver's seat and had flung open the rear doors. While oxygen was pushed into her lungs, King and the EMT picked up the stretcher. The wheels dropped down, and the three of them flew into the E.R.

A doctor was waiting. He glanced at the woman, then checked between her legs. "Dilated three centimeters," he said, and then barked out an order: "Take her up to a high risk D.R.!"

Suddenly there was a rush of activity, and the stretcher went flying down the hall, an orderly pushing, with a nurse running next to him holding up the IV; another nurse was bagging her; one of the interns monitored her heartbeat. Two minutes and they were gone, racing around the corner about a hundred miles an hour, heading for the elevator.

All of a sudden, King had nothing more to do. As it always happened, he had a moment of letdown. They had moved fast, and they had done everything they could, and all at once it was out of their hands. They were finished; he could go home now. Home. It had become an ambivalent word lately. Where *was* his real home? With Toni or with Mom? Christ, he didn't want to start thinking about that again.

Then it hit him, like he'd been hit with a baseball bat. Now he remembered where he'd seen the woman they'd just brought in. Suddenly he remembered her face and her name.

"Holy shit, Mike, that was Betty! Betty Cannon!"

27

Same night

Deedra came out of delivery room 3 with a smile on her face. All right, it was ten P.M., and she hadn't slept more than three and a half hours the past two days, but so what? She had just delivered, with the help of the mother, of course, a beautiful, healthy, full-term, perfect baby boy. It didn't happen often enough. Too many babies with too many problems. It got her down. Some days, she didn't think she could stand it anymore. But tonight, it had gone so nicely. Labor was short, the parents had done natural—Jesus, there had actually been a *father* there!—and everyone was happy. Including Deedra Strong.

And then, without warning, she saw his face with that strange frozen smile, felt his breath on her cheek, his weight on her chest, his—damn it, she had *promised* herself she'd never think about that night again, never! She had to stop and lean against the wall. She felt she had to vomit. She *wanted* to vomit, to get rid of him, of the memory. Why did it keep coming back to her like this? And always in such vivid detail! She checked the hallway. She'd been doing that ever since . . . ever since. She tried to stop, but she just couldn't help it.

Oh shit! She sucked in a deep breath, her hand over her rapidly beating heart, willing herself to calm down, to forget about it, to stop being so fucking *scared*. That's what she hated most. She'd always been so much in control of her life. She'd always been so strong. She was a runner; she played basketball; she was tough; she'd grown up on the streets of Harlem, Jesus Christ, there was *no one* who could get the best of her! And he'd turned it all into a lie and a sham and a living nightmare. She couldn't walk down the fucking hallways without looking over her shoulder. She couldn't hear a footfall, not anywhere, without flinching, without turning to check.

Especially in the hospital. How could she have been so stupid! She should have seen the signs, should have known better than to let him into the center at night. But . . . she *knew* him. And he was respected; she had thought he was a friend, for Christ's sake! How could she ever trust anyone, ever again? How could she ever have sex again? Just the thought of it sent shudders through her body.

Dee stopped and breathed deeply. In a minute or two, her heart stopped racing, and she made herself think about something else. Work. Her patients. She walked down the hall, thinking she'd get coffee at the nursing station. They had a good coffee maker and real milk instead of that powdered stuff. It looked very calm and quiet there as she came down the hall. She expected to see her friend Natalie, but there was only a guy she didn't know and, oh good, Nancy Dryer. She loved Nancy; Nancy was one of the old-style no-nonsense nurses, a woman in her sixties, very sure of herself, very caring, very competent. The two of them were bent over some charts and Deedra, silent in her spongy walking shoes, came up to the desk without their hearing her. She cleared her throat.

"Yes?" Nancy Dryer's startled frown cleared. "Oh, hi there, Deedra. What's new?"

"A seven-pound, thirteen-ounce, bouncing baby boy."

Nancy grinned. "Oh good. That's a great feeling."

"Deserving of a good cup of coffee, that's what I figure."

Nancy laughed. "Help yourself. John just made fresh."

Dee had just reached out for the pot when the elevator behind her slid open to release a babble of sound. Startled, she turned. A gurney was being pulled and pushed full speed ahead, surrounded with emergency people. And a cop. Aw shit! She'd had a minute and a half of feeling good. Some poor soul . . .

And then, with a lurch, she saw the familiar bulky figure in a heavy jacket coming out of the elevator. George. *George!* Oh my God, oh my God! She tried to call his name, but the sound froze in her throat. She was unable to move, totally paralyzed with terror, while he, half running, caught up with the rest of them. Her mind was racing, her pulse hammering in her throat. It can't be, it can't be! No, no! Please!

She forced her feet to move, her mouth dry with fear. He

hadn't seen her, even though she was standing practically in front of him. It was something awful, the look on his face—! She ran after them, feeling as if she were running through a bad dream—not really moving, just running and running and running.

The cop was trailing behind. She touched his arm, and he wheeled to confront her. He was so young, her own age. "Officer! What is it!"

"A shooting." He had a funny look on his face.

She grabbed his arm. "Who? Who? You've got to tell me! I've got to know. That's—"

He backed away from her a little, and then she recognized the look in his eyes. He was apprehensive.

She was dimly aware that her voice was high and cracking with urgency. She must seem crazy to him, but she didn't care.

"Take it easy, lady—"

"I'm a doctor!"

"Okay, okay, Doc. Just take it easy. Someone's been shot, but there's already doctors there."

She opened her mouth to say all she wanted to know was *who* was it, *who*? Oh, to hell with him. She knew what he was doing; he was trying to calm her down. She didn't *want* to calm down; she wanted to know. She pushed by him and continued running, but as she watched, frustrated, they pushed the gurney into one of the high-risk delivery rooms, and the door closed behind them.

George was there, leaning up against the wall, his whole body sagging, his shoulders shaking, his head buried in his two hands. One of the paramedics stood next to him, a hand on George's shoulder. George was sobbing. She could hear it as she got closer. Oh Jesus! It *was* Betty! Of course it was. She had really already known that. Nightmare of nightmares! It was Betty in there! What did that cop say? Shot? Betty, *shot*? Oh God!

There was a loud buzzing in her ears, and the walls seemed to pulsate under the bright fluorescent lights. For a moment, Dee was sure she would faint. She put her hand out, leaning against the wall, grateful for its cool solidity, closing her eyes against the woozy sensation. Betty, oh God, it was Betty. Why? Why her? She was so good, and she was *pregnant*! It wasn't fair! It wasn't fair. God, why are You doing this to us? Dee thought. Save her, save her, make this go away! I still need her!

A gentle hand touched her arm, and she opened her eyes to find herself looking at a pair of startling light eyes filled with such tenderness and compassion that she immediately burst into tears.

"I'm sorry," he said. It was the paramedic. "I'm so sorry. Are you related?"

"Related! She's my sister. . . . She brought me up; she's been a mother to me!"

She had thought she had her crying under control; she was wrong. Tears began pouring out of her eyes, and she felt painful sobs being torn from her body. His arms went around her, and he patted her back . . . just like Betty used to do when she had been little. Dee opened her mouth and wailed like a baby. He held her closer. Oh God, it was so good to have someone else's strength to lean on. And then she struggled to free herself. "I have to go to her! I have to see her!"

"They won't let you in."

"I don't care, I don't care; I have to talk to her!"

"She can't hear you—"

"Goddamn it, I *know* she can't hear me! I still have to talk to her! There's something I have to tell her—"

"Tell me." He wasn't going to let her go, and in a way, she didn't want him to. But she felt so bad, so bad. Just last week, sitting at the kitchen table, drinking tea together, Betty had put her hand over Dee's and said, "Now listen, baby, I don't want to hassle you. But I can see something's eating at you, and I think I know what it is."

"That's enough, Betty," Dee had answered tightly. "I told you that's off limits! I'm not going to tell you, and that's final."

"Dee, there's nothing wonderful about keeping quiet. It just means he gets away with it."

"Betty, quit it, will you? It's bad enough, without *you* nagging me!"

Betty quickly hid a look of pain. She got up and began fussing with the tea kettle, but Dee realized she'd really hurt her. Well, tough, she'd thought. Now maybe she'll leave me alone and stop asking that same question over and over again.

He had warned her, his face up against hers, his horrible breath blowing on her, spittle spraying over her cheek: "You tell anyone, and I guarantee you'll be in deep shit. It'll be your word against mine, and nobody will believe you. Remember the black girl at St. John's? And it won't only be *you*; it'll be your sister, too, who's out looking for a job.''

She *had* to keep her mouth shut; she had to. She couldn't tell Betty. Since that night, whenever she'd called, her sister's voice had been cool and distant. She'd thought, *Well, too bad, Betty, but I'm not obligated to tell you everything.* She'd thought she had forever to make up, to make everything right between them. She'd thought they had all the time in the world. And now, suddenly, like a visitation from hell, all their time had been snatched away from them.

She heard a strange, dreadful sound. A moment later, she realized it was her own voice, crying out her pain. A torrent of sobs wracked her body. Now it was too late. Now she was never going to have a chance to tell Betty that she was sorry, that she loved her, that she wished she could tell her. Oh God, how she wished she could!

Those strong arms around her never faltered, never weakened their hold. And suddenly, the thought flashed through her head: I don't even know his name. And it calmed her and at last, she was able to stop. She tried out her voice. To her surprise, it worked. ''Is she dead?''

Just the tiniest pause. ''No, but . . .''

''Brain dead,'' she guessed, and he nodded. ''Oh God!''

''We kept the oxygen going so the baby would have a chance. They're doing a C-section right now.''

She glanced over at George. Poor George. Here she was, so busy feeling sorry for herself, but it was his *wife*, his sweetheart who was lying in there, barely alive. He looked like someone who had been beaten. ''I should go to him.'' Now when she made a move to back away, he let go instantly.

He shook his head. ''He can't hear you; he can't hear anyone right now. He says he wants to be alone.''

She looked at her savior and tried to smile. ''Thank you. Thank you for . . . for all your help.'' She took in a tremulous breath and looked at his ID badge. CRAWFORD, KING, it said. ''Your name is King?''

''Short for Martin Luther King . . .''

Now she really *looked* at him. Part black, the best of both worlds, really nice-looking. And tall. For a moment, his face was very familiar to her. But of course. He was a hospital paramedic; she must have seen him around.

"Look, thanks very much. You've been terrific. But I have to get in there." She assumed he knew she meant the delivery room, and he did, because he didn't fight her on it and, in fact, began to walk down the hall with her.

Dee opened the door, and immediately one of the nurses came, stern-faced, to shove her back out. Then the nurse did a double take and murmured, "Sorry, Doctor. But . . . are you scrubbed?" Dee shook her head. "Then, I'm sorry, but . . ."

Behind her, Dee heard King's voice, also at a murmur: "Nurse, this is Betty Cannon's sister. And she's a doctor here—"

"I *know* she's a doctor here."

"Sorry. Of course you do. She could scrub."

A stubborn set of the lips and a stubborn shake of the head. "She'll have to wait. We've got enough to do." The door was closed firmly.

King reached over and took Dee's hand. She looked down at the two hands as if neither one belonged to her. She realized that she was probably in shock. She had to try to pull herself together. King had just said, She's a doctor here. She repeated the words to herself. I am a doctor here. I am a doctor here. But it didn't seem to make her feel any more real. But maybe she could play the part of someone who was ready to give comfort.

Straightening her shoulders, she found herself able to walk over to George and speak his name. He looked up, and she had to bite her lips, so as not to gasp aloud at the sight of his ravaged face and empty, red-rimmed eyes. "Oh, George!"

The tears in his eyes spilled over. "She's gone, Dee. Betty's gone."

"No. She's still alive," she lied.

"They say she's in a coma. That's not alive."

"Some people come out of a coma, George." She couldn't believe she was talking this nonsense. Brain dead was *dead*!

"I saw it. I saw it happen; I saw her; I saw what they did to her. Dee. Please. Don't tell me stories."

"They're delivering the baby right now."

His face crumpled. "Tonight—it was just a little while ago— we were talkin' . . . talking about what to name her. We were—" He stopped, his voice clogging, and shook his head. "Not now, Deedra."

She held out her hand to him, but he no longer saw her, so

she turned away, wondering where she had to go now. She was no good to him right now, and he couldn't help her, either.

"You did your best." It was King Crawford. What was he, a mind reader? "I couldn't get anything out of him, except 'Go away.' "

She looked at him and gave a bitter laugh. "Yeah, and that's what I got from him, too. So what good did I do?"

They began to walk together toward the nursing station. "You did what you could. He's in shock . . . oh, but you know better than I do. You're a doctor."

"Some doctor," Dee muttered. And then she stopped dead in her tracks. "Do I see what I think I see?"

At the end of the corridor, the elevator doors had just opened and were disgorging three people and television equipment. There was no mistaking Ham Pierce.

"I don't believe it! I don't believe it! Who the hell gave him a pass to come up here with his ghouls to take pictures of us!"

Without waiting for an answer, she began to run up the hall, then sprinted. She could fairly feel the adrenaline shooting through her. She was enraged, and it was wonderful to feel something at last, to find her emotions and her thoughts and her muscles all chugging away in good working order. No way was that damned TV snoop going to get anywhere near Betty. And if he tried to stick his microphone anywhere *near* George, she'd mess up Ham's pretty face for him!

Halfway there, she was already shouting at him. "Who let you up here? You have no business here."

Pierce turned to her, his face startled, then stubborn, then truculent. "Are you in charge?"

"I'm in charge of Betty Cannon. That's who you're here to put on display, isn't it?"

"I'm here to cover a news story, that's all. What's your problem?"

"My . . . 'problem,' Mr. Pierce, is that my sister is in extremis and in labor and in a coma, and it's none of your goddamn business . . . no, nor the public's, either! Can't you let decent people alone?"

"I know Betty Cannon, and I have a great deal of respect for her. My intent is—"

"Respect? Like hell! That's why you're here with your cameras and your microphones—to show your 'respect.' Well, we don't need that kind of respect!''

She could hear his condescending sigh even before he got that look on his face, the look that said he was going to have to deal with a crazy person. She launched herself at him, beating on him with her fists, screaming, hollering, not even listening to her own words.

Hands pulled at her, hands held her arms. Somewhere she could hear Nancy Dryer's voice, saying, ''You'd better leave. I'll take care of her. You'd better leave.'' And then Deedra let herself stop battling, let herself relax. She stood, head bowed, breathing hard, feeling stupid, even though she heard Pierce and his people leaving.

The first person she was aware of was not Nancy but King Crawford. Every time she had lost her cool tonight, he had been there for her. She started to think about how that made her feel, and then she heard voices down by the delivery rooms; she turned to see someone holding up a small bundle. A baby. Betty's baby.

Quickly, she ran back down. George was refusing to even look at it. He was like a man shell-shocked. Deedra held out her arms. ''I'll take her,'' she said. ''Give her to me.''

28

April

Toni looked up from the damn budget and straightened her back, groaning a little. Every muscle in her body was tense and aching. She looked over at her favorite cartoon, enlarged to giant size and pinned up on the bulletin board facing her, and waited for it to make her laugh. It was an old one, by Shel Silverstein, showing two men shackled hand and foot to the wall of a very tall, very narrow, windowless dungeon with a barred grating way up at the top. One of them was saying to the other: "Now here's my plan . . ."

That was her, all right, pinned to the wall, no escape possible, too many problems, not enough money. But this time, she was shit out of plans. Her Women's Health Center, the place she had pinned so many hopes on, every day became more crowded, more chaotic. There was no way three part-time doctors and a part-time social worker could handle the tide of disaster that poured through the door.

What she wanted to do, she decided, was absolutely impossible. She wanted to save this whole generation of inner-city women. Alone, she wanted to do this! It was impossible. That entire part of New York was an island of disease. She was seeing women with advanced cancers, too late to help. She was seeing diseases everyone had thought were wiped out in this country: measles, TB, syphilis.

Her efforts, however well-meant, were nothing more than a Band-Aid on a gaping wound. She had set up special times for PAP smears, for breast exams, for anemia testing, HIV testing. But that was only a drop in the bucket for her patients. The worst off never showed up at all; too many of them had lost all hope and couldn't think beyond the moment. She kept trying; she kept sending out flyers urging them to come in, saying, "We'll be here." And what did she get? The shaft! A memo from the head of her department, "reminding" her that PAP smears and blood tests "are not profitable." Shit! She grabbed the memo, crumpled it, and sent it flying into the wastebasket.

That's what you got for resisting; you got what Betty Cannon got: a shot in the head. Every time she thought about Betty, she felt sick. Betty Cannon had been the symbol of everything hopeful for these people . . . and now, tragically, she had become the symbol of futility. And Dee! Before she'd even had a chance to heal a little—*this!* Hadn't she suffered enough?

God, how did people *endure* the perpetual terror? How did Dee? She'd battled all the odds to get where she was; and if any dedicated doctor could work miracles in the ghetto, she could. But would she ever be able to feel safe again? And why the hell wouldn't she name the bastard? Toni had talked herself blue in the face, trying to convince her that he couldn't possibly do anything worse to her than he had already done. But Dee wouldn't listen. What she was doing now was pretending, going through the motions of being okay, hoping it would all go away by itself. Oh hell!

She pushed herself up from her chair and paced, sending a baleful look at the papers on the desk, filled with columns of hateful figures. She had a lovely moment of imagining herself just sweeping the whole desktop right onto the floor and leaving it to be swept up by the night cleaners. Of course, that's what she'd like to do with all her worries. Wouldn't *that* be terrific!

She had just about decided that she had to get back to balancing her budget when a smiling face appeared around the door jamb.

"Howdy, ma'am. I was just moseyin' on by when I saw your light on. Don't you know it's past six?"

He was really adorable, she thought as she looked at him, fighting back an answering smile. The tanned skin, the dimples, the pale mysterious eyes, that great grin. And then she reminded herself that of course he was handsome and appealing; he was a television personality. He took care of himself, groomed himself. But she had to face it. Real or fake, the sight of him did terrible things to her equilibrium. She had to resist him. This was impossible, absolutely impossible. It was unprofessional, it was stupid, it was counterproductive and, oh, let us not forget, Toni, it was cheating.

Lately it had occurred to her that she'd been the Other Woman twice in her life! Twice!

Well, the thing with Arch was easy to figure. She'd been a virgin, though she had hidden it under a barrage of sophisticated sexy talk. And Arch had come on so strong! He had aroused feelings like none she had ever experienced before. He was the first man who told her she was exciting . . . sexy . . . *alluring*. He described, in marvelous detail, just how she made him feel. He had been irresistible.

If her folks had ever found out Arch was black, her father, especially, that bigoted, narrow-minded bastard—! Oh, it had given her such pleasure to think how crazy it would make her father! She would lay her pale arm across Arch's broad brown belly, let her white fingers curl around Arch's brown-skinned penis, and chortle inside. If he could even imagine her riding that big dark stallion, her back arched, her hair flying, sweat pouring in a river between her bouncing breasts . . . oh, God, he'd have had instant cardiac arrest!

So, yeah, it was easy enough to figure out what she was up to, with Arch, and it was called getting even. But to have gotten involved again—with Eliot, *another* married man—after all the pain and heartache she'd suffered with Arch? Her father would have said that Eliot was white, at least, but Jewish, for Christ's sake! Was her affair with Eliot just another nose-thumbing aimed at her father? Sometimes when she thought about it, she had to shake her head in disbelief. One of these days, just for fun, she was going to take herself to a friendly shrink. One of these days.

And now *she* was the cheating one! She was so bad! How had this life happened to a strictly brought-up Italian girl from Bensonhurst—schooled by nuns, trained by Mother Church, hit across the head by her father for any transgression! Probably because she thought she was smarter than all of the above. But how smart was she? She couldn't balance a simple budget, and now a man was standing in her office doorway, and she couldn't keep her hormones from running amok! That made her laugh aloud.

Ham took this for an invitation and sidled in, seating himself in the chair facing her desk. "I've discovered a great little place for dinner. An Afghan restaurant, down on Columbus and . . .

91st, I think, yeah, 91st. Oddly enough, it's called Afghanistan. They serve pigs in blankets, and there's no cover charge. . . ." He looked at her expectantly and then added: "Afghan. Blanket. Cover. Get it?"

"Ham, I have too many problems to laugh at bad puns."

"You're good at solving problems. I don't worry about you."

"Swell. Try worrying about my patients, then."

She paused, shaking her head. "Like—this is so typical—in comes Marylou, yesterday, not two months after she assured me she would always use a condom, and she's pregnant. Sixteen years old, high school dropout, can't even hold a job at McDonald's, and *this* is going to be a *mother*? So I take her aside and I get a pleasant expression fixed on my face, and I very gently ask her, 'So what happened to the condoms?' And she says, 'Well, I couldn't find them, and Lance, he tol' me I could wash myself with Pepsi, and I wouldn't get no baby.' ''

Toni threw her hands up. Ham slid her a smile and said, "Did you tell her you don't ask her to do anything you don't do yourself?" He winked.

Oh shit! Toni thought. The last goddamn thing she had intended was to bring up the subject of sex in front of this man. She should have kept her mouth shut. They had to stop, that's all. They just had to stop seeing each other. Letting the thing die a natural death was not going to work. She was going to have to kill it.

"I'm a married woman!" she burst out.

At this, Ham threw his head back and roared. "Excuse me? What brought *that* on?"

"You know damn well what brought that on, Ham." She tried scowling at him.

He looked around quickly, then reached out a lazy foot, catching the edge of the door and swinging it shut. "C'mere." He sat back in the chair, his legs stretched out in front of him, motioning her to come to him.

Toni, standing by her desk, gripped the edge with both hands, hard. "No," she said.

"Then I'll come over there."

She held out a hand, shaking her head. "No, Ham. I mean it."

"What's going on, Toni?"

She was doing this badly, she knew it, but to hell with it.

Badly, goodly, it had to be done. "Ham, we've got to stop seeing each other. Don't shake your head at me. We've got to, and you know it. You *know* it! This can't last. In fact, I've gone too far!"

"We haven't gone nearly far enough."

"I'm serious."

"So am I, Toni. And you know damn well we *can't* stop."

"No such word as 'can't.' "

Ham rolled his eyes. "Give me a break, will you? No such word as 'can't'? I haven't heard that one since sixth grade!"

In answer, she turned away from him, and he instantly apologized, adding in a much different tone, "What about the feelings we have for each other?"

She sucked in a deep, painful breath. "We can't have those feelings."

"No such word as 'can't.' Sorry, sorry. But, come on, Toni, look me in the eye and tell me you're not dying to be in my bed right this minute."

She met his gaze and said frostily: "Only a child demands gratification of every wish."

"So you admit it! You admit you want me!"

"Quite beside the point. The point is, we're finished. This can only lead to disaster."

"Why?" Stubbornly. "You could leave him."

Toni could feel the blood draining from her face. "Leave him! What makes you think I'd ever leave him!"

His mouth tightened, and she watched his hands ball into fists. "You've made your feelings very clear . . . or so I thought."

"I never said a word—"

"I'm not referring to what you *said*, Toni." His eyes, those strange, light eyes, held hers.

Now she was blushing, and that made her mad. "I hate those sexual innuendos. I can't help what you thought . . . or think. I only know what I have to do. I'm not going to see you again. Period."

He took one or two steps toward her and then stopped. His face was absolutely still, and his eyes had gone blank, the way he often made them do. "Okay. But, I repeat, what about the feelings we have for each other?"

"What feelings?" She kept her voice deliberately cool, then allowed herself a tiny smile. She knew he'd hate it. He did. But instead of arguing with her, he turned on his heel and was out the door. Gone.

For a moment, Toni just stood there, not really believing he could leave without a word. All this intensity, all this talk about their feelings for each other, and all of a sudden, it's over? She felt . . . abandoned. She wanted him back; she wanted to run after him. And then she told herself that he had probably slowed his steps, in the hope that she'd relent. He was probably just down the hall, lingering a little, waiting for her. Her heart lifted, and she ran out into the corridor. Which was empty. Footsteps coming around the corner made her begin to smile. But it was just an orderly. Ham really *was* gone, and she found herself blinking back sudden, unexpected tears.

Quickly, she got back into her office and kicked the door shut, cursing her own stupid ambivalence. She'd done the right thing. She wasn't going to bawl; how could she walk out there with her eyes all swollen and red and her nose running? She wasn't going to succumb to girlish histrionics. He was just a man, that's all, a guy who had turned her on. And she *had* done the right thing, goddamn it!

She looked at her messy desk, gave it a Bronx cheer, and announced to the walls, "I'm history!" Grabbing her purse and turning out the light, she marched herself back out into the hall and decided, quite on the spur of the moment, to walk down the stairs, and once on the stairs, thought, "Hey, let's see if Janet is still in her office."

She and Janet Rafferty had done lunch a couple of times, just by chance, and it had been nice. Actually, she and Janet were a great deal alike. And, as it happened, Toni was on the loose tonight—Eliot was trying to make a relationship with his son David over dinner, and she was not invited. Even if he were free, he was the last person she wanted to see right now. Another woman, that's what she needed. Maybe Janet would like to grab a bite with her.

But when she got to Janet's office, the door was closed. That was unusual; she was probably gone already. Toni was a bit surprised at the letdown. She realized she had really been looking forward to a little girl talk. And then she heard, from behind the door, a file cabinet drawer slamming shut. She was there . . . oh, but maybe she was busy.

She knocked and Janet called out, "Come on in, whoever you are."

She was behind her desk, twirling in her swivel chair. When she saw it was Toni, she stopped. "I was just thinking about you," she said.

"And I was just thinking about you. And about dinner. What do you say? I hear there's a great new Afghan restaurant down on Columbus and 91st."

"Sure . . . why not? I've never eaten Afghan . . . whoops! That sounds a little dirty, doesn't it?" She giggled, and struck by something else funny, began to laugh. Then she looked at Toni and stopped and put her hand over her mouth and said, "I'm sorry."

Toni eyed the other woman. Janet was a bit flushed, not a lot, just a bit, and her eyes were almost too bright. They nearly glittered. She seemed . . . wired. Whatever it was, Toni thought, was very subtle, just enough of a difference in her behavior to make you wonder what was going on.

"Are you okay?"

"I'm terrific!" She started to push herself up from her chair, but it rolled, and she plopped back down. Again, she laughed hilariously.

Now Toni became all doctor. She wasn't exactly alarmed, but something was wrong. She marched over, and as soon as she got close, she knew what it was. Janet was drunk, just a little, but definitely drunk. She looked around for the bottle, but there was no bottle in sight. She remembered the closing file cabinet drawer. A secret drinker?

She had just opened her mouth, not quite knowing what to say but determined to say *something*, when the phone rang. Janet picked it up, and Toni was amazed how sober, how ordinary she sounded, all of a sudden.

"Yes . . . how nice of you to call. Well, I was . . . working late. No, no, I'm afraid not. Dr. Romano just walked in a minute ago, and I believe we're going out for dinner. Hmmm, yes. Well, I don't know."

She was grinning like the Cheshire cat; you could almost hear her purr. It was a man; it had to be a man. Toni had already seen her in action, and she knew. She'd found out, since that day when she saw Janet chirping at Havemayer, that she had a bit of a reputation around the hospital. But, so what? Toni had

had a bit of a reputation when she was young and single. You did what you had to do in this world.

"Well, I'm sorry," Janet said, "I just don't know." She hung up the phone, smiling.

Oh, God, Janet thought, let me just keep a straight face. She wanted to laugh; she wanted to laugh out loud and scream in triumph! So, the great Dr. President Eliot Wolfe couldn't stay away! Well, she was so glad she could tell him no. He was always doing it to her; let him have a taste of his own medicine. Let him miss her, let him think about what he's missing tonight. He deserved it, always calling her at the last minute!

And then she pulled herself together. Come on, Janet, pay attention. That's his wife standing on the other side of the desk. What if Toni asked who it was! Well, she'd say some guy she met on a trip to Bermuda, something like that.

But Toni didn't ask who it was. Toni just stood there for a minute, like she was thinking about what to say, and then she said it, what Janet was hoping she wouldn't say: "Janet, you've been drinking, haven't you? Is something wrong?"

Was anything wrong! She opened her mouth to say something flip, and to her amazement, she began to cry. "Oh God, it's so awful, being out there!" She stopped, sniffling, and wiped her eyes carefully so as not to smear her mascara. "No, I didn't mean that. It's just . . . oh hell, it's just been one of those days." She gave Toni a big smile. "You know what that's like."

She doubted very much whether Dr. Toni Romano knew what it was like, being out there all by yourself, with only your looks and your charm and your wit. Toni had everything: a powerful, handsome, rich husband; the prestige of being a doctor; fame; social standing . . . everything! She didn't have to make eyes at stupid, piggy men in order to make her way.

There was a gorgeous drug salesman who hung around the cafeteria between calls, Rafael, Raf they called him. The young nurses were always fluttering around him. Janet had noticed him from the very first; well, it was hard not to. He'd sit there like a king, sideways in his chair, leaning back against the wall, his legs stretched out into the aisle, looking as if he owned the place. He looked like Robert Redford, dimples and all, only with salt and pepper hair. A few times, she caught him giving her the eye; and a few times, she considered maybe giving it a shot. But she always decided against it. A salesman? Forget it!

For the past couple of weeks, he'd been really looking her over; she couldn't miss it. There were times, as she was walking to a table with her lunch tray, when she could feel his eyes boring into her back. And sure enough, when she'd turn, ever so casually, and look toward that end of the room, he'd be looking right at her, with that adorable, sexy little smile.

Well, she had to admit, he was tempting. And anyway, Eliot was giving her a very hard time lately, and she was ready to try something new. So when she walked by Raf, she began to let her eyes meet his and to give him her own sexy little smile. It was fun to flirt and feel young and attractive.

Well, today she had been eating lunch alone, and he had come right up to the table and sat himself across from her, looking her straight in the eye and grinning. God, he was gorgeous. And he didn't waste a minute, just came on to her, telling her he'd had his eye on her for a while; he'd like to see her away from this crowd, get to know her better. Could she get out now for an hour? His car was parked right down the street. What nerve! she thought. She knew damn well what he was talking about. He wanted a quickie; he wanted to drive her to some cheap, hot-sheets motel!

"I'm very busy."

He looked so disappointed, like a cute little boy. "How about later? Or tomorrow?" She shook her head. If he wanted it so badly, let him work harder for it.

"I gotta tell you, I'm real sorry," he said, leaning across the table to get closer to her. "You really do something to me. But you must be used to it. I'll bet you have to beat them off with sticks. Well, I got news for you. I don't give up easy."

She sat at the table for a few minutes, toying with her food, but she wasn't hungry anymore. She was filled with excitement. Eliot had been so cold and distant lately, she'd begun to think she'd lost it. She'd found herself staring at her reflection, trying to find the flaw that was making him pull away. But it wasn't her at all, she knew that now. She was still sexy, still able to call the shots.

When she got up and headed out of the cafeteria, she could feel herself strutting a little on her high heels. To hell with Eliot. If he didn't want her, well, someone else would.

And then she heard Raf's voice. He was laughing. "The red-head? She's head of nursing; I've heard plenty about her." He whistled. Janet's heart stopped beating; she felt suffocated. "I hear she'll go with just about anybody. So I figure, let me get mine. I'll bet that body's in good shape for an old babe." He laughed in a nasty way. "Old meat's better than no meat!"

He was . . . he was talking about *her*! Oh, that bastard! And then, one of the other guys said, "Whoa, Raf, better not. AIDS."

Oh, God! She had almost made a total fool of herself over a stupid salesman who couldn't even speak English properly! She could feel her face flaming, and she almost ran to the elevator, she was so ashamed.

Once in her office, she allowed herself a few tears of self-pity. She was getting old; she wasn't married; she didn't even have her children with her; and everyone in the hospital talked about her. What the hell had she done with her life? She leaned against the closed door, feeling despair creeping over her, and buried her hot face in her cupped hands.

"I don't know what to do!" she heard herself say aloud.

And then, she knew. She lifted her head and allowed her gaze to settle on the bottom drawer of the metal filing cabinet in the corner. Now it called her, as if it had a voice. Here I am, here I am. Forgetfulness. Peace. Serenity. Comfort.

No. She couldn't. She mustn't. She hadn't slipped since January. The last time she'd been tempted, she'd fought it off, so proud of herself! And then she heard his mocking voice again, in her head, laughing, laughing at her, making fun of her. She felt so stupid and humiliated . . . ugh! She couldn't stand even thinking about it.

Without thought, without volition, she went to the filing cabinet and knelt before it. A memory flashed through her head of herself in church, hundreds of candles flickering in front of the Virgin with her carved robes, her carved face, praying in supplication for help with this affliction. Of course, the statue did nothing for her problem, nothing, it never had. Now she bent her knee before an altar that would offer her real relief.

She opened the drawer. It looked just like any other file drawer. But way in the back . . . She pulled it farther out and reached behind the packed files. Her palm met the cool smoothness of glass; she curled her hand around the narrow neck and pulled it out. A fifth of Absolut vodka, unopened, of course it was unopened, it was her bottle of faith, the bottle that symbolized her victory over booze.

Swiftly, she opened it, tipped the bottle back, and took a gulp, waiting for the first jolt that would begin to erase her humiliation and pain.

And it had been working just fine, until Toni came in. How'd she know, anyway? She had to be super-smart. Several people had come into the office this afternoon, and nobody had had the least little idea! She was a lady who knew how to hold her liquor.

"Janet," Toni was saying, "why don't we get out of here, before—"

Janet had to laugh. Really, Toni was so sweet, so good to take care of her. "Yeah, I know," she said. "I fell off the wagon. I didn't mean to. . . . It's just that . . . oh hell. I'm sorry. I didn't mean to. . . ."

Toni took her arm. "Are you AA?"

"Yes."

"Do you want to call your sponsor now?"

"No, I want to sober up first."

"Okay. Let's get out of here. Get your stuff, and I'll get you home."

It was so nice to have someone else doing the thinking. She could just float and let Toni take her. She felt loose as a goose. They got into an elevator and went down and got out and all the time, Toni's hand was under her elbow, steering her; and all the time, Toni was chatting. Janet was aware that, left on her own, she might stumble. But nobody looked at them funny; in fact, nobody looked at them at all. Hey, this was terrific.

They turned corners, and they went down empty hallways, and then they ducked through one of the empty clinics, and then they were in the back of the E.R. Unexpectedly, they came to a halt and Janet almost lost her balance. Toni had stopped and was greeting a tall, young doctor with dark hair that flopped over his forehead.

"David! What are you doing here?" she said.

He threw his head back and laughed. "Excuse me, I work here. What are *you* doing here?"

"I thought you were having dinner with your father," Toni said. He started to answer her and then, suddenly, he focused on Janet, and the look on his face changed. It was like a double take, and then he smiled at her and what a smile it was! Am I imagining this? Janet asked herself. He looked dumbstruck. At *her*? "And what are *you* doing here, and why hasn't Toni introduced us?"

Janet was speechless.

Toni laughed. "I would have thought Janet Rafferty needed no introduction. Janet is director of nursing."

"Director of nursing." The way he said it, it sounded like a love song. She was becoming quite breathless—and suddenly very sober. "Of course. I've heard your name," he said, shaking her hand. "What I can't understand is, why haven't I seen you before?"

"Maybe you have and didn't notice."

"I would have noticed. Believe me, I would have noticed." His voice was layered with meaning.

More bullshit? Janet thought. She'd had quite enough of *that* from men today. But he looked like he meant it; he sounded like he meant it. And he hadn't let go of her hand yet. No, he meant it. Something was happening between them; her heart was beating very fast, and she found it confusing to look into his warm, brown eyes. What was going on? Why did it feel so . . . *right* to have him looking at her so tenderly? She didn't even know him. Hell, she didn't even know his *name*. Now he let her hand drop. Their eyes were still locked. It was such a queer feeling, and so lovely.

Next to her, she heard Toni laugh a little. "I guess I should finish introducing you two," she said, amused. "Janet, this is Dr. David Wolfe. My stepson."

Even through the fog of enchantment, she could feel the jolt of it. David Wolfe, David *Wolfe*. Oh, Jesus Christ, God almighty! Eliot's son!

29

The same day

Eliot got up from his desk and paced. What the hell was Toni doing in Janet's office? It made him nervous. But, of course, it was nothing, just hospital business. Probably nothing to do with him. They were both on the new gender-bias committee. Sure, that's probably what it was.

But why had Janet turned him down for tonight? She always cleared her calendar whenever he called her. She was always waiting for him, eager and pliant. Furthermore, he had already told her he'd be having dinner with his son tonight, and it had been *she* who suggested they might squeeze in an hour or so of romance . . . dessert, she had called it.

It made him edgy . . . out of sorts; he found he couldn't settle down to anything. He never should have given her that necklace on Valentine's Day, the one he'd bought for Toni. That was a mistake of major proportions. He wished to God he'd never done it. But he'd been so pissed at Toni, he hadn't thought. Well, he was paying for his stupidity. Ever since then, Janet had been hinting that she expected some kind of commitment. That was a fantasy! It was probably his own fault. In the beginning, he had complained about Toni—not a lot, but apparently too much. That was *another* mistake. He wasn't going to leave his wife. Was Janet up to something? No, she'd never say anything to Toni! That would be so stupid, and she wasn't a stupid woman.

He couldn't just keep pacing until seven-thirty when David was due. So he sat down and began riffling through the pile of mail the substitute secretary had put down for him. It wasn't sorted the way he liked it. Nothing was the way he liked it, not since Betty got shot. Christ, what a nightmare. Every day, he went up to the ICU to look at her. Was he hoping for some change? If so, he was a damned idiot. She was not going to come out of it; it was only a matter of time. He put his head into his hands and closed his eyes. He would never become old enough or tough enough, not to mourn senseless death.

After a few minutes, he lifted his head, stretched a little, and went back to his desktop. He ought to get to his mail, but he didn't want to. So he picked up Section C of today's *Times* and flipped to the back, looking for the theater reviews. It had been a long time since they'd been to a Broadway show. Maybe he'd call for tickets and surprise Toni. And maybe, if he was very lucky, she'd go with him.

A large photograph caught his eye. Obviously a publicity photo, perfectly posed and lighted, big perfect smiles full of perfect teeth: a couple, not young, yet not quite middle-aged . . . a brother and sister? They looked very alike, with large round eyes and round cheeks . . . and then he realized that he was staring at this picture because he'd seen these people before. Where was it? It came back to him: Sam's office. They were Sam's patients.

He looked for the accompanying story. The headline gave him a jolt. THEATER TEAM IN FAILED SUICIDE. Now his interest was total, and he scanned the article quickly. "Tim and Brenda O'Connell . . . over the years . . . famous play . . . only hit . . . *The Gingerbread House* . . . Tim O'Connell had apparently tried to get backing for a revival of his show and had failed. . . . Friends say that, in recent years, he had begun to fantasize about backers for his show and would become depressed when his wife tried to remind him of the reality of the situation. . . ."

Oh Christ! Eliot slapped the paper down and drummed his fingers on the desk. It wasn't so long ago that he'd found them in Sam's office, sitting patiently, waiting. Had they *ever* gotten to see him? Maybe not. If Sam could forget he was on rounds from one minute to the next, he could have forgotten more than just one appointment. How many of Sam's patients had suffered because he was impaired? He'd waited too long to confront Sam. He had not done what he had been supposed to do—as physician and as friend. He had been a coward.

He had to talk to Sam. He *had* to. He reached his hand out for the phone and instantly felt his gut knot. Listen, wimp, he told himself, this time, just *do* it! It was six-forty. Sam was probably home, but he'd try his hospital office, just on the off chance. He'd rather talk to him here, in neutral territory. And Sam answered the phone himself.

"Sam, you're there. Good. Can you come down?"

"Eliot?"

"Of course it's Eliot."

"Sorry. My mind was on something else."

Eliot paused, then looked at the O'Connells, smiling out of the *New York Times*, saved from death by an elevator operator who smelled gas and went to make sure everything was all right. How many others?

"Sam, we need to talk."

"Sure, old buddy. How's tomorrow lunch?"

"Now would be better."

"Sure, okay."

Eliot thought he heard something in his friend's voice, wariness, maybe, or guilt. But he was so nervous about this, he could be imagining it. How was he going to be able to say, "Sam, old buddy, there's something terribly wrong with you." Jesus! But he had to. Sam had to stop practicing until they found out what was going on, that's all there was to it.

Sam must have left immediately after they hung up; not even ten minutes had passed when he shambled in, drawling, "Scotch, please, bartender. And make it a double."

Eliot poured them both drinks from the rarely used bar built into the bookcases. "Well, what do you know," he commented, "Chivas Regal. Your favorite."

As he offered the glass to Sam, he gazed at his old friend. To look at him, you'd never think anything was the matter. On the surface, he was unchanged, just as rumpled and crumpled and shaggy as always. The face was broad, strong featured, homely, probably, though not to Eliot. He knew Sam thought of himself that way; it was why he had grown that enormous mustache— "to hide," he'd said.

I can't do this, Eliot thought, in pain. "How about those Mets?" he said, lifting his glass in salute and taking a sip.

Sam gave him a look. "You're not a Mets fan! Lillian's the Mets fan!"

"I am now. You know Lillian!" That made them both laugh. He lifted his glass again. "Cheers!" They both drank.

Sam plopped down into one of the easy chairs, and Eliot took the one facing him. "So?" Sam said, smoothing his mustache, as he always did when he was bothered. "What's your problem, young man?"

"I have to have a problem to see my oldest and best friend?"

"In a word? Yeah. I think you have a problem, and that's why you wanted to see me right now, this minute, not tomorrow, not lunch—instantly, at once, posthaste, without delay." Sam was now smiling at him quizzically. "So? What's the story, Eliot?"

"I don't know what you mean."

"You've always been a rotten liar, Ellie, you know that?" Something tender in Sam's voice made Eliot want to cry.

"But seriously, folks . . ." Sam went on. "You know and I know you didn't ask me to come down to chat about the Mets. And I don't think you want my advice on how to save Harmony Hill Hospital."

Eliot's throat tightened; he was unable to speak. He had to turn his eyes from Sam's knowing gaze.

"It's about this, isn't it?" Sam said, after a moment. He leaned forward and tapped the newspaper, still open to the O'Connell story. "Well, *I* think it was my fault, too. I've had it. I have to quit."

"Wait a minute, Sam—" He stopped as Sam held up a hand.

"No, no, it's my fault. I let them down. I missed appointments. I think that once I even forgot who they were—right in the middle of a session. No, don't interrupt me. I know everyone's been covering for me: you, Irene, my secretary, the residents, the whole department—even my patients! I've been grateful, believe me, I've been grateful. But when something like this happens—" He broke off, then took in an audible breath.

"It's time for truth. It's been like living in a nightmare. I stood my kids up; they were taking me out to dinner for my birthday, and I forgot all about it. I blew up at my secretary a couple of days ago, for no reason, and made her cry. Yesterday, I left the hospital to go home and . . . oh God, Eliot, I got lost going home! I didn't know where I was! Now I can tell you I was on Riverside Drive, but yesterday, it was a blank. I walked and walked, up one block and down the next, and then I lucked out. The doorman said hello and held the door open. The minute I saw him, I remembered. But one of these days, Ellie, I'm not going to."

"We'll find out what it is; we'll get it fixed."

Sam looked at him with sad eyes. "Just let me finish. I'm pretty good, today; it may be a long time before I'm this good again . . . and, when it happens, I'll probably have forgotten I was ever here!"

"Sam!" Eliot was on his feet, coming to his friend's side. "Sam, don't! We don't know what it is yet. It could be anything, you know that. We'll get you a complete work-up, we'll—"

"Oh, Ellie, I've known for a long time. I went to Leahy Clinic last year, when I first began to have . . . lapses. I've *had* the complete work-up. It's Alzheimer's."

"No!"

"Yes, Eliot, that's what it is."

"You can't be sure; other conditions present the same way. . . ."

"Come on, you're talking to a doctor here. A smart guy, remember? Listen, Ellie, they took a very good look at my brain, and it's . . . it's . . ." His voice wobbled.

"Oh, God, Sam, if only I could—" He choked, his voice caught, and suddenly he was weeping heartbrokenly. "I can't stand it, Sam!"

Sam leaped from his chair and stood by him, putting a hand on his shoulder. "Don't cry for me, Ellie. Please don't. I've got it all planned out. I'm not going to let myself become a vegetable. I've got it all written down, right here." He tapped his chest, then reached into his jacket and pulled out a crinkled sheet of paper. "I was afraid I'd forget, if I didn't. I'm giving it to you, and you destroy it, okay? After . . ."

"What is it?" He knew what it was; he knew after *what*. He took the sheet of paper, numbly.

"Your marching orders, old buddy. And . . . I nearly forgot . . ." He reached into another pocket and came up with a plastic vial, shaking it and making it rattle. "Can't do it without the little red pills." Sam chuckled a little. "Come on, Ellie, take it. When I'm no longer in my right mind, or even in my wrong one, you'll give them to me. You'll make sure I swallow them."

Eliot swiped at his wet face with the back of a hand. "Christ, Sam—"

"Hey. I'd do it for you. And I know you'll do it for me. Right, old buddy?"

Eliot could not talk. He tried to look at Sam; he tried to answer, but all he could do was cry. Sam took his hand and pressed the bottle of pills into it, folded the fingers over it, and held it tightly.

After a while, he let go and stood up. "I'd better go. Irene worries when I'm late, these days." He gave Eliot a wry smile. "Take it easy, okay?"

"It stinks," Eliot finally managed.

"You bet it does. But you're going to help me when I need you, and that makes me feel a helluva lot better."

Eliot listened to the sounds of Sam's footsteps, moving out of the office and into the corridor. He strained to hear until he realized Sam was probably outside. He stood up suddenly. He should have gone with him; he should have put him in a cab. Sam had said he could forget, any minute! He ran to the doorway and then stopped. What if he was seen with his eyes red and swollen. It was only a moment before he was running full tilt to the entrance—in time to see Sam getting into a taxi. That was okay, then.

He started back to the office, and there in the corridor, deep in conversation, were Havemayer and Voorhees. Voorhees was doing most of the talking, poking Havemayer's arm with his index finger, for emphasis. They heard his approach and broke off, both looking startled. And guilty? He thought so. He knew with a chilling certainty that they had been talking about him, discussing how to get rid of him. And their uneasy smiles and hearty hellos convinced him. They did not invite him to stop and chat, and he did not pause. I know what you're up to, he thought grimly, and you're not going to get away with it.

Back in his office, he poured himself a good, stiff drink and sat in his chair, his legs stretched out and his feet resting on the desk. Goddamn it, he didn't have time to waste, thinking about those two. He was going to lose his oldest, closest, dearest friend . . . no. He had already started to lose him.

Day by day and bit by bit, the Sam he had always known and loved—the comic, the wit, the rumpled academic, the trustworthy and nonjudgmental friend—was fading away. This was only the beginning: the loss of memory, the momentary confusion, the occasional lapse of decorum. Later, it would be harrowing, as all the knowledge and all the intelligence—all the personality, the person himself—just drained away. There would be nothing left to Sam except a mindless body that drooled and stared and had no control of any of its functions.

"No!" he shouted aloud, his feet coming off the desk and hitting the floor with a thump. "No! No!" He swallowed back his tears and took a large gulp of Scotch, waiting for its warmth to smother his agony. He wasn't ready to tell anyone else in the family, not yet. They would be devastated. Lillian—! Oh God, this was going to kill his mother.

David would be here soon; he had to get himself under control. But he kept remembering Sam's big, broad hand on his shoulder . . . Sam, comforting *him*! Well, Sam had always comforted him. Even as a kid, orphaned and lonely, he had been the one to take care of Eliot. And he was still doing it.

Then the memory came back, full and complete. He could even smell the wood burning in the big stone fireplace at that camp up in the Adirondacks. He and Sam had gone up alone, to Elizabethtown, a little hamlet way up in the mountains, closer to Canada than to New York City. They were going to "hunt." In truth, Eliot's colitis had kicked up, and this was Sam's cure.

One night, they were sprawled in the big chairs in the cabin, watching the wood fire burn, cooking hot dogs and eating them right off the stick and drinking Jack Daniel's. Eliot was supposed to be on a strict diet: bland foods, no liquor, no coffee, nothing greasy. But Sam had laughed and said, "My boy, I am putting you on Dr. Sam's Special Colitis Diet. You eat everything you really like, because, if you really like it, it doesn't give you colitis." It had been three days of eating everything he wasn't supposed to, and he was fine. In fact, he felt better than he had in a long time.

They would go out in the morning, with food and booze, and walk until they found a tree big enough to lean against; then they'd sit and eat junk food and drink whiskey and get high and talk. And talk and talk and talk. And then they'd come back and nap, and when they woke up, they'd cook burgers or hot dogs in the fireplace and drink some more. And talk and talk and talk.

Mostly, Eliot realized later, he'd talked and Sam had listened. Then, about three days into their week, sitting in their chairs watching the sparks fly up the chimney, Sam had looked at him and started laughing. "No, it's not that you're funny-looking. But I just realized: you came up here with two of the biggest suitcases I've ever seen, and here it is, Tuesday, and you're still wearing the same shirt.''

Eliot laughed, too. "You know Arlene," he said.

Arlene had packed and repacked and repacked his bag, until he was nearly crazy from it. She couldn't decide if he would be cold or hot or if he would be out in the woods or inside or maybe it would rain or maybe it would snow—how did people dress up there, she wanted to know, as if they were going to a fancy hotel instead of a log cabin without running water or plumbing, in a little clearing in the forest.

"Arlene was up until six in the morning, the day I left, packing for me," he went on. "Even after I told her I didn't really need so much, that it was fine the way it was. I nearly missed my plane . . . because she wasn't quite finished. She was convinced I *had* to have a sport coat packed, in case we went to a restaurant. Isn't that funny?'' He expected Sam to answer with a joke.

But Sam didn't. He leaned forward in his chair, cupping the glass of whiskey in both hands, and said, seriously, "No, old buddy, it isn't funny. It's sad. And even more than that, it's . . . oh, hell, it's . . . not normal, Ellie. She's *sick*.''

"I know Arlene's a little extreme, but—''

Sam held up a hand and shook his head. "She's *sick*. Don't look at me like that. From what I've seen and now, from what you're telling me for the past three days, she sounds manic depressive.'' He stopped, looking deep into Eliot's eyes, waiting. Eliot could not talk. As soon as he heard the words, he was afraid they were true.

"One week, up and moving like a tornado, almost unable to stop—right?—the next, in bed with a sick headache or something—right?'' His eyes bored into Eliot's.

Stubbornly: "You could be wrong, you know.''

"Yes, I could. But I think you certainly ought to check it out. Aw, look, old buddy, I'm sorry I've made you feel bad.''

"Yeah, Sam, I feel bad; I feel awful. But, mostly, I feel relieved!'' He wept a little, for his lost love and his lost hopes. Whenever he thought back on that scene, what he remembered was the comforting feel of Sam's strong hand on his shoulder. Like today.

Just like today. He took another slug of Scotch. Much better. No, not really much better. In fact, he didn't need any more. He got up and went to the john, poured what was left down the drain, splashed cold water onto his face, and peered into the mirror to make sure he looked okay. He actually looked human. Now he could face his son; hell, he could face anyone or anything.

And when he came back out into his office, David was walking in, a great big slaphappy grin all over his face.

"What happened to *you*?" Eliot blurted.

"A woman, a wonderful woman!"

Eliot grinned back at his son. He'd never seen David like this, never. This woman must be extraordinary. "That sounds good. How long have you known her?"

"Ten minutes!"

"David—!" Eliot objected.

"I know. I know, it's crazy. But I knew it the minute I saw her; I just knew. This is *it*!" He stopped and pondered his own words and then laughed. "I really *am* crazy! But, Dad, I've never felt this way before, not about anyone! I can't believe she works right here, in the hospital, and I only met her by accident!"

Eliot sat on the edge of his desk. "So," he said, "who *is* this paragon, and when do I get to meet her?"

"Oh, God, Dad, you know her! I mean, Toni introduced us! You *must* know her!"

As soon as he heard the word "Toni," Eliot's mind began to jibber. Oh no! This couldn't be happening. It couldn't be, it *couldn't* be! He found himself unable to respond.

David laughed gleefully. "Oh, come on, Dad! She sits on your administration committee!"

Eliot's heart froze; his whole body went completely still. He stopped breathing. He tried to keep his face expressionless. He could never let David know what was whirling through his mind, *never*. I'm sorry, son, but the woman you're so crazy about has been sleeping with me for months. Oh, Christ! What a mess!

"And the real miracle . . . she feels the same way!"

What? What was David saying? She feels the same way? She couldn't.

"We're having dinner tomorrow. And the day after. And the day after that—"

"David, for God's sake." His voice came out much sharper than he had intended. "You just met the woman!" Then he dropped his voice; he didn't want to sound too agitated. "Just exactly what did she say to you?" It was pipe dreams, that's all. Eliot well remembered his response, the first time he had been close to Janet Rafferty. She was a seductive woman; he couldn't blame his son for being taken with her.

"Exactly what did she say? She said yes."

"To *three* dinner dates—from a total stranger?"

"That's right, Dad. She said yes, yes, yes."

I have to tell him, Eliot thought; he even opened his mouth to begin. And then, he thought, I can't, I can't. What the hell is she up to? Has she completely lost her mind? And then the word came to him. Of course. Blackmail. She thought she could get to him through David. Well, if she thought that, she was dead wrong! Still, there was an awful weight in the pit of his stomach, a weight he recognized, after a moment, as fear.

30

Late April

The woman sat at the foot of the examining table, her back very straight, her eyes focused on a point somewhere over Toni's right shoulder. Toni was used to this; many women were embarrassed in the gynecologist's office, no matter how often they came in. Even with a female doctor. Even with her.

"All right now, Joy, I'm going to lower your robe and examine your breasts." She did so and was glad the woman wasn't looking at her. What she would have seen was a look of horror. The woman's breasts, shoulders, upper arms, were a mass of bruises, some old and healing, but many of them recent. Very recent, would be her guess. She bent closer. Teeth marks! Oh God, another one. She cast her mind to Joy Martino's file; it had showed no history of beatings. So she'd have to begin at the very beginning. Gently, Toni raised the gown and draped it around her.

"Joy! How did this happen?"

"It's not what you think! My husband doesn't hit me."

"Then how did you get these bruises?" Did any of them ever admit it, the first time? Battered women were usually deep into denial. But she had to get through the defenses; this woman needed help. Toni waited; no answer. "You can't keep on taking this kind of punishment, Joy. I'm only trying to help you. Won't you let me? Please?"

Joy, who had cast her eyes down, now looked up. Her big, dark eyes were swimming with tears. "I—it's—my little boy. Geraldo. He's so beautiful, and I love him so much, but I'm—I'm beginning to hate him!"

"Your little boy?" What could she mean? What little boy

could dole out this kind of punishment? "How old is he?" And, she wanted to add, how big?

"Four."

"Four!" She did not bother to hide the disbelief in her voice. If she was covering for her husband, it was the weirdest coverup Toni had ever heard. "Look, Joy—"

"Doctor, wait. I know . . . I know it's hard to believe. But my little boy . . . See, my husband and me, we couldn't have babies. So, last year, after my sister ran away, we took her two, Geraldo and his little brother, Justin. Justin's just a baby, he's a year and a half. He's such a good baby, doesn't give me no trouble. But Geraldo—" She broke off, her face twisting, and began to cry bitterly. "I don't know what to do anymore, Doctor, I'm going crazy with him!" She sobbed for a moment or two, then brought herself under control. "He's . . . he's a crack kid, Doctor. We knew Lucinda, that's my sister, we knew she was smoking crack. But we didn't know it was gonna make Geraldo so crazy! That's what he is, Doctor, he's crazy! He's broken all my nice things—he throws them when he gets mad— and this—" Here she pulled down the gown, exposing the ugly bruises once more.

"What does he do?"

"When he gets real mad, he goes crazy, screaming and yelling and throwing himself around. I kept thinking, if I could just hold him tight and keep talking very quiet and calm, he'd calm down, you know? Like you're supposed to do with temper tantrums. That's what the baby doctor said to do. But nothing works, nothing. Yesterday, I picked him up when he fell down and hurt his knee. I was just going to take him into the bathroom and clean it up and put a Band-Aid on, and he began beating me with his fists and kicking, and then when I didn't put him down right away, he just bit me! Hard! I wanted to throw him out the window! Every day it happens, every day! All the time! I'm so scared! I'm scared for the baby!"

Her hands were in her lap, balled tightly into fists. Toni put her own two hands firmly over them. "Joy, you must get yourself some help with him."

"Help! We can't afford no help! And you want to know what else? He's *good* with me; I can't ask nobody to stay with him."

"There's a support group at the hospital. I'm surprised the pediatrician didn't tell you."

The woman opened her mouth to speak, closed it, then sagged. "I haven't had him to the doctor since a year ago. I was ashamed I couldn't make him behave better."

"Well, no need to be ashamed anymore. You aren't alone, Joy. Unfortunately, there are a lot of crack babies . . . and a lot of very nice women like you trying to take care of them. It's a good group; it's run by a very nice woman. Carolyn Wolfe is her name. You'll like her. I'm going to give you her phone number. Call her; she can help you."

Fifteen minutes later, Toni was alone in her office. She wanted to cry; of all the thankless tasks mortal woman had ever been asked to do, bringing up a baby affected by crack was the worst. Many were apparently born prone to violence. And few of them were as lucky as little Geraldo, with a mother and father who loved him and wanted to take care of him. Most of them were abandoned, left to the tender mercies of the system.

There were, she remembered reading in the *Times*, half a million of them in the United States. They were small children now, but they were all going to grow up. Then what? The thought of half a million violence-prone teenagers unable to control themselves . . . it was a nightmare that was going to come true.

She started pushing papers into neat piles. The phone rang. She eyed it, thinking, I'm not supposed to be here now. Let Gloria take it, out front. But Gloria must have gone to the bathroom, so she picked it up.

"Dr. Romano here."

"Hi, Toni. I got something you're gonna like."

"Besides you, King?" It was amazing how happy she always was at the sound of his voice. A few months ago, she hadn't even known him and now—? She couldn't imagine her life without him. Eliot didn't know it, but they talked a couple of times a week, and whenever their schedules allowed, she took him out for a meal.

"No, no kidding. I've got Charmaine."

"What? Great! She's okay, isn't she?"

"She looks okay to me." He laughed, and over the phone, she could hear the familiar sound of Charmaine's distinctive four-note giggle. A sound she hadn't heard for a long, long time. "Are you gonna hang over there?"

"I am *now*."

"We'll see you in a few."

Toni hung up the phone and twirled herself in her swivel chair. Maybe there *were* some happy endings in this place, after all. "Yo!" she called. "Gloria! You still here?" She knew Gloria was still here; she hadn't come by to say good night.

A moment later, Gloria appeared, short, chunky, dark-skinned, bright red hair, courtesy of L'Oreal, putting on fresh lipstick without benefit of mirror. She had unerring aim.

"Yo yourself," she said. "What's up?"

"I just had a call from King. He found Charmaine!"

"Hey, great! I was really worried about her. Did he say what happened with her?"

"Only that she looks okay. And I guess she *is* okay, because she's coming in with him."

"Good. You really had high hopes for that one."

"Yeah . . ." Charmaine had been the one bright light in this place, when King had first sent her in. The first time Toni talked with her, she was very aware of those eyes, fastened on her face, trying to bore into her brain. Total concentration. And Charmaine remembered everything, literally *everything*, every word, every pause, every joke. You never had to tell her anything twice.

After sitting in on one meeting and listening to the other girls talk, she stood up and said, "Yo, my boyfriend really conned me good! I was supposed to get pregnant—for *him*, you got that, *I* get pregnant to prove *he's* a big man!" She got a big laugh with that one; many of them had heard it. In fact, many of them had the same story. "And I was so dumb, I thought I had to! But Dr. Toni told me I ain't gotta do nothing I don't want to. Dr. Toni says I am entitled to say 'no' to *anything* I don't want to do." She paused, then added with a little smile, "Except school. Right, Dr. Toni?" That, of course, got another big laugh; they had all heard Toni's theme song, over and over and over: "Stay in school. Stay in school. Make something of yourself and stay in school."

Soon, Charmaine was showing up every day, being useful, straightening up, sweeping, spraying Windex on every surface, watering the plants, welcoming the new girls, drawing them in with her quick smile and trendy getups. She looked like one of them. Well, of course she *was* one of them. Only different.

Charmaine chose the Pill. "That way, no boy can talk me out of using it," Toni heard her telling the other girls. "But you pick what feels right to *you*. And remember, you gotta stick *with* it. And *always* use a condom.'' She sounded like an echo of Toni.

But she was more than just a clever mimic, as Toni had discovered when she heard Charmaine admonishing another teenager: ''Don't you listen to what that bad ass says! 'Hey, baby, I ain't putting one of them things on *my* johnson!' What does *he* care? *He* gonna have a baby, or *you*? And you sure he don't have AIDS? You listen to *me*, Jolene! I know that dude, and he's plain no good!''

It had occurred to Toni, right then, that when school was out for the summer, she had to make a job here in the clinic for Charmaine, at least part-time. And if she wanted to give Charmaine a job, she'd damn well have to pay for it herself.

''Funny, how she just disappeared like that,'' Gloria said now.

''Tell me about it!'' Toni said. ''It kept me awake many a night, let me tell you. And I'd just told her how well she was doing, that I thought I was going to have a job for her in the summer, a *real* job, keeping the appointment book and doing the filing. I'll never forget the stunned look on her face when I told her. I thought surely *that* would keep her coming around! But enough about mysteries, let's talk about your vacation. Where are you going?''

''Alaska.''

''Alaska!'' She stared at Gloria, who began to laugh.

''Well, at first I figured we'd go home to San Juan and lie on the beach and catch a few rays. But then, when I thought about visiting not only my old grandmother and my mother and my father, but also my aunts and my uncles and my brothers and my sisters and my godchildren and . . . I said to Rosario, '*Alaska*, baby.' '' They both laughed. ''When I get back, you gotta fill me in on the lovebirds. So keep your eye peeled, will you?''

''What lovebirds?''

''Come on, Toni, I know you're busy, but he *is* your stepson. Show a little family feeling! Gossip a little!''

''I don't know that much about his private life. He's a grown-up, Gloria, not a teenager. And anyway, I don't see that much of him.''

''I don't either, usually. But the other night, at Ditto's, Rosario and I were having a few drinks and a late dinner and who should walk in but those two: Janet and him. Well, Rosario had had a couple of drinks, and when I said hi to them, he was on his feet immediately playing the host and inviting them to sit down with us. And they did. Well, that David, he's a great guy! He reminds me so much of Dr. Wolfe . . . your husband . . . his father! He's warm and caring and—well, *you* know. He's one of the few doctors in this world who doesn't think he's God!''

"Warm and caring," Toni repeated, bemused.

"Yeah, yeah, just like—"

"His father . . . my husband . . . Dr. Wolfe. Well, thank you, Gloria, I'll tell Eliot what you said. He'll be pleased.'' Inwardly, she was wondering where *she* was when all this warmth and caring was being handed out. But maybe she wasn't so warm and caring with *him*, either.

"Anyway," Gloria said, "they're a big item at the hospital. Everybody's making book.''

"On what?''

"On whether there'll be wedding bells, of course.''

"You'd think people would have better things to talk about than someone's private life.''

"Yeah, sure.'' Gloria laughed. "But when there's a romance at Harmony Hill, believe me, nobody wants to talk about anything else!'' She gave a big, throaty laugh. "Lemme tell you, if I was gonna fool around on Rosario, I would *never* do it any-- where *near* that hospital! He'd hear about it before I got home that night!''

Toni felt uneasy. Was Gloria giving her a message, letting her know that she and Ham Pierce had been seen? That there had been gossip about them? Lucky she'd got out while the getting was good! Now, if anyone asked her, she could truthfully deny anything between them. It was over.

She walked Gloria to the front door so she could lock it after her, and there they were: a grinning King and next to him, looking very tiny in the crook of his arm, a dejected, contrite Charmaine, her head down, her eyes shyly lifted.

"Oh, Charmaine, I'm so glad to see you!'' She drew them inside and locked the door. Then she held her arms open, and Charmaine walked into the embrace.

The girl felt so small, so frail. "Have you been eating right?'' Toni asked, smiling into Charmaine's round, dark eyes. "You're very thin.''

"I—I may have dropped a pound or two."

Toni kept waiting for a smile from the girl, some sign of life. Instead, she looked . . . what *did* she look like? Frightened, Toni suddenly realized. She looked scared. Oh God, not of *me*.

"Charmaine has something to tell you," King said. Toni's heart sank. "Come on, kiddo, that's why we're here, remember?" To Toni, he added: "It's a big secret, but we decided it's time for Charmaine to tell, and let's *do* something about it. And it's *you* she wants to tell."

Oh shit, Toni thought. She's pregnant. Her eyes closed, and she took in a breath, thinking, I mustn't show anything.

"Oh no, Dr. Toni, it ain't that!"

Her eyes flew open. "It ain't what?"

"It *isn't* that I'm pregnant. That's what you thinking, isn't it? But I'm not. It's just . . . it's that . . ." Her eyes brimmed with tears, and her voice shook a little. "Shit, I can't even say it."

Gently, King said, "You gotta, Charmaine. It's going to be fine. You know it is."

"Oh, Dr. Toni, I can't work here! I can't! I can't go to be a secretary! I don't even go to school anymore! I can't read, Dr. Toni. I can't read, so how can I have a real job?"

Toni took the girl's hands in hers. "Is *that* what sent you running away from us?"

"I got a job in a factory. It pays good, and the other women are nice. And . . . and . . . you don't have to read."

"You're going to learn how to read," Toni said. "Don't shake your head at me; you're very smart. Yes, you are." She smiled. "It won't take you long. Gloria has a nice, long list of reading volunteers. She'll find you a really good teacher and by next fall, you'll be able to go back to school and finish and graduate."

Now the eyes were wide with wonder. "Really, Dr. Toni?"

"Cross my heart and hope to die . . . That's what we said when I was your age. It means, yeah, babe, count on it!"

When Charmaine went off to the bathroom to put on new makeup, King turned to Toni. "Toni, listen, I gotta talk to you," he said in low, urgent tones.

Laughing a little: "You *are* talking to me!"

"Charmaine's not the only one with a secret. I've got one,

too." He took in a deep breath, smiling self-consciously. "I like Dee; I mean, I *really* like Dee."

"You mean, *my* Dee?"

He smiled wryly. "Well, I've been hoping to make her *my* Dee. But . . . We've been out together for coffee, and lunch a couple of times, but she won't see me at night. Wait—" He held up a hand. "Don't remind me. She was raped; I'm very aware of that. And I know about post-trauma syndrome. So I never made a move on her, nothing, not even a touch on her hand! I don't know what to do! I'm going crazy!"

"Maybe," Toni said carefully, "maybe . . . she's just not interested."

"No, it's not that. A couple of times, when she was real upset, and I held her, it was okay. It was better than okay. I could tell it felt good to her, too. And now all of a sudden—"

"Look. King. How many rape victims have you brought in to the E.R.? I know you're great with them; some of them have been my patients, and they tell me. But you have to remember, it takes a very long time for trust to be restored, a *very* long time." He looked so sad, she couldn't help adding, "I'll see what I can do. I'll talk to her. I'll put in a good word for you." Anything, to see him smile.

Charmaine reappeared, and the conversation stopped, but after they had left, Toni couldn't stop thinking about King. As much as she loved him, she found herself wishing, every once in a while, that he'd left well enough alone. Was that sinful? God, she wished she knew. She wished she knew how to handle this thing better. She kept thinking how nice it would be if she could just tell everybody. And then she thought about explaining herself, over and over, and then she just wanted the whole thing to go away. Was she an unnatural mother? It was making her crazy that she didn't know what to do or even what to think!

Every time she had these thoughts—and she had them frequently—the one person she always thought of was Lillian. She sat herself down and let herself sprawl, her legs out straight in front of her. Lillian. There was something about Lillian, something very straight, very clear, and very tolerant. Toni knew that Lillian wouldn't fuss about King at all. She would just accept the situation. And him.

To Lillian, she could pour her heart out, could confess how remorseful she felt, all these years later, about giving away her own child. She could cry, with Lillian, cry and cry until the pain was all cried out of her. Startled, she thought, Where did *that* come from? Crying? She didn't need to cry! What she needed, she decided, was a hot bath and a cold drink. And that meant she really should rouse herself, and get the hell out of here.

When the door suddenly opened, she nearly jumped out of her skin. Her heart began to hammer. Hadn't she locked up? Oh God. A man strode in; even as she tried to think what she was going to do and how she was going to call the police and how she was going to get out of here—all of this racing through her head at the speed of light—he came into view, and she sprang to her feet.

"Ham! What are you doing here?"

He laughed. "I've come to see you, of course."

"Well, that's just too bad, because I was about to leave. Hours are long over, you know, and I'm terribly sorry, but you'll just have to excuse me—"

She stopped talking suddenly. She had to stop; his mouth was over hers. He was holding her tightly, and the taste and touch of him was making her dizzy. She knew it was all over, the pretense that she didn't think about him, didn't care about him, and didn't want him. She was lost, and she didn't care. Didn't care? What was she, crazy?

Pulling sharply away from him, she said, "Ham! Ham! The window. I can't be seen here like this—"

"Good. I was planning on taking you home with me."

She was like someone bewitched, not caring where they were going or how they got there. They went in his car, and as he pulled the car over to the curb, he put her hand on his erection, and she gasped. He laughed; they were both laughing as they ran to the front of his building, then slowed to a dignified pace for their entrance into that imposing lobby. She had to admire the evenness of his voice as he greeted the doorman, the receptionist, and the elevator operator in a sonorous, somber tone.

Once inside the apartment, however, he slammed the door and turned, kissing her so hard she could feel his teeth against hers. They grabbed at each other, moaning, growling, murmuring half phrases, tearing at each other's clothes. She needed

to feel his bare skin; she was desperate to rip off all this stuff
that was in her way. They struggled together, kissing each other
passionately, laughing as they fumbled. Her panties were still
trapped at her ankles when she dropped to the floor, still clinging
to him, pulling him down over her.

He covered her face and neck with quick, hot kisses, digging
his hands into her hair, pushing his tongue into her mouth, biting
her lips, her neck, her breasts. She was begging him, pleading
with him to take her, take her now! Chuckling deep in his throat,
he entered her. She was so wet, he slipped deep inside her, and
she groaned with pleasure at the feel of him. She was pushing
her hips up to his, she was clinging to his buttocks, panting,
sweating, crying, ''More! More! More!''

Condom! she tried to warn herself, but she wasn't listening.
And then she was gasping for breath, unable to speak, unable
to think, unable to do anything but come and come and come.

A few minutes later, having more or less regained her senses,
she thought, Look at me, lying on the carpet in Ham Pierce's
foyer, covered in sweat—and probably lint—every bit of lipstick
eaten off, and this big, sweating, exhausted male body collapsed
on top of me, and I'm in bliss. And then she thought, Shame on
you, Toni Romano. You preach condom and feel so fucking
superior because you're saving all these poor, young, ignorant
women and then, when push comes to shove, you only want to
push and shove and to hell with everything you preach, to hell
with safe sex!

She laughed ruefully. At the sound, Ham rolled away from
her a little and turned on his side. Leaning on one arm, he
looked into her eyes, smiling.

''Now you know this is real.''

''Ham, don't start. I'm—''

''I know. You're a married woman.''

''Actually, I was about to say 'I'm not kidding.' But, yes, I
am a married woman, and this is wrong.''

He bent, placed his warm lips on her shoulder, then said,
''Wrong, maybe. But you love it. And I love it. And it's about
time we seriously discussed what we should do about it.''

''We already went through this; I don't like playing the same
scene twice.''

''But—''

"Ham. Stop it." She extricated herself from his embrace and stood up. "I can't do this to my life, I just can't! Please try to understand. We're both adults, Ham, come on!" He got to his feet, not answering her, putting his clothes on slowly.

Conciliatory—because she had after all been just as eager as he had been, maybe more—she smiled at him and said in a softer tone, "I really admire the programs you've done on Betty. The TACK people say they've gotten over three thousand dollars in contributions already. And Dee tells me that George watches the tapes over and over, and each time, he says it lifts up his soul."

"Dee says that?" He couldn't help but smile, and she knew the praise had pleased him. Somehow, that pleased her. "Well . . . thanks but . . . I don't think it's helping *Dee*."

"What do you mean?"

"I see her around, and we talk. And I think she's headed for big trouble—"

"What *kind* of big trouble?" I see her every day, she thought with some asperity; if anybody's going to spot something wrong, it would be me, wouldn't it?

"I don't know. But there's something about her lately. I hate to say crazy but . . . *crazed*, that's more what I mean. There's something crazed behind her eyes."

"That's very poetic," Toni said, hoping her voice did not reveal her annoyance, "but it doesn't tell me anything."

"I'm sorry, Toni. Didn't mean to step on your toes."

"You didn't. I just . . . look, Dee isn't crazy, or even crazed. She's been through so much; that's probably what you're seeing."

"That's not what I'm seeing. Look. I know you're the doctor, and I'm just a lowly television reporter, but give me a break. It's my business to look behind the facade and see what's really going on inside a person."

I hope to God you don't know what's really going on inside *me*, Toni thought, or you'd lock the door and tear off my clothes again and take me to bed and never let me go. "I hear you," she said. "I'll talk to her tomorrow." She bent to retrieve her purse from where it had been flung into a corner, and when she straightened, he was right behind her. His arms snaked around her, and he pulled her in close to him.

"Don't leave," he whispered. Then, to her stupefaction, as

he nuzzled into her neck, he added: ''Don't leave, and I promise I'll lock the door and undress you and take you to bed and never let you go.''

31

May

Dee sat in a straight chair pulled as close to the hospital bed as she could get and draped herself over the rail so she could look straight into Betty's face. Her sister looked so placid, so calm, so peaceful . . . nothing like the real person, Dee couldn't help thinking, *nothing* like! Her eyes welled up with tears again, and she blinked rapidly. She couldn't waste time crying; she'd cried so much already.

"I'm sorry, Betty," she said to the smooth, untroubled face, the face with no emotion, the face with no animation, the face with no life, really. And, in fact, Betty wasn't really alive; Dee knew that very well. Only the life-support system kept her breathing. But George was not ready to face reality. George was still waiting for the miracle to happen, waiting for Betty to come out of the coma and be alive.

Oh, Jesus, it was such a nightmare! Why Betty, who had always been so vibrant, so active, so alive? The tears came again, and this time, she let them roll down her cheeks, unchecked.

"It's my fault," she moaned. "My fault!" That was her personal nightmare: that she had caused all this. After the rape, she should have toughed it out, kept her lousy fears to herself! But no, she'd given in, spending her nights at Betty's place, so that Betty couldn't help knowing how often she woke up screaming. No way her sister was going to sit still for that! Betty had been all set to stop going out nights with the TACK patrols. But when she found out what was going on with Dee, forget quitting!

"Not after what happened to *you*, baby!" she had said, her whole face set with determination. "That bastard—whoever he is, and one of these days you *are* gonna tell me—that bastard's

319

gonna pay! Meantime, I'm gonna do what I can to make sure it doesn't happen to any other woman, not around here, not as long as I draw breath!''

And now she didn't draw breath! No breath in her body, just the oxygen pumping in and out, mechanically. Dee put her head down on her arm and whispered, ''Oh Betty, I'm such a loser! Can you ever forgive me?''

''Dee!'' The voice from the doorway startled her. She wiped at her wet face with her sleeve and turned. It was Ruth, a worried little frown between her brows. That worried little frown was appearing between the brows of all the interns these days, Dee thought. She knew she wasn't quite herself. She was struggling like crazy to keep herself from curling into a little ball and letting herself sink into oblivion. She was working so hard to act like a regular normal person, and she was aware that she was falling short.

As chief resident, she was supposed to be the shoulder they all cried on, the strong shoulder they all leaned on, and she knew they were becoming disturbed . . . maybe annoyed. She gazed at Ruth's pale, placid face, the frown lines, the supplicating posture. Poor Ruth, she must be getting tired of baby-sitting me. That's what she was doing here; she wanted to make sure Dee ate lunch.

Sure enough, she said, ''Come on, Dee, you really have to eat. It's lunchtime.''

''I'm not hungry.''

''I know you're not, but you've already lost too much weight. If you're not careful, Dr. Toni will put you into a hospital bed—''

''And I'll end up with a tube up my nose. I know, I know. She already warned me.''

''The guys are saving us a table at Ditto's. We'll have baked ziti, yum, yum.''

Dee had to smile. ''All right, Ruth, I know I'm in bad shape, but I'm not that bad. I know baked ziti is yum yum.''

She was actually laughing as they left the room and ran for the elevator. She was laughing harder than the joke deserved. Her emotional volume control was out of whack. But laughing was better than crying, right?

Ditto's was mobbed with hospital personnel, as usual. You could hardly fit past the bodies lined up two deep at the bar—

all men, of course, and, of course, every one of them turning to
eye every female passing by. Every table was filled, and each
filled table also had a couple of people hanging out. Dee spotted
Gilbert and Alan sitting at a table over in the corner, bent over
their mugs of beer, talking. It was slow going, getting to their
table.

You couldn't help hearing Gil Reid's voice; he never talked,
he pontificated. She really didn't like him; he was so goddamn
self-important, so sure he was right about everything. He was
going to be a lousy doctor, competent enough in the technical
department, but as for compassion . . . zip!

"Nearly useless these days, as a chief resident. She's screwed
up three of my schedules already! How come Dr. Toni hasn't
told her to shape up? She's playing this so-called rape of hers to
death! She was no virgin! No, you take it from me, she did
something to ask for it—!''

Ask for it! Dee could feel her scalp tighten. She was cold all
over. If she moved, she would kill him.

In a moment, Ruth was standing over Gilbert, her voice quivering with rage. "You stupid shit! You asshole! What kind of
thing is that to say? Hell, what kind of thing is that to *think*?
You're sick, you know that? I don't know how someone like you
got by the admissions committee!''

Her voice was so loud that heads turned at tables close by.
Dee didn't even have to think about it; she was there in a second,
next to Ruth, her hand on Ruth's shoulder, saying, "Okay, that's
it. Let's lower our voices and calm down.'' Not that *she* was
calm, but the last thing she wanted was a scene here at Ditto's
where everyone from the hospital hung out. Within ten minutes,
the story would be all over Harmony Hill, with added details,
none of them necessarily true.

Gilbert's face paled and then reddened. Good, he ought to be
ashamed. He jumped to his feet and held a chair out for her,
kind of babbling something or other, she couldn't be bothered
listening. She paused, just for a moment, wondering how the
hell she could possibly sit down at a table with this sexist son of
a bitch and then *eat*, for Christ's sake. A huge portion of baked
ziti had been set down in the middle of the table. She looked at
it, oozing melted cheese and puddles of red grease, and felt ill.
She could not possibly choke it down.

But she had to stay; she was the chief resident. Telling herself that had kept her sane on more than one occasion, lately. I am the chief resident in OB/GYN; I have responsibilities, and I cannot fall apart. Her magical incantation. But it worked.

She took a chair, nodding to Alan. Ruth sat next to her. There was an embarrassed silence, nobody quite looking at anyone else. Then Alan leaned toward her and said earnestly, "Look, Dee, I think Gilbert's full of crap. But, well, we worry about you; we worry about you a *lot*. I mean . . . well, you're our chief, Dee, and you haven't really been here, you know what I mean?" He paused, cleared his throat, and said hesitantly, "Maybe . . . rape counseling?"

She was ready to give it to him, *really* give him a piece of her mind! She didn't need any spoiled rich white kid giving *her* advice! She opened her mouth to tell him exactly what she thought and then thought better of it. "You think I'm acting . . . peculiar?" she said carefully.

"Aw, Dee, come on! I'm only—hey!" This last was addressed to two men who were pushing by, jostling his chair and nearly knocking his beer over. How rude, she thought. She looked up, ready to give whoever it was hell, and then quickly looked away. Havemayer and Voorhees, strutting through the room to their special table, hardly acknowledging the existence of all the peons.

"Isn't that your running partner? Doesn't he at least say hello?" Alan teased.

"He's not my running partner. He never was my running partner."

"Oh yeah, he just happened to be in the park at the same time as you all the time, right?"

"I really don't know, Alan, and you want to know something? I really don't care."

"Okay, okay, okay!"

"I haven't seen Dr. Voorhees since—I haven't seen him in ages. Look, I don't even run anymore."

Another silence fell over the table. They all thought she was scared. Well, she wasn't. Well, maybe she was.

Quickly, Ruth put a hand over hers. "Look who's sitting over there with the big boys," she said. "Dr. Carlsen, our very best favorite!"

Gil quickly said, "They should really give the job to Dr. Toni. Carlsen's an idiot."

"What strings did he have to pull to get chief of service?"
Ruth wondered aloud. "Every woman in the hospital hates him!
How could a jerk like that go in for OB/GYN, anyway?"

Dee wanted to say, How about our very own jerk, Gilbert
Reid? But she didn't. They were trying so hard to change the
subject, to get her mind off her troubles. Nothing was going to
get her mind off her troubles. Nothing. They were so naive; they
had no idea about real life!

Now they were on to the Bachelor Brownstones; Christ, those
buildings were never going to be used for people who really
needed them! And Gilbert was happy about that! "I don't know
about you guys, but I don't see why doctors should have to put
their lives on the line for a bunch of faggots and dope addicts."

"You wanna know something, Gilbert? I pity your patients,
I really do."

Stubbornly, his mouth set, he said, "When I'm in private
practice, I won't accept AIDS patients. There's nothing saying
I have to."

"I say you have to!" Ruth was red in the face, and her hands
were balled into fists. "No doctor has the right to refuse to treat
anyone! It's unethical, it's . . . it's immoral!"

Gilbert curled his lip and he said, loftily, "I have a wife and
family to think about . . . I'm about as eager to deliver AIDS
patients as I am to put a pistol to my head . . . oh."

Again, they were very carefully not looking at her, not talking, hardly breathing, it seemed to her. Shit, was there no end
to his stupidity, his total insensitivity to every other person in
the world? She looked up and stared at him until he met her
eyes, sheepish.

She felt tears starting. Again. It was happening all the time
lately. Betty was gone. There was nobody in this world she could
run to, nobody she could talk to.

None of them understood what she was going through. The
sudden memories—total, complete, intact—that assailed her unexpectedly. Feeling the weight of him again, shoving himself
into her, smelling him . . . ugh! She hadn't told anyone about
her sudden, cold sweats. Or waking in the middle of night,
terrified.

The dreams, the terrible dreams of him, coming at her, smiling that weird smile, saying those horrible things to her in that
soft voice, so creepy—"You're going to love this, you know

you're going to love it. . . . I know all about black women; black women gotta have it.'' And then the feel of him, forcing himself, laughing a little—oh, she couldn't bear it, she couldn't think about it. And yet it came to haunt her every night, making her flesh crawl. And now, horribly, Betty was in all her dreams, she was always running to Betty for safety, like she always had. And then waking up, the terrible moment when she remembered all over again that Betty was gone.

Under the table, where they couldn't see, she gripped her hands together tightly. She had to hang in there; she had to. She could not fall apart.

She felt a shiver on the back of her neck. There were eyes on her, eyes from across the room. She'd been feeling those eyes ever since he had sat down, and now she just couldn't pretend they weren't there, staring at her, willing her to turn around, *turn around*. She heard that laugh, *his* laugh, and she swallowed to keep herself from throwing up.

She couldn't stand it anymore. She had to get out of here. She had to do something, anything! Abruptly, she pushed herself up, knocking her chair over. She didn't pick it up; she didn't say good-bye; she didn't wait for anything; she just elbowed her way past the crowded bar. Behind her, she heard them calling her, but she didn't care. She had to get out of there!

Outside, she walked quickly toward the hospital, taking in large gulps of air, forcing down the sick feeling. After a few minutes, she felt almost sane, sane enough to start thinking about what she was going to do.

She went in through the E.R., and the minute she walked in, she saw King Crawford. He was chatting with one of the nurses, his back to her. She paused for a moment, thinking how nice it would be to talk to him. All she had to do was walk over there. She'd say his name, and he'd turn and give her that big, lazy grin. He was such a cute guy. She knew she'd feel better . . . Now wasn't that weird, thinking that about someone she hardly knew?

He'd called her a couple of times, wanting to meet for lunch or a drink. She'd had lunch with him, but she was afraid. He was a normal, healthy guy. Sooner or later, he'd put the move on her, and she'd freeze. She liked him fine. He was strong without being macho. He was sweet. But he was a man, and right now, no thanks, Deedra Strong was not having any. Not even any of *that*. She sighed and got out of there.

Her first stop was the neonatal nursery where baby Winifred Cannon lay, wrapped in a pink blanket, in her crib. Next to the really sick babies, with their wizened little bodies and their wrinkled skin, baby girl Cannon looked huge, almost fat. As Dee stared down into the crib, her finger gently stroking one soft, brown cheek, the infant gazed at her. It was like looking into Betty's eyes. Deedra snatched her hand away as if it had been burned.

From behind her came Marie Campbell's calm voice. "You won't have to come up here after today, Dee. She's doing so well, we're sending her to the regular nursery. She can probably go home in two days—"

"Go home!" Dee choked out. "To what?"

"Oh, God, I'm so sorry." Marie's hand was instantly on her shoulder. "Every time I think about what they did to Betty, I get mad all over again! I don't suppose there's any change . . . ?"

Dee's eyes filled again. This time she let the tears overflow. She was getting so damn tired of swallowing them. Her throat hurt from it. Wordlessly, she shook her head. Marie's eyes were pools of sympathy, and Dee had to look away, had to leave before she broke down completely. Suddenly, she knew exactly what she had to do.

She couldn't bear waiting for the elevator, so she took the stairs two at a time, up to the ICU. Con Scofield was on duty. Dee desperately did not want to have to make conversation with Con, and she was happy to see that the nurse was totally engrossed in some work. Dee tiptoed past without saying anything.

George was sitting on a plastic chair taken from the lounge, right outside Betty's door, his shoulders slumped, his head bent to his chest. Maybe he was sleeping. Poor George, she knew he was up all night, most nights; you could see it in his red-rimmed, blasted eyes. She walked very quietly, and when she got close, sure enough, he was fast asleep, snoring a little. On her tiptoes, she very slowly, very cautiously moved the door handle and silently opened the door, sliding herself into the room. She closed the door tightly behind her, and then held her breath, as she always did when she came in here, dreading that first moment when she had to look at her sister's blank face again.

She turned and let her breath out, painfully. A little moan escaped her, and she clamped her hand over her own mouth. She didn't want George to hear her and come in; she wanted to be alone with Betty, at least for a little while.

The room was small and bleak. The one straight chair was still pulled up close to the bed, and there was a small bouquet of daisies on the bedside table. George. Poor George.

She sat on the chair, leaning over so that her face was very close to Betty's. This wasn't any Betty she had ever known. She remembered how every feeling was always mirrored on Betty's face: joy, delight, anger, compassion, sadness, disgust, fury, love . . . oh, God, love! Burying her face in her two hands, Deedra felt the sobs strain at her throat but made no sound. She must not allow herself the luxury of weeping aloud. George might hear.

"Betty, if you're anywhere that you can hear me, I want you to know I'm so sorry I never told you who did it to me," she barely whispered. "I feel so awful, Betty. Sometimes I wake up in the middle of the night, and I'm cold with sweat, crying. Crying in my sleep, Betty!" She was beginning to cry again. She had to stop.

Sniffling, she wiped at her wet nose with a tissue from the table and took in a deep breath. In a shaky voice, she went on. "Ham Pierce is doing such nice programs about you, Betty. You'd blush. I didn't want him to, at first, you know how he can be. But he's telling everyone that you're exceptional . . . *exceptional*: that's his word. One of them was the story of your life; he got old snapshots and stuff and showed how you pulled yourself up. Oh, Betty, there was that picture I always hated. You remember the one, when I was eleven and had made a solemn vow never to wear dresses again, and you made me put one on; remember that? Did I give you a hard time about that! But you were even more stubborn than me; there's the picture to prove it."

For a moment she sat, holding Betty's limp and lifeless hand. How could this be Betty's hand? She knew Betty's hands; they had bandaged her and braided her hair and rubbed her back. When Dee was nine years old, she had broken her arm roller-skating on the broken sidewalk. She had whimpered for nights in her sleep from the pain, and she still remembered the feel of Betty's broad, warm, comforting hand gently rubbing her face.

"Oh, and there was a program about TACK, too, with the whole crew, and all of them saying how it was *you* who did it all, you who got it started, and you who kept it going. Oh God, Betty . . ." Her voice was failing her again. She stopped and cleared her throat. Then she let go of the slack hand and smoothed Betty's hair.

"Betty, listen to me. I love you. You were my mama; you *are* my mama and the best mother there ever was; I want you to know that. I can't stand seeing you like this. I swear to you, I'll take care of your baby girl; I'll raise her like you raised me, and I'll love her like you loved me. And all the good you did in the world, I'll try to do it, too. I swear to you, Betty; I swear it."

She was amazed to hear the strength in her own voice, amazed not to be fighting the sobs and the tears. She was dry eyed and resolute, and she was ready. She kissed Betty's forehead and, for a moment, leaned her hot cheek on Betty's cool skin.

It was an easy reach to the plug in the wall. She didn't even have to get out of the chair. One pull, and the respirator fell silent. And finally, it was all over.

The elevator sighed to a stop on six, and Toni Romano stepped out. An urgent high-pitched whine was signaling a flatline. Someone had just stopped breathing. Without having to think about it, she began to run toward the sound. It was still just as frightening, just as sickening, as the first time she had ever heard it. It meant failure; it meant that, no matter how careful you had been, how brilliant a doctor, how inspired, how caring, how *correct* . . . death had beaten you anyway. Alice Rodriguez slid into her thoughts. Sometimes, you weren't careful or brilliant or caring enough. She shook the image of Alice away.

Con Scofield was not sitting at the nursing station; that meant she was already on the scene. Quickly, Toni scanned the battery of screens. There! Room 3! She was halfway down the corridor, at a run, when she realized that it was Betty Cannon's room! Thank God it was over.

Then she noticed that Con Scofield and George were out in the hall, both banging on the door of room 3. Something was wrong. As she got closer, George hollered, "Someone's in there; someone's gone and unplugged Betty!"

"Dr. Toni!" Con was panting a little. "I think it's Deedra."

"Deedra?"

"I think so. I saw her on the floor a little while ago—"

"Couldn't be Dee!" George insisted. "Dee loved Betty like a mother!"

Softly, Con murmured, "Who else?"

Who else, indeed? Dee must be in worse shape than Toni had thought. "Why can't you get in? There's no lock on this door."

"Something's jamming it," George said. "But I'll get in there! I'll get in there if I have to pull the door off it's hinges!"

"Wait. Let me." Leaning her head against the door, Toni called, "Dee, are you in there?"

Silence. Then: "Yes." Next to her, she could hear George make a tiny sound, not quite a sob.

"Let us in, Dee."

"I will, as soon as I'm sure she's gone."

"Dee, you have to let us in. You can get into a lot of trouble. It's not worth it." How could she say in front of George that Betty would soon be dead, anyway? She turned to Con and asked: "How long?"

Consulting her wristwatch: "Three minutes."

Again, Toni called through the door. "Dee. Listen to me. It's all over. It really is. It's okay. Now let me in."

A moment later, there was the sound of furniture scraping, and then the door opened. Dee stood there in the middle of the doorway, her face a mask, her body rigid. "Oh, George—" she started, but he pushed by her as if he didn't see her.

"George, please! I did it for her! Betty would never have wanted to stay attached to a machine, not able to see us or hear us or talk to us!" She crumpled then, her whole body curved into itself, her face buried in her hands.

"Nobody asked you to do that! Nobody wanted you to do it! You shouldn't have done it! Betty, baby, don't go!" George flung himself down, wrapping his arms around his wife's inert body. Nobody else moved. A moment later, Toni heard him moaning, "You're gone, baby, you're gone, you're gone. . . . Oh Jesus, what am I gonna do? What's gonna become of me?"

Toni put her arm around Dee's shaking shoulders and, turning the girl, walked them both out of the room. As she closed the door behind them, Dee said, in a dead voice, "I'm not sorry,

Dr. Toni. No, I'm not sorry at all. I'll take my punishment, but I'm not sorry.''

Toni squeezed her shoulder. "We'll talk about this later,'' she said. She knew from the look and sound of her that Dee was in shock. There was no sense in trying to ask her why she had done it, what had made her suddenly decide. And anyway, Toni thought she knew.

Sometimes a comatose patient could be kept "alive" for a year, or two years . . . even longer. It turned into a nightmare for everyone. You went and visited and you looked at this un-moving, unfeeling, unthinking person, and because you couldn't stand knowing there was no feeling or thinking, you began to make things up. You thought you saw eyelids flutter; you thought an involuntary groan meant she was waking up; you thought when you said hello, she squeezed your hand . . . just a little, but a squeeze. You told the doctor, "Today she smiled a little,'' and the doctor looked at you with kind, sad eyes, and said noth-ing.

Con was back at her post; when she saw them approaching, she came running out and put an arm around Dee. "I know what you need, young woman. You just come with me.''

Toni watched them walk into the tiny nurses' office behind the station and immediately reached for the house phone and punched out Eliot's number. "This is Dr. Romano,'' she said; an instant later, she realized that this was one of the many sub-stitute secretaries who had been filling in since the shooting. Quickly, she added, "Dr. Wolfe's wife, and it's urgent.''

A moment later, Eliot was saying: "What is it?'' She told him, tersely. "Don't move,'' he said, "I'm on my way!'' To her surprise, she felt reassured and relieved. So that's why everyone around here loved him so much!

Damn these old elevators, Eliot thought. I should have used the stairs. Toni had never called him before on the red phone, so the moment he heard her voice, he knew it was something se-rious. And when she said, "Betty is dead,'' in that tense tone of voice—just that, "Betty is dead,'' no comment, no emotion, no details—he *knew* something had happened that he wasn't going to like. The elevator doors wheezed open on six.

Toni was waiting for him at the nursing station, her whole body taut, her eyes searching the corridor. As soon as she saw him, she began walking toward him, and when they met, she was already talking.

"I'm glad you're here." She reached out and grabbed his hand, holding it tightly. "Betty was unplugged."

"Christ!"

"Exactly."

"I knew we should have kept a closer eye on George."

"It wasn't George." She expelled a loud breath. "It was Deedra."

"Oh, Christ, one of our doctors!"

"Betty's sister," she reminded him.

"I know, I know, she's under considerable strain, she's been through a lot, and she's very young. But, bottom line, she's a doctor in this hospital."

They started to walk briskly to the nursing station. His mind was racing, trying to figure out all the ramifications—how to contain this, how to deal with it, oh Christ, how to deal with Ham Pierce! He groaned, without realizing it.

"What?" Toni's voice was sharp with worry. Then it softened, as she added, "Oh God, how stupid of me. You must feel terrible. She was more than just a secretary, wasn't she?"

Inwardly, Eliot flinched. What was *wrong* with him? Betty Cannon was cruelly dead and cruelly gone, too young and for no goddamn good reason! And all he could think about was his own precious reputation, his own precious position, his own precious hospital. That's not how Lillian and Philip had raised him!

"I can't allow myself to think about it right now. Right now, I have to think about how the devil I'm going to handle the media, and especially Ham Pierce. Pierce will crucify us if he ever finds out."

"What do you mean 'if'?"

He groaned. "Right. It's almost a given, isn't it? And once *he* has the story, every reporter in the city of New York will be swarming all over us, pushing mikes into my face and your face and Dee's face and George's face—" He broke off. "I can see the headlines now: MURDER IN HARMONY HILL HOSPITAL . . . RESIDENT KILLS SISTER IN HER BED . . . or, at the very best, MERCY KILLING AT HARMONY HILL. But they won't have any mercy on *us*!"

They'd be after him first, of course. He was beginning to

know what it was *he* had to say. The announcement would be brief and professional: Betty Cannon died today at one fifty-four P.M. from head wounds inflicted by an unknown gunman two weeks ago. She had been in an irreversible coma since the shooting. That sounded right . . . and, in fact, it *was* right. Maybe he should say that she had "succumbed" instead of "died." And, of course, how could he have forgotten, they must add that her newborn was normal and healthy.

He probably should add something personal, about his own loss; he'd have to think about that. But the main thing was, they all had to tell the same story. He and Dee and George and Con Scofield. Oh, and Toni, too. Con would have to handle the other nurses. He'd get them all together, now, before any questions were asked.

The media! If he didn't handle this right, they'd smell something funny, and then they'd be out in force, talking to everyone they could get their hands on. Disgruntled employees. Former staff doctors. Nurses with a grievance. Janitors who didn't get a promotion. He shook his head.

Toni put a hand on his arm. "Poor Eliot. What a mess. Damn, I should have been more tuned in to Dee."

"*You* aren't going to be held responsible."

"*Held responsible?* I *am* responsible! I knew she wasn't quite herself, but, God, I had no idea, no idea at all that she might—! Oh, this is awful! Poor Dee! Poor Dee!"

"I'll tell you something even worse. Betty's case was coming up for review at the ethics committee meeting tomorrow. Her condition had deteriorated. I was going to talk to George right afterward; I know what I would have said, and I know he'd have agreed. It was over. Damn it, if only she'd waited one more day. One more day!"

Now he looked around. The male nurse on duty was making himself invisible, busily scribbling on charts. He spotted Con Scofield back in the office, her arm around Dee Strong. "Where's George?"

"In . . . with Betty," Toni said.

Eliot turned to the nurse who was bent over his papers. "Get Mr. Cannon. Tell him I have to talk to him. *Now.*" The young man practically ran.

In a few minutes, they were all crowded into the little office:

George Cannon, Con, Dee, Toni. And himself. Eliot closed the door and leaned against it. The rest of them kind of huddled together, their eyes fastened on his face.

"I'm sorry, George."

The big head lifted, revealing George's face, creased with sorrow, the dark eyes bloodshot, bleak with pain, swimming with tears. He looked a hundred years old.

"Betty's out of her misery now," he said. His voice sounded rusty, as if it hadn't been used for a long time. "Betty's at peace. I ain't sorry I did it—"

Deedra turned to stare at him. "George Cannon! What are you saying! You didn't do anything!"

"Deedra, you be quiet now. I'm a man, and a man's always ready to take his punishment."

She grabbed his muscular arm, tipping her head back so she could look into his eyes. "George, I don't want you to do this. Everyone here knows that I—"

"Hush now. Anything you say can be used against you!"

Eliot interrupted. "Nobody's going to use anything against anyone," he said. He looked into the eyes of George Cannon, who returned his gaze without flinching. Eliot moved to his side and put a hand on his shoulder. "I'm going to miss her, too," he said, surprised to hear his voice quake with tears. "You don't have to protect Dee. I will."

George's eyes overflowed, and he mouthed, rather than said, Thank you.

Clearing his throat, Eliot backed off and spoke to the entire group. "My gut reaction is that nobody has to know what happened. There's no reason. Betty was in a terminal situation; everybody knew that. I'm just thinking aloud now, but it seems to me that all I have to do is make a simple statement that she's gone."

He looked at each person in the room, in turn, and each of them nodded. Until he got to Dee.

"I don't want anyone to lie for me," Dee said. "I'm ready to take what's coming. I did what I had to do. I'm glad I did it; I did the right thing. If Betty had been able to talk, she would have *told* me to do it and—" She broke down, sobbing.

Eliot said, "No reason to destroy a promising career. We were planning to disconnect tomorrow anyway."

She looked at him, studying his face. "Are you telling me the truth, Dr. Wolfe?"

"Yes, Dr. Strong."

She took in an audible breath, clasping her hands tightly together. Then she let it out and looked over at George.

"Come on, Dee," her brother-in-law said hoarsely. "We gotta call the minister. We got arrangements to make." He walked her out of the room, his arm around her shoulder.

When Con went back to work, there they were, alone together, he and his wife. His wife. He looked at her. They had drifted so far apart, she was like a stranger to him, someone he hardly knew. He felt that everyone close to him was fading away and disappearing. Betty. Sam. Toni.

"Eliot!"

"What?"

"You were . . . moaning, sort of."

"Was I? Yeah, I guess I was."

She eyed him. "Are you okay?"

"Yes, of course I'm okay. No. That's a lie. I'm not okay."

"Poor thing." She laid a hand on his cheek. "Everything's on your shoulders, isn't it? God, what a job! I'm glad I don't have it." They stood together like that, her hand on his face, for a minute or two. He wished it made him feel better. Oh, it made him feel *better*, but it wasn't like it used to be. Sadly, he thought, Toni, I haven't even been able to tell you about Sam. It's too personal.

"Come on, Eliot," she said. "Let me buy you a drink from the cabinet in your office." She took his hand and tugged at him. He was so close to tears, but he could not permit that to happen. He went with her, but he was beset with loneliness. She was being so sweet, so understanding. And so distant. It hurt him to realize that this warmth and compassion was reserved for strangers.

32

Late in May

At three in the afternoon, the Harmony Hill cafeteria was the closest it ever got to quiet. A group of nurses, taking a break in the corner, shrieked with laughter at something a young doctor had just said, and the drug salesmen sitting at their usual table near the Coke machine were talking loudly, as they always did. Still, Toni could hear the canned music that was supposed to soothe the savage medical breast but was not usually audible. She listened and then wished she wasn't able to hear it; an orchestra of cloying sweetness was playing her least favorite song in the world, "Feelings."

Toni was sitting at her table of choice, the last one in the center, facing the entrance. She could see every person who came in. That was the idea. She and Ham had a signal worked out. She would sit at this table at three, if she was free, and he would walk by. They would greet each other loudly, with surprise. Then they would chat.

Somewhere in their conversation, he would mention a time— "You should catch 'MacNeil/Lehrer' tonight at seven," or, "My cousin's coming in and wants me to meet him at the airport— can you believe eleven-thirty?"—something like that. If she said, "Okay," or something positive, he knew she'd show up at his apartment at the hour named. If she said, "That's too bad," or "I wish I could," or something negative, he knew she couldn't make it.

It was childish, she knew. It was silly, and it was probably not even necessary for them to play this little game. There was such a thing as a telephone. But somehow, it pleased them both. It teased them both. It added spice. In the end, they only man-

aged to see each other once or twice a week—not much for
ardent lovers. And that reminded her: it was now three-ten, and
where the hell was her ardent lover! Five more minutes and she'd
have to leave. She'd had to do that before, and he'd given her a
hard time.

"Take it easy," she had warned him. "You don't own me,
you know." He looked so wounded that she had tried to soften
it. "I know it feels like it, but we're *not* a couple of kids meeting
in the college dining hall. Our lives are more complicated than
that. We have to forgive each other for whatever comes up in
real life."

"And, first and foremost, I don't own you," he added, with
a wry smile.

"And you don't own me," she had agreed.

But she had really been looking forward to it today. She
needed the sweet oblivion of making love. She'd had a lousy
night worrying about Dee, who was still suffering over Betty.
Not that Toni blamed her; she'd had some experience recently
with guilt and she knew it could wear you down. She'd tossed
and turned through most of the wee hours of the morning, while
next to her, oblivious and peaceful, Eliot slept on. He had com-
pleted his experience with the death of Betty Cannon. It wasn't
keeping him awake!

In the old days, they would both have been up half the night,
talking about it. They were so far apart these days, it was hard
for her to remember how they used to feel about each other.
Nowadays there was nothing left but anger.

Ah, there was Ham, coming down the aisle right now, pausing to greet people, a big smile on his face. There was a thrilled
little flutter in her chest, at the sight of him. She wasn't sure
what she felt for him, but she certainly was hot for his body, no
question. Later today, they'd be together in his big bed, wrapped
around each other, as close as two people could get; and it was
going to be so good, because everything else in the world would
fade away and disappear. When they were screwing, there was
no room in her mind for anything else but her sensations. He
made sure of *that*.

It seemed to take him longer than usual to get to her table.
She bent her head over the cup of cold coffee, lifting it to her
lips, pretending to drink. Then he was next to her. She caught

a whiff of his after-shave and felt that little lift again. Oh, she was in the mood, all right!

They greeted each other very casually. He was seemingly on his way out, when he stopped and snapped his fingers, and said, "Oh, Dr. Romano, the tape I was going to get for you . . ."

"Yes?" Bad news, she knew it.

"It isn't available today. Maybe tomorrow, okay?"

Disappointment swept over her like a cold shower. "Oh sure, no problem. Just give me a call." She hoped her voice sounded normal; her lips felt numb. And then he was gone, and she was left feeling very goddamn abandoned. She had been planning to feel abandoned in a very different way tonight. Shit! And then, for the millionth time, she cautioned herself not to let this thing get out of hand.

Anyway, she had other, more important matters in her life to think about. Like her son. Last week, they had had lunch together at Uno, down near the Museum of Natural History. The place was full of young people; well, it was a young people's place. She had looked across the little table at him and thought again what a great kid he was. She was so damn proud of him . . . Arch would be proud of him. On impulse, she had reached across the table and put her hand over his. With a shock, she saw that they were identical: long-fingered hands with that funny, crooked pinky. Her eyes filled a little, and she said, "King, I'd like to meet your folks."

She was smiling; she was happy; she was expecting joy and delight from him. He said, "No."

"No?"

"Why should I? Nobody in your family knows about me."

"My husband does."

"Yeah, and he really loves me, doesn't he? He really wants me to meet the rest of the family, doesn't he?"

She felt herself coloring—whether with anger or chagrin, she couldn't tell. "That's Eliot's problem."

"Well, I hate to tell you, but it's my problem, too. I mean, shit, you gave me away. No wonder he sneers at me."

"He didn't sneer. He just doesn't know what to make of you, of the whole situation! It's not easy, you know."

"Hey, it hasn't been so easy for me, either!"

They stared at each other, and suddenly she realized he was *angry* at her; he was angry at *her*! He had popped back into her life, uninvited, and she had welcomed him with open arms, had told him the whole story about her and his father . . . had fallen in love with him! And this was her reward?

"I did my best, King, and I've lived with my sadness and regrets. But maybe now it's time to move on . . . for both of us."

"Oh, you think so! How do you think it feels, growing up knowing your own mother threw you away!"

"King!"

"Well, it's true! If you had loved me, you'd have kept me. I used to lay awake nights, when I was little, trying to figure out what it was about me that was so awful that even my own mother didn't want me. I figured it was because I was a nigger."

"King! Don't use that horrible word!"

"Yeah? Well, it was said to me plenty by other kids."

Toni winced with pain. "Oh God. I'm so sorry. I'm sorrier than I can say that you had to go through that. I'm sorry for all of the pain I have caused you. Listen to me. Not a day went by that I didn't think of you."

"Yeah, sure." His voice was bitter.

Toni took in a deep breath. "We can keep this up forever. Or you can tell me what you want me to do."

"Okay. Here it is. I gotta stop being your dirty little secret. Either you tell the world I'm your son, or you can forget about me. And I mean that."

The moment he put it to her, she realized that to lose him was insupportable. "Okay. You got it."

"What do you mean?" He looked so startled, she couldn't help but laugh.

"I mean okay. You know what okay means. Yes. Si. Da. Oui. I'll do it. It's going to take a little time . . . now, don't look at me like that. I can't run a story in the *Daily News*. I have to pick the time and place very carefully. This is a big deal, King. First I'm going to tell Eliot's mother; she's the real head of his family. You'll agree that they deserve to know first, right?"

To her immense relief, after what felt like an endless silence, he smiled at her and said, "Hey, Toni, you ever notice we have the same hands?"

Sitting in the cafeteria, thinking about it now, she held her hands out in front of her and smiled. And when she looked up again, Janet and David were coming toward her. They didn't

see her yet; their eyes were glued to each other. It was so obvious
that they were lovers, it was almost funny. But it wasn't funny,
it was sweet. Anyway, it was *supposed* to be sweet.

Toni regarded them as they came closer and closer, the way
their bodies yearned toward each other, the way they had no
interest in anything else outside themselves, the way they touched
and smiled. Do I think that's wonderful? she asked herself. No.
Being in love that way, shutting out the rest of the world, might
be okay for them, but it was not for her. She simply didn't have
the time. Or the energy. Or the inclination. And if she was
honest with herself, she had never had. She had fooled herself,
and in doing so, she had fooled Eliot, as well. Poor Eliot.
Wouldn't he be better off without her?

"Well, wadda ya know, the wicked stepmother. Hi, Stepma."
David and Janet were standing by the table, both of them grinning. David bent to give her cheek a kiss, and she felt a little
twinge of guilt. The way things were going, she might not be
his stepmother for much longer.

"Hi. Sit down."

"Janet will, I can't," David said, his voice bubbling with his
happiness. Toni had never seen him with anything remotely approaching this exuberance. It must be love, she thought. Well,
good for Janet. "It's back to the E.R. for me!" David said.

"Do I hear something in your voice that says you're not exactly thrilled about getting back to the E.R?"

"You got it, Toni."

"It's so easy to get burnout there."

He shook his head. "It's not burnout exactly; it's not the
pressure. But you know, in the E.R., you work with a patient,
the patient goes upstairs, you never get to see what happens,
you never make a relationship. It's in one door and out the
other."

"David needs personal interaction," Janet finished. "He's
so empathetic, he can't stand it when he can't follow up. It's
such a waste of a marvelous talent!" She and David exchanged
a look of adoration and smiled at each other. It was so goopy,
but obviously it was something David really needed, Toni
thought.

"So what's the solution?" she asked.

"I'm going to take a residency in family practice. That's what
I really want to do."

She smiled at him. "You know, it's not always so wonderful, following through. You have many . . . 'disappointments' doesn't begin to say it." An image of Alice, lying broken on the sidewalk, flashed through her head.

"Janet and I have talked about that, and we've decided it's worth it."

Maybe *they* would be Albert Schweitzer and Mother Teresa, since Eliot and I never quite made it. The thought made her smile, and she was still smiling when Janet, having kissed her beloved a prolonged farewell, sat down opposite her.

"Boy, has he changed!" Toni said. "I have to hand it to you, that's the quickest transformation since Superman came out of the phone booth."

Janet blushed a little. "He hasn't really changed, Toni. He was always tuned-in and thoughtful and committed and—oh God, everything!"

"I guess you think he's okay."

"More than okay! He's terri— Oh. Sorry. You were kidding. Of course you were kidding; I should know that." She paused, and added, "And, you know, he doesn't mind that I'm smart. He likes it. Jim . . . Jim was sweet, a nice guy, but he did not like me to sound too clever; it threatened him. It threatened him that I had a degree. His way of dealing with it was to laugh at me. He laughed at me a lot, and I told myself, hey, this is the way he is, this is how men are, nothing I can do about it.

"But David is so different. We discuss work together!" She stopped and laughed self-consciously. "Oh, you wouldn't know how fabulous it is for me. You've been married to a doctor for years. You couldn't be a threat to him."

"Yeah, right."

Janet gave her a swift, puzzled glance and then kept on talking. "Oh, it isn't just that, Toni, of course not. He's such a delicious, sexy guy. We have a lot going and . . . I want to marry him!"

"And how does David feel about this?"

"I haven't told him. I don't dare. I'm terrified he'll turn and run."

"I don't think that David will turn and run, Janet. He looks positively besotted."

They both laughed at that.

"It's so nice to be able to talk about David," Janet said.

"Other women, even my friends—or so I thought!—keep 'warn-ing' me, for 'my own good!' He's young. He's Jewish. He's never been married. Aren't I worried he'll eventually start look-ing around for a younger woman? Doesn't he want children *of his own*?"

"They're just jealous," Toni said.

Janet gave her a big, warm smile. "That's what I mean. You're so accepting. My God, he's your stepson; if anyone had a right to raise objections, it would be you." She paused. "You're such a good friend to me."

To her surprise, Toni was touched by this declaration, her eyes filling. She couldn't trust herself to speak, just smiled and patted Janet's hand.

Janet must have seen this. She stood up. "You got a few minutes? Let's take a walk. It's gorgeous today," she said brightly.

Grateful, Toni blinked back the tears. Piling together all the papers she had brought in order to pretend to be working when Ham came by, she got up, and together they walked out onto 96th Street.

"Notice anything unusual?" Janet said. Her voice lilted with laughter.

Toni looked. Clumps of young doctors and nurses sat on the front steps, sunning themselves and chatting. Wheelchairs were busily going up and down the ramps. Taxis were pulling over to the curb, and people were getting out. She smiled to see a young woman and her husband putting their new baby carefully into their car. An ambulance went tearing around the corner, lights flashing and sirens hooting, on its way up Riverside Drive. She wondered if it was King. Soon, she'd be able to introduce him to Janet. She'd be able to introduce him to the whole goddamn world! It was going to feel so good!

"I don't see anything unusual," she said. "Tell me."

"No protesters. No placards. No marchers. No TV van. No . . . Hamilton Pierce." She gave Toni a meaningful look with the last couple of words, and Toni had to work very hard to keep her face neutral. What the hell did she mean? She couldn't know anything; they'd been too careful for that. Hadn't they?

"I guess we must be doing something right at Harmony Hill!" Toni said lightly, and they began to walk toward Riverside Park.

"I'm so happy with David," Janet said. "Half the time I don't even think about the future. And then . . . I think about the future! My family, his family!" She made a face, and they both laughed.

"Of course, Eliot *might* have a hard time with this, but he's a reasonable man." Toni stopped, thinking to herself, But *is* he? She wasn't so sure anymore. "You know what! I think you should have a talk with Eliot, person to person!"

"Oh, I couldn't . . . I already . . . uh, I don't think David would like it." Janet forced a merry little laugh and turned back toward the hospital. "You know men; they like to think they're taking care of us. Especially David. Oh no, I think he should be the one to talk to his father!"

"Sure. Okay. You know what's best for you. But I still think—"

"While we're on the subject of romance," Janet said with some hesitation, "what's with Ham Pierce?"

Once in a conversation might be happenstance, but mentioning Ham twice! She was going to have to defuse this one, quick. "What do you mean, what's with Ham Pierce?"

"Well . . . for a while there, it looked like he was . . . well . . . after you."

"He was after an interview. But I'm a virgin!"

To her relief, Janet just laughed.

Oh really? Janet thought, carefully not looking at Toni. She didn't want to grin or laugh. You really think I'm so easily fooled? Me, the Queen of the Cafeteria Pickup Squad? Oh, God, if you knew how many years I've sat at that table, and at other tables, waiting for that signal, or other signals!

Conrad Havemayer, yes, the sainted and blessed and godlike Dr. Havemayer, used to go to the Coke machine and fumble around for the right change, and she would always be nearby, ready with a quarter, and under cover of the clatter of the machine, they would negotiate. He always wanted her to just appear at his office for a quickie on his leather couch and she always wanted to get at least dinner out of it. And she usually won because Havemayer was horny and sex made him hungry! Oh, God, the stories she could tell!

She put a hand on Toni's arm. "Toni. I don't give a shit who you have an affair with, not even if it's Ham Pierce. Honestly. These things happen to everybody, and don't ever let anyone bullshit you into thinking otherwise. People have affairs because they're needy, because they're lonely. . . ." She paused and laughed a little. "People have affairs because they feel like it! Look, Toni, you're outspoken, and I've found that any woman who feels free to speak her mind—especially around this place— is suspect. I oughta know. People have talked about me plenty, and I learned ages ago to just let it roll off my back."

"Janet, thanks for the kind words, but you're wrong."

It was a snub. She shouldn't have talked so much, especially about something she was only guessing at. There was no talk about Toni and Pierce in Harmony Hill that she had heard, and she usually heard everything. She thought of ten different things to say and finally settled for a simple "Sorry."

"Forget it. I know he's around a lot lately . . . always wanting another story. That's *his* problem. He can be an awful pest."

"I think he wants more than a story from you," Janet said with a little laugh.

"Enough already! Just because you've fallen in love, don't start projecting your feelings onto the whole world!" More laughter. "So tell me, why can't you ask David to marry you? I'll bet he would!"

"I . . . it's complicated, Toni. I have to make sure it's okay with David's family."

"That's crazy. David's a grown man. He doesn't need his parents' permission!"

"I . . . well . . . they're a prominent family, and I'm a no-body."

"Me, too."

"They'll think I'm marrying him for his money."

"Same here."

Now they were both laughing hard. What Janet could not admit was that David *had* asked her to marry him, and she had been putting him off. She was scared to death that Eliot would tell him. She figured, the longer she kept the relationship with David just the way it was, the better off she was. She didn't want Eliot to feel pushed into a corner; she didn't want him to feel that he had to tell his son the truth.

She had really sweated bullets for a while. David wanted to get married right away and to hell with his family and what people might say. She thought for sure he was going to announce his intentions and dare his father to stop him. Oh Christ, she could write *that* scene! But she finally sweet-talked David into keeping it their own little secret for just a while.

"Don't even think about the family, Janet. Either they get used to it, or they don't. I'm on your side."

Oh God, couldn't her life be simple for once? A couple of weeks ago, she'd been screwing Toni's husband. Ouch. Put that way, it sounded cheap and mean. But it hadn't had anything to do with Toni! And as far as she was concerned, it was in the past now—over, done with, and finished. At first, being with Toni had been a little embarrassing, but now it was like the thing with Eliot had never happened. She hadn't really loved him; she had been so lonely, and he had fit into her fantasy, that's all it had been. It was just . . . one of those things, like it said in the song. God, to think that it was over Eliot that she began drinking again—! Unbelievable! Meeting David had turned her life around 180 degrees.

Suddenly it started to rain, one of those sweet summer showers. As if they could read each other's minds, both of them tipped their heads back, lifting their faces to the soft rain. Then they looked at each other, and Toni said, "Are we crazy, or what?" and Janet answered, "Or what!" Toni took off her white coat, and they held it over both of them as they ran like hell down the block.

They were very close to Harmony Hill when Janet spotted Eliot, of all the goddamn people, handing some old guy into a taxi. When he straightened up, he glanced in their direction and for a horrible moment, their eyes met, and he got the most frozen look on his face. Just for a moment, but for that moment, she was in a panic, thinking, Oh shit, what am I going to do when we get there; what am I going to say? She didn't want to stop running because Toni would wonder why. And then his glance slid away, as if he hadn't seen them, and he went back inside. She said a silent prayer of thanks.

A minute later, they reached the lobby, a little out of breath and a little damp, but in a good mood. Toni said, "Listen, Janet, let me talk to Eliot about you and David.

Not about marriage. I'll convince him, don't worry. You
just leave it to me.''

Oh Christ. That's all she needed! Janet watched Toni run for
the elevator, her mouth opening and closing like a fish, unable
to tell her. No, don't! Keep out of it! Christ! She'd lied herself
right into a corner. Well, it was time to stop all the deceptions.
She turned and headed for the E.R. She would tell David right
this minute.

I'm going to call Lillian right this minute, Toni thought. I should
have done it weeks ago. She's not going to have palpitations or
shriek or faint or anything like that. On the other hand, she
might take it very hard and be very angry and very hurt. Hell,
she might even decide that Toni was a despicable person, on
several grounds. She'd had an illegitimate child. She'd given him
up. She'd kept it a secret. She'd tricked her husband. God, the
list of everything she'd done wrong was pretty long.

Well, it was a chance she had to take. King was right; he
deserved better from her. And if the Wolfes wouldn't accept
him? So what? So be it! *She* accepted him! At least he would
never again have to think of himself as her "dirty little secret."
Oh God, she'd done *that* to him, too! When the elevator came
to its creaky halt, she practically ran down the hall to her office,
to make the call.

Half an hour later, she was in Lillian's blue and yellow
breakfast room with its trellis wallpaper and Mexican tile
floor. Lillian had taken one look at her and poured her a stiff
drink: Stolichnaya on the rocks.

"Why the drink, Lillian? The sun's not over the yardarm
yet."

"I think you need it. You sounded terrible over the phone,
and I must say, you don't look much better. So . . . drink
up. You said you have to come talk to me, so . . . talk to
me."

Toni laughed a little. "If I drink up, Lillian, I won't be able
to talk at all."

"Is it Eliot?"

"No, no. Eliot's fine. It's just . . . I have something to tell
you that I should have told you a long time ago, and it's very
difficult."

"What could be so terrible? It's only me, you know. I'm so fond of you, dear. There's nothing you can't tell me, you know that."

I hope so, Toni thought. Well, there was nothing for it but to just say it. "Lillian, a long time ago, before I met Eliot, I had . . . an affair . . . with a doctor, a married man—" She felt tears clog her throat, and she stopped abruptly.

"It happens." Lillian sat, her hands folded in her lap, her face composed.

"And . . . I had a baby." Toni looked at her mother-in-law, searching her face for a clue to her feelings. But Lillian just nodded. "I had a baby, a boy, and I gave him up for adoption. I never even saw him." Again, she had trouble talking, and stopped, trying to collect herself.

"That happens, also," Lillian said. She gave Toni an encouraging smile.

"I—he found me. I mean, my son has located me, and we've seen each other several times, and he's a wonderful young man, and I want the family to know about him and—"

"Does Eliot know?"

Startled: "Of course he knows. I told him first. But it's very hard for Eliot. He's hurt that I had never confided in him."

"Yes, yes, that's Eliot. He'll come around, I'm sure."

"There's something else. It's . . . a little touchy. Oh hell, Lillian, let me just say it. My son's father was black."

"A little touchy, yes, but no biggie."

No biggie! Oh God, that was so Lillian! Toni burst into sudden, grateful tears.

"Antonia, Antonia, don't, please. It'll all work out, you'll see. Everything will be okay."

"Oh, Lillian," she sobbed, "you don't know what it's been like! I've been so selfish, so concerned with myself. I've hurt everyone: I've hurt Eliot and my child and myself and you. . . . I've been so dishonest, and he's such a terrific kid, and I've managed to hurt him over and over again, and I've been torturing myself with this, and here you are, and you're so wonderful, so understanding, you say exactly the right thing—oh, Lillian!"

She wept and then, when the tears stopped pouring out and she was able to calm herself, she looked over at her mother-in-law, a tower of strength in a Chanel suit and genuine oriental pearls, and managed a watery smile. ''Lillian, I can't thank you enough.''

A tiny smile played at Lillian's mouth. She looked directly at Toni, and said, ''You think you're the only girl who ever had a baby out of wedlock?''

33

June

"Goddamn it, I hate to say it, but it looks like you win, Wolfe! I'm giving up the fight on that fairy hostel . . . hospice—whatever the hell you call it."

Eliot looked across his desk at Barney Goldstone and thought for the hundredth time that if Barney weren't so obnoxious, he'd be funny. There he sat, looking like a slob, his shirt billowing out of his pants, his tie askew, his thinning hair rumpled, oblivious to everything: his appearance, his own boorishness, oblivious even to Eliot's barely hidden distaste.

"Ellie, Ellie, what's with the I-smell-shit look! What did I say? Hey, a fag is a fag. I'm known in this town as a man who means what he says and says what he means!" He paused, to laugh, and added: "Whatever the hell *that* means. Hell, Ellie, I know you don't like me, and to tell you the truth, I'm not too crazy about you, either—"

"Barney!" That was Arlene, using her best aggrieved-but-polite tone. Eliot did not turn to look at her; he knew from long ago the exact expression of disapproval that was doubtless on her face. She had been roaming the office, giving it the white-glove inspection, straightening every picture on the wall, rearranging every plant, examining all the photos on his desk.

A few minutes ago, she had picked up his wedding picture, lingering over it, and now she set it back down, hiding it way behind all the other pictures on his desk. She thought Eliot wasn't noticing, but he was as aware of her presence as if she had been emitting a signal. Just knowing she was anywhere nearby had the same effect on him as fingernails on a blackboard.

Barney ignored his wife's plea for some kind of civilized behavior. He continued, shaking his index finger, then rapping it on the desktop for emphasis. "Well, it is a fag hospital. Who the hell else gets AIDS?"

"Who else?" It gave Eliot great pleasure to tell him off. "Intravenous drug users. Prostitutes. Spouses of the same. Hemophiliacs. Children of—"

"Awright, awright! We all know it's a wonderful group of folks, just the people you want across the street. Say, Ellie, how about turning one of them fancy co-ops in *your* building into a homeless shelter?" He guffawed and slapped his thigh. "How do you think you'd like *that*?"

Time to end this charade, Eliot decided. "So what's the catch, Barney? There's always a catch, with you."

"No catch. Just good business. Okay, Ellie. Here's the deal. The hospital buys our house. Or, if you don't like that, how about this? I give the house to Harmony Hill—a contribution— and you guys buy us our new place. Which, by the way, Arlene has already picked out, haven't you, sweetie pie?" He leaned back in his chair and reached out to give her a grab on her tush.

Eliot waited for the earth to open up and swallow them all. But instead of exploding, instead of walking out in a huff, she giggled. Giggled! I guess I didn't have quite the touch, he thought. I never heard that.

"Give up your house? I thought you loved it!"

"Ellie, you ever fix up a house in this city? No? Well, lemme tell you how it is. It's hell, pure hell. Right, sweetie pie? Yeah, Arlene is getting nuts from how long it's taking and all the *agita* from those lousy workmen, not one speaks English, not *one*! Where the hell do they find them? You know how many times they've taken the banister apart and put it back together wrong? Backward. Upside down. Inside out. Don't ask! I'll be dead and buried before that fucking place is finished. At least that'll make you a rich widow, sweetie pie, and you could at least afford to finish it!" He threw his head back, roaring at his own humor.

"But seriously, Ellie," he continued, "seriously, Arlene and I are fed up with renovations, and now that the neighborhood's gonna go down . . . well . . . we figure we'll get a co-op on the East Side, dirt cheap, while the market's in the toilet. I'm telling you, we can work something out together."

"You want to name a figure, Barney? A very low figure? You know the state of Harmony Hill's finances."

"Let's not be crass and crude, Ellie! My lawyer will talk to your lawyer, and then we'll sit down. How about it?"

Eliot pretended to be pondering. He was very pleased about this but did not dare show it. Barney was crass and crude, but he was also smart and shrewd, and if he thought Eliot was getting exactly what he wanted, he'd find a way to bollix it up. That real-estate switch was not going to fly. The executors of the will had started finding objection after objection. Landmarks was already sniffing around. And at last count, fourteen Abraham cousins had decided to contest the will. So Barney could have stayed put. They would all probably be dead and buried before Harmony Hill was allowed to take over those buildings.

"Okay," he said and stood. Barney got the signal. He stood too and snapped his fingers for his wife to follow him. Eliot watched them leave with mixed emotions. He wanted to feel sorry for Arlene, married to a lout, but at the same time, he couldn't help but envy her this somewhat weird but obviously satisfactory relationship.

He said he would talk to his lawyer; so, true to his word, he immediately picked up the phone and called, and of course, Jerry wasn't available. He left a message, thinking there would never be a call back. He must remember to ask someone someday why lawyers never returned phone calls.

He got up from his chair and began to pace, restless. He checked his watch, gazed out of the window, saw nothing, checked his watch again. Damn it, he had to clear his head for lunch with David, which was next on the agenda. It was not going to be pleasant. Oh, Christ, what an understatement. At best, it would be confrontational. At worst? World War III.

To hell with this. He marched out of his office and out of the hospital, looking neither right nor left. Once he thought he heard someone call his name, but he just ignored it and kept on going. By some miracle, a cab pulled up, disgorging a hugely pregnant young woman and her hugely nervous husband. He got in and headed downtown. Ditto's was out, naturally; too many people from the hospital. He had made reservations at Amsterdam's. David was off today, and they were planning to meet at the restaurant.

What in hell was he going to say to David? How was he going to broach the subject of Janet Rafferty? He'd tried to talk to her first, but she had been stupidly stubborn. Adamant. She wouldn't even see him in person, insisting that, if he wanted to talk, it had to be over the phone.

He had asked her what she thought she was doing with his son, and the minute he heard the words coming out of his mouth, he was sorry. Sure enough, there was the irritated intake of breath on her end of the phone. He hadn't wanted to antagonize her; he had wanted her cooperation. But before he'd had a chance to say anything else, she had spoken and her tone had been mild.

"Look, Eliot, David and I love each other."

"Leave him alone, Janet. He's a nice young man with a promising future. He deserves—"

"Better than me, I suppose," she ended his thought, an edge to her voice. "That's a lovely attitude. That's going to really help!"

"I didn't mean . . . that's not what I wanted to say. Come on, Janet, it's not as if we're total strangers, you know."

She laughed, and he had not liked the sound of it. "You know what I think, Eliot? I think you're jealous! Well, I'm very sorry. But we really do love each other."

"You have a . . ." He cleared his throat. He didn't like saying this. "You do have a certain reputation. Aren't you worried what David will do if he ever hears those stories?"

She had laughed. "Oh my God, is that supposed to be a threat?"

"Don't try so hard to act tough. Of course that's not a threat. But let's face it—"

"Look, Eliot, I'm sorry. We had something nice, you and I. But you know as well as I do that nothing was ever going to come of it. You were never really interested in me. And this is different. This is real." It was so like a woman, he thought, to try to make a great romance out of a man's lust. She'd done it with *him*. Well, she wasn't going to pull the same trick on his son, not if he had anything to say about it. David was young and single and vulnerable.

The cab pulled up in front of Amsterdam's; he was glad to stop thinking about his conversation with her. It had left him with a bad taste in his mouth.

As soon as he walked in, he spotted David sitting at a table in the front section, two martinis in frosted glasses already on the table. David, grinning, gave Eliot a buoyant wave. As Eliot walked to the table, he couldn't help thinking how good his son looked. That little boy he still remembered so vividly had grown into one helluva man. What did Carolyn call him? A hunk, that was it. Yes, he decided, David Wolfe was probably a hunk. No wonder Janet went after him!

After they had raised their glasses in a silent toast and had each taken a sip, David leaned forward. "Yes," he said, "I'm wondering why you've asked me here today. What's on your mind, Dad?"

"What's on my mind is your . . . whatever it is with Janet Rafferty," he blurted.

David colored, the grin instantly disappearing. "What do you mean, my 'whatever it is.' That sounds damned insulting!"

Hell. He couldn't seem to approach this subject without putting his foot in his mouth. "Your . . . romance, then."

"I don't like the sound of that much better."

"Okay then, David, you tell me. What's going on between you and Ms. Rafferty?"

"She's the woman I'm going to marry."

"You can't."

"What's with you, Dad? From the first moment I met her, you've been on my case. She's a lovely woman, educated, intelligent—as you well know. So she has a couple of kids, and she's a couple of years older than I am! So what? I love her, she loves me, I'm ready to settle down, and she's it. What's your problem, for Christ's sake?"

"You're not making this easy, David. I'm only looking out for your welfare." He drew in breath, wondering just how to proceed. What was the nice word for a tramp? "How do I say this?" Eliot went on, pained. "She has something of a . . . reputation."

David dismissed the subject with a disdainful wave of his hands. "Oh for Christ's sake, Dad! Don't you think I've heard all that crap? Who the hell listens to hospital gossip? And anyway, what was she supposed to do, a young widow? Commit *suttee*? If she were a man and slept around a little, nobody would say a word. In fact, he'd be congratulated. Look, Dad, this is the 1990s, and we're all grown-ups here. I've got news for you: I've slept with other women." He smiled. "So it really doesn't bother me that she's slept with other men."

Eliot had to take a very deep breath and force himself to speak. He had hoped he would never have to say it. But now he

had to. There was no other way. He had to save his son from
making a terrible mistake. "And what if one of those men . . .
was your father?"

David took a deliberate sip of his martini and gazed at Eliot
over the rim of his glass. His eyes were cold and unreadable.
After a moment, he put the glass down. "I wouldn't think less
of her, necessarily." He paused. "But I sure as hell would think
less of my father," he said.

But I'm a nice person! Eliot found himself thinking. I'm a
nice guy; I've always been a nice guy! It wasn't me; it was her
. . . she came after me; she came on to me; she knew I was
married; I never would have even looked at her if she hadn't—!
I haven't done anything so terrible; I haven't done anything other
men don't do every goddamn day.

His voice choking, he said, "David, my intent was not to
alienate you. I only want what's good for you."

"Then stop. I don't want you to say another word. I know all
about it. She told me. So stop. Let us get on with our lives. I'm
going to marry her, and I suggest you get used to the idea.
Okay?" His eyes were boring into Eliot's, and Eliot found himself nodding.

He was back in his office an hour later, unable to remember
what he had eaten. He knew he must have eaten something,
because his stomach was churning. Why was everything in his
life falling apart all of a sudden? He and his wife weren't getting
along; his best friend had a horrible, incurable disease; one son
was HIV positive; his other son was marrying a slut he himself
had fucked!

The phone on his desk buzzed sharply, Betty's signal that an
important call was on the line. He caught himself. Not Betty,
of course not. Betty was dead, had been buried amidst hundreds
of weeping mourners a week ago. Betty. He missed her; he
really missed her and the way she thought and the way she
handled things. This one . . . Miranda, that was her name . . .
this one was a bit scattered. A good typist and nice phone manners but not as calm and unruffled as Betty had always been.
His mother had always said that Betty had her head screwed on
straight—what a funny, old-fashioned saying that was. As usual,
his mother was right.

Of course, he couldn't help noticing that, since Betty had
been shot, there were no more inside stories about Harmony

Hill Hospital on "Voice of the City"—except about Betty herself. He didn't want to think it, but it was becoming more and more a probability as the weeks went by and Ham Pierce remained conspicuous by his absence. Betty, Betty, how could you? he thought. And then answered himself. She hadn't been a racist; she hadn't blamed every white person in the world for her own troubles. If Betty Cannon had been feeding information to Hamilton Pierce, she must have had a damned good reason . . . or had thought she did. Still, it made him feel sick.

The buzzer went off again, calling him to attention, and he picked up the phone. "Eliot Wolfe," he began, but before he had a chance to say anything else, the female voice on the other end, without introduction of any kind, assaulted his ears. It took him a moment or two to realize that it was Irene Moore.

"He's gone! Eliot, I only went to take a shower, I swear to God it wasn't more than maybe five minutes, yes, five minutes at the most! I came right out. I didn't even use the loofa, and I swear I left him sitting on the bed in his pjs, and when I came out, he was gone. I was talking to him, that's how quickly he went, well, I didn't worry about it, I mean, most of the time, he's fine, just like his old self, you'd never know that he—"

She broke off, and Eliot heard her make a strange, strangled sound, something like a sob. "But now it's *hours*, and Hilda didn't notice a thing; she's deaf as a post, and she doesn't lift a finger if I'm not here to tell her—"

"Irene!" He barked into the phone.

There was a sharp intake of breath, and then she wailed. "Oh, Eliot!" and began to cry loudly.

Eliot spoke very slowly and calmly. "Irene. Listen to me. Breathe deeply. That's right, in and out, in and out. Good. Now, calm yourself, just don't say anything for a minute. I'm here; I can wait."

After a few minutes, she spoke, sniffling a little but otherwise reasonably contained. "It's Sam. He's gone, Eliot."

"When did he leave?"

"Around nine this morning."

Eliot checked his watch: two-thirty. "So he's been gone over five hours. . . ."

"I looked for him; I went all over the neighborhood; I asked all the doormen and Rav at the newsstand; I even asked at Häagen-Dazs—Sam does have such a sweet tooth; he's always there when he thinks I'm not looking—and even at the super-market. Of course, our doorman saw him; he opened the door for him; Sam said good morning and headed uptown, and nobody's seen him since, and he hasn't called, and he hasn't had lunch, and lately he forgets to eat. Eliot, I'm worried, I'm worried sick; please, Eliot, help me. I don't know what to do!''

He believed it. She was dithering. She was probably hysterical. He said something soothing to her, but already his mind was racing. A list was forming in his head: call Sam's office upstairs, call his service, have him paged in the hospital. Call Ditto's . . . and if all that failed, call the cops.

Irene was still babbling, going on and on, her voice shrill with panic. He found himself losing patience with her. For once, she could turn off the histrionics and behave like an adult human being!

He was finally able to interrupt her. "Irene. Take a drink. Calm yourself. Take it easy. Can you call someone to be with you? Do it. I'll handle this.''

She sobbed with relief. "This is so awful for me, Eliot, you have no idea what it's like for me! I feel as if my whole world is disintegrating! We were planning a trip to Paris.'' Here her voice began to quake. "Oh, Eliot, we were going to get *married* there! I just can't live this way anymore; it's too painful!''

He made noises at her, glad when he was finally able to hang up and cut her voice off. He couldn't stand listening to her go on and on about how much this was hurting *her*. Sam was the one who was losing bits and pieces of himself. And he, Eliot, was the one who was losing Sam.

Tears sprang to his eyes, and he pushed himself up from his desk. It would be folly to give in to emotion. Sam had to be found. He reached for the phone and gave a series of orders to Miranda. When he was sure she understood everything, he sat back and regarded the phone on his desk as if it might tell him something. But it remained stubbornly silent.

Ten minutes later, all the calls had been made; everything and everyone had been checked; and no Sam. He was nowhere; no, that wasn't right; he was somewhere, but *where*? And was he alive or dead or something in between? No. He mustn't let his imagination take over, mustn't let himself get morbid. Firmly, he told himself that everything was going to be all right.

Sam had wandered away; he had memory problems; but sooner or later, he'd realize where he was, and he'd go home.

Now he called the police, described Sam and what he was wearing and said he would bring a photo if Sam hadn't returned home by nightfall, but they said they would come to his office now and pick it up. Eliot sat in a state of . . . what? Shock, maybe. Suddenly, it was real; it was too damn real.

He had to tell his mother. He didn't want to, but what if Sam showed up *there*, confused, maybe hurt! Oh, God, the thought was awful. He wished he could share this with Toni—there had been a time when Toni would have been there for him. But he did not want to call Toni and take a chance that she would dole out that remote, disinterested benevolence to him.

Well, it had to be done. It would worry her, but Lillian was feisty as hell. She'd be out there, looking for Sam herself. Just imagining his mother in one of her impeccable linen suits, scouring the streets of New York, made him smile. If anyone could find a needle in a haystack by sheer willpower, it was his mother. Just thinking about it made him feel better.

And then she surprised him by bursting into tears. "Oh, my poor Sam, my poor boy!" she lamented.

Eliot held the receiver to his ear and closed his eyes against the pain. He had somehow forgotten that his mother was elderly. She wasn't going to take care of him. She couldn't fix everything. In the end, he was all alone with this, all alone.

34

A few days later

"You sure this guy hasn't got a girlfriend on the side, or some-thing?" the cop was saying.

Eliot gritted his teeth. He would love to just throw the god-damn phone across the room. But that would be stupid, and it would accomplish exactly nothing. The officer was only doing his job, right? But it made him furious.

Evenly, clearly, he repeated for the one hundredth time in the last three days, "Not this guy." He took in a breath and blew it out before continuing. "Dr. Bronstein does not have a girlfriend or something. Dr. Bronstein has Alzheimer's disease. He suffers temporary loss of memory, but he is a respected member of—"

The detective interrupted him. "Okay, Dr. Wolfe. I hear you. We have to ask these questions. Believe me, you'd be surprised how many men of his age just take off one day. But, don't worry. Most of them show up within a week. Mid-life crisis, usually."

"It's been three days. My—his mother . . . it's been hell on her."

"I understand, Dr. Wolfe. Look. I know it's been three days; that's the bad news. The good news is, we haven't found his body. Don't worry, we'll find him for you."

"I—okay," Eliot said, his shoulders sagging, and he sud-denly realized how tensely he had been holding them. "I'll call again later this afternoon."

"Good idea." There was just a hint of condescension in his voice.

Eliot slammed the receiver down into the cradle and pushed the phone to the middle of the table. "Fuck!" he spat.

Toni reached across the table and put her hand on his; when he looked over at her, her eyes were soft with sympathy and, unless he was very mistaken, misted with unshed tears. He felt a surge of . . . was it love he was feeling? It had felt like love last night when Toni had slid over until their entire bodies were touching and began a slow, deliberate, delicious seduction of him. Thinking about it now made his heart speed up a little. Maybe there was hope for them, after all. Since Sam's disappearance, she had been wonderful. They had actually been talking to each other.

They were sitting next to each other at the round table by the window that overlooked Central Park. They had eaten brunch there—if you could call choking down half of an English muffin and a cup of coffee eating brunch—and had tried to buy a little forgetfulness by reading the Sunday *Times*. But it hadn't worked because, there in part two of the main section was a big story, headlined: "DR. SAMUEL BRONSTEIN DISAPPEARS . . . Prominent Psychiatrist Analyst of Many Broadway Stars and Prominent Artists."

He picked the paper up and looked again at the old photo of Sam, a younger Sam, the mustache unflecked with gray, the grin he knew so well— His eyes filling, he slammed the paper down and said, "Fuck!"

"Eliot, please, don't look at that article. It's horrible. All those horror stories . . ."

He knew what she was referring to. The writer had done her homework, mentioning other missing prominent men. One had been spotted in South America, spending the money he had embezzled. One had gone on a "spiritual quest to Tibet." And one had been found floating face down in the East River. He had wanted to avert his eyes when he read that, and now he wished he could somehow avert his mind. It was real. Sam could very well be lying in a ditch somewhere, maybe beaten, maybe dead. He got up and began to pace nervously in front of the window, trying hard to soothe his troubled heart with the verdant expanse of Central Park below.

When the phone shrilled, he jumped a little. Toni picked it up immediately. That was another thing he was grateful for; she had been fielding all the phone calls. This time, she signaled him with a smile. Good news! At last! He looked a question at her, and she mouthed: He's okay. She held out her hand, and he moved quickly to her side, grasping it. As soon as he was close, he could hear Irene's piercing voice. She was weeping and talking all at the same time, and Toni was saying yes, yes, yes, yes, we'll take care of it, don't worry about it, and at last, saying "Gotta go, Irene, talk to you later!" she hung up.

"They found him; he's fine. He's okay, Eliot, he's okay." Eliot suddenly felt dizzy and swayed a little. Her grip tightened on his hand. "Sit down. He's tired; he's bedraggled; he's a little confused; but he hasn't been hurt. He's okay." He could hardly concentrate on her words, but he did register "okay" and kept repeating to himself, Sam's okay, Sam's okay.

After taking in a deep breath, he had Toni repeat the whole thing again, and then she added: "He's waiting for us at the Thirteenth Precinct house. You know, the one by the 86th Street transverse."

"Us? What about Irene?"

Toni rolled her eyes and threw her hands in the air. They had both been suffering with Irene's multiple phone calls, the last one at four this morning. She had gone on and on about herself: she was so lonely; the apartment was so scary at night; oh how she was suffering; oh how she was worrying; oh how this was driving her crazy . . . ! On and on and on and on.

Finally, he said to her, "Irene, do you know what time it is? It's not helping anybody for you to wake us up." Irene probably hated him now. Tough.

He thought he'd handled it so quietly and quickly; he thought Toni was still sleeping. But she turned to him the minute he hung up and said, "Why'd you do that? I'm not sleeping! Who could sleep with Sam wandering around somewhere out there . . . or maybe dead. Why didn't you give me the phone? I wouldn't have been so easy on her."

"The woman is frantic. She loves him! She's very worried about him!"

"Oh really? She never says one word about Sam. I keep hearing just one word over and over, Eliot, and that word is *me*."

"You're exaggerating. She's crazy about him."

"Oh, Eliot! Men are so dumb about this kind of stuff!" She laughed, leaned over to kiss him on his cheek, and went to sleep.

So they were both tired this morning, but he was more tired than she was because he had lain awake for another hour, trying not to think of what might be happening to Sam that very moment.

"Irene's useless," Toni was saying now. "She's a baby. She says she can't go, that she can't stand it, that she's never been able to deal with sick people, that she can't deal with the squalor, the police. She's sorry, but she just *can't*. I say we're better off without her, frankly."

At the end of this recitation, she heaved a great sigh, and he nodded in agreement. "How I ever could have thought she was the perfect woman for Sam—! Never mind. You're right. We don't need her emoting all over the police station.

"But wait—! You said Sam is confused. *How* confused? In what way? How badly? What should we prepare ourselves for?"

"Shhh." Toni got up and came around the table, taking his arm. "She didn't specify. Whatever it is, we'll handle it when we get there. Hey, kid, we're doctors, remember? We know how to do this stuff."

Before they left, Eliot dialed his parents' apartment and was relieved when his mother answered. It suddenly struck him that Lillian *always* answered the phone! How come he never noticed that before?

"Lillian, they found Sam. He's okay. He's with the police. Toni and I are going to get him."

"And Irene—?"

"Irene is . . . well, um, not behaving quite like—"

"Irene's a total loss, I could see that from minute one!"

"We'll bring him here and then—"

"No. You'll bring him here. He'll *stay* here. He's my boy."

"Lillian, you have no idea what you're taking on."

"Eliot, I'm not a saint. I'm not planning to put on an apron and do it all by myself. I can afford plenty of help, and we have plenty of room. And . . ." Her voice quivered a little. "What other choice do we have? Put him away? I couldn't live with myself! Eliot, listen, years ago I promised myself I would always take care of Sammy, and I'm a woman of my word. So that's that. See you later."

Eliot stood holding the phone, blinking back unexpected tears. And then he took himself in hand. He had a feeling there would be more reason for tears yet to come.

In the station house, the sergeant behind the desk was ex-

pecting them. He gestured them to a hallway on their left, saying, ''Detective Rizzulo is with Dr. Bronstein.''

Eliot hardly waited for all the words to come out before he
was on his way. The door was closed. He opened it without
knocking, and there, facing him, sitting in a chair, needing a
shave, his clothes rumpled and stained, was Sam. New tears
stung Eliot's eyes.

''Ellie! Hey! What's up, Doc?'' His eyes moved to Toni, right
behind Eliot. ''Hi!''

''How are *you*?'' Eliot said.

''A pain in the ass. This officer told me I've been missing for
three days. I went out to sneak a cigar—you know Irene and
smoking!—and the next thing I know, I'm sitting under a tree
in a park, and I don't know where the hell I am. Me, who's lived
in New York his whole life!'' He grinned at Eliot. ''Tell me, I
have lived in New York my whole life, haven't I? I mean, I didn't
forget *that* much, did I?'' He laughed.

For one stunned moment, Eliot didn't realize Sam was kidding, and his heart froze. Then, he heard Toni laughing, and he
was able to relax and even to smile back at Sam.

''Jesus, look at me,'' Sam said. ''Irene's gonna throw a fit,
like we used to say when we were a couple of kids. Hey! Where
is she?'' Into the rather extended and uncomfortable silence that
followed his question, he said, ''Oh. Yeah. Well. Irene's a
frightened woman, you know. She's afraid of all kinds of things,
but mostly, of being alone. And hey, when you're with a guy
who's slowly losing it, you *are* alone!''

''Sam, don't,'' Eliot said. He hadn't known he was going to
feel this bad.

Sam got to his feet and brushed himself off. He laughed ruefully. ''Hey, old buddy, I don't want to make you suffer, but if
we're going to handle this thing, we have to face it.'' He started
for the door. ''So. Where do we go from here?''

''To Lillian.''

Sam laughed. ''Where else? I had a great cup of coffee, thanks
to the officer here, and three doughnuts.''

''Four,'' the detective corrected. ''You ate one of mine, remember?''

''Is it a capital crime to steal a doughnut from a police officer?'' Again, he laughed, and again Eliot felt a constriction in

his chest, in a place he knew damned well was not where his heart was. Nevertheless, it was his heart that was aching.

Sam crooked both arms in invitation. "Okay, Ellie and . . . okay, folks, let's go."

"Damn it, Toni," Eliot said later, as they rode home. "He couldn't remember your name! I'm not sure he even knew who you were, but he's too damned ashamed to say so. And I don't think he quite knew who Philip was, either. Didn't you notice? Didn't you get it? He covered up, he covered up beautifully. But I saw!"

Sitting next to him in the backseat of the taxicab, holding his hand—it felt to her like he had been hanging on to her hand forever—Toni drew in breath and ordered herself to be patient. They had deposited Sam with Lillian, and she had shooed them out of the apartment. "You two look awful! Go home and be nice to each other—*if* you know what I mean!"

Toni knew what she meant. Oh, God, what a mess. She'd stuck by him while Sam was gone because how the hell did you *not* stick by someone when he was in such despair? She had put everything else in her life on hold to give him a little comfort, a little warmth in a world that had suddenly turned ice cold for him. He'd told her about a thousand times how strong and capable she was, how much he needed her, how he loved her being there for him, what a fabulous woman she was. She was so tired of being fabulous. She was tired of being strong and capable. She was tired, period.

Oh, God, there he went again. "Toni, you're so wonderful; you're so good to me, to all of us. And poor Sam! What does he have? Irene! Irene, who couldn't even bring herself to come to Lillian's to see him! I'll bet right this minute she's lying in a bubble bath, stoned on Valium."

"Oh, Eliot! Give me a break! Bubble bath!" She couldn't help laughing. "Come on, at least Irene is being honest. She's not pretending to be Florence Nightingale. Imagine if she wasn't able to admit her own weakness. He'd be there with her, and she'd be in her bubble bath, and then what do you think would happen to him?"

"You have a point. But she upsets me."

"I know." She patted his hand.

Eliot slumped a little into the corner of the seat. "I hate this whole thing; I'm mad at it. I'm mad at seeing Sam deteriorate;

I'm mad at this damn disease; I'm mad at not being able to do anything about it.''

''And maybe you're mad at your mother,'' Toni said.

''What are you talking about!''

''When we walked in with Sam, the door was already open. She was standing there, her arms open to receive him, and she hugged and hugged him. She called him 'Sammy'—Eliot, think, have you ever in your entire life heard your mother call any person by a nickname? Think, Eliot, think how she was behaving. I've never seen her like that before, not with anyone, not even with her sainted Philip.''

''So? I think that's terrific!''

Like hell you do, Toni thought, but she said, ''I don't think so.''

''I hate it when you get that tone in your voice . . . the tone that says you have a secret *I* don't know!''

Toni bit her lips to keep from saying what she wanted to. ''All right. I'm sorry. All I know is, if it were me and my mother, and I saw her hug and kiss someone else and use endearments, stuff she never did to me, I'd be mad as hell!''

''Well, I'm not you, and I'm not mad.''

''Hurt, then.''

''Not hurt, either.''

''Okay, Eliot, you're not hurt. You're not angry at your mother.'' She hesitated, and then added, ''And you're not hurt and angry at David, either?''

''I don't deny I'm down over David. You got *that* one right! Damn it, my son is about to destroy his whole future.''

''Oh, Eliot! Just because she's older and was married!''

''And has two little kids, whom she has abandoned. Every man deserves a woman without a past.''

''Eliot! I don't believe I heard you say that! Hell, you married me!''

''That was different. She has a reputation.''

''Gossip. Ugly gossip. Haven't you learned, after all these years, what a hotbed of gossip a hospital can be? It's worse than a small town. Hell, it's worse than an Italian neighborhood!'' She laughed. He didn't.

''He's a laughingstock.''

''He is not. He's a wonderful young man who is highly regarded by everyone at Harmony Hill. I don't know where you get these ideas, Eliot. I really don't. Come on, he's in love. Give him a break!''

''I could tell you things about his lady love—''

''Look, Eliot. She's a friend of mine.''

''Not Janet Rafferty!''

''Yes, Janet Rafferty. We have lunch together, or dinner . . . we see each other at least once a week. Eliot? What's the matter?'' She peered at him over there in the corner, scowling, looking terribly grim. ''Eliot, she really loves him, she really does.''

''Love! She sees my son as a meal ticket, that's all!''

''You sound like an old man who's over the hill and is jealous of his handsome young son! And I'm sure that's not the case.''

''You don't know what the hell you're talking about! She's a tramp!''

''A tramp?'' The word sounded so ridiculous, she couldn't help it; she just burst out laughing. ''Oh, Eliot, give me a break!''

Rage suffused his face, turning it crimson. When he spoke, his voice was a knife blade. ''I've been sleeping with her. That's right, me—old over-the-hill me!''

Toni found herself unable to speak. What the hell could she say? He was *cheating* on her? With *Janet*? She couldn't get her brain to settle on that thought and make sense out of it.

She looked away from him and found herself meeting the cabbie's wide, interested gaze in the rearview mirror. At first, she was stricken. Oh my God, he's heard everything, she thought; then she mentally shrugged and, seeing the big ID card on the dash next to the meter, silently told him, Well, Maxood Rafshid, number 303568D, that's how life goes in the Big Apple. You've seen worse, right?

She turned back to Eliot with some trepidation, but now he was looking very regretful, stammering his apologies. She held up a hand. ''No, no, Eliot. I don't need to hear anything else. I want to tell you something. I used to think that if I ever found out you were unfaithful to me, that I would kill you. But you know what? Now that it's happened, I don't give a shit.''

She watched his eyes blank out, and it felt good to know she had hurt him. Just look at us, she thought. He's been banging Janet. Silly old me, I had the crazy idea that she was my friend! What really hurt—oh yeah, she'd been lying when she had said she didn't give a shit; she did!—what *really* hurt was the betrayal by another woman. And then she realized that was bullshit. What really hurt was that her straight-arrow husband had been cheating on her.

But come on, Toni, she reminded herself, who the hell are you to talk? You've been fucking your brains out with another man! Loving it! Looking forward to it! And without a single thought for your straight-arrow husband!

So what are we doing together? Why the hell are we calling the same place home? Why are we so busy pretending? Obviously, whatever we used to feel for each other is gone. Our marriage is brain dead, just like Betty, just like Alice's baby— kept artificially alive, looking healthy, but dead at the core.

A feeling swept over her, a feeling she could not put a name to. Was it regret? Sadness? Nostalgia? Fear? Maybe a little scared, maybe a little regretful, maybe a little sad and nostalgic, too. But mostly, she realized suddenly, free. *Free.*

Now she regarded Eliot, seeing him as from a great distance, noting what a good-looking man he was, how strong and capable, yet she could feel nothing, nothing at all, not even cheated.

"Eliot," she said quietly, "since it's truth time, let me tell *you* the truth. I've been having an affair of my own." She watched his face crumple. "I'm sorry. But . . ." She pulled in a deep breath and blew it out. "We're done for, Eliot. Surely you can see that. The patient is terminal. It's time to pull the plug on Toni and Eliot."

From the front seat of the cab came a groan and a heartfelt "Aw, lady!"

35

Mid-June

The Channel 14 van was pulled up in front of the studio, motor running. Ham jumped in the front, while Carol, his camerawoman, got into the back. It had been raining for days, but finally, it had stopped. A good thing, since Dr. Voorhees had called this press conference for outdoors, across the street from the hospital. He wouldn't say why he had chosen this rather odd place, but he was very insistent. Not in front of the hospital, across the street from the hospital. The insistence was what really interested Ham. It confirmed that something was not kosher at Harmony Hill, and *that* meant a good, juicy story and maybe a couple of points on the ratings.

He knew something was up, anyway. Voorhees had called him early yesterday and offered him an exclusive. "I have a big story for you, Pierce, and I'm willing to give it to you alone, but I have to tell it, live, on your show. Interested?"

Was he kidding? Of course Ham was interested. But he wasn't going to do it, no way. Voorhees was a bit volatile. To put him on live, without rehearsal and without knowing what the hell he had in that peculiar head of his, was asking to be sued. He turned Voorhees down.

"I think you're going to regret your decision, Pierce. But never mind. Maybe it's better if everyone finds out at the same time. I'll see you at the press conference. Noon sharp, tomorrow, across the street from the hospital. Remember that: *across the street*."

When his producer found out he'd said no, she was mad as hell. "We need a shot in the arm, Ham! If you think he's got

something really lowdown and dirty, why not keep him for ourselves?''

"You know me, Rita. I love to take risks. But there's something about this guy . . . I dunno . . . he's a loose pistol. I don't
want him on live, and believe me, Rita, neither do you.''

As the van bumped along, heading for the hospital, he thought
about Voorhees. An odd duck, single, solitary, plenty of old-
fashioned manners that felt phony to Ham, and no warmth, no
warmth at all.

He wished he knew why the guy gave him the creeps. He'd
always been perfectly polite with Ham. Nobody at the hospital
had ever said anything, except for Betty, of course. But every
once in a while, he did or said something that made Ham wonder.

Like the other night, at Ditto's. Ham was there with Wolfe's
daughter Carolyn. He planned to do a piece on her new program
for battered women and children and had been after her for a
year now for a story on her parenting program, but she hadn't
let him in. Confidentiality. And she wouldn't even give him an
interview outside the hospital.

Now she needed him, so now she was willing to talk. So
there they were, sitting at the bar, sipping at vodka tonics, mind-
ing their own business, really into their conversation.

"It started when I took in a couple of battered women and
their kids, one or two, that's all. It was against hospital regulations. But they'd been so mistreated, I just couldn't let them go
back!''

"So you found yourself with a crash pad for abused women
and children.''

Carolyn raked her fingers through her hair nervously and gave
him a sharp look. "This is confidential, Ham. I'm not kidding.
I want a story done about the plight of these women and these
kids! I mean, they're trapped! They can go back home and get
beaten—and worse—or they can go on the street. . . .''

"I know, I know . . .'' he said, in his best soothing tone.

"But I can't let you say that I'm sheltering them. They would
come down on me so hard, the hospital *and* the city! They could
close me down, and then what would become of my mothers
and my kids?''

She really cared, she really felt for them; he could see it in
her eyes. It wasn't her precious program, it was the *people*.

"Maybe it's time you came out of the closet," he suggested. "Everyone in this town knows what a problem we have with domestic violence. Going public with this will bring so much interest. I'm telling you, Carolyn, you'll get money; you'll get backing; the hospital won't dare to close you down. Damn it, this city needs *more* people like you, people who are willing to put their careers on the line for the poor and downtrodden."

She grinned at him, pleased, and then sighed. "Come on, Pierce. You know what they'd say. 'The toilet isn't the right height; there's no shower; where's the full kitchen; where's my permit.' " Her voice rose with every word. "There's got to be a way to rescue these people!"

Suddenly, from behind them, came a loud pronouncement— "The trouble with those people, Ms. Wolfe, is we give them *too* much, too easily!"

They both whirled around, and there at a nearby table, a light little smile on his tight little face, was Dr. Warren Voorhees, sitting alone.

"Let me tell you something, Ms. Wolfe. What those little bastards need is more discipline. Their parents don't give a damn. All they care about is that Welfare check! You know why their neighborhoods are so crime-ridden? Because they're all addicts. You know as well as I that they bring their troubles on themselves!"

This guy sounds like a Nazi, Ham thought. He was all for blowing him off and getting back to business. But not Carolyn. She wasn't about to let him get away with it, not her.

"A two-year-old child is not a criminal, Dr. Voorhees. My mothers can't help being poor and uneducated. It's not their fault they're being abused—"

Voorhees gave a little laugh, his lip curling. "Not their fault! Ah, but they could just walk out! So why don't they? Because some women *like* to be dominated, Ms. Wolfe."

"I don't believe you just said that," Carolyn said through clenched teeth. Ham, watching this scene with great interest, thought, Oh, so that's what "white with rage" means. Every bit of color in her face had drained away.

Voorhees seemed not to notice. "Not consciously, of course. But subconsciously, they want to be victims."

"If men weren't abusers," she had said coolly, "there wouldn't *be* any victims."

"With all due respect, Ms. Wolfe," Voorhees said in that smug way he had, "you're very young and very green."

Making a strangled noise in her throat, Carolyn whirled on the bar stool, turning her back to him. She downed her drink in one gulp, then banged her glass down so hard that a couple of ice cubes flew out.

"Terribly sorry, Doctor," Ham said. "We're in the middle of a private conversation. I hope you'll excuse us."

As he turned back to the bar, holding two fingers up for a couple of refills, he thought gleefully, maybe Carolyn Wolfe's little shelter was confidential, but what had just happened with Voorhees was *not*. Catching sight of the doctor's reflection in the big mirror behind the bar, he saw him lick his lips, like a cat with cream. A split second later, the self-satisfied look was wiped away, instantly replaced with the public face, stonelike in its immobility. He would have liked to watch this guy for a while; he gave you a sense that something was about to happen. But Carolyn was talking, so he pulled his attention back to her.

Thinking about it, he realized how much Carolyn was like Toni, the way she stood up for what she believed in, the way she talked with her hands, the way she had of mimicking other people's speech. She even had that habit of running her fingers through her hair when she was fired up. Just like Toni.

He smiled to himself. He always smiled when he thought of Toni. He was crazy about her . . . well, sort of. He really went for her, but now, damn it, who knew what she thought was going to happen? She was separated—not legally, she had said, but hell, she was living alone and fucking him in her marriage bed. That was legal enough to make Ham Pierce very nervous. The trouble was, he wasn't sure what she wanted from him . . . besides his cock. Of course she wanted *that*; they all did! Every time he finished with her, she was one happy woman! He knew he was goddamn good in bed. Hell, he was the best!

The van pulled to the curb about halfway up the block to Harmony Hill. The street was blocked with television vans and TV personnel, not to mention the all-news radio stations—he recognized a couple of them—and someone from the *Amsterdam News* and even Siegel from the good,

gray *New York Times*. It was a beautiful crystal-clear day,
not too hot and not too humid, so of course there was a
mob across the street from the hospital. They were spilling
over into the roadway. Normally, a doctor's press conference was a big yawn, and it might collect the occasional
passerby. But this—! He'd bet most of them had no idea
what it was all about and couldn't care less.

He cared. What's more, he knew it was going to be big,
whatever it was. That's why Voorhees had been so tightly
coiled the other night. That's why Ham had sensed something
was about to happen; it was that manic quality. He wished
he knew what it was, but it really didn't matter. It could be
anything, anything at all. Christ, it could easily be right off
the wall.

He threaded his way through the crowd, calling out the station's call letters. They parted for him, like the Red Sea for
Moses, his camerawoman trailing right behind. They were just
in time. As they got to the front of the mob, there came Voorhees, smiling that tight little smile, wearing a crisp tan suit
without a wrinkle in it and a striped shirt with a tightly knotted,
skinny little tie. His eyes were like bullets. Clustered behind
him was a group of doctors from the ethics committee . . . aha,
that was a good clue. Who had done something unethical? Ham
wondered. Of course, there was nobody there from administration and no sign of Dr. Eliot Wolfe.

Voorhees positioned himself so that he faced a battery of
mikes and cameras straight on. "I have a brief statement," he
announced. "And then I'll take questions."

A murmur went through the crowd. Voorhees stood very still,
waiting for his audience to quiet down and give him its full
attention. He soon had it. Then he gave that weird little quirk
of a smile and began to speak. No notes, no nothing. Just started
to talk.

"Today, it is my duty to reveal to the public a cover-up at
Harmony Hill Hospital." There was an immediate buzz to
which he held up a hand, and then continued speaking, a
little louder. "The president of this hospital, Dr. Eliot Wolfe,
has knowingly and deliberately kept secret the murder of Betty
Cannon." Now, no hand could hold back the noise from the
crowd. Voorhees stepped back just a bit from the microphone, looking very goddamn pleased with himself. Ham

suddenly realized that this was exactly a thirty-second sound bite, and he shook his head in admiration. The guy was too perfect to be real!

The hand was up again, palm out. "Yes, murder. I say murder, because I have reason to know that a doctor practicing in Harmony Hill Hospital secretly entered the room where Betty Cannon lay comatose, and without authorization of any kind, unplugged the respirator, thus causing Mrs. Cannon's premature death." He looked around, deliberately, slowly. Working the crowd, Ham thought.

"Furthermore, ladies and gentlemen, it is my duty to report to you that the hospital's president, Dr. Eliot Wolfe, extracted a vow of secrecy from everyone present—including his own wife, Dr. Antonia Romano, much touted as one of New York's best physicians.

"As a member of the hospital's ethics committee, I strongly condemn Dr. Wolfe's actions and demand his immediate resignation."

The shouting erupted before the last syllable was out of his mouth. Ham got in the first question. "Dr. Voorhees . . . can you tell us, was Dr. Wolfe present when Mrs. Cannon's respirator was unplugged?"

"I have no way of knowing. However, it is my understanding that he was called to the scene by his wife immediately after it happened. Yes? NBC?" And he turned quickly away.

Inside, Ham was rejoicing. So! All Wolfe's high and mighty crap about ethics was so much bullshit! It was about time he got what was coming to him, the hypocritical schmuck! And then it struck him that, Jesus, *Toni* was implicated . . . and she had never said a word, never even hinted! Shit! How had he missed that one?

He turned to his camerawoman, talking fast. "Stay up close and get everything that's said. When Voorhees leaves, come into the hospital. You'll find me in the president's office." Now he had to fight his way back out of the mob and then dodge traffic crossing the street.

He pushed his way into Eliot's private office, leaving the little secretary squawking and squealing behind him. The buzzer on the president's desk was going full blast as Ham came barreling through the door.

"Are you aware of what's happening out there, Dr. Wolfe?"

Wolfe looked up. He looked completely cool, completely calm, completely collected, and suddenly Ham felt sweaty and grubby and overly excited.

"Yes," he said. "Dr. Voorhees was kind enough to come in earlier to inform me." His voice betrayed no emotion whatsoever.

"Then why the hell aren't you out there, answering his accusations?"

"I will not dignify his assertions with my presence."

"Then it's true."

"No comment."

"Is any part of it true? Was Dr. Romano part of it?"

"Part of what?" His voice was edged with irritation. Good. We're getting to him, Ham thought.

"Part of the conspiracy?" Surely Wolfe couldn't let a word like "conspiracy" just slide by!

But he could. "No comment," he said.

Ham leaned forward, hands on the edge of the desk, very earnest. "Look, Wolfe. I've had dealings with the man. There's something off kilter about him. As far as I'm concerned, he could be making it all up."

"No comment."

"We're on the same side."

"No comment." Said very slowly and distinctly.

"Dr. Wolfe, they're going to crucify you!"

"Starting with Channel Fourteen?"

"Oh, for—! Look, I know there's no love lost between us, but this time, I'm on your side. Think. Haven't I been doing positive stories about Harmony Hill? You know I have. You must know I'm doing a story with your daughter."

"No, you're not."

"What do you mean? She's willing . . . hell, she's eager."

"Well, I'm not. Those are children and parents in crisis, Pierce. They're extremely fragile. What they *don't* need is being badgered for the gory details by the likes of you."

The likes of me, Ham thought. The fucking, arrogant, patronizing, condescending prig! He smiled at Eliot through clenched teeth and said sweetly: "I'm good enough for some people in the Wolfe family."

Wolfe frowned a little. "Just what is that supposed to mean?"

"No comment." He only paused long enough to see that his shot had hit the mark. The noble brow was creased; the noble jaw had dropped; the noble eyes were clouded with confusion.

"No comment," he repeated with satisfaction and exited, gently closing the door behind him.

36

Later that day

Toni stood in the doorway, staring at him, looking as if she'd like to murder him, so he leaned back deliberately, laced his hands behind his head, and pasted a calm look over his face.

"Damn it, Eliot, Voorhees just accused you of a *crime*!"

He smiled at her, knowing that his unruffled appearance would irritate her. He didn't care if he irritated her; in fact, right now, he *wanted* to irritate her. "You should include yourself," he said. "It seems to me he mentioned my wife. And unless I am sadly mistaken, you are still my wife?" He kept his voice low, but even he could hear the sardonic edge on it.

He watched her get mad and then fight it down. She sucked in a deep breath and tried to match his phlegmatic manner. She should have known better; she was Italian. She made her voice soft, but he wasn't fooled. "You can't just sit here after that man has maligned you," she said. "And yes, me, too. You think because you're a Wolfe, you're invulnerable."

"Forget the nasty cracks about the Wolfes, if you don't mind." Now she had made him good and mad! "We'll manage somehow, even without your help."

"Eliot! Come on! Just because you and I are on the outs . . . look, you were right; we're both in this. Can't we talk about it like human beings, like colleagues?"

All of a sudden, she wanted to act like a human being! His lips tightened. "I've put a call in to my lawyer. Until I hear from him, there's nothing I can do. *Should* do," he corrected himself. "And if you'll take a bit of advice, Toni, you shouldn't comment, either."

She was beginning to look a little desperate. "Eliot, I didn't

373

want to worry you unnecessarily, but . . . Dee is going on 'Voice of the City.' ''

"What?" He came to an upright position, all attention. "She's . . . what?" Oh God! What next?

"Dee is going on Ham Pierce's program. Tonight, Eliot. In"—she looked at her watch—"in two hours. I tried to stop her, but she's like a woman possessed. She would only say over and over that she had something important to say, and that she wanted the whole world to know. And she refuses to tell me what it is. Eliot, she's going to *confess*!"

"Maybe not."

She regarded him, half-sorrowful, half-exasperated.

"Obviously, if she won't tell you what it is," he explained, "she certainly won't tell me. I did my best to protect her; if now she has decided to go ahead and expose herself, there's nothing I can do about it."

"You know what they say: 'if you can keep your head while all about you others are losing theirs . . . you must be crazy!' ''

"*Someone* has to keep his head around here. Look. If Dee tells the truth, nothing will happen to her—no court in this state will have anything to do with prosecuting a distraught family member. Voorhees will have no leverage; and, by the way, Toni, you and I will be off the hook."

Bitterly, she said, "And if *we* get off the hook, everything's okay, right?"

"Toni, you're not being fair. And that's naive. Voorhees can't know very much—he didn't accuse Dee, after all—and he certainly can't have any *proof*! He's after my job, that's the bottom line."

"I'd rather be naive than what *you* are!"

That was not worth answering. Why in hell was *she* so angry? He had always taken care of her, cherished her, supported her, and been proud of her! He'd awakened next to her for so many years, had looked across the table at her, had gazed down into her eyes when they made love. He had trusted her absolutely.

And she had gone to the arms of another man and had made love to him! She had betrayed him once again. At this moment, he almost hated her.

Who was the man she had slept with? The question haunted him, invading his work, his sleep, his every thought. He had found himself, ever since that horrible cab ride, looking at every man she had come into contact with, wondering, imagining. Havemayer, Harrison, Jim Chu! Even Ham Pierce! God, it was making him crazy! Who was it?

She looked him over carefully, a cold, distant set to her face. "Does this mean you refuse to protect one of your own doctors?"

"I know how to protect my doctors. But I intend to wait until I have talked with my attorney." She was making him very angry. "And you are out of line, Dr. Romano."

She turned on her heel, her fists clenching and unclenching, and got the hell out of there before she killed him! Out of line! Mr. Godalmighty President had spoken, and she could not bear to be in his presence for one more minute!

Besides, she was due to pick up Dee. She was going with her to the studio. If Dee was going to do this ridiculous self-sacrificing thing, she wanted to be there for her. And anyway, maybe there was still time to talk her out of it.

When she got upstairs to her office, she found her answering machine blinking. It had to be Dee. But when she pushed the playback button, the first message was Janet. Again.

"Toni, I know you're hurt and bothered, but if you knew all the facts, I think you'd feel differently. I wish you'd meet me so we could talk. I'm not going to give up!" Toni made a little noise with her lips. She wasn't going to give up? She could keep it up forever. No way could they be friends.

After the beep, it *was* Dee, talking very rapidly, almost too fast to be understood. But Toni did get that she'd be about five minutes late; she couldn't help it; things kept coming up. So much fussing over five minutes? What was with her? Maybe Ham shouldn't be letting her go on live.

She was reaching for the phone to talk to him when it rang. It was Dee again, still talking too fast, but sounding up. "Oh, Toni, I'm so glad you're there; I'd rather talk to you than a machine, and anyway, you don't have to take me . . . to the studio, I mean. You could be there if you want to, but you don't have to—"

"Dee!" Toni interrupted, laughing a little. "Slowly, slowly." Ham wouldn't take advantage of her situation, would he? Of course he would. "What do you mean, I don't have to go. Of course I'm going. I wouldn't miss it."

"Oh, I didn't mean that, Toni, I didn't mean I wouldn't want you there. It's just . . . well, King, King Crawford, he's going to take me. I mean, he asked if he could. He *wants* to." There was a lilt in her voice. "Oh, Toni, he's so nice. I wish . . . I don't know what I wish. Yes, I do. I wish I wasn't so afraid of getting close to a man. King is nothing like . . . *him*, nothing, nothing! But I just can't seem to relax."

"You will, you will," Toni soothed. "I happen to know that King is an unusual and wonderful young man, and he'll be patient with you. I also happen to know," she added coyly, "that he really likes *you*."

"I know. I just wish . . . oh well. Maybe after today."

"After today?" Toni countered swiftly. "Why, Dee? What's going to happen today?"

"You'll see."

"Listen, Dee, are you sure this is a good idea? Are you sure you really want to do . . . whatever it is you're going to do?"

"I've never been more sure of anything in my life."

Dee and King, Toni mused. She smiled to herself. When Toni tells Deedra that King was her son, Dee would *flip*! And so would Eliot, she thought. He still hadn't come to terms with it. He hadn't liked it one bit when she told his mother. He was being so unreasonable in general. She had been wondering if maybe she and Eliot ought to talk about divorce. Hell, he had moved out and gone to Lillian's. Not too many people knew why. What they had been saying for public consumption was that Eliot felt he should be there to help with Sam for a while.

She gave a quick glance around her office—everything was shipshape, nothing left behind—and locked up. On her way downstairs, she found herself thinking again about Dee and King. How did she feel, as mother of the groom, about him marrying a black woman? She was no racist, that was for sure. After all, she'd slept with Arch and would have happily married him if he'd been available. But, for King . . . well, he was half-white and could go either way. Choosing Dee meant he was choosing to live in the black world and to father black children and, in this city, that was choosing a lifetime of bigotry, hate, and discrimination.

King was in the studio already when she got there. As soon as he saw her, he smiled and gave her the A-okay sign. She felt a twinge of guilt that she hadn't yet announced him as her child to the whole world. Look at him! Anyone would be proud to claim him! So what the hell was she waiting for?

One of the assistant assistant something-or-others, a busy young woman named Debra, gave Toni a nod and motioned to a line of chairs close to the set. "You know where to go, Dr. Romano."

"Thanks," Toni said and quickly glanced sideways to see if King had caught the implication. Of course he had; he was her kid, wasn't he?

He came over. "I didn't know you'd been on the show," he said.

"I haven't been." After a second, she realized she wasn't going to get away with such a short answer, so she hastily added, "I've been here a couple of times . . . a kind of consultant. Where's Dee?"

"In the ladies' room. God, you women have to pee a lot!"

"She's nervous. I hope to God she's not about to do something very stupid and self-destructive."

"Brave, yes. Stupid, no." He put a comforting hand on her shoulder and gave it a little squeeze.

Just then, Ham and Dee both came in and took their seats under the bright lights: Ham in the easy chair and Dee perched tensely in a corner of the loveseat. The big monitors overhead suddenly came alive with a giant image of Dee licking her lips; a shot of the two of them; a smaller Dee, seen over Ham's shoulder; and the giant himself, Ham Pierce, larger than life.

Toni regarded his likeness on the big screen. Not for the first time, she wondered just what she was doing with him. Would she want to live with him? She didn't think so. But then, how to explain her breathlessness at every first sight of him, the first kiss, the first touch. Well, that was easy. It was lust, that's all, and forbidden sex, to boot. She wondered if that would change, now that she was contemplating freedom.

The familiar theme sounded, played by trumpets, and the title came onto the main monitor, and the announcer's voice gave them—" 'the Voice of the City' . . . Hamilton Pierce!" More trumpets, fading away; then Ham's voice, very earnest, very serious, introducing "a young doctor from Harmony Hill Hospital, here in response to accusations made yesterday and seen by all of you right here on Channel Fourteen . . ."

Then the camera focused on Dee, who looked straight at her

unseen audience and licked her lips. Her right eyelid was twitching a little, Toni noted.

"I am Dr. Deedra Strong, chief resident in gynecology and obstetrics at Harmony Hill Hospital. Yesterday, Dr. Warren Voorhees announced that a doctor at Harmony Hill had unplugged Betty Cannon's life-support system. I am that doctor." She stopped, blinked back tears, cleared her throat.

"Betty Cannon was my sister. She raised me from childhood. There was nobody in this world I loved more than Betty. As a doctor, I was aware that her condition was hopeless, and as her sister, I knew that she would never want her life sustained artificially."

She paused and cleared her throat again. Toni let out the breath she had been holding. It was just as she had thought and not as bad as she had feared. Dee sounded calm and intelligent and rational. Much as she hated to admit it, it looked as if Eliot might be right.

She expected Ham to pose a question now, to keep the discussion going. Instead, the camera stayed on Deedra, who licked her lips again and continued.

"Dr. Voorhees has accused Dr. Eliot Wolfe and his wife, Dr. Antonia Romano, of a criminal act. Well, I'm here—" Her voice shook a little and she broke off. In the big monitor, Toni could see the gleam of tears swimming in Dee's eyes, then falling, rolling down her cheeks. "I'm here," she continued, "to accuse Dr. Voorhees of a criminal act. . . ."

Now Toni dropped her gaze from the monitor to stare at the real Dee, who had leaned forward even farther toward the camera, her arms wrapped tightly around herself. What in the world—?

"On the evening of February sixth, Dr. Voorhees rang the bell at the Women's Health Center on 123rd Street in Manhattan, where I was on night duty. It was after hours, and I was alone, closing up." Her voice was flat and even, wiped clean of emotion.

"I recognized Dr. Voorhees, both from the hospital and from an occasional accidental meeting while running, and he had treated me for shin splints last year. I, of course, admitted him."

Again, a pause. Dee took a sip from a glass of water and put it down. The camera stayed fixed on her face. Her eyes, Toni thought, looked enormous.

"Dr. Voorhees said he was glad I was alone, he wanted to . . . to talk to me. He seemed a little . . . peculiar to me, but I figured that it was late, and I was tired. So I took him into the back, into the office. He closed the door behind us; I remember noticing that because it was odd. Nobody else was around.

"And then he . . . he began to talk, very intensely. Not . . . normal. First he said that he knew I came to the park every morning to run, hoping to meet him. When I said that wasn't true, he paid no attention, just kept on. He said, 'Don't think I haven't noticed how often you let your arm brush against mine when we're running together. Don't think I haven't been aware of what you're after. I know the way you look at me,' he said. That's when I got scared. I had never looked at him in *any* way!

"I tried to calm him down, I said he was mistaken, and if I had offended him, I was sorry. He smiled at me and said, 'Oh no, you haven't offended me, Deedra. And I sincerely hope you won't now.' And then . . . and then . . ." Her voice wobbled, and she stopped to take another drink.

Oh my God! Toni was thinking, Oh my God! It was him! It was Voorhees! Voorhees! She had racked her brain, after the rape, trying to figure out who it was, who was sick enough! But never in a million years would she have guessed Warren Voorhees! That buttoned-up little tight-assed prick. She had thought he was gay!

"And then," Dee continued, "he came after me. He . . . grabbed my arm and told me I was a . . . He said I couldn't get away with teasing him and then say no. But I kept saying, 'No, no, you're wrong, and I don't want to do this.' . . . He said, 'Look what you've done to me,' and he put my hand on his—" She came to a halt again, and now tears were rolling down her cheeks.

Ham's deep, soothing voice said, "It's all right, Dr. Strong. You don't have to go on, if you don't want to."

She had bent her head down to hide her tears. It came back up quickly. "No, no! I want to! I'm sorry, I'm sorry for getting upset."

"We understand; we understand completely, Dr. Strong. Just go on when you're ready. We can wait."

"He . . . he forced me!" she blurted. "He became angry with me. He told me I was lying, that I'd been leading him on and I had to . . . to 'come across.' He pulled me close to him and tried to kiss me. I . . . I fought him, and when I did, he grabbed my hair, and he hit me with the back of his hand and then he *kissed* me. I struggled and struggled, but I couldn't get away from him, and he pushed me down onto the floor. I was crying and begging him not to do this, to please stop. But he got very angry and told me he would beat me senseless if I didn't stop fighting him. And he meant it. I could see it on his face.

"I . . . we . . . women are always told it isn't worth losing your life. I kept thinking that, I kept saying it to myself, over and over again, while he—" She halted and cleared her throat and wiped her eyes with the palm of her hand. "He ripped off my clothes and he . . . he raped me. He kept smiling, so I closed my eyes. I couldn't stand seeing that smile.

"He raped me," she repeated. "And he kept saying I really wanted it." She shuddered and looked down. Then she raised her head so that she was looking the world in the eyes, and her voice became strong.

"Dr. Warren Voorhees raped me."

There was a long silence. Toni could hear her own breathing very clearly. She turned to look at King. She had been so engrossed in Dee, in her face and her voice and her words, that she had virtually forgotten he was there. As she faced him, he met her eyes and nodded. "Yes. She told me," he whispered. "I told you she was brave."

"Oh, God, how horrible for her! And all this time, she's been at the hospital, having to deal with him, having to pretend . . . ugh!"

Ham was saying almost the same thing to her. "And you have continued to work at Harmony Hill . . . ?" His voice was heavy with sympathy.

"That's right."

"Has he ever said anything to you?"

"No. He . . . he acts as if it never happened. One day . . . one day not long ago, he even came up to me and said, 'Say, I don't see you running anymore.' " She closed her eyes briefly.

"How did you respond?"

"I just stared at him. It was so unreal. I wondered if he was ridiculing me, but he seemed genuinely curious. I don't remember what I said. I just wanted out of there!"

"I'm sure nobody could blame you for that. But this terrible thing happened in February, Dr. Strong. Why have you not come forward before now?''

"He told me, that night—I remember every word because he had that weird smile on his face—he said, 'And I wouldn't try telling anyone if I were you. I'll make sure your career as a doctor is finished. In any case, nobody will take your word against *mine*. You're a black woman; everyone knows black women gotta have it.' And I was afraid! Who would believe me against him?''

"And you decided now to tell the whole story.''

"Yes. When he attacked Dr. Wolfe on ethical grounds, it made me sick! I just couldn't keep it a secret anymore. I couldn't!'' Now she broke down, sobbing into her hands, and a moment later, the camera was off her and onto Ham.

"This stalwart young doctor has risked everything, reputation, career, privacy, to save other women—not only from rape, but from the shackles of silence! I applaud her, ladies and gentlemen; I salute her; I acclaim her! Show her your support and your empathy. Call 555-1234.'' He paused and smiled broadly. "I should have known my viewers. I didn't even have to ask. They tell me the switchboard is already lit up like Times Square on New Year's Eve. Thank you, fellow New Yorkers . . .''

And then, the fat little Pillsbury doughboy was dancing across the screen. Toni jumped up, ready to run to Deedra, but King beat her to it. He stood by her side, his hand poised over her shoulder, and you could see, even at this distance, that he was aching to touch her, but he wasn't going to do it, no matter how badly he wanted to. His hand shook with the tension.

Dee looked up, her face streaked with tears, and when she saw him, she cried, "Oh, King!'' and leaped up, into his embrace. His arms went tightly around her, and he put his lips to the soft curve of her neck. He was facing Toni. On his face was a look of such bliss, it made her eyes sting with sudden tears. She and Eliot had had that kind of feeling in the early days . . . hadn't they?

Later, after the show was wrapped up, she and Ham put the two kids into a cab and watched as they both turned to wave out the back window. They looked like teenagers out on a date. Once Dee had finished talking and then had finished crying, she had become euphoric. Toni wondered just how long *that* would last.

As if he could read her mind, Ham remarked, ''I give her till tomorrow morning to come off that high. And then she'll have second thoughts. She'll probably come to you to tell her she did the right thing.''

''She did. That scabrous bastard!''

Ham laughed. '' 'Scabrous!' Where'd *that* come from?''

''God knows!'' She laughed, too, glad to think about something other than Dee's ordeal—or her own misery. At least Dee had been in good hands. Ham had done right by her, not pushing, not insisting, and had been so gentle. On their way out, people kept popping out of offices along the corridors. ''Great job, Pierce!'' ''That'll show Mike Wallace how to do it.'' ''Your ratings must have been off the charts!'' ''You deserve a Pulitzer for this one!''

It was the first time Toni had ever seen him with his peers, and she was gratified to see that he was highly thought of. She thought he was good at what he did, but she sometimes had trouble convincing herself that what he did mattered. There were a lot of people out there in television land who trusted him and who apparently needed his voice. God, she must've been a doctor too long, thinking that if you weren't in a ''caring profession,'' you were unnecessary.

Ham put an arm around her, and she turned to give him a startled look. They had an agreement: no public displays until her separation was legal. But he was on a high of his own, and he was oblivious.

''God, Toni, do you realize what this means?'' he was saying. ''I'm going to be on the front page of every newspaper in the city tomorrow morning! I wouldn't be surprised if *Time* and *Newsweek* didn't pick up on this! Oh Jesus! This is the best thing that's happened to me in a long long time!''

He bent and opened the door of a white stretch limo that had been parked at the curb.

''For us?'' she said.

He laughed. ''Nothing but the best for the best!''

They climbed in and as soon as they were seated and the car pulled away, Ham got out a bottle of champagne. ''There are glasses in that little cabinet next to you,'' he said. He was really enjoying himself, playing lord of the limo. Toni wasn't quite sure whether *she* was enjoying herself. What did he mean, it was the best thing that had happened to him? And where was

Dee and her pain in all of this? He had been so good with her, so sweet, so understanding! Was it just a practiced performance and nothing more?

"What about Dee?" she asked.

"What *about* her? She did great! And when she couldn't hold back those tears . . . Jesus, I hadn't dared hope for that!"

"Ham! That's terrible!"

"No, it isn't. Hey, I didn't say I *wanted* her to cry so people would call in. All I'm saying is, she cried, and it made them mad, and it put them on her side . . . on *our* side, Toni! That's what my show is all about: uniting people to fight for justice!" He leaned over to kiss her, but she put a hand on his chest.

"Wait, Ham. What about Dee's pain?"

"Hey, this was the best thing she could've done for herself. She told me she's been a zombie ever since it happened. And you saw her after the show! That's catharsis, baby!"

"Well, it sounds to me like you don't care about her."

"I care, all right, but I can't get too involved, or I'm no good at my job. You should know about that. You keep *your* distance. You told me yourself you don't always pick up on everything."

Her spine froze. She remembered perfectly well where he had learned that little piece of information. It was right after Alice had killed herself, and she had poured her heart out to him. And here he was, attacking her with it. "I may not pick up on everything," she said, "but I usually do okay."

"Toni, Toni, you're a wonderful doctor. You're beloved! You don't want that sicko wandering around the hospital anymore, do you? Hey, bottom line is, a bad guy is gonna get what's coming to him! Is it so terrible if it also takes my ratings right up out of the cellar?"

A little voice way in the back of her mind was asking, Were his ratings so bad before? He'd never said so. Had he just been using Dee? But, come on, Toni, lighten up, she told herself. He was like a boy who'd just made the winning home run, guileless and full of himself. It was kind of endearing, wasn't it?

He bent to her lips again, and she let him kiss her. She wanted to melt, as she always did, but that stubborn little voice kept bothering her, telling her to grow up, pay attention, and see this man for what he was. Ham's mouth covered hers, and he pulled her in close against him, his big hands warm against her back. Then she felt his tongue, exploring, probing, and heat rose in her loins. It was no use. She was going to give in.

Go away, little voice, she ordered silently. Don't bother me right now.

37

Two days later

Sun was streaming through the windows of Ham's bedroom, glinting off the gilded screen and dappling the dark walls with bright, moving flecks of light. Toni sat very straight, propped up against half a dozen plump down pillows, leafing lazily through the Sunday *Times*. She was nude, enjoying the warmth of the sunlight on her shoulders, and the nice cool breeze from the river. Three small television sets, side by side on one of the bookshelves, were all on, but silent, and she was doing her best to ignore them.

Ham always turned all of them on, first thing every morning—to catch the competition, as he put it. To laugh at them and comment on how stupid they were was what actually happened. But that didn't stop him from picking up their better ideas. She'd noticed that, right away.

Now he came into the room, bearing a large wicker tray with coffee, bagels with lox and cream cheese, and a glass jug of orange juice that glowed in the sunshine like a huge golden jewel. He, too, was naked, and the sun burnished the golden hair all over his body, setting his skin aglow. Oh, the wondrous things he could do with that body—! Even now, not ten minutes after a long, lovely session of lovemaking, just thinking about him made the breath catch in her throat.

He set the breakfast tray down in the middle of the bed and leaned over to give her a kiss, when he suddenly stopped, mid-lean, and straightened, all attention on the busy little TV screens.

"Yo! There I am!"

She looked. And there, indeed, he was, looking very intent and empathetic, his lips moving without sound. The camera

moved to Dee, her lips moving without sound. Then came another switch, to the gaunt, ascetic face of Warren Voorhees. At
that moment, Ham upped the volume on the remote and suddenly the room was filled with Voorhees's voice, blaring, "Cat-
egorically deny all accusations made by that young woman. No
further comment."

"Turn it down, Ham! In fact, turn it off! We need to hear him
telling more lies?"

"Shhhh." His eyes did not leave the television sets, but he
did lower the volume. "Hey, babe, this is a breaking story! It's
my story! I have to keep up with it, you know. I might have to
go in today. Thank God for the creeps of this world; otherwise,
I wouldn't have a job!"

"You're thanking God for *Voorhees*? After what he did to
Dee? And who knows how many other young women? Ham!"

"Well, it's my job. Voorhees would be who he is, with or
without me. Hey," he interrupted himself, holding his hands up
in surrender. "It's not my fault if the American public dotes on
other people's misfortunes!"

Now the commentator was beginning to give background and
Ham's head automatically swiveled back toward the sets.

"Right here on Channel Fourteen, where city stories are always first . . . Hamilton Pierce, well-known investigative reporter . . . Dr. Deedra Strong accused Dr. Voorhees of
rape. . . . police custody . . . charged and released on his own
recognizance . . . suspended from all duties and privileges at
Harmony Hill Hospital, by its president, Dr. Eliot Wolfe."

And then, there was Eliot, staring out, looking right at her.
Without thought, Toni pulled the sheet up over her breasts. Then
she laughed at herself. He had such an amiable and earnest
appearance, and he looked so young! If it weren't for the white
hair, he could pass for forty. He was saying, "Dr. Voorhees has
been suspended by this hospital as of this morning, and we will
take the appropriate action if he is found guilty. Meanwhile, I
feel it would be unconscionable—"

Click! His face and his voice disappeared all at once, and she
turned to Ham. "Hey, he was just getting interesting!"

He laughed and eased himself onto the bed, saying, "If you
don't mind, I'd rather not have breakfast with your husband.
Particularly not when he's getting interesting!"

He reached out for the frosted pitcher of juice and murmured,

"Mimosa, my dear?" She should have known he wouldn't have just plain old orange juice, not Hamilton Pierce. No, for him it had to be freshly squeezed OJ with Möet champagne!

She took her glass from him and sipped. "Perfect." She waited a minute and then said, "Could we please have the television back on? I *do* work there, you know."

He didn't like it, she could tell. He never liked it if she went against him—even in something as small as this. How do I so unerringly manage to pick them? she asked herself. Then, she added, "And I feel so sorry for Eliot. Poor Eliot."

That did it. He turned to her, his eyes alight with interest. "Why poor Eliot? It seems to me he's handling it very well."

"You know how many problems there are at the hospital, Ham. Can you really believe he feels as calm as he looks? No, no, I know Eliot. I'll bet you he's having an attack of colitis this minute!"

Ham poured them more Mimosa, then lay back and stretched out his long legs. "Colitis, huh? Who'd ever guess that the stonefaced, stonewalling Dr. Wolfe had any nerves at all? I had an ulcer, but it hasn't bothered me for years."

"Lucky you. Eliot's colitis kicks up every time he has problems. And poor Eliot, he came to a hospital already *full* of problems! I don't think he was counting on that when he took the job. He saw Harmony Hill as his inheritance, sort of."

"Yeah, yeah. I know that story. He was always talking about his hospital."

"How do you know that? He only says that in private."

Ham leered at her, very pleased with himself. "Ever hear of the private secretary?"

"Betty? Betty used to tell you things?" No! No, he was bullshitting. He had to be. Betty would never—! Never!

"You should see the look on your face!" He laughed. "I didn't think *anything* could surprise you. But don't worry. She never gave me anything really important. She liked your husband. Hell, she loved him. She was always protecting him from me. She was always telling me it wasn't him; it was the system. But she hated the fucking system in the hospital, so she was always on the lookout for anything she thought was wrong. Hey, that was okay with me; it gave me some good leads. I really miss her."

"Is that why you've been letting up on the hospital lately? Because you don't have someone there to give you *good leads*?"

"Of course not! To tell the truth, I kind of like the guy, myself. He really means well; you know what I'm saying? Hey, it couldn't have been so easy to walk into that hotbed of mediocrity and deal with those prima donnas. He's a bulldog; I'll give him that. He never gives up."

"Yeah, well, he had so much to live up to. The Wolfe reputation can be overwhelming. I mean, that's why he went to D.C. in the first place, and it's also why he stayed there for thirty years. He had to prove to himself that he could do it on his own, and he did. He was a damn good doctor! His patients loved him! He could've stayed there forever. If he hadn't been passed over for head of his department, he'd still be there."

"But then we wouldn't have met," he murmured and nuzzled into the curve of her shoulder. A little chill raced down her backbone. He rolled over to be closer to her, and all the plates and glasses on the breakfast tray sent up a rattle. "Ham! You're going to knock that tray over, and I'll never get my breakfast!"

She was laughing, but he wasn't. Honestly, men! "Whatever you say," he gritted and moved away. He picked up the sports section of the paper and disappeared behind it. Okay, if that's how he wanted it. She took the first section and continued to leaf through, looking at the photographs and headlines. Maybe someone she knew had done something newsworthy. Besides that animal Voorhees.

Aha! Here's one. "HEALTH CARE COSTS FORCE CUTS. Five large, primary-care hospitals bite the bullet." It was a big story, full of lists. And then the words Harmony Hill leaped out at her and she focused, reading rapidly. "President Wolfe has announced the closing of half a dozen satellite clinics. 'We can serve the same people right here in the clinic area of the hospital,' Eliot Wolfe told reporters. . . ." She let her eyes slide down. Uptown Dentistry. Walk-in Substance Abuse. Women's Health Center.

"Women's Health Center! That bastard! He didn't even have the balls to tell me first! This is a helluva way to find out. Goddamn it!"

She flung herself out of the bed, rattling the breakfast tray and bringing Ham's head out of the sports section. "Toni! What's going on?"

She had a vision of herself, stark naked, furious, fists clenched, standing in the middle of Ham Pierce's elegant bedroom. But to hell with how she looked. "Eliot! That bastard has closed my Women's Health Center! Closed it! Without a *word*! I'll kill him!" Tears of rage began to pour out of her eyes, and that made her even angrier. She hated feeling so goddamn helpless!

Impulsively, she picked up the phone and dialed Lillian's number, half expecting Eliot himself to pick it up. Hoping he would. But it was Lillian. She had to damp down her anger and try to talk in a halfway normal voice.

"Lillian, hi, it's Toni."

"Yes, darling, I recognize your voice. How are you?"

"I'm fine, Lillian." Slow down, Toni, slow down. "And you? And Philip? And Sam?"

A tiny pause. "And Eliot?"

Oh, damn. She didn't want to discuss their problems with Lillian, she really didn't. She didn't even know how much Eliot had told his mother. So she decided to skip it altogether.

"As a matter of fact, Lillian, I was calling to speak to him. Is he around?"

"I hope it's about the two of you making up, dear, if you don't mind my saying so."

"Oh, Lillian . . ." What could she say to this great old dame, who had been unfailingly nice to her? Not to mention the fact that her lover was sprawled on the bed, leaning on his hand, taking in every word.

"Never mind, Antonia. I'm sure you and Eliot will find your own way."

"Is he there?" Let's change the subject.

"He's at the hospital, in his office. I'm sure he'd love to hear from you."

Now she had to laugh aloud. "Oh, Lillian, you are shameless."

"I certainly hope so, dear. I'm very concerned about the two of you, very. And so is Philip. And I do think, with this Voorhees thing, he needs you more than ever."

Toni made placating noises into the phone and hung up. Damn! He was *never* there when she wanted him!

"Oh boy, when I get ahold of him, he'll be sorry he was ever born! How could he *do* this to me? To *me*? He knows how important that center is to me. Hell, to all those girls, all those women! And Charmaine! Oh Jesus, I have to go up there—''

''Whoa! Where do you have to go?'' She was already racing around the room, putting on her clothes, picking up her things, hopping as she struggled with her shoes.

''To the center, of course!''

''Hey.'' He had gotten out of bed and was trying to hold her still. ''Hey. I thought this was going to be our romantic morning.''

''Yeah, me, too. But did I know that son of a bitch would pull a stunt like this on me? He can't get away with it.''

''He can get away with it. He's the president.''

''He's going to be one sorry president when I finish with him.'' She took his arms and put them down at his sides. ''Ham, I'm sorry about this. Give me a raincheck. I have to get up there.'' She gave him a good, slow, hot kiss and then scooted away from his embrace. ''I'll call you!''

''When?''

''As soon as I'm finished!''

''When will *that* be?''

''How long does it take to commit murder?'' That made him laugh. Good. Ham laughing was preferable to him sulking.

When she jumped out of the cab at 123rd Street, she expected few women to be at the center. Sunday hours were short, and the weather was gorgeous. But the place was jammed, and it looked from outside as if everyone in there was talking at once.

And they were, she discovered as soon as she opened the door. There was such a din, it was a wonder anyone was able to hear her enter. But everyone's head swiveled as she came in, and then a sound came out of all those throats, a sound like despair.

''Dr. Toni!''

''What are they doing to us?''

''Wadda we gonna do?''

''Not fair! Not fair!''

''Why'd you let them?''

''Wadda we gonna do?''

They were all crying. Oh Christ. Exactly my question, Toni thought. What are we going to do? What in hell are we going to do? One thing she must do right now, she suddenly realized, was to gather together all the charts and all the papers that were in the back, in her desk. She'd show them to Eliot; she'd point out that there *had* been growth in the past couple of months, not anything spectacular, but growth nonetheless. She'd show him how her girls weren't getting pregnant so often, only 5.2 percent of those who had been coming to the center for a period of two to four months. She'd give him a list of all the girls who had entered drug treatment programs, explain how many of them were in Carolyn's program. He'd be forced to keep the center open when he saw what was happening here.

And then she said to herself, Who are you kidding? Nothing had been able to convince him. Why should anything be different today?

As she stood there, a small body hurtled through the air and into her arms. Charmaine, her shoulders shaking with sobs. She could hardly believe it. Charmaine, who always hung tough, who always teased the other girls when they gave in to self-pity. She was so tiny, so thin, it was like holding a ten-year-old. Toni looked around the room at the stricken faces and thought, They're all babies, abandoned babies. This country, this city, this hospital, the whole goddamn world has thrown them away and has turned its back on them.

They need me, every single one of them, she realized. It's not just that their clubs are gone, that they don't have a hangout. This was home to them because their actual homes are so awful. This was home to them because it was safe and because the people here cared about them.

Finally, Charmaine lifted her head. "Oh, Dr. Toni," she wailed, "what are we gonna do?"

"We'll think of something," Toni said, with more firmness than she felt. "I'm going right now to talk to Dr. Wolfe at the hospital. I'm going to tell him he can't do this to us." And I hope, she thought, that he'll even let me get the first word out.

"Now, listen up," she continued, speaking to the whole room. "I'm going to explain to the people at the hospital how important this center is. I don't know if they'll listen to me—"

"They'll listen to you, Dr. Toni, I know it!"

"Thanks, Jennifer. I hope you're right." Now she had their attention. "We can— Oh. Hello, I didn't know you were here." Deedra and King had just appeared from the back. Dee looked like death.

"Where *were* you? We've been calling and calling your service."

"I'm here now. Charmaine, why don't you pour juice for everybody; and, here—" She dug some bills out of her purse. "Send a couple of girls to that nice bakery on Broadway and get doughnuts or something."

Now she turned to Dee and King, motioning to them that they should come back into the office to talk. They walked together without a word; nothing at all was said until the door was closed behind them and then Dee burst into loud sobs.

Without thought, Toni took the young woman into her arms, not an easy task since Dee towered over her. And indeed, after a few minutes, Dee giggled through her tears and said, "I can't cry anymore or I'll drown you."

"Don't be silly." Toni reached up to pat her shoulder. "Cry all you like, I know how to swim."

Dee gave a shaky smile and pulled away. "I'm okay, I'm okay. Only . . . oh God, Dr. Toni, I feel so goddamn guilty!"

"Tell her she's nuts. She won't believe *me*!" King said.

"You're nuts," Toni announced, deadpan, but neither of them cracked a smile. "Okay, what's the problem? Why do you feel guilty?"

"Well, obviously I started it. I mean, if I'd kept my mouth shut, like I promised myself I would, this place wouldn't be closing. It's all my fault."

"Excuse me?" For a minute, Toni didn't know what she was talking about.

"Didn't you hear the report on Channel Fourteen? No? Well, they said this center is being closed because it's unsafe! And we all know *why* it's unsafe, don't we? Because of *me*! Because of what happened to me! And because I couldn't keep my mouth shut!"

"Dee, do you know how crazy that is? That's not at all why they're closing us down, and you know it. Just think for a minute. They've been threatening to close us down since before I got here! We're not cost-effective, Deedra! That's the beginning and the end of it. That unsafe crap is for the public! None of it's your fault!"

Dee tried to smile; then her face crumpled, and she began to cry again. "It's all for the best, I know, I know. But I can't help it, I feel so bad. I'm sorry, I'm sorry, but . . . George . . . he's taking the baby, and they're going to . . . Rockland County, to his sister's place in the country. And she's going to take care of Winifred and now . . . I know I didn't have the time to really take care of her the way she should be taken care of, and George's sister is a wonderful mother, and I can go see her as much as I want and everything . . . but it won't be the same, nothing's the same, and now I don't have any family, no family at all!''

"Oh swell, thanks a lot," King said, rolling his eyes and hugging her. He smiled at Toni. "I told her she's marrying me, and she said yes."

Dee looked at him. "I thought you weren't going to tell anybody but family."

King slid Toni such a stricken look, she could feel a tearing sensation in her chest. Here she was, feeling so bad about all those kids out there and not one thought for her own! She had not been a good mother to King. She'd been no mother at all. And she wasn't doing a helluva lot better at this very moment.

But that didn't mean she couldn't change. She took a deep breath, surprised at how difficult it was, for once, to open her mouth and tell the simple truth. But she had to. And she had to start somewhere.

"Dee, listen, there's something you should know. Something I want you to know." She waited until Dee's big, brown, wet eyes were fixed on hers. With her heart pounding, she said in a low voice, "I'm King's mother. His birth mother."

It took Dee a few shocked moments to take this in. And then, her whole face became transfigured with what could only be joy. "No shit!" she said, her voice shaking. "Oh my God, then you're going to be—"

"Your mother-in-law. So watch out!"

They hugged; they kissed; they all said thank you, thank you. She wasn't sure who was thanking who for what. And then they hugged and kissed some more.

Finally the time came to break away from this little island of delight and go back into the shark-infested waters of reality. It was a little weird to be so happy when so many sad things were happening to people they cared about. "Do me a favor, kids. Stay here and try to be of some comfort to these girls. I've got to go to the hospital and talk to Eliot. Don't give up hope, not quite yet."

She marched to her desk, emptying the files she needed into

a huge Macy's shopping bag, thinking, *I know whose fault it is, all right, and I'm going to see him right this minute.*

She charged through the lobby of Harmony Hill, heading right for Eliot's office, rehearsing in her head what she was going to say, looking neither left nor right. It was Sunday, a big day for visiting, so the lobby was busy. But there was a peacefulness about Sundays that made the hospital seem quieter and calmer. People were dressed up, carrying plants and flowers, or heading for the gift shop.

And there was Eliot, practically in her path, standing with his arms folded across his chest, gazing up at his noble ancestors. She almost barreled right into him. She skidded to a stop, crying out, "Eliot! I need to talk to you."

He turned to look down at her, theatrically calm. "Why, hello, Eliot, how are you?" he asked in a sticky-sweet tone that instantly put her hackles up.

"All right, all right. Hello, Eliot. How are you? How's it going?"

"Not badly. I feel pretty good, to tell you the truth. I just got a call from Conrad Havemayer, who demanded to know why I had not consulted with the advisory committee over the suspension of Warren Voorhees. And I had the enormous pleasure of telling him that there *is* no advisory committee. And when he asked me exactly what I meant by that, I told him, 'I just disbanded it.'" Eliot laughed. "I just had to come out here and tell my forebears that the hospital is back in Wolfe hands once more."

Back in Wolfe hands! He couldn't be serious! She was almost rendered speechless. But then, his expression changed subtly, and he added in a quite different tone, "I only wish I could share this with Sam." And he broke off, tears filling his eyes.

For a moment, her heart melted, and she felt sorry for him. But she remembered why she was there. "Did you also tell your forebears why you closed my Women's Health Center without a word to me, not even a friendly warning?"

"I didn't know we were friendly these days, Toni."

"Please don't be cute with me. Our personal relationship should have nothing whatsoever to do with our professional relationship."

"Exactly, Dr. Romano." He gave her that smile she hated so

much, gloating at having the upper hand. "I informed your superior, the head of your department. Going through channels is proper procedure. And that is all I am required to do."

She hefted the heavy shopping bag. "I brought records with me, Eliot. I brought facts and figures. Just tell me the truth: is any of it going to do any good?"

"Toni, you've known for months this was bound to happen."

"There are fifty or sixty young women in there right now, Eliot. They're mourning; they're in despair because this is something they desperately need. And now you're taking it away from them, without any warning."

He spoke very slowly, as if to make sure she could understand. "I don't know why you didn't prepare them, then."

"You bastard! You close the place, without warning, and it's *my* fault? I'm sorry, Eliot, I can't take this anymore. I can't continue to work here under these conditions."

"I'm very sorry to hear that. We will miss you."

"I . . . you . . . you can't—"

He smiled again. "Oh, yes I can. I'm the president. I can do pretty much what I want. Haven't you been telling me that since I got here? Well, now I'm doing it, so stop complaining."

He turned on his heel and strode away. Toni stood where she was, rooted to the spot. Well, damn it, he really meant it. She was fired. She looked after his retreating, soldier-straight back, thinking, *My God, at this moment, I almost love him, the bastard!*

38

A week later

Toni came out from room 1251, blinking back tears. It was so hard to say good-bye, particularly to people who were depending on you. But it was her last day at Harmony Hill, and she had to bid farewell to all of her patients, one by one, had to hold their hands and hold back her own tears when they cried. God, some of these women she'd seen through every kind of problem over the past year—problems and joys, babies and hysterectomies, false hopes and false alarms. Everything.

She had come to know so many of them intimately, and now she was deserting them. It was all over. She wasn't supposed to care about them anymore. She was supposed to walk away and just forget about them. At this moment, she had the worst headache of her life.

Ham had made reservations at the Four Seasons for dinner tonight—a late dinner, nine o'clock—and had told her to wear her Sunday finest. She only hoped she was up for it. He was doing his best, she realized that; he was trying to cheer her up. It was sweet. He was like a teenager in some ways, with his little secrets and surprises, so she'd agreed to it, although without any real enthusiasm. He was probably going to pull out all the stops, with champagne, and he'd promised her a couple of surprises. Maybe she'd get a little gift. It was all in honor of her getting fired by her husband; that's what he'd said.

Then she realized that she was standing still, here in the hallway, thinking about Ham Pierce, because she didn't want to leave Harmony Hill. Everything was finished; her office had been cleared out last night—over a year of her life was now packed into three rather small cardboard cartons. But she couldn't make herself move. Once she went down in the elevator and out the big front door, it was all over—done, ended, terminated.

Shut up, Toni, she told herself. *You sound like a soap opera—a not very good soap opera. Just get yourself down the hall and get yourself a cup of coffee and get yourself outa here and get yourself a life!* It made her laugh; that was better, much better.

She was at the hot beverage machine, watching the spurt of weak coffee half miss the cup, when she became aware of a large group of people gathered around the TV in the lounge. Something was happening. She checked her wristwatch. It was "Voice of the City" time. Oh, God! Suddenly she remembered; this morning, as he had kissed her good-bye, Ham had said, "For surprise number one, make sure you catch the show tonight!"

Alan Pasternak had caught sight of her from the lounge and was motioning for her to come quickly. So she hurried in. Ham must be doing something about the hospital. Come to think of it, he'd been smiling and secretive this whole past week; he had something up his sleeve, for sure.

When she walked in, the group clustered close to the set parted to make room for her. She kind of half-noticed how totally quiet it was; and then her attention was riveted to the screen because there was the street outside the Women's Health Center, in living color, with women walking in and out. And there was Deedra, and oh my God, there she was, herself, half-running, a frown on her face, hair looking like Frankenstein's bride. Is *that* what she looked like? Ouch!

"The Women's Health Center on West 123rd Street as it looked last week . . ." Ham was saying. There were brief scenes, without sound, of a club meeting; of women waiting and chatting; of Gloria Gomez filling out forms with patients . . . all the activity that went on all the time. When had he been able to get those pictures? She had specifically forbidden him to come inside . . . and until she walked out of the front door tonight, she was *still* in charge!

Then Ham's voice: "This is how it looks today . . ." And there it was: closed, dark, desolate, the plants beginning to wither in the window, a big, ugly chain and padlock on the door.

Alan leaned close to Toni and murmured, "You missed the beginning. He's calling this show 'The Wolfe Pack.' "

"The *what*?" She turned to look at Alan, her mind racing.

He nodded. "Right. W-o-l-f-e. Good old Ham Pierce is giving it to all the Wolfe doctors. . . . He's saying that one family
has virtually owned a major metropolitan hospital for three generations, and the upshot is disaster. . . ."

"Oh my God." Toni breathed. So this was Ham's first surprise.

Now the program had moved from the center, and the picture
on the screen was of the dear, departed dental clinic on Amsterdam Avenue. "The Wolfe Pack." It wasn't a news story; it
was no more than a malicious, undeserved attack on the whole
family. Philip. Even Lillian. But why? What was the point? He'd
just told her—in bed, yet—that he was beginning to *like* Eliot.
This was nuts! What the hell was he up to?

Then, once again, her eye was caught as Eliot's face appeared
on the screen. She remembered when that was taken; that day,
Eliot had been so furious with a militant group of anti-
abortionists who were harrassing and threatening all the patients. His mouth was open, and his face was grim. But there
was no sound and not a single shot of the crazies who had been
screaming and thrusting pictures of bloody fetuses in front of
nervous young girls. No, none of that, just an angry Eliot.

And Ham's voice-over wasn't explaining what happened that
day, not at all. He was talking about Eliot's having been passed
over for department head at John Quincy Adams Hospital in
Wash—*Wait a minute! I told him that! Oh, God!*—"And Eliot
Wolfe, not six months later, with no qualifications whatsoever,
came begging for the job of president of Harmony Hill Hospital,
which because of his family connections, was *handed* to him!"

Toni stood stock still, sick to her stomach. She had given
Ham that information, she had told him while lying in his arms.
Did you have to evoke confidentiality with your *lover* nowadays? Did you have to get it in writing, that what you said to
him in the privacy of the bedroom was not for publication? Did
Hamilton Pierce know her so little, that he would think this was
something she would enjoy? He had to be stupid to do this. He
had to be heartless. Christ, he had used her! That's all he had
wanted her for! He was a shit!

The thought of his skin touching hers made her flesh creep,
and she wanted to go hide somewhere. Better, let her go
scrub. She felt so unclean, so trashed. Her face burned with

shame. What kind of idiot was she to fall for the oldest line in the world, from the oldest kind of creep? She couldn't even stand to see him on the television screen; looking at him made her feel scummy. And for this bastard, this low life, this piece of garbage, she had given up a perfectly fine man and a twelve-year marriage—no, wait, they'd had an anniversary while they weren't talking to each other! Okay then, a *thirteen*-year marriage. All the more reason to put Ham out of her life.

Poor Eliot, she thought. I've got to go to him. I've got to find him. "The Wolfe Pack." What a horrible thing to do to a family that's always been decent and altruistic! O God, if you're good and kind and merciful, she prayed, Lillian and Philip are not watching this.

The den in Lillian and Philip Wolfe's apartment had not been redone since Billy Baldwin. The red plaid carpeting was the same, a bit worn, but still good; the green leather furniture was still supple and glowing. The television set, a console with fold-back doors, was new, as were the large white cards with their black block printing, taped around the room to help Sam remember: "TELEVISION" "TELEPHONE" "LIGHTS" "ON" "OFF" "VIDEO TAPES."

Right now, the television was on, a little too loud, perhaps. Philip sat erect in the wing chair. Lillian was on the loveseat next to Sam, holding his hand. This had become a habit with them. Usually, she couldn't be quite sure who was holding onto whom, but tonight, she knew. He was comforting *her*. And God knows she could use it, the way that Pierce was carrying on. First he had picked on Eliot. It was so unfair, she thought, blaming him for all the hospital's problems . . . and to bring up his disappointment in Washington! That was lousy! And now, now he was starting on Dr. Eli, who had been loved by absolutely everyone! And with good reason, by the way!

She pulled her hand from Sam's and got up. "I'm turning this off!" she announced. "This is disgusting!"

"Don't touch that, Lillian!" Philip said sharply, waving her off.

What! Philip so abrupt? It wasn't like him at all. So she turned her attention back to what that horrible Pierce fellow was saying, and it almost gave her a heart attack. "Jewish hospitals," he was saying, "have always looked after their own, first and foremost. That's why they exist. When New York was still New Amsterdam—''

"Philip, listen to him!'' She glanced over at him. A spasm of pain crossed his face and was instantly wiped away. She had to turn it off. "That lousy anti-Semite! Philip!''

"Lillian, sit down please. I want to hear this.''

"Well, I don't want you to hear it. It's too upsetting.''

"Maybe you're upset. It's not bothering me.''

"How can it not bother you? Of course it bothers you! I know you better than that!''

"Sit down, Lillian,'' Sam said. "You'll give yourself a . . . a cornea.''

The poor boy, Lillian thought. He meant coronary. That had been happening more lately: him forgetting words he'd always known perfectly well. He wasn't so bad yet, just little lapses now and then. But she had to prepare herself. It was only going to get worse. She could do it; she was strong. She only prayed she would live long enough to see Sam through. But enough. Enough.

"I'm not giving myself anything, sweetie pie,'' she said to Sam. And she sat, steeling herself to watch this repulsive program to the bitter end, no matter what.

The screen showed Philip at the hospital dinner in his honor last year, where everyone had got up and toasted him with such praises. But the voice on the television was saying nasty things, horrible things, *untrue* things. "Honored, but we should ask why? *Why* does Dr. Philip Wolfe deserve special recognition? For outliving his contemporaries? For taking over the *family business*—which happens to be a hospital receiving public funds? For being good at raising money? Money is always of prime importance to certain segments of the population, as we all know . . .''

"Philip, I'm turning it off this minute!'' Lillian cried.

Philip's pale eyes blazed. "No. I want to hear it *all*.''

"And then I hope you're calling Jerry!''

"I don't need a lawyer. I need peace and quiet.''

Lillian subsided once more, letting herself sink back onto the loveseat. But she couldn't sit back and relax; she couldn't. This was horrible. It was like being stabbed all over by a thousand knives. She couldn't listen to another word. So she turned off her ears—she knew from long years of experience with her mother-in-law how to do *that*—and let her mind move onto something else.

Not that there was much good news to think about. It felt like the world was falling in on all of them. It looked like Eliot and Antonia might be getting divorced. Sam would never, ever get better. And that lousy Irene—! Every week, she came "for a little visit." But she would never go out with him, not even for a walk. She sat across the room from him, always on the edge of her chair, always looking at her watch because she was always on her way somewhere else, to see someone else, so she only had a minute. To think that everyone had considered her a member of the family, that Sam had been ready and willing to *marry* her. *This* was the thanks he got!

Irene rolled over onto her stomach—she was sick of watching the stupid show, anyway—and said, "Rub my back, darling."

Dougie obeyed instantly. He always did. He was such a darling. "Why don't you take off your negligee?" he wheedled.

"All right, but later." He was so young, and it was still early; she didn't want to let him see her aging body, not in full daylight! Ronnie Harrison did good work—the man had golden hands—but still, Dougie was *so* much younger than her.

Ham Pierce's voice went on and on behind her, talking about Eli Wolfe and Philip Wolfe and Eliot Wolfe. Boring! "Turn it off, darling, would you?"

"Sure." There was a click, and then silence. "I don't know why you turned that on, anyway. Who cares about that stuff?"

Irene chuckled low in her throat. "I'll have you know that Dr. Eliot Wolfe thought you might be dangerous, Dougie. He warned me about you."

"What'd he say? Tell me exactly!"

"Never you mind! Oh, all right! He said beware of young men with floppy dark hair who hang around and give you roses, that's what he said."

"And he was right!" Dougie said, his voice growing husky. "And I think I'll prove it to you right now!"

"Oh, my darling!" Irene murmured in her sexiest voice, the one that wowed them in *Passion Fruit*, thinking, oh God, not again! Forget what everyone always said! Having a young lover was not a bed of roses!

* * *

Barney Goldstone and his wife Arlene were having drinks in
their media room, the only finished room in the house, a marvel
of high-tech black and gold glitz, featuring a sixty-inch Mitsu-
bishi television screen, now showing a sixty-inch shot of Eliot
Wolfe looking unhappy.

Barney, ensconced in his favorite Ettore black leather chair,
slapped his thigh with glee and whooped. "Atta boy, Pierce!
You may be a nigger lover, but boy, you sure know how to put
it to 'em! Right up the old—"

"Barney!" his wife scolded, sounding shocked.

"Aw, can't a fella have some fun?" He swiveled to look at
her, sitting in her matching chair, knitting a mile a minute on a
pair of argyles. "Hey, sweet socks, bring your body over here.
I feel like biting your neck!"

"Oh, Barney!" But she giggled. "I can't think what you have
against the Wolfes. Philip Wolfe kept your mother alive for
years."

"Maybe that's what I've got against him. . . . Now sweetheart, don't get that look on your face. It was just a joke. Dr.
Philip Wolfe is a saint. No, no, it's Eliot I mind. Your ex. I love
seeing him get it. Dr. High and Mighty, thinks he's a cut above
me. Hell, he thinks he's a cut above *everyone*. The schmuck
didn't even have the brains to treat you right, honey bunny."

Arlene blushed and put down her knitting. "Now, that deserves a great big kiss," she said. She got up and went to him
and bent over him.

Barney put his hand under her skirt, running it up the inside
of her legs. "Yeah, angel thighs, I do deserve it. It took me to
open you up—haw, haw, haw—figuratively *and* literally, you
know what I mean? Yeah, sweet cakes, between me and Lith-
ium, you're doin' okay, right?"

Now his hand had reached up the final inch, and she jumped,
giving a little shriek. Then she giggled and slid down into his
lap. Barney immediately began unbuttoning her blouse. "Yeah,
I don't mind watching your ex get cut down to size," he said,
his eyes still fixed on the screen, while his hands busily went
about their task. "Hey, maybe he'll resign!"

Toni came into Eliot's outer office, a trifle breathless, just as
Ham was talking about Philip. The secretary was gone, of
course—it was long after regular hours—so she just barged

through. And stopped at the doorway, thinking, *oh, poor Eliot*. His face was chalky, his lips clamped tightly together. She'd never seen him look so bad.

"And the result is that the Wolfes consider themselves an imperial family that can dictate priorities. So if upper-crust families want a new pavilion for their little aches and pains, why, they get it. But if the sixty-eight percent of Harmony Hill's patients who are poor African-Americans and Hispanics need a drug treatment center or a women's health center or a dental clinic in the neighborhood . . . forget about it! *That's* where the doctors Wolfe have always pinched pennies—in the ghetto!"

"Eliot! Turn off that garbage!"

He nearly jumped out of his chair, he was so startled. He tried for a smile but failed miserably. "I'm surprised to see you," he said.

"Why? Just because we're separated doesn't mean I don't care about you."

"But I fired you!"

"Yes. As a matter of fact, today's my last day. But what he's doing—! I thought I had his number, but in my wildest dreams, I never imagined he'd pull a nasty stunt like this! It's a fucking hatchet job!" She marched herself up to the set and snapped it off. "There! Much better!"

Eliot was silent for a moment. Then he said, "I never thought he'd dare make anti-Semitic remarks on the air. Jerry called me after the first one to say we have an actionable suit against Pierce."

"You're gonna sue him? Great!"

" 'Actionable suit,' " Eliot repeated. "Only Jerry!" He laughed briefly and bitterly. "I shouldn't be laughing about anything right now. It's not just me. God, that bastard Pierce has gone after my grandfather and my elderly *father*, for God's sake. What can I say to Philip? What have I done to him by taking this job?" He put his head in his hands. "My life is a wreck," he said, muffled. He sat, head bowed, for a few moments, then straightened up and looked at her forlornly.

She didn't have to think about it. In a moment, she was standing at his side, her arms around him, pressing her lips against his hair. He buried his face in her breasts and held on to her for dear life. It's really all *my* fault, she thought. I'm the one who

ran off at the mouth. I'm the one who's *always* running off at
the mouth!

"You can't blame yourself, Eliot. Ham Pierce thrives on dis-
sention and trouble. If he hasn't got a legitimate crisis to exploit,
he makes one up. This one, he made up. You'll win your case."

"The case isn't the issue. You know as well as I that, in this
town, if you're accused of something on television, that's it. It
becomes fact. I could prove, with my own facts and figures, that
he's a liar, that I had to do what I did, that there was no other
way, that I'll make certain the same services are provided right
here, that if we don't do this, the whole hospital might very well
fold! I could do all that, Toni, and there aren't ten people in this
city who would believe it!"

"Yes they will. Yes they will." She had no idea in the world
whether what she was saying was true or not, but she couldn't
stand to see him suffer like this. She tried to move away from
him, but he clung harder, holding her so close she wondered
how he could breathe.

"Oh, God, Toni, my life is a wreck. David isn't talking to
me because of Janet. Carolyn isn't talking to me because her
program is in jeopardy. You aren't talking to me because . . . I
don't know *why* you're not talking to me!"

Toni had a sudden flash. Inside this tall competent man lived
a little boy: a scared, insecure, hurt little boy. Oh, women joked
about it all the time: men, they're such babies. But even as they
said it, they weren't willing to believe it. Certainly, she had
never believed it about *Eliot*. He was older and wiser; he was
cooler and more mature. He had seemed so powerful to her that
she had been unable to see there might be another side to him.
Where was it written that the same person couldn't be strong
and vulnerable at the same time? Wasn't she both? If she had
only recognized this sooner, she might have been a better wife.

"I feel so alone!" he went on. "You're not with me, and
Sam's not with me, and who else do I *have*?"

Toni made what she hoped were soothing noises, but he wasn't
really hearing her.

"Why *aren't* you talking to me, Toni?" he went on, wistfully,
letting her go at last.

"But, Eliot, I *am* talking to you. I'm here, aren't I?"

"Not the way I want you to be." He must have seen something in her face, because he immediately apologized. "I'm

sorry, I don't want to press you. But . . . there're so many things troubling me lately. Look Toni, medical school led us to believe that we were going to help people, heal people, save people, *cure* people. And I *believed* it, Toni. But there's so much happening right now that I *can't* help or heal or save! Damn it, it all feels so fucking futile!'' He had stood up and was mindlessly straightening the same pile of papers over and over.

"Eliot, you're only human. I realize that a lot of people think all doctors are gods, but we don't have to agree with them!'' She gave him a small smile.

He groaned. "I've been so arrogant, thinking I had all the answers. But I can't save Sam. . . .'' He paused and groaned again. "Oh, God, Toni, Sam asked me to help him commit suicide when he's lost everything . . . when he's not in his right mind and not in his wrong one either—that was the way he put it. Isn't that just like Sam, to make a joke out of his own hopeless situation! God, I love that man! How can I do it? And how can I *not*?''

"Of course, you have no choice. Poor Eliot. What a tough number that is.''

"Toni, I promised him; I gave him my word, my solemn word. And I keep wondering, when the time comes, am I going to be able to make myself do it?''

"When the time comes,'' Toni said. "You'll do the right thing. You always do.'' And like a lightning bolt, the realization hit her that she meant it, that it was *true*. Eliot was the genuine article: a truly decent, honest, caring human being. What in God's name had she been *thinking* of, this past year? What had made her think that her cause was holy and his was trivial? She had been trying to keep her center open, yeah, but *he* had been trying to keep the whole goddamn hospital open! And she had not helped him, not one bit. In fact, she had withheld even the simplest kind of support. Like all those fund-raising functions it had pleased her to sneer at. She could have turned out once or twice and attempted to charm a few rich people! She stared at her husband, as if she had never seen him before—and maybe she hadn't.

"And it's not just Sam! My parents . . . God, my parents are getting so old!''

"And you can't stop *them* from getting older . . . or from dying, either. Hey, it's pretty humbling stuff, I know.'' She wanted so badly to go to him, put her arms around him, comfort him. But did she have the right?

"And . . . now Eric!" Eliot went on, pain creasing his forehead.

O Jesus, she prayed. Not yet, please, God, don't let him die now. "Has something changed?" she asked carefully.

"He's in the hospital in San Francisco. He's got pneumonia." The last word was said in a charged tone.

"Oh, God," she moaned. "I'm so sorry."

She had been very busy feeling sorry for herself all day. Job ended, marriage over, big romance kaput. Big fucking deal. She had her health; she had her son; she had a job offer at Mount Sinai Hospital—and, she suddenly knew, she could damn well have her husband back again. If she wanted him.

"Toni?" he ventured after a moment, his voice shaky.

"Yes?"

"I want you to come with me."

"To California?"

"Yes. To California. I have to go. I . . . I need you, Toni. I need you to be with me. I'm not sure I can do it alone."

She's been so angry with him all year, and now, suddenly, it was all gone. Evaporated, as if it had never been there. She had allowed her animosity to obliterate all the good things they'd had together. But the good things had really happened; they were real. Was that enough for a second chance?

"I'm not going to give up on you, you know," Eliot said. "I'm not going to give up on *anything*. I've decided. Let Ham Pierce do his worst. I intend to stay right here at this hospital— in this office, in this job—and prove him wrong! Most important, I'm going to prove to myself what I can do!"

"You can do plenty," Toni said. Just listen to him! *This* was the Eliot she had fallen in love with! And then she cautioned herself. He sounded like a new man, but there was no such animal.

He gazed at her with melancholy eyes and said, "I love you, Toni."

"Oh, Eliot—!" She couldn't help it; she began to smile at him and shake her head. He was doing his best to seduce her; what's more, it was working! "Eliot, what am I going to do about you?"

"Come to California with me. For starters. Say yes, Toni. Please?"

She thought of and rejected several dozen arguments against. But what choice did she have? She couldn't say no; she couldn't let him go out there to face God knows what all alone. She squared her shoulders and tipped her head back to look him in the eye.

"All right, Eliot," she said, "I'll go to California with you."

"I'm warning you; I'm after more than a trip to California with you." Now his eyes were warm and his voice tender.

"Maybe I am, too. You never know." She smiled.

"You mean it?"

"I really mean it," she said.

Either she was marching boldly into a brave new future or stepping into the abyss. She wasn't sure which.

Marcia Rose